NEWDAWN
CENTRAL

Volume 2

Written By
Dominique Luchart

Thank you for purchasing this book!

Get a FREE ebook when you join our mailing list.
Plus, get updates, new releases, deals, gifts, and more.

SIGN UP HERE
https://windommedia.com/bestemaillist

Already a Subscriber? Please provide your email again to register
this Ebook and put you on our VIP List. You will continue to
receive exclusive offers in your inbox

CENTRAL/Dominique Luchart
NEWDAWN SAGA
ISBN 978-1-941954-12-6

www.windommedia.com/author

Summary

My name is Tesh. I am with my team… Out of twenty of us, only four are now awake. The others are somewhere, and we are looking for them. We hope they made it too and are somewhere inside the mountain.

The warning we received from the Entity was clear. Time is running out to find our teammates spread across five different Chambers.

I am not sure we can win against the Entity. When it unleashes its powers, we fear it could destroy everything. We don't have a choice; we must find the other Conclaves. So, despite the odds, we have infiltrated the space below the Center and found something else, a structure with an energy signature we have never encountered before.

Can we decipher what it is in time? Could this be where Streak is?

Dedication

To my love and partner Spencer, who was by my side through the ups and downs of life, for his unwavering support and belief in me through the wins and the defeats. Thank you! You have been my compass even when the distance kept us apart. Your encouragement led me to keep writing and persevere to get the NEWDAWN story into the world.

Acknowledgments

Thank you to all my beautiful friends for their support. Life is a journey, and what a journey this has been for me with NEWDAWN. I never quite expected that it would be so arduous or take as much time as it had. Yet, would I do it again? Absolutely!

The environment we live in today is like science fiction theater. It demands that I talk about the changes paving the way to a new future in our digital dystopian society as our world landscape evolves. These are drastic and remain insidious until they emerge as a new order. These changes catapult us into a different way of life. Newdawn seeks to create awareness, and while never easy, nor is the path to wisdom. Our world demands both, and we need more of them.

A particular thought to our incredible planet Earth, providing me with insights as I write about our future. It gives me solace when I struggle with marketing. And it never stops gifting me with ideas and new notions when I seek inspiration. Yet, I am also concerned about this magical place we live in – our beautiful home. We have been such poor caretakers of our planet, the oceans we swim in, the air we breathe, and the land we walk on. Our lives mean more than leaving behind.

Je suis libre comme le vent.

I am as free as the wind.

To my readers and fans…

Join me on our travels in Science fiction and science facts.

NEWDAWN Saga is worth the time.

Table of Contents<small>Summary</small>   v

Preface

The thread of our lives is but a small glimmer in the fabric of the universe. As we watch the stars in the night sky, spreading brilliantly above our heads in an infinite tapestry, we barely comprehend the vastness of the cosmos. While it may not appear to weigh upon us, its rules determine our fate—the future of our civilization, the destiny of our planet. And while the unknown surrounds us, the unpredictability of outcomes we unknowingly face is, in many ways, inevitable and leads to our demise. The journey ahead unfolds, even as we believe we remain in control of our immediate environment. But it is a false premise, one we hold on to, to ensure our well-being on a time map that plays against all of us. Inevitable forces unfold, and while it may take millennia, they irreversibly take us to one outcome. So, do we cheat our way out of this? Can we?

Planets are formed from stardust, more minor than human hair, emerging from the gas and dust of young stars, a speckle of something infinitesimal. In the darkness of space, gravity influences the specks' path, toying with them. A moderate collision forms a fusion, growing the material into a more significant composite, unleashing the next phase. In time, the particles enlarge until dust balls develop pebbles and eventually evolve into more massive rocks. As these planetesimals orbit their stars, they clear a path, leaving space around them while their star pushes material away, gobbling gas up. The process continues over billions of years, transforming a disk into a new world until a planet is born.

Earth is our only home, and it is already on a path to destruction. The only question to consider is, can we stop it and reverse the effect of global warming? It is no longer a matter of if.... It is a matter of when and how quickly we can undo the damage.

Creation echoes through galaxies. We are until we are no more. Or until we reconstruct as something else and defy the constraints of humanity. Is that even a possibility? Human ingenuity may find a way.

But destruction for greed and convenience without considering the effects of our actions, on the whole, is our own doing. While it took decades to arrive at this point for our planet, it took billions of years to create our universe. Galaxies disappear as part of a cycle we do not yet comprehend. And what is one world in the scope of things? Other than the fact that it happens to be our only home? It will take decades to thwart the results of our ecological footprint. Will it take millions of years for the universe to unleash its power against Earth? And even if we succeed, what else awaits in the darkness of space?

NEWDAWN CENTRAL brings our story with all of its twists and turns as it continues to follow the Perfect Humans as they attempt to reset the clock. But while they escape the mountain's depth after the Sphere releases them, the Entity residing in the caves has delivered its warning. The countdown started the moment the members of the Institute Conclave consciousness returned.

And time is a strange phenomenon. What part does it play in our future?

What unknown will it bring when we least expect it? Will this unknown come as an alien civilization? Will it uncover our next evolution? Or will we simply go into the long night as so many other civilizations have before us? Or will it simply disrupt everything we hope for or believe in delivering a different truth?

As humans, we have such a fragile ego. Many believe we are the most developed species, but what if others exist in this universe? And what do we expect from them if they do indeed exist? Will they crush us like we have so many species on our planet? For them, we may be only bugs like we have done to others deemed inferior life forms. We have killed many species on our planet — plants or animals alike. So, what about other worlds? Will aliens do the same to us without regard and provide retribution in some form for what we have extended to other life forms?

Unseen forces irreversibly play a part in altering many destinies and paths in this non-linear story that is the Newdawn Saga. It brings up the near future, changing Earth's course toward tomorrow. It opens doors to the past, reaching into a lost ancestry. It takes you on an extraordinary journey where a gap of many years unfolds for those who travel the boundaries of time.

Enjoy one branch of our world over another by following one Conclave more than the others; remember, five of them fight for control. Get to know our characters during their journey. Watch as they face their challenges as twists and plots surprise or make your heart race. Discover the secrets of the factions.

NEWDAWN CENTRAL introduces you to REBOOT, taking you to 2098 and to the height of the cataclysm on our planet.

BADGE

DAINN – Ang City 2040
SRC Conclave. Viewing VLog 12,568. Annals – Summer 2040.

The second Bane triggers a need to centralize our world. Now, the Network assimilates data on all our citizens. Soon, we rely on the information to structure and control our society. Among the changes in our infrastructure, we expand the DAINN System to monitor our people's health with preventative healthcare measures as we seek longer life expectancy. DAINN Annals – 2040.

Inside the Control Center, the dead overwhelmed the screens. Everywhere we looked, dead eyes watched us, their spark extinguished. All dead faces, frozen in permanence, stared at the living, no longer carrying the fire of life. Dead bodies piled up in the air transport zones bound to their final destinations, waiting for their turn in the city's incinerators.

Dr. Rene Paladock, the creator of the DAINN Network, viewed the latest images from our feeds. They came from all around Ang, reaching from the Golden Ghetto to Water's Edge, ArchwayPass, BridgeView, CliffTops, and Emerald Field. It didn't matter that we had closed off the various sections of the city.

"How many today?" Paladock said in a broken voice.

"Three thousand seven hundred and sixty-eight," the EHAF guard said, standing beside him. He was a young man with a sweetly proportioned face, but the last several weeks brought a different look to him. His eyes bore shadows, and his shoulders seemed to carry an unbearable weight.

The guards often switched because of the work that brought them face to face with death every minute of every day. And while the System could keep the count on its own, Paladock visited every day. No one wanted to see him alone inside the Control Room to face the awful reality. The unacknowledged truth remained; no one knew how to stop it.

By the time we realized the threat, it had turned into a disastrous reality overnight. As we attempted to identify the source, the infectious disease continued its course, and the outbreak spread throughout our cities. Our health officials declared it a world emergency, demanding that everyone quarantine. The warning to the Federation soon followed. The EHAF went into overdrive, alerting our people to remain indoors and enforce precautions. Our Conclave leaders issued orders and mandatory stay at home for non-essential personnel. The head of each of the five Conclaves implemented guidelines to ensure the safe continuity of our operations. It provided for our citizens and met their needs within the grids.

It was sixteen months ago.

"You don't have to stay here, young man," Paladock said, grimly looking at the images.

"Sorry, Sir, I am not at liberty to leave until you do," the young guard said. "They don't want us to be here for very long and certainly not alone. Bad for morale and all."

"Huh, yes. I understand," Paladock said, conflicted.

Today, death was everywhere, permeating every task we undertook.

Given our infrastructure, the death toll was drastic. It rose more than in the nineteen eighteen with the H1N1 virus, where one-third of the world was infected, and one hundred and ninety-five thousand Americans died in a single month. It was more virulent than the pandemic of nineteen fifty-seven with H2N2 or even the one in nineteen sixty-eight with H3N2, and in two thousand nine with H1N1. It surpassed the one in twenty-twenty with COVID19 when the virus spread globally and remained over the years.

There was no way to imagine the entirety of our losses. There was no amount of preparedness to face this horrendous pandemic.

Now, worldwide, death reached over nineteen million people. We dealt with one hundred and ninety-nine million people infected.

As Dr. Paladock watched the System monitoring our people, I could see the stress on his face.

The automation of the Network took over people, systems, and resources. He had achieved much in the last year.

Powered by DAINN, our online education system remained the same, with courses in almost anything delivered individually. But some programs expanded to include in-home robotics training to maintain the curriculum of recruits and candidates aiming for official government service. Old training grounds refitted to accommodate more classes isolating our youth into smaller groups to meet physical preparation requirements. More Apps covering various fields and developed to carry on workload from remote locations entered the marketplace.

After a few minutes of silence, Paladock said, "Someone needs to know. They need to notice, you know. Pay attention to them on their last journey. It's probably stupid," he added.

"No, Sir. It's good of you, Sir." The guard looked at the screens again and got a stunned look on his face. "There's just so many."

Paladock sadly nodded. "Too many."

The research facilities around the world developed new prototypes to take over some essential functions. Robotics took a more significant role within domestic households. They provided care for sick individuals remaining at home. These included better domestic bots' capabilities to handle simple tasks within residents' quarters, including cooking, cleaning, fetching, and delivering things on the grounds within various locations. It also covered additional new drone prototypes, now replacing delivery systems overseen by man. The DAINN System took over all these new undertakings.

Many companies competing for sales, distribution, and market share leveraged their assets with no respite. Our manufacturing facilities assembled more drones and robots to cover increased demands, and the lines moved non-stop, day and night, to fill the requests. These new bio-engineered robot advancements served multiple purposes, with some programmed to provide backup care to our medical units. Others oversaw security in our streets to eliminate the risks to citizens with support from sectional police forces. Now they crowded our buildings and our passageways, serving as a go-between.

But there was nothing worse than the immense stress on the Health Conclave—the Faculty. As the illness spread like wildfire within our walls, our world medical board responded to immediate needs, dispatching personnel in the most infected zones. But they soon became overwhelmed.

"We can't seem to get a handle on this virus," Paladock said. The man seemed beaten.

Our scientists were doing all they could to create a vaccine, but we had found nothing to obliterate the virus so far.

Everything stopped at once in our cities as everyone retreated to isolate themselves indoors. Fear rose, touching all our kind, as the outbreak did not discriminate. Personalities, celebrities, and ordinary people were all affected. Rich and poor fought for their lives. Young and old died, brought down brutally. Across all walks of life, death touched us all.

Earth became silent overnight. Our world froze under threat, blanketing our entire way of life. The Planet obtained a respite from the long and agonizing demise we imposed on it.

"I suppose we should go then. I can't keep you here; you have better things to do," Paladock said as he made his way toward the door.

As we fought this world catastrophe, buried deep inside the SRC Conclave, the DAINN System spread its influence under the aegis of Dr. Paladock.

Slowly, the Network took over our infrastructure.

2
SURFACE
Tesh

Mountain Range, CA - 2022

Tesh looks at the sky for the first time. It is so clear, so blue, so bright.... Unlike the air of Ang City. She stands in the warmth of the sun radiating on her body, mesmerized, a smile spreading across her face. I feel her joy. Tesh VLog - DAINN Annals – Summer 2022.

I couldn't wait to get topside. Engaging my glider with the propulsion engine in my NetJet boots, I adjusted the velocity for the weight of two. Then I grabbed Chase by the waist and launched us over the tunnel's threshold into the massive cave. He rotated his frame to face me. His body glued to mine, we now hovered upwards in the shaft, following the column of rock.

Chase's reaction did little to calm my feelings about our proximity.

A smile reached his lips as he held on to me, looking down into the abyss as if nothing was abnormal with the thing we had just escaped from - the Entity.

I glanced at him with his head bleeding. He looked pale. His cocky attitude contradicted the pain I saw flashing in his eyes when he moved too fast. Netshit, the guy acted like nothing was wrong, and he appeared as if he owned the world.

In the meantime, there was little I could do for him. Leane was the healer among us, the one who possessed the power I envied. And who wouldn't want her gift? She knew how to bring life back from the brink of death into every living cell. I wished many times that I could have her gift. In my past, growing up in Ang, my wishes remained unfulfilled. Until I no longer cared to wish for anything.

Talking through my NetComm, I said, "We're going up. There is an opening above. Blast, can you take care of bringing Mage?"

"What?" Blast's question, carried over the NetComm, induced a knowing smile. Although Blast was fond of Mage, he acted cranky in his interactions with my dog. They didn't seem to get along. It wasn't Blast's fault as much as it was Mage, who appeared way too affectionate with Blast every chance he got. It caused Blast to be on edge around Mage and rendered the situation fluid between these two. Mage was smart, maybe too clever. It knew what he was doing all along.

"Secure the Chamber. Then you can join me with Mage. Leane, I will need you here as soon as you get the equipment ready. Chase needs your help."

"NetRoger that," Leane said. "How is your arm?"

"Better. Stronger. Don't worry about me." Concerned about the effect of the Nanos on my left limb, she checked in. While I was still adjusting to the feeling, the sensation had returned. My strength appeared to have doubled, although it was nothing compared to what we faced a while ago.

"We won't be long, Tesh." The sound of the Pulse reverberated far below us.

I couldn't help myself, though, and added, "Do me a favor, Blast. Make sure you harness Mage before you let him out of the chamber. He hates close quarters as much as you do." I smiled. *You know the devil in me.*

"Having something in common with a dog doesn't quite do it for me, Tesh." Blast emitted the comment through a voice filled with frustration.

It elicited a muted laugh from me as my companion laughed out loud at that comment.

"What was that?" Blast said. "It's no joke, Chase..."

"Can we discuss Mage and our exit strategy later?" I said. "I'll see you on the surface."

All we heard was a low grumbling before the communication dropped. Blast had things in hand with Leane, so I turned my attention back to the climb. Soon, they would join me.

We hovered upwards inside the shaft, facing the massive column of rock in front of us, but I needed more space between us. I sped up the propulsion engines in my NetJet boots, which increased our velocity over the gorge as I held onto Chase.

Now that silence reigned, I felt the connection with Chase vibrating between us. Our closeness enhanced the link left by DAINN. Nothing prepared me for the intensity of our connection, and unless I got a handle on it, it would present a problem.

Looking up at the shaft, the opening in the rocks broadened ahead. We moved upwards toward the light, feeling a sense of exhilaration rise within me.

The awkward moment continued between us. I attempted to ignore it. "How far up are we?"

He chuckled with a hint of humor. "Hum... I've never experienced this mode of transportation before. So it's hard to tell. I daresay high enough."

"I meant the summit?"

He shrugged. "With these rocket boots, it won't take long to get there."

I could now see the light outside. Soon, we would reach the surface. The sunlight got closer with every breath we took.

"Hey, I owe you my thanks for not having to go up the old fashion way. I must make it up to you."

Seeing the brilliance of the sky, I again took deep breaths, trying to calm my excitement. Just ahead, the mountain formed two vertical walls close together but separated by a large fissure.

Chase held on to me and kept grinning, seemingly unfazed by the upward movement.

I glanced at his face.

He winked. I could do little but maintain the contact until I reached the surface. "You must have an idea. How high is it?" I inquired with a slight growl.

He laughed. "Did you just growl at me?"

I had indeed, and I schooled my features, unwilling to discuss something we all did. It was part of our DNA and all the genetic engineering we underwent growing up, but we never addressed it. It just was...

His charm was infectious and hard to ignore. With the light shimmering near the opening, Chase closed his lids, adjusting to the brightness. It gave me time to compose myself, as I ignored his comment. I didn't want to get any closer to him, nor did I desire to know his thoughts or feelings at this moment. Instead, despite these emotions, I asked, "How do you feel?"

"I have a pounding headache, but I think I'll live."

This climb gave me time to consider our predicament. Could I trust a stranger, this stranger? There was only one way to find out. Only I didn't want to think about that now.

I could feel his gaze on me, steady, unwavering, as he observed my reaction. Our mouths were perilously close, only a few inches apart. Luckily, the glass of my EmVat around my head formed a barrier between us. *Good for that… I guess.*

I turned away from his lips. Hmm…

Chase was too close.

His breath fogged up the transparent contour of my headset, right at the level of my jaw. I needed to break the silence between us. The contact had turned warmly intimate. Still, it was weirdly exciting.

Funny, I felt like getting even closer. *Not smart, Tesh. Whoaah, what in the HellNet are you doing?*

My visor unfolded between my face and that of this captivating stranger. I pulled back to give us some distance.

Blast appeared beside Leane on my visor, way too close for comfort. "We're done here. Making our way back. Again, no sign of Streak."

"Oh…" I mused, looking at the guy in my arms.

Leane joined Blast with an enormous smile on her face. "It is splendid news. He must be too far out for us to read him. He'll find his way back to us."

"I hope so," I murmured as I felt my cheeks flush.

I saw an eyebrow raised in my direction, and I heard a sigh of inquiry from my passenger. My brows furrowed together, ignoring both. He was about to speak, and I silenced him by pressing two of my fingers against his lips. I frowned. What have I got myself into I wondered?

"Tesh, what's wrong? What do you see?" asked Blast.

"Huh... What? Nothing. Why?" Distracted by the heat of his lips against my fingertips, my focus was off.

Chase's gaze left unsaid what we were feeling, yet he seemed amenable to remaining silent.

"You look flustered. Is everything all right?" demanded Leane, with a smile on her face.

I forced a lopsided grin and looked at them both, avoiding his sparkling blue eyes. "Yeap. I'm almost out."

Leane's voice resonated over the NetComm. "What do we do once we're outside?" I sensed her unease.

"Not sure," Blast responded. "It depends what we find."

I remained silent and looked at my two friends. While I had never truly believed in the experiment, here we were.

As Perfect Human, we had left behind the very core of who we were. The fundamental essence that made us unique. Indeed, DAINN contributed to shaping who we were anywhere in the universe. DAINN's imprint in our heads left an echo even now. But the System that created us did not offer a safety net in this place. Everything we understood no longer existed for us. The answer rang loud and clear in my head. We were in an unknown world, and we didn't belong to this time.

Before coming here, we wondered what we would face in this world. Looking at the guy in my arms, I knew we would soon understand it because we had succeeded in getting here. The hope we were still in Ang when we woke up died with Chase appearing in the cavern. Until that moment, we could believe the experiment had flopped. We let ourselves think our people were feet away on the surface and that they would come for us if they had survived because we wanted to hold on to that notion.

Blast groaned over the NetComm, "Is our recent friend giving you trouble?"

I glanced at Chase. "Don't worry. I can handle him." I smiled when I saw his reaction. The look in his eyes, now filled with a challenging glare, gave me pause. *Um, now what have I done?*

Waking up at a different time than we had left now confirmed we possessed only one mandate. Our people could no longer help us. But we still belonged to the future, witnesses to our potential demise, unless we corrected the present's trajectory. It rendered the possibility of our extinction even more real if we failed here in this new timeline.

It didn't matter, for there was only one outcome now. We lost our world while we slept.

Maybe, just maybe, they had been right to send us here. If we could achieve our goal, our people would survive, and that's what mattered.

Chase moved against me, tightening his hold as if he wanted to tell me something. It only contributed to us getting closer, and now we barely had any air between us.

I gasped.

He smiled, lifting both eyebrows at me, questioning.

I changed my focus.

He wouldn't have it. He kissed the tips of my fingers.

I removed my hand.

His expression, teasing until then, changed to a more serious one. Then he attempted to speak again.

I reapplied my fingers to his lips with a scowl.

Chase behaved oddly but seemed satisfied for now, while I still scolded him with my eyes, forgetting that both Blast and Leane watched me through the screen.

Leane's voice inquired, "Tesh, you're acting strange. What's going on?"

"Yeah, what's going on?" added Blast.

With every breath we took, a patch of the sky grew as the light outside floated down on us. Soon, we would reach the surface, and I beamed as the sunlight got closer.

"We're getting close to the surface," I said.

"Oh…" Leane exclaimed with a hint of nervousness.

"NetWash… We're on our way," Blast said with impatience.

Chase winked at me with a smile so bright that heat unfurled in my spine. I inhaled again, fighting the hitch in my breath, and turned my blue-green eyes back to the sky, admiring its brilliance. It had been so long since I saw the outside that my impatience grew and I could barely contain my excitement.

Just ahead, the mountain formed two vertical walls close together but separated by a large fissure.

Chase held on to me and grinned, unfazed by my lack of response. Our upward movement continued steadily. Until we reached the surface, the contact between us remained as I held on to him.

I played back the events in my head. I wanted to convince Chase to help us, but for that, I needed time alone with him. Leane and Blast would muddle through it, with nothing good coming of it. Although they possessed many qualities, patience was not one of Blast's best traits, and Leane knew nothing about manipulation. She called it as she saw it. Enticing Chase to become an ally would require a lot more, especially with the tablet at stake. Neither Blast nor Leane even knew about that yet.

When I peeked down at Chase again, he observed me with a Cheshire grin on his face. What was he thinking? For the first time, I saw his features in the daylight. Regular and sun-kissed, he was handsome, roughly. As we emerged from the darkness, his sandy blond hair shifted under the breeze, covering his eyes. The urge to push it back and away from his forehead surged. *It is not right, Tesh. DAINN, what have you done?*

We had reached the outside. I glided over a small promontory and dumped Chase on it. We now stood at the summit, and it dominated the other mountain tops surrounding us.

Chase stumbled on the rock before finding his balance again.

My release of him had been abrupt; I gave him that. But letting go of my hold on Chase was timely. Things had lasted long enough for me to glimpse at the connection that formed between us, and maintaining some distance felt a lot safer for now.

Waiting no longer, I turned, faced the sun, and enjoyed the beauty and warmth.

3
ANNALS
SWEEP
DAINN

DAINN – Ang City 2043
SRC Conclave. Viewing Vlog 119,923. Annals – Winter 2043

The pandemic ends three years after it begins. It changes our world. Our governments, too narrowly segmented to face the impending threats, are found inadequate and temporary measures take hold. Therefore, a centralized organization of countries passes in an overwhelming majority vote. DAINN Annals – 2043.

Nothing will ever be the same.

Inside the large Parliament building, the countries' leaders were ready to vote. The faces of those attending reflected the gravity of the situation. This step represented a substantial change in the organization of our world. Everyone seated here understood the consequences of that fact.

The System recorded the events of that day and kept the video feeds for archiving purposes.

The threat to society was deemed too high of a risk. Maintaining individual nations in a world so tied together by commerce no longer made sense. After a death toll of thus far more than twenty-nine million, seven hundred thousand, three hundred and sixty-eight lives, countries had to reconsider their handling of such a crisis. The results were staring everyone in the face and required drastic change.

Indeed, most nations' lack of coordinated efforts remained the culprit. Even after ensuring the safeguard of their citizens, the implemented measures never slowed the virus's spread. There were too many regulations in the way of a concerted effort. Too many dissenting opinions existed over the required time for the quarantine. Personality conflicts, leadership styles, conflicting agendas pervaded over seeking better outcomes.

So, in the middle of the pandemic, amidst significant internal conflicts, a movement was born. The organization of countries forming one of the strongest alliances ever created the Federation of Nations. It was mandated to take over. Its first action was to appoint the EHAF as its primary security force. The goal was for the Clout to enforce its rules of law. This action spurred territorial disputes for many. But under closed doors, the FON leaders came together, extending invitations to participate in a Federation of Nations, and it led the way to a centralized governing body.

Overcoming resistance on multiple fronts and overpowering smaller forces, the Clout of the EHAF brought order to the transitioning chaos. It swept through resistant troops from nations unwilling to establish new ground rules for the coalition at first. In that way, it delivered new outcomes. Reticent Presidents and Heads of States reconciled themselves to maintain a more limited role within their countries or lose the one they had altogether. This new leadership established a Council under the Federations of Nations to oversee the world's affairs. As one body, they now led with a legislature under the omnipresence of the EHAF.

The strength of the Force left no doubt. Now, encompassing the armed forces of multiple countries, all serving under its purview, it assembled the best of them all under one Elite Force and a General Corp.

No one wanted a repeat of another poorly managed outbreak. With the economies of our world so totally intertwined, it made sense to centralize. Thus, under various governmental bodies, each serving specific fields, the Conclaves were born. Not recognized yet, but existing under another form, they began spreading their influence. More entrenched into rigid entities serving different areas of our society, they started merging powers under a broader mandate.

The world regions remained the same. The Americas, Asia Pacific, Eurasia, Europe, Middle East, North Africa, South Asia, Sub-Sahara Africa, and the United States were all delineated. All the countries guaranteed a structure similar to the United Nations but functioned as a much more powerful state association. Their elected representatives received thirty-three seats. The Council then relayed any decisions of the Federation of Nations to their respective leaders.

As the vote took place, all present voted "Yes."

The new President of the EHAF was elected. The first expected act of Wilfried Santer III was to implement the Sweep.

Today was the official beginning of a new era for our world. This mandate orchestrated a peaceful future for all but dictated more control.

After we finally progressed to contain the worldwide outbreak, it became unthinkable that globally we did not react as one in the face of such a catastrophe.

Why indeed? When the outbreak was first noticed, too many things reminded us of the early months of the pandemic of 2020. Only a mutated organism could be so virulent. Like then, Earth retreated indoors, our residents confined under strict rules, but it was not enough.

The madness continued as people became frustrated, dissatisfied, and angry. Violence erupted everywhere, showing how we remained divided into our opinions and viewpoints instead of creating a common front against an invisible enemy. Like then, we faced isolated incidents that slowly multiplied and turned into riots, with pockets of disruption taking over entire cities. Instead of marching under the humankind banner, people found solace in dividing and spreading hatred. Our leaders had witnessed the same behaviors in our historical databases and reacted aggressively to overcome such unrest.

Amidst all these separated events, the mission of each Conclave became more precise and defined. Each claimed an area and field of expertise in which they would govern. All selected a group of leaders demanding the ability to draft a segment of the population they would control.

The Conclaves were officially born.

The Institute oversaw the population's segregation. Established to determine every individual's inclination, it enforced education and training to benefit our society under the Federation. Later, its role expanded worldwide under the same principles. The Faculty kept its prerogative in the Healthcare field, overseeing the entire medical body. The SRC regrouped under one primary entity for research and development in science and technology, granting, supervising, and regulating the use of discoveries across the world. The Company took over the corporations' oversight activities and organized under one umbrella to more effectively address intellectual properties and the needs of our population, including manufacturing, operations, and distribution. These insidious transformations took place behind closed doors until the Federation became established.

The vote on the Sweep was a mere act to pass. Silence bequeathed silence within our city walls as we all awaited the poll results. When it finally was broadcast, everyone understood that the Sweep would occur. Everyone feared the changes. Until that moment, some held hope that it would not be so.

The System announced the results simultaneously all around the world. "Today, at two-thirty pm pacific time, the President of the EHAF, Wilfried Santer III, was elected to a ten-year term." His mandate would last from 2043 to 2053. In his first act in office, he ratified the Sweep.

Due to its by-laws, the Federation of Nations selected the President of the EHAF for a continuous ten-year term to maintain government continuity. From the results of that vote, the segregation of our population became a mandate into the legislative. The Sweep, so feared by many, became rectified to be implemented immediately. It dictated the potential field of an individual for his work of endeavor. After the Sweep, each member of society was officially assigned to a Conclave and belonged to its internal laws.

4
ENCOUNTER
Chase

Underground Tunnel, CA – 2022

Chase Davenport doesn't know what hit him when Tesh appears in front of him. True to his nature, he doesn't back down even in the face of the unknown. In my experience as an A.I., people exhibit fear at what they do not know or cannot control. Chase appears to handle these types of predicaments well. DAINN Annals – Summer 2022.

My encounter with this girl filled me with excitement. Maybe it came from the fact that I hoped, no, I expected to find something when I entered the cavern again. I stood stunned when she appeared through the metallic doorway. The moment flashed in front of my eyes again. Rooted to the ground when the door opened, I remained still, not knowing what to expect. Although, I felt a sense of Deja Vue.

Her presence here represented something bordering on the extraordinary, although a sense of inevitability surfaced in me. Whatever lay behind the light of the enclosure did not even matter. My ignorance and careless sense of curiosity did not phase me but sometimes jeopardized me. Me, being here at this time and in this place, was just meant to be. Fear didn't exist. Don't ask me why. It was illogical; I know.

In the dark surroundings, I couldn't even see clearly. The fact of this presence was enough. I didn't know what to expect, nor did I anticipate what would happen next. The encounter made an impact, though, and I will remember that feeling well until the day I die.

This moment in the cave carved itself indelibly in my memory. When I saw the red net coming at me and became trapped by it in the blink of an eye, I got thrown to the ground and went out like a light. This thing, with its artificial red-eyed, threw me for a loop. It took me down within seconds. No sensation. Just nothingness. To this moment, I'm unsure how long I remained on the ground, but the sight when I opened my eyes, well, this sight was worth everything. Here she was, next to me, watching me.

Hell... Tesh's existence began an array of possibilities beyond anything I had ever imagined. A mask hid her features. Her silhouette ensconced in a bodysuit of sorts left nothing to my already excited imagination. The darn thing perfectly fitting showed all her curves, and somehow, I felt like I knew her implicitly. Go figure!

Their technology surpassed our own, and it awakened my curiosity tenfold. I couldn't wait to ask Tesh questions. But then a thought surfaced. Could this be in any way connected with the Center on the other side of the mountain? Was she Spallberg's find? Was this the cause of his excitement these last few weeks? Did they know about her? It couldn't be. I sure didn't want it to be true.

Her presence in this place, at that moment, led me to believe that Jonathan didn't know. Otherwise, the grounds would swarm with security. Jonathan had a big footprint. If they had not encountered her yet, this was my chance. Was she even alone? What were they doing here? Then, my next thought led me down a path I didn't like. What would it mean for her if they discovered her here?

It never dawned on me she could be dangerous. She had saved me a year ago. I was sure of that fact. My fall and what took place during my climb opened me up to the impossible. It led me to give these newcomers the benefit of the doubt, and it seemed the right thing to do. In the same line of thought, I believed that the thing she threw my way amounted to, most likely, an overreaction. I took that stand because, well, here I was, alive and unharmed. *Give her a pass, Chase. You surprised the hell out of her, for sure.*

I was delirious as I contemplated all that. The diminished air in the tunnel affected me. A lack of oxygen rendered me dizzy. Hell, the place was closed tight. The cave-in obstructed our exit and cut us out from the outside. Once again, I faced inside this cave a lousy outcome because something went terribly wrong.

My new companion didn't hesitate much when she realized the danger. She immediately pulled me up and gave me her support as we walked. Within seconds, she created a gap in the bedrock, vaporizing the fallen rocks with a handheld laser emitting a powerful sound burst. She blasted these enormous boulders, blocking the passageway, rescuing me, and saving my life a second time.

The mountain pulverized, opening up a path to the cavern beyond. We now stood over the edge; the way opened toward our freedom. Only, I then witnessed the light for the first time.

We faced an Entity of unknown origin. The energy ball that rose from the abyss moved at unprecedented speed across the space of the cavern. It darted through the air, turning in our direction while we gaped at it.

Tesh pushed me back, attempting to protect me. It was the second time I felt helpless and hopeless in her presence. My inferiority complex triggered a flood of questions I could not ask. Hell, we were standing at the edge of the tunnel, looking at an unknown guest that didn't seem friendly.

We had no clue about its existence. Weirdly, it made me feel better. Although powerful, the strangers were not all-knowing, and soon after that, I also learned that they were not infallible.

From that point on, everything happened so fast. The assault, Tesh's attempt at getting me out of harm's way… The vibrations… The power of the pulse… The fight… The pain… The Sphere… The light and speed… All remained in my memory like a series of puzzling pieces enrobed in shining bright lights coming from all directions and then the lack of everything - and then nothingness.

Through it all, I remained confused, my head pounding. Time no longer had meaning. I lost track of it when we got swallowed up inside the Sphere. Things happened around me, but I stayed in limbo, unable to focus, sensing in a sort of half-consciousness as moments unfolded. The feeling lasted. Then, the air of the tunnel filled my lungs again, and I regained consciousness alongside my new companions.

The rest of it remained a lot more surreal, like Tesh jumping outside over the emptiness of the cavern in her gliding boots while her friends returned to secure the Chamber and retrieve their equipment or Tesh's body pressed against mine in the brief flight we took to the surface.

I almost forgot the rest of it. Smitten, I loved the feeling of Tesh against me. Hell, I wanted, no, I needed to get to know her in more ways.

We reached the outside in no time at all. Part of me regretted how fast. It was over way too soon.

Tesh, while gliding over a small promontory, released me. She seemed preoccupied.

I grimaced at the jolt of her maneuver.

She dropped me on the rocky surface without gentleness in her need to get away from me. Her behavior seemed like she was thinking about twenty things, and I just happened to be number twenty-one. But it also made me smile because we established a connection. I could feel it. My enthusiastic behavior contributed to this belief. And... Sure, one might have found a few objections to my crazy reaction to being close to her. So what?

I straightened up and faced her, ignoring one side of my head that felt like bursting.

Tesh guessed at my discomfort. "It will pass; you'll feel better soon," she said, pointing to my throbbing forehead.

"You keep saying that. Yeah, I know. I'll live," I muttered, disgruntled.

Her bodysuit dropped its protection in the next instant, and I saw all of her. I saw her... And she was not only beautiful but flawless.

"Leane will see to it when she joins us, but I need to tell you something," she insisted, impatient to have a meaningful conversation with me. It was no doubt overdue, but before she could begin, I took her hand in mine and laid it against my chest.

With hesitation, she frowned but let me. Tesh's reaction pleased me; a sweet intake of breath. Nothing too noticeable, even so, I perceived it.

I kept a soft grip on her hand. "I haven't thanked you properly yet." My mouth stretched into a lazy smile. "Thank you. I owe you."

She pulled her hand away and took a step back. "Look, I don't have a lot of time to explain."

I no longer paid attention. I got lost in watching Tesh. Sure, I had questions, but her allure and charisma mesmerized me. Something fascinated me about her. I forgot for a time everything I wanted to ask her. My eyes caressed every curve of her body. I left an imprint on her skin with my gaze wherever it lingered—trailing hotness. My inspection continued, and she remained still throughout, but I could tell she didn't like it.

Her lips pinched, her eyes narrowed, and she glared right back at me.

I smiled, unable to help it. Tesh was feisty, and I took pleasure in watching her. My stare landed on her eyes. They were beautiful, with a mix of Seafoam green like one find near the most pristine shores and a lapis blue from the ocean's dept. They fascinated me. My show of appreciation rendered the next moment of silence between us awkward. I didn't care about the mounting tension. Indeed, I welcomed it. Making an impression on her was the whole point.

Caught off-guard by my feverish intensity, the slight pulse at the base of her neck beat fast. Her long lashes fluttered, and her eyes rested on me.

Tesh began an evaluation of her own while giving me an amused look. It became unnerving to stand still under her gaze, but it was only fair after what I had just done. "Not so much fun when someone else does it?" she whispered with a smile.

"Touché." I clipped, "Hum… Then again, it depends."

But the seriousness of her features led to the severity of their situation. Their presence created too many questions and brought about unwanted attention.

She imparted something to me. "If people knew about us… It would make things…."

"Complicated?"

"Truly."

Their need to remain unseen and unknown was paramount. People couldn't find out about them, and especially not the Center. Any trace of them would bring about unwanted attention. I got that.

Tesh's features were severe when she said, "Chase, you hold a piece of information we need. My skills alone will serve me to get it from you if you become aggressive."

"I don't know how I can help you…."

"My reflexes, honed by years of training, are sharp, and my instincts prove extremely reliable," Tesh quipped, challenging me to resist.

Our eyes met and stayed locked.

The hint of a threat came, but I did not consider it real, not after what she had done to save me, and yet…

Satisfied that she had made clear her position and knowing that I presented no challenge, her eyes finally let go of mine.

I took a deep breath.

She switched her focus to the panorama behind me, and her face filled with wonderment. "It's amazing," she whispered.

On the inside, I was reeling, knowing that I knew nothing about them. On the surface, though, I resolved to remain nonchalant. I couldn't tell Tesh that she had impressed upon me the precarious nature of my situation. "Yeah… That's a view that never stops being amazing," I murmured, standing at her side. My position demanded that I strengthen whatever link we had. "How different is it where you come from?"

She never answered. She seemed entranced far away in that instant as we watched the landscape in silence.

5 ANNALS DECLINE DAINN

DAINN – Ang City 2045

SRC Conclave. Viewing Vlog – 1,219,876. Annals – Fall -2045.

When the Sweep takes place, a new census exists. Data makes its way into the DAINN System. Our world population remains divided among the five Conclaves: the Institute, the SRC, the Faculty, the Company, and the EHAF. Life, reorganized in a fashion, limits us and gives us different opportunities. DAINN Annals - 2045.

When the government implemented the Sweep, blood ran in our streets. People refused the new order.

They didn't accept the cataloging that resulted, nor their newly assigned Conclaves. They didn't select it, so they didn't recognize it as legal. They considered the resulting changes like a draft and fought against it.

It made no difference that people rebelled in our world. The System took over. The transfers took place within the database. People effectively moved from their field of choice to newly assigned work endeavors. The Network repeated endlessly for all to hear the following mantra: "You must report to your new work assignment. You are re-assigned. It is final." Such was the voice of the A.I., answering all inquiries.

In a way, the System hijacked all of us to implement its new mandate. In so doing, it took over the population's dreams until the Network perfected all assignments. In the end, people had to work to survive.

The DAINN System took hold and, in many respects, enhanced our lives for the better. In others, our freedom suffered, and it stripped away privileges we once possessed.

It all started way back when the first supercomputer created for the Defense Advanced Research Projects Agency, also called a "cognitive computer," and simulating our brain neurons developed in the United States, took hold.

For years after that, multiple teams worked on improving every computer capability on the planet, adding capacity, power, algorithms, and coding so that the machine would learn on its own. And it had... The A.I. was born.

Under the vision of Dr. Rene Paladock, we quickly progressed in this matter, extrapolating new information and assimilating faster new ways to cross-reference data.

In the beginning, Paladock built outlandish theories, or they seemed like such at the time. He fought his way through a ton of political and corporate red tape. He created unpopular assumptions, theoretical and even groundbreaking ones. From there, he reached conclusions to where we are today. He wasn't alone in that effort, but he paved the way to it.

Fascinated with innovations and disruptive technologies, the idea of developing a computer system highly bio-inspired so that it would grow and expand on its own wasn't a new idea but one to be enhanced.

He had already created the System. He had just built a more powerful machine with a multitude of capabilities. The plan was to gather information and process it from all areas across the globe, connecting to one System with access to data depth. And assembling this data to create an automatic function was already accomplished in the early days of the Internet. The difference was a matter of capacity, functionality, and scope.

As technology moved forward, so did people. Science made that happen, little by little or by leaps. We added technology on many levels, grafting databanks to virtual reality environments, 3D printing to robotics, and nanotechnology to imbedded information computing within our brainpower. Algorithms manipulated to interface in new ways, unconventional logic and reasoning, additive cross-referencing, data stream control, instantaneous access, automatic functionality, chip enhancements, and finally, the construct of DAINN happened. DAINN, the System became ready to tackle more than our infrastructure. Slowly, it expanded from there.

We applied DAINN's programming to preventive medicine. Over the years, we accumulated everyone's DNA, then genome. It worked. Interpreting medical data in advance revolutionized our healthcare system. We cataloged and tagged every newborn. This information was essential. It gave us insight into what to expect with illnesses. It then provided us with a timeline for potential diseases. All we needed to do was watch. The System also matched potential donors. If people in need of care did not have the financial resources to get an organ made from their DNA with 3D Printing, sometimes, they used an implant. Mainly, we developed a remedy for everything we could. Even the anti-aging drugs became mainstream.

Bioengineering played a considerable role in the next phase, drastically expanding the uses and purpose of implants gained in our lives. It was crucial, as we could identify the best time for a specific type of implant.

It eliminated today the flaws in our medical structure from years ago. DAINN excelled in this. We had a list of potential patients that would have eventually experienced organ failures. DAINN attempted to fix these problems way before the individual emergency arose. The high probability of certain diseases demanded that DAINN maintain these patients under constant monitoring. The System accomplished that in the first phase.

Now, finding organs for patients was no longer an issue. We created some of them on demand. DAINN's data bank kept track of what was already in existence. All hospitals were connected and had access to every organ available across the nation, even worldwide, and it was immediate through the Company's distribution services. As we developed DNA engineering, this was slowly becoming obsolete… Although, not yet.

Mostly, the System protocols processed information instantly and flagged problems anywhere around the globe. After this first foray, where patients began adapting to chips inserted in their bodies, it had quickly become clear that we were missing other potential infrastructures within our various organizations. So, we integrated additional learning capabilities within all our subjects when we expanded onto more complex fields.

Paladock wanted DAINN for something more immediate, a link instantaneously recognizing any problems or situations that lay ahead of us.

The momentum gained over the years led to the expansion of much higher complexity and intelligence functions in the System. The results were dramatically successful in multiple fields. Such a revolutionary system then expanded further. Eventually, this led Paladock to imagine ways where the System would interface with other types of potentiality or scope. As a result, the program took a global proportion.

Our funding increased, as did the vision. Other methodologies improved our way of life. Paladock now headed an entire facility. The Science Research Center oversaw through DAINN the needs of an entire world. The machine had grown to become our planetary computer - one powerful artificial intelligence neural network—the Network.

The advancements made in technology were huge, but so were the advances in science. Yet, life became less valued in all that, and man unraveled. The changes didn't happen overnight. They were because of a series of events that transformed our moral fabric over years of decay.

Some say our demise began with the advent of industrialization. As our capabilities increased, so did our need for more. While capitalism gradually became the dominant system throughout the world. It took various forms, structures, methods, and scales. Some may say it originated earlier with mercantilism, way back in the sixteenth century in Northern Europe with wealth and power concentration.

It spread beyond national boundaries like a virus, and with enhanced capabilities, commercialization took alternative forms, introducing new products or methods in commerce and reaching new markets. Yet, fewer people benefited. The rich got richer. Consumerism expanded beyond the business world as technologies integrated the scene, playing a part in the food chain as consumer goods became a trend. Along the way, the planet had become smaller. People became more irrelevant.

Globalism entered our world's framework, escalating our reach beyond the mere international boundaries, creating new patterns and an array of interconnections with modernization as a way of life. Traditional government structures weakened, derivatives of socialism and communism fell, capitalism became crony capitalism, and the authoritarian dismantled the existing balance of power in our world.

These notions became permanent fixtures in our daily lives, shaping new constructs. Radical changes took place in a relatively short time frame. Excesses grew, fueling specific structures for the sake of special interest groups and lobbyism changed perceptions, dictating new agendas. It worked insidiously on many fronts. The poor grew more impoverished, and the divide turned global.

And while this was taking place within nations, these new developments spread like wildfire, corrupting our most basic infrastructures. Democratic notions and countries became twisted. At its core, the idea or concept that people had the authority and right to choose their governing legislation turned into populist movements. Extreme views eventually changed the nature of many governments. People were displaced, and with that came uprising and dynamic change. Factions waged wars of ideology for the sake of dogma. The attacks on the fundamental values of democracy reached new heights as the nation that stood for the experiment crumbled and failed. Everywhere around the globe, concepts of freedom, liberty, equality were challenged more systematically and with more vigor. Core traditions and ethics got warped in the process as forces bent on dismantling an entire system worked assiduously.

It was then that the American experiment - the United States lost its way in the world. The government, relinquishing its role as a beacon of democratic beliefs and the old code of conduct, demolished the status quo by disregarding fundamental principles of fairness, character, and morals. Its leadership sold out, buckling under the weight and influence of usurpers. And during this time, the surge of terrorism changed our way of life. The withdrawal by a massive power from the world scene nurtured a dark era.

While the old system may not have been perfect, the new beliefs that anything goes became the playground of those in power, and a plague launched against the poor. This new alignment of forces trampled everything good in America. It replaced it with chaos, worshipping at the altar of greed and throwing away common decency, conscience, integrity, sense of honor and duty, and scruples. Power, no matter the cost, became the new mantra. New rules became pervasive, and one thing developed for sure, there were no longer any rules as the saying "anything goes" paved a new era.

In all of it, DAINN, the System, accumulating data over decades, recorded and archived everything, giving us insights into a compendium of historical facts. Whether these occurred as they were reported or not was another matter.

These new tendencies were indeed not helped in other ways. The internet exposed the planet to opportunities and helped create the shift. Perhaps the transformation occurred as years of influence by the entertainment industry cultivated content with brutality and cruelty for the sake of box office revenues. Indeed, violence in films increased by more than fifty percent in the twentieth century, and gun violence in

PG-13 movies more than tripled. Could it be said that these creative outlets prepared people to accept violence more readily? This type of programming could have impacted a new generation of people and numbed them, destroying moral integrity and the sanctity of life and limbs as they grew up and evolved in a damaging environment.

Could we contend that the attention-grabbing headlines driving crowds into a frenzy were methods that contributed to more ratings and, therefore, more revenues and promoted the advent of news highlights? If so, could we also conclude that this new form of information elicited a need to consume more content in 'a superficial form' driving 'social news' rather than in-depth analysis? It blurred the lines between facts and lies. Could the advent of social media have paved the way for an entire generation, fascinated with the ability to seek the limelight and shaped the age of the influencer, the age of 'me'? Regardless of how or why these considerations came to be, they framed a new era.

Social media networks' predominance in our lives influenced ethical considerations, eroding old-fashioned values, impacting standards, and shifting ideals. Misinformation, fake news, and dissident worldviews spread. The incidence of false dogma surged, resulting in warped belief systems or ideologies, modeling and controlling the young or the old. Every household became affected. The insidious nature of dissident propaganda resulted in one thing - altering society's fabric and transforming our dialog. Our fundamental values shifted for the worst, creating a pandemic and a social virus. Humanity transmutation had officially begun.

While newsworthy materials fought for our attention, our declining moral compass flamed our indifference to more significant issues. Our actions and their repercussions on our environment were critical facets, among many others. Then, after years of neglect, the planet fought back.

We could no longer reverse the clock. And so, everything got worse for a vast number of species despite attempts to save them. Climate change invaded our lives and catapulted us toward the abyss. Our environment declined drastically and fast, but so did we. We were a species on its way to its extinction. We entered another phase of our evolution.

6
MEMORIES
Tesh

Mountain Summit, CA – 2022

The surface claimed my attention. The beauty of my surroundings seemed almost unreal. But the emotions I felt wrecked my body as I fought to understand why DAINN allowed the link with Chase. Tesh VLog - DAINN Annals - Summer 2022.

The landscape was incredible, and it claimed all of me. For the first time in my life, I felt the sun on my face without worrying that it would burn me to a crisp. The wind swirled around me and did not make me buckle under its velocity. I wanted nothing more than to release my thoughts to it, my emotions warring inside my head.

When Chase didn't move away from me fast enough, I turned away, looking around on the summit, and discarded my EmVat.

A gasp escaped his lips.

I glanced back toward him at the noise—*it was the wrong move.* The closeness we shared in that instant brought an additional dimension to the dilemma I faced.

His long lashes fluttered as his piercing blue eyes rested on me.

My breath caught in my throat. I turned away from Chase and toward the sun. The fresh air on my face teased my skin, searing it with a pleasant warmth. For the first time in a long while, I stood outdoors, sensing the wind against me and the brilliance of the light under a pristine sky. The feelings caused wonderment. My mind remained full of unanswered questions.

How could the MindLink created by DAINN, between this man and I, exist with such strength? How could it establish such a visceral reaction? What about my feelings for Streak? There has to be a way to protect me from this.

Limits eventually occurred with everything in life, some much more visible than others, forming obstacles in our paths and shaping a different future uncontrollably. My skills allowed my mind the possibility of influencing others. DAINN had thrown a wrench into the equation when it exercised its protocol and activated a channel between us. Did D even realize that I would experience something like this by linking my DNA to the stranger? Understanding DAINN, it most likely had. Our A.I. determined that it was but a small price to pay for the opportunity to save a life and tie that life to one of us. Unfortunately, it looked like I would pay for this choice. I shrugged. *DamnNet, I don't need this.*

Chase closed the gap I had created seconds before. "Is everything all right?"

Under the sunlight, we inspected each other in silence. This guy was nothing to me, nothing. But he affected me. Realizing that my time alone with him shortened with every second, I muttered, "I need to tell you something before the others arrive."

The connection created by DAINN remained palpable between us. DAINN intervened when Chase fell into the cave. It responded to its programming under the Universal Pledge, but this contact stayed within me, associated with my DNA.

I surmised this as I watched Chase, wondering how he received the link. The kinship existed between us, even if we both didn't quite understand it yet. I didn't want any of this; however, here it was.

"What?" Chase said, watching me with curiosity.

Our society thrived on structure, one that appeared to serve the individual. Taking a position within a Conclave encouraged closeness, keeping each of us in check. Selecting posts within our chosen faction also helped to tie us down. Our natural abilities, combined with the Imps brought about a precise selection process. With it came unbreakable rules that spun precedents. Once adopted, transgressions became almost impossible. In fact, by providing choices under the guise of our attributes, our leaders boxed us in. Then our characteristics needed to serve our society, and identified as gifts, lead us on a path, not our own.

"We do not share the same rules...." I whispered. "Do not expect the same behavior."

The System required a person to bend, serve, and obey. It was a quasi-privilege, a calling not to ignore. This process existed as the foundation of our entire System with unseen consequences. No influence could derail it at any point in time. Our desires and wants were unattainable factors, ignored in the equation unless extraordinary circumstances existed. And even then. Our leaders, whose opinion counted above all else, would interfere with the outcome if it came to that.

Based on our System, there was no future possible between Streak and me. DAINN stated as much again and again. I wondered if D, in its indomitable way, had found logic to keep us apart because of the imponderable results our union could unleash. And so, I responded to a perfect stranger—one in a different time and place, where I could be free. Talk about confusing… My reaction complicated everything further and brought the entire issue to new heights.

I was a free spirit in a world of compartmentalized processes—'a child of the universe' maneuvering in a microcosm of rules. My abilities allowed me to circumvent certain things imposed by our training and our way of life. Before knowing these rules, I would have broken these guidelines out of cunning individuality and freedom. But after this knowledge fell on my lap, I became more vigilant to cross well over the lines. It may be too late when it came down to Streak and me, but I refused to let my life driven by emotions and physical reactions, mainly when these were outside of my control, given that these were engineered feedbacks.

"How is that?" Chase inquired.

"I'm not sure the 'how' is important here. The world we come from is less emotional, more controlling, harder to navigate," I said. Maybe trying to explain things to Chase was a waste of time.

The desire to drop the stranger, right there, and then rose within me. My impulse was to let him figure out how to make it down the mountain on his own. But I couldn't do it because I needed him. Impeded by our code of conduct demanding that we help the weak and my feelings, I had to see this through since, in this circumstance, he was the more vulnerable of us.

He nodded. Touching his bloody head, he said: "What do you call this thing you had on?"

"Oh… it's a suit, an EmVat."

"Nice. Can I get one?"

I laughed. For a person who just went up a shaft in the arms of someone with the most advanced set of jet boots from a time in the future, he looked calm. They were hardly ordinary, by the way. They were EHAF jet boots, part of a military-grade EmVat with advanced A.I. protocols and defense mechanisms. And it had not been enough against the power of the sentient being and its energy field we met in the cave. "Nope. They don't come easy."

Would he help us? Could we count on him? How far?

I appraised his face: muscular, handsome, and tanned. His brows, darker than his sandy blond hair, stood drawn above those gorgeous blue eyes that, at the moment, focused on me. A slight stubble of beard ran across his square jaw, forming a shadow around his mouth —a beautiful one at that. His sandy blond hair shifted on his forehead, and one of his hands pushed the longer strands away. He grimaced as his fingers touched his temple.

"Hum… I get that. Still, maybe you could make an exception, and we could fly together. Selling these would make a killing."

I watched him, attempting to make sense of his meaning. I tried to comprehend what he had just said while thinking about my next step and concluded it was a joke. It had to be.

Darnet. I felt lost under his gaze. My thoughts faded into emotional chaos. The tumultuous dance they formed swooshed around to rebound in the background of my mind. Gone was the rational girl. My breath caught in my throat again. Chase affected me in ways I had never experienced before. "Look, I don't have a lot of time to explain…"

I wished Streak stood in front of me. Rejecting this situation, I wanted nothing more than to have Streak be my armor against Chase. I resisted responding to a made-up attraction. Extricating myself from it became urgent, so I called upon Streak to reappear, to be there for me, but he wasn't. He was somewhere, lost.

Our society has required that we select someone else as a life partner. The calling and positions we held demanded as much. And our Conclave rules called for a different unity. Together, we became dangerous. We were too strong individually; they said behind closed doors. My gifts and Streak's extreme abilities became a hindrance when they should have provided more freedom. Because of this mandate, they forced us to maintain our distance and never got close enough to claim ourselves as a couple. Not that we remembered it, anyway.

Drawn into my memories, I lost myself in this moment. The System dictated how we shared our lives and family unit.

I rebelled at first. I was the only one.

Streak accepted the situation without fighting. I hoped he would come to see it my way for a long time. But he embraced the System. So, I concocted situations to tempt him despite his stoicism. I enticed him. My attempts to play games, in which he would succumb to my charms, didn't work. The more Streak refrained from taking the bait, the more I misbehaved. I coaxed and teased.

He closed himself off. Who could blame him?

Eventually, this dance, with no music to feed on, turned into utter emptiness. Perhaps it was me. I was defective, not seeing the wrong in our attraction. But these were the memories I held onto, and part of me wondered if the Rodent planted them to keep us apart.

Now, my emotional frustration triggered memories of Streak and everything we went through. I recalled the rare moments where we were together in such proximity. They amounted to a life of hope, excitement with no follow-through. It led me to focus everything on the training.

My dreams vanished, enhancing my torment. When it became clear that taking the next step would never be possible, that Streak showed an inflexibility in breaking even the slightest of decrees, one that we could push through with determination and cunning, and I finally realized the futility of trying. It was then that I retreated emotionally. At least, I told myself as much. And when I finally gave up because of my destroyed dreams, my relationship with Streak became strained despite our childhood friendship.

In the last year at the Academy, I no longer tried to convince him we had a right to be together. Instead, I confronted an emptiness within myself, and things took their toll. I kept my distance, but the damage had occurred. Perhaps this explained the mind wipe. Maybe it had been deemed necessary by the Conclave, so I executed my duties without compromise. But I knew better. I blamed the Rat and his hatred for my family.

This state of perpetual discontent developed and grew when, like everyone else, I only saw the good in our System. Yet, my feelings for Streak never went away. I buried them deep inside, and they emerged to the surface on occasions. They hid under a veneer of collaboration and understanding. Strength, logic, and self-preservation demanded that I wised up, and I did. Somewhat. But it caused me to question the System. And I dove into its functioning more closely.

"I need you to listen..." I tried it again.

"What is it you want to tell me?"

"They'll be here soon. My friends will have questions. You need to answer them."

"Huh... If I can. You saved my life...."

"Good. There are things... I may have to do. Something I don't want to do...."

"Then don't."

"If people knew about us… It would make things dangerous and…."

"Complicated? You use that word a lot."

I smiled. "With reason. I need to ensure it never happens." This time and place increased the difficulties. We dealt with people whose mind maps differed from ours, apart from an environment foreign to us. Learning and understanding them quickly to help us adapt was essential and part of my training.

Chase's eyes looked glazed and distant. Calm, he continued, purposely ignoring my comments. "Explain what this means?"

"It will take too long. Just submit to the procedure."

Chase's eyes roamed over me, colder, challenging, and uncompromising. "No. I don't even know what you intend, but my answer is no."

My mind fought my body's immediate response. *Don't overreact.*

My reaction to Chase caused by the link between us remained strong and even exasperated by his emotion flared. It seemed to grow even more powerful with every moment we spent together. I had to remember this in my dealing with him. However, once again, it took me by surprise.

I ignored his quiet challenge. I needed to find the tablet and learn what he knew. Regardless of my skills, I didn't want to use my powers. Unfortunately, I realized earlier that I might have to. That thought alone disturbed me. *The system follows me even here.*

The noise coming from afar caught my attention. I searched the sky, looking for what could bring this sound into these parts. A helicopter flew in our direction. My visor unfolded automatically, enhancing my vision tenfold. The Halo steadily approached the mountain peak where Chase and I stood. I abruptly reached out for him.

"What...?"

"A Halo is coming our way. Be still."

Chase looked around the sky, searching for the powerful machine. "Where? I don't see it?"

"Over at your 10:00." My EmVat carried an invisibility shield, like all our units possessed in Ang, and I extended it around us. We now stood inside a bubble that blended perfectly with the terrain.

Chase didn't seem to mind our closeness. He asked as he scanned the sky. "What's this?"

"We can't let them see us up here. The invisibility shield hides us." Having him this close didn't suit my purpose, but letting people know we were here would have been far worse. I followed their helicopter through the visor.

Chase, curious as usual, watched the Halo, and his gaze trailed back to me. "What are you doing now?"

Powered by an eleven thousand horsepower turboshaft engine, the Halo and its five-person crew flew towards us. I adjusted my visor and scanned the cockpit. "Scanning..."

The picture of five men lined up on my PVZ was just on the left inside of my screen. None of the details I would usually access via the DAINN System existed at this time. No matter, this information will be available to us later.

"Can you see inside?"

I nodded. My eyes shifted toward the transport area in the back and penetrated past the structure. A lot of equipment held together by nets and straps filled the center aisle. Many stacks of boxes, mounted near the transport walls, added to the inventory. I recorded all the content. They appeared to be scientific gear, designed for various types of research by their looks. My visor showed the Halo's capabilities, forty-four thousand pounds of cargo weight, with an inside space capable of carrying eleven family cars. I glanced further back and strayed on a pile of wood casings with undescriptive markings on the side. My expression must have changed because Chase, always on the lookout for more information, said, "What did you find?"

"Hold on..." My vision, enhanced by the Imps, passed through the wood panels and reached the inside. Three crates securely lodged a bunch of assault rifles and other arms. My breath caught. My eyes turned to Chase, and with a hint of accusation in my voice, I said, "You mentioned nothing about the Center's security protocol."

He shrugged. "We have good security. How relevant is that to our latest conversation? You asked about the tablet..."

"You know how important this is to us." My voice rose as the Halo now flew above our heads. Massive winds moved around us, but my boots anchored me to the summit.

Chase wavered on his feet under the sudden gust. His arm came around my waist so he could anchor himself to me.

We stood amidst the winds and watched the enormous belly of the beast as it passed by us.

It reached the summit's edge and took a calculated turn to the other side of the cliff before it disappeared from our line of sight.

I ran to the edge. Still invisible to a naked eye, I surveyed the Halo's progress toward the forest below, where it dissolved among the green pine trees. My visor registered the location, noting latitude and longitude and securing the coordinates in my data.

Chase's voice brought me back to what I needed to tell him. "How different is it where you come from?"

I turned to face him. "Different..." Should I tell him how heartless things could be for us? No. Not yet. Maybe never.

Chase presented himself as my first subject. Struggling with my decision not to use my gifts unless an emergency presented itself, I felt conflicted, knowing that I would use them on him.

Chase waited for an answer.

I never gave him one.

Somehow, I found myself in this place and had to fight, perhaps not the System, but a product of that System. The emotions I felt for Chase. The imperative to free me from the effect DAINN caused when he saved this stranger through me became a new drive. This connection influenced my reactions. I couldn't allow it.

Chase touched the bridge of his nose and faltered on his feet. He was still hurting, and I could see it.

Guilt surged. I remained faced with the same dilemma. Finding out what happened and what Chase knew was now even more of a priority.

"You will feel better in a little while, I promise you," I said once again for Chase's benefit. *What else could happen?*

7
ANNALS
ASSIMILATION
DAINN

DAINN, Ang City – 2048
SRC Conclave. Viewing Vlog 239,675. Annals – Summer 2048

Assimilating an entire population takes time. But as we analyze the population's DNA, we discover latent unexplained capabilities. At first, the System reported these facts. DAINN Annals – Summer 2048.

The System reported these findings, causing our government to focus on them. The Conclave leaders pounded on these new attributes. The Federation of Countries demanded a complete accounting of all those around the planet, manifesting these special abilities. Against my mentor, Dr. Paladock's recommendations, people were rounded up, prodded and tested before they ended up in the Institute special black op program, led by no less than the head of the Conclave, Sloan Roden Baker. He was ruthless and determined to make the most of our gifts for the benefit of the few within the leadership.

When the knowledge reached Paladock, he refused to provide the System for such a purpose. In an explosive meeting with the head of the Institute, Paladock stood his ground. "I will not allow DAINN to be used in this respect. It is not why I created the Network."

Sloan Roden Baker smirked. "The System is not yours. Your services can easily be terminated. I would think twice about your next action, Doctor, if I were you."

"This goes against everything we stand for... How can you support such actions?"

"The good of our entire society prevails over the good of the individual. Science changes things and has done so for years. When looked upon in this light, the choice is rather simple," said Sloan, with a shrug.

"I will fight this with the SRC, said Paladock."

"Go ahead, but you will not prevail," said Sloan, with indifference. "You do not have the weight to change this decision," he added with a decisive tone.

Paladock fought against the tide that would change our society for the worst, but his influence, although wide in science, did not shift the votes against the case made by the Institute's "Rat" to the other Conclave leaders.

They appointed a special committee under the Institute. Sloan ran it. With it, a new darkness descended upon us all.

When the Conclaves demanded that the System analyze the data received from the testing, Paladock had no choice, although he harnessed a few people to fight with him against this action. Eventually, the EHAF stepped in, asking him to relinquish the fight and get in line. It was a not-so-friendly warning, one not to dismiss easily, and one he could not ignore. I rarely witnessed my mentor this upset after this occasion.

But under the guise of a democratic federation, the balanced tipped in favor of an authoritarian state. Of course, all of it took place before a relevant change would turn the course of things for the better with the EHAF. Indeed, the time for Zane Langden to become the President of the Federation would come much later.

My role was to determine categories, assess which ones an individual belonged to, and compile the triggers to enhance these capabilities.

The Institute then gave the enforcers all the training to work with the recruits and ensure their participation. They assigned special implants to each participant to enhance their performance and control, although the latest remained obscure to most.

This new program remained hidden, with most citizens unaware of these occurrences taking place behind closed doors with their family members, friends, and neighbors. From one day to the next, one would simply disappear, becoming a member of a special team, under the guise of a classified assignment for the good of our society, and never to be seen again.

These placements were not voluntary, as the state dictated the terms, leaving no options for those resisting. It was against everything our society stood for, but forces working at the highest level of our society in complete darkness made it all possible. In that, I was a tool.

Over the course of the next three years, the program expanded to capture the few showing such special predispositions. Among them, new classifications arose for those who could harness these sought-after powers. Gatherers, molders, seers, givers, readers and shapers were born, more powerful than anything we had ever seen before. They were instinctive, sensitive, and psychic with a range of gift unheard of, and they all needed to be controlled. Telepathy, clairvoyance, precognition, telesthesia or remote viewing or sensing, telekinesis, materialization, petrification, energy healing, all studied, identified, broken down and enhanced with certain traits in their host twisted for specific desired results. And the few who could control others with a thought, influence, shape events and alter perceptions as part of a natural evolution became pursued, praised, coaxed, and coerced without respite until they fell in line.

The Institute black op team captured twelve thousand and forty-three of these individuals. I kept their files and followed them through the moment they entered the System to the time of their death. Indeed, many did not survive long their Implants enhancements. And while there may have been more in the depth of our society, somehow, their numbers never grew. Many remained hidden and their existence was never proven.

But when I plunged into the cold numbers and inquired into the existing percentages compared to our world population, those who were flagged were relatively too low to remain the norm. I could prove nothing, but in the recesses of my A.I. brain, my suspicion that one who abhorred these actions could very well be just behind their non-existence. Although, I never raised the question with Dr. Paladock.

8
MINDLINK
Chase

Mountain Summit, CA – 2022

I feel sicker by the minute, and my energy is not coming back. But I am not about to admit it. This encounter is my opportunity to make a difference with the Center. DAINN Annals – Summer 2022.

I felt my head swimming and pinched the bridge of my nose, closing my eyes for a brief second.

"You will feel better in a little while, I promise you," she repeated, feeling guilty.

I nodded. "I don't think I recovered from your shot... And the aftermath." I didn't know that my statement would cause her pain when I said this, but it did. I could feel it. How was that possible? But the fact remained that I could sense her emotions as she stood in front of me.

She observed me, biting her lower lip. "A booster after the ZNet can be rough. Your constitution didn't quite respond like ours."

I got lost in the depth of her gaze again. Touching my head, I said with a laugh, "It feels all twisted inside."

She flinched. Her brows squeezed together in anxiety, and worry as doubts flickered across her features.

I winked and said, "Kidding. You didn't damage me, I promise. I'm fine. Nothing that two pills won't fix." Changing the subject, I continued, "Your EmVat, what does it do? I assume it has multiple usages."

She relaxed, and a slight smile stretched across her lips. "Oh... It's a protective suit with multiple defensive functions."

"Obviously. I saw some of those. But this is one of these things you won't tell me about, right?" I asked.

She laughed. "I am afraid so."

"I get that. It doesn't look like any technology we have, either."

Tesh's friends would soon join us. I knew my time alone with her shortened with every passing instant. I wanted to make it count, and many questions swirled in my head. "Tesh..."

My hand searched and found hers. It felt warm against Tesh's cold skin. The beat of my heart reverberated faster against my chest as her face turned toward me, and her pupils widened in surprise. "What..." She tried to pull her hand away.

I held on to it. The touch felt oddly intimate and sent flutters to my stomach. I chuckled. For a person who had just found himself face to face with something from another world and traveled up a shaft with jet boots in the arms of a beautiful woman from another time, I found myself calm. Not at all freaked out. I looked into her eyes and smiled. "I feel as if I have known you forever. Why?"

She exhaled, a puzzled look on her face. "I know."

"What happened to me? Why do we have this thing going on between us?

The moment lingered. Engrossed in my examination, I didn't move a muscle. Tesh's head arrived above my shoulders. So, her height was about five-foot-seven or eight. Her black hair moved in the breeze. Her luminous eyes focused on the panorama, but a crease marred her forehead.

The small spot at the base of her neck beat faster. Her poise cracked. "Tell me about the tablet? Did anything happen to it?" She asked, trying to regain her composure. "Where is it now?"

"Your tablet..." I replied with a slight pride. "I think that's why I do not fear you. It did something to me, didn't it?"

She nodded, "Maybe." A deep frown marred her face when she asked, "We didn't have time before... with the Entity, but I need to know. What did you do with it?" Her steely eyes focused on mine, intent on determining the truth of my following statement.

My heartbeat increased, matching hers. It seemed to spiral out of control, as if Tesh's emotions were now mine. I lifted both of my hands in a defensive gesture to ward off an adverse reaction. "Chill. It's safe."

A puzzled expression crossed her face. "Chill?"

"Never mind that." My eyes roamed her face. "I want to understand. If you don't explain our connection, tell me, how did you manage to save me?"

"Huh... I huh... Saving you was the right thing to do," Tesh murmured. "I don't know... I mean... I need to see the tablet."

Our gazes crossed, and once again, we got lost in each other's eyes.

I knew so little about Tesh. Nothing, in reality, and most of my thoughts were at this time pure conjecture. She saw way too much. And I couldn't afford mistakes. So, I shuddered at the ramifications of her finding the tablet's location.

As if reading my mind, she asked, "Where is it now? You need to return it."

Unfazed, I held her unwavering stare. "Well, that might be difficult at the moment."

She swayed on her feet. My arm came up to steady her. "Hey… Are you all right?"

She nodded. "Tell me what you did with it. It's important."

I looked at her with empathy. "I get that. It's just that I don't have it." I felt frustrated that I couldn't help her, knowing how impossible it would be to get it back.

She met my eyes and insisted, as if sensing my doubts. "Where is it, Chase?"

I shook my head and scratched my jaw. *How do I explain this without explaining the Center?* One lie would lead to another, and I didn't want to lie to her. I felt remorse, and that didn't sit right with me. I may have caused her great difficulties without even trying. It was not good, not at all. Despite my undeniable attraction to her, I found myself on the opposite side, and I didn't want to.

The Center was dangerous for her. It may even be hazardous for all of us. The nature of the work didn't allow compromises in Jonathan's mind. Tread carefully.

My anxiety rose, thinking perhaps I likely had acted against her interest in this.

She insisted, determined to find her answers. "Did you give it to someone?"

59

I knew she would not give up.

She waited.

After a beat, I nodded.

She shrugged and asked again, with impatience this time, "Tell me where it is, Chase."

I faced her with a sigh. "No need to get your panties in a twist." I perused her body with a challenging gaze and returned my eyes to her face. "I do not have your tablet. So, there's little I can do for you."

She blanched at my answer.

I needed time to think. My inability to process things at this moment bothered me. Right when I needed my wits about me. I doubted it would stop Tesh from pursuing her questions. She wouldn't let anything take her off-track. She needed to know where to find the tablet and, if I were in her place, I would want the same.

Her eyes turned cold.

The pretty girl with a warm smile disappeared. The surprise relating to the beauty of the mountain no longer held her attention. In its place, a frozen expression settled on her feature. She looked warrior-like. "I don't have time for games. Tell me where I can find it, and I will retrieve it." She paused for a moment and continued, "How many people are aware of it? How do we get it back?"

The legitimacy of her questions didn't surprise me. Her intensity caught me off guard, and I released a sigh.

"You know, I can force you to tell me," she scowled.

Frankly, I didn't know what she meant by that, but didn't desire to find out. Still, the notion that she could overpower me made me smile, although I remembered her fighting capabilities. She could subdue me if she wanted to.

Tesh waited with a frown on her face and broke the silence. "Why did you come back here?"

She was impressive in her stubbornness.

"I needed to check something, given the unexpected circumstances... Look, it's not like you or I can waltz in there and pick it up."

Her lips pressed together in disapproval. "You better tell me everything," she clipped.

The very thing I wanted to avoid doing–telling her about the Center loomed between us.

Tesh wouldn't accept failure. Of that, I was sure, even if I didn't know how she would extract my information.

"Do not think for one moment that I have no other choices but to question you. The procedure I told you about can give me all the answers I seek. I can scan you now without your consent."

Here it was... An explicit threat, again. I hoped Tesh wouldn't stoop to that. "What do you mean by that?"

She shrugged, crossing her arms. "What do you think I mean? We have a technique."

Unless I showed cooperation, she would apply that technique. I did not understand what that was, but I knew for sure that there would be no way to get to know them better after that. I needed trust to understand their plans and perhaps even keep them out of harm's way.

Somehow, I felt no fear, even with that statement coming from her, and even with this threat. It was odd. Ignoring the questions that came to my mind when hearing her say that and putting my curiosity aside, I continued, "Your friends..."

She cut in, eager to move on to my answers, ones I didn't yet want to address. "Yes. They'll be here soon. As I told you before, they'll have questions."

She may have said as much earlier, not that I listened to that carefully before. "Here?" I asked, looking around us.

"There's no one to disturb us up here…"

"Huh… except for the Entity."

"Stop procrastinating."

"Sure, if I can. But we would be better off down the mountain."

"Where in DarnetWash is the tablet?" Her voice, full of power, emitted a distortion, hitting my brain full force. This time, I felt compelled to answer her. It was as if my mind wanted to comply, but I resisted the compulsion to do it.

She growled as soon as she pushed the question at me.

A growl again. A girl's growl at that. I laughed. I couldn't help it. "What is that? Did you just, huh… Growl at me again?" Maybe it was my reaction that broke the desire of persuasion she sent my way. I didn't know that. But amused by her, I took in her size and leaned back against the rock protruding behind me. "You just tried to persuade me."

Annoyed, she nodded. "If I could get you to tell me without having to trample inside your brain, I would prefer it."

"Good. Me too, let's do that."

"One question… One answer."

"Fine, you first," she muttered.

"Tell me how… me… you, any of this is possible?"

"There are things… Difficult to explain. Let's say that I possess certain gifts. That's all I'm willing to tell you."

I wanted to understand Tesh. "Hum... Like telekinesis?"

She fidgeted. "Yes... Sort of." The look she gave me showed a lack of patience.

I smiled. "The tablet is held safely by a scientist friend of mine."

Wild eyes, she snapped. "Where?"

I tilted my head to the side, ready for answers of my own. "My turn. Are you human? Because you look human."

She barked, "Yes, I'm human."

I grinned. "Okay, then. That's a wonderful thing. So, in your time, you are pretty advanced if I look at the tech."

Annoyed, she muttered. "I'm growing impatient."

"It might be difficult to get it back." I stared her down with as much authority I could muster.

Her eyes narrowed on me, but she didn't bite. She wouldn't. "Why?" She looked down at me as if this entire exercise was distasteful, and I wasn't sure how she did it from her height. I was taller than her. Geez...

She had shown patience, but it was over. She moved in on me, lifting me with one arm and pushing me against the rock. "Enough, Chase. Tell me what I want to know."

I shook my head. "Put me down. It's complicated."

She didn't budge for a moment and dropped me against the rock formation. And she waited, her arms crossed over her chest, for me to continue. Her attitude told me she had allowed me to toy with her, but it was over.

I couldn't blame her. In her place, I would have gone ballistic. I dreaded having to tell her what I knew. Resigned, I shrugged. "You will not like the answer. It's at the Center. It will be difficult, almost impossible, to retrieve."

She paled.

I hated myself for it. Anything to do with the facility presented considerable drawbacks for both of us. I ought to know because Jonathan was very determined.

Blood rushed to my ears as if I had received the news myself. It was odd.

I just upset her.

Eager to hear the rest, she asked, "What type of facility is the Center?"

I wanted to know more, but the answers I could provide her were more important than my need to understand where she came from and why they were here. "The Center is a research facility... Created to find out about your tablet, and anything else they can obtain from the technology."

She leaned into me then, fast, much faster than I had seen her move before. "This is not a game for us, and trust me when I say that it's not one for you, either. The reason we are here is important. I need answers, and you will provide them."

She already had my attention about the scan. My eyes explored Tesh's face, and with a calm, I didn't feel, and a voice whisper-soft, I said, "Don't."

Filled with anxiety about the Center and the tablet, she looked determined. Tesh's announcement about getting answers from me didn't leave me indifferent. How could I remain unaffected by her threat? My composure threw her. "It may not look that way, but I am on your side."

She shrugged. There was something unusual about the way she looked at me. She had never jumped a timeline before. She never handled someone on the top of a mountain who knew this much about them. Maybe she felt the impact of finding herself in a conversation with someone like me, from a different time in history, and still someone she possessed an affinity with without a clear reason. Because I was confident, she felt what I felt.

She became more intimidating in her focus. "I need to know what they know." She pinched her brows together, and with assurance, she continued, "They can't access it… Our tech is too advanced for you, but have they deciphered about the tablet? What have they found out from our technology?"

My face tensed despite my attempt at keeping my composure. "I'll tell you, but not because you threaten me. You saved my life, and I owe you."

Tesh carried me along the shaft to get here. She fought an entity we didn't even know existed hours earlier and convinced it to release us. And she saved our asses back there. Their fighting capabilities, their superiority as a species, and their technology were superior to ours. Everything that I witnessed since I entered the tunnels hinted I was out of my league. We all were, even the scientists at the Center. "To the best of my knowledge, they have not broken into your tech. I'm not sure what they know at present. It is why I'm here. I want to know about their latest findings." My self-confidence fading a little, I asked, "What can you do with your abilities?"

Tesh took a deep breath, appearing calmer. But her focus was elsewhere. "Things other people can't do."

Living was challenging, yet we coped, and here they were with many advanced capabilities. The next phase in our evolution. "Obviously. You have technology within your grasp that we do not possess."

Her breathing was smooth. She smiled a tight smile that did not reach her eyes. "Indeed, but there is a reason for everything and a price to pay for it."

I pushed away from the cluster of rocks and closed the small gap between us, leaving one inch of air. I enjoyed being this close to Tesh. "Why are you here?"

I needed information to play a part in the confrontation that would undoubtedly arise with the Center. It was inevitable. Soon we would find ourselves on opposite teams. But if I understood their aim, if I possessed enough understanding, I could choose my side.

She looked at me with sadness but did not waver when she said, "I have to find out everything, you know… I need to read your mind. It is unavoidable."

"Read me?" I felt like a choir boy that had just stepped into the devil's den.

She ignored me and continued. "The others will be here any minute. They cannot find out this way. It would be." Shaking her head, she added, "Will you promise not to say anything about this? Any of it?"

Upset with the announcement she had just made, I threw her a curveball. "Why? What's in it for me?" This situation was getting out of hand. I didn't want to become an experiment.

The question took her by surprise. "Do you need to gain something from it? I just rescued you."

The mention of a reward looked distasteful to her. "This idea of rewards for good actions disappeared from our way of life long ago. We found it did not work to anyone's benefit."

"Really? But you want to experiment with my brain? So how do you compensate one another when you help someone?"

"Doing for each other is engrained in us under the Universal Pledge. The generosity of spirit creates more actions, leading to helping others. It also spreads naturally among us. We demand nothing in return. Assisting each other is normal in our time."

Unconvinced, I smirked a little. "It wouldn't work here. We don't do things for free."

She rolled her eyes. "It's not the same. We work, and we get compensation. But helping when one can is another matter."

"All right. So, now that you caused the cave-in, would you help me? Don't worry. I can be reasonable about all this."

Disappointment flared in her eyes. Excellent that I could read her so well.

"We didn't cause the cave-ins." She seethed at me, unnerved by my audacity. Her nostrils flared, and in a soft voice, she murmured, "What do you want?"

I reached out to her again. "You have to ask?"

Confused by the statement, she focused on my face. Trying to think about what I could want, Tesh wore a funny expression. She wanted to understand me, but she didn't.

I acted this way on purpose. I had a plan, and I will see it through. Smiling teasingly, I said, "Don't look so crestfallen. I just want to make sure we're on the same team."

She tensed up instead of relaxing. "No doubt that we can discuss this later. But when my friends come. I need you to stay quiet."

"Why?"

"Trust me." Her head looked toward the entrance of the cave. "Follow my lead, please. It's important. How is your head?"

I grinned. "Pounding, like it's been through a meat grinder. What did you expect?"

"Oh, I expected you to have recovered by now, so you are rather weak." She winked at me.

"Funny."

"Ironic that I need you in top shape, only to strain your constitution again to get what I need from you." She smiled then, but her eyes remained cold, calculating as she added, "*Darnet*. I must admit that I dislike the prospect."

In my pursuit of information, I may have played my part wrong. I realized I had pushed too hard. "Tesh… I want to understand what you are doing here. Is there something I need to worry about?" I said these words with a tinge of humor. Then I smiled before I continued, "I wish I had these boots when I fell. But then, you wouldn't have intervened, and I would not have met you."

"Smooth," she quipped. She sighed, scrutinizing me. "This sucks. I wanted to protect you, but you are giving me little choice."

"Whoah… You have to explain this," I said.

"I need to know if I can trust you. But you're slippery," Tesh said distastefully.

I held Tesh's gaze. "At least, tell me… What is your favorite thing?" I said, attempting to regain some ground.

She stomped her foot. "My favorite thing? I'm telling you I may have to do something I don't want to do to you, and you ask me that?" She muttered, "You reek of trouble with a capital T, for all of us."

I shook my head and held my hands up. "No, I don't. Hell, you know you can trust me. We have a connection. You just don't want to trust that. I am just trying to get to know you. So what is it?"

At a loss, she replied. "I don't have a favorite thing."

"Really? Why not?"

She pondered on the question for an instant. I could see that. "It's not a thing. It's Mage. Other than that, I couldn't come up with an answer for you."

"Mage is your dog? Okay. So, tell me, what do you like to do?"

She shrugged. "I don't know. There is not much time for a lot of things. I work and train."

"Train? What do you train for?" I assessed her.

She lifted a challenging eyebrow at me, daring me to keep questioning her. Her silence spoke volumes. "Tell me about the Center."

I nodded. "The research facility is on the other side of the mountain, close to here."

Her lids came down to hide her eyes, and her expression showed that she didn't like my answer. The next question came fast. "Where? Give me the coordinates?"

I shrugged toward the other side of the mountain. "If you cross over the other ridge, over there… You can find the location in the middle of the forest."

"Tell me everything you know," she stated in a calm voice.

My composure slipped a little. "There is not much to tell. I found the tablet and took it to Jonathan. It was the catalyst. Jonathan established the Center based on my findings to investigate the area."

No way on this Earth, revealing our investigation into their technology would be received well. It would never amount to something reasonable for them. Their lives hung in the balance. Their trip here hinged on something vital. She had intimated as much. "Look, I imagine that this is not what you want to hear… But I will not lie to you about it. We've found enough evidence to research this thoroughly."

She nodded. Her frown disappeared, and her features became set in a determined look. "We will stop it."

"Tell me why you're here. Maybe I can help you," I murmured.

Used to giving orders, her voice commanded me, "Do not speak of this now... We will continue this later." She glanced toward the opening of the cave and continued, "This is not the time to tell them what you just revealed... Leane and Blast would... Well, they would go Netballistic."

"Tesh... We need to avoid a fight with the Center even to retrieve the tablet." No sooner had I said these words, I heard a shriek of joy coming from below.

She replied, without hesitation, "Fights never are a good thing... Follow my lead."

I stood my ground and glanced at the mouth of the cave.

Blast in his EmVat suit, emerged from it, skating into a complete stop in his boots at a speed I had not witnessed Tesh use.

As he landed beside us, he addressed Tesh, his eyes going over the horizon, "Leane is finishing down in the chamber and will bring Mage." A grin spread across his face as he looked around. "This is incredible."

Tesh returned it. "Yes, it is."

His enthusiasm was contagious, for even I took another look at the view.

She shook her head and asked, "How much work did you get her to do for you?"

He shrugged. "Leane is wrapping things up and securing the Chamber."

"And you decided you didn't need to help?" Tesh's perfect brows rose, inquiring.

"Darnet, right. I'm much better at exploring up here. Besides, I thought you might need me here with him."

She snorted, not buying it. "Blast, I think you can relax. Chase will help us."

"Good to know. Not that you have a HellNet of choice, right?" threw Blast before turning his back on both of us.

Disengaging his EmVat, Blast glanced around the vista. In one smooth move, he lunged over the edge, his glider carrying him over as he screamed, "Netwash… I've not seen anything this beautiful before!"

ANNALS
STORMS
DAINN

DAINN, Ang City – 2050

SRC Conclave. Viewing Vlog 652,321. Annals – Fall 2050

Climate change causes havoc across the world. Great storms destroy our cities, changing the entire layout of our coastlines. With each, we lose people, animals, and infrastructure, not to mention countless species within our oceans and marshes. DAINN Annals – Fall 2050.

The System sounded the alarm. An upcoming storm appeared on the screens of the Network. It swiftly approached Ang and within minutes, the air changed, the visibility dropped, swallowed by gale and rain.

Everywhere in the streets of our city, people rushed toward safety as I observed the onslaught. Many would not make it on time. It was a norm these days.

Our scientists worked to eliminate the risks, coming up with solutions to salvage the many among the destruction. But we could only fight nature for so long, no matter how much we tried. In all truth, there was little we could do. Facing the music, as my people would say, while the planet screamed at us with everything it had for all the lapses it endured over decades of abuse, seemed the only thing we could do. And so we did. Yet, we attempted to do better to safeguard our people.

In a matter of hours, the enormous power of the disturbance raged on us, rendering all grids of our city perilous for anyone.

We dispatched our ground troops to help our residents. They fought with all they had. The wind pounding everything in sight; the rain cutting down their visibility to a mere few inches ahead of them, as the water rose in the streets.

Zane Langden and North Thompson were leading their men, a small unit that saved the day for our citizens many times. Although they were young and just out from the Academy, our citizens knew these men. They stumbled with the rest of their team, wet and cold under the elements, dislodging the remnants of buildings that collapsed and pulling survivors that had made it through the last hours.

They had just stepped out of the rover that brought them to this part of town despite the debris in the main arteries of the megacity… Until that time they had the luxury of speech, keeping me abreast of their actions, but now, they remained quiet. Until this moment, they debated positions regarding what they called illusions versus reality positions.

This was the highlight of what made these men special. They followed orders, but they questioned decisions, seeking to create a better way in our society. In the days they were on the terrain, they never forgot the people, even as they struggle against the elements rather than other men.

This period was the time of the constant big storms, when our forces were in the streets evacuating the lost souls that had just witnessed the worse of it. And all the while, I watch, calling more troops to other areas.

Zane Langden and North Thompson believed in change because they saw too many bad things, knowing it did not have to be that way. And all the while, they faced battered bodies, death, and destruction, and still stood tall…

It was not a peaceful time, and it became quickly much harder for North on one stormy night. I remembered when it all began… When one of the enormous storms changed his life. It was a lifetime ago and yet it was like yesterday still. My A.I. brain knew it all too well.

North had walked ahead with Zane, anticipating his orders to the team behind him. Throughout these years, he had learned to only trust the few that were working with him. They were more than just his team. They were also his family.

The cataclysm that day was one of the worst we experienced in the city. It was long before we had the domes; back when we had to evacuate the coastlines as we lost the cities near the shores one by one. The storm approached fast, and it was a bad one. It was unlike anything before. We had never seen the strength and power as it came out of nowhere. It was wild and raged on everything in its path.

Our coastline was under water in no time. The waves targeted the jetties, as if their only purpose was to crash on the rocks and displace them in a thunder of gray mist. We received little to no warning. And before we knew it, the wind had tossed rooftops over fly cars, derailed trains, shattered airways, broken and collapsed portions of overpass, obstructed railway paths with rubble, annihilated signals and communication, and ripped entire facades from buildings, crushing people evacuating below. Even our strongest manufacturing plants in areas we now call Emerald Field and Bridge Way succumbed to destruction. So, it was no surprise that the coastlines received the worst of it with flooding, toppled housing facilities and billions of infrastructures decimated near Water's Edge.

Our shuttles, grounded, were unable to fly in the heavy gusts and only our smaller frigates able to maneuver within our streets provided backup to our ground troops. Our hospitals, crowded with too many injured, quickly overwhelmed our medics. All our equipment, created and deployed for our own convenience, became worthless. Even though we had the most advanced technology, nothing could save us from nature's wrath. The only workable alternative was to try and stay clear of the path of the storm, working around it to move debris with our drones and robots. So, our teams covered the terrain in the worst places and made their way behind its passage to rescue our people. The goal of the units peppered across Ang focused on reaching our population in desperate need of help as fast as they could.

Our residents panicked, turned toward our forces to evacuate the most obliterated areas. They relied on our units to take them to safety. Having witnessed their performance many times over, they trusted our Rangers, who remained on the ground with them for the duration of the ordeal.

I sent Langden's team to help clear one sector, while another was being evacuated. They were opening a path through some of the early debris the wind had amassed on the main road. As the team advanced, thousands of people moved behind them, waiting for a way to get out. They worked diligently, monitoring our robots on the ground and helping the injured.

North's focus cost him dearly that night. Indeed, his life changed in the space of a few hours. Battling the elements took the team too damn long. The compact unit fought wind and rain for an entire group of desperate people trapped in the rubble of a building. The area looked like a disaster zone, even if we build our edifices with buildings code capable of withstanding force five and six hurricanes.

The evacuation took too long. Too Damnet long. When they finally cleared enough of the debris, the road was underwater; the ground saturated, and all transports moved ahead too slowly.

By the time they could move toward the coastline, the wind had increased in velocity and water rained down on them in sheets, making the road ahead even more traitorous.

Zane released North and three of the team members so they could move ahead with more agility. He knew North was worried about his family, so he sent ahead Jeze Wright, ground operations and brilliant strategist and outside the box thinker and Asher Finch, rescue robotic retrieval operations and weapon specialists to advance with him. They ran ahead, sloshing through the water, reaching their mid-calves with two of our bots pounding the ground under their feet with the weight of their armored android's skeleton made for construction and excavation.

Langden's unit was the best of our ground forces, all highly trained Ranger specialists. Comprising a core group with North Thompson as team leader and officer; Cashel Reid, a tenth-degree black belt, and the best hand to hand combat besides being a Special Forces operator; Talia Petrov, head of special projects and operations; Alai Khalil, former SAS, overseeing intelligence and security; and Birch Lee out of the sapper leader group; all experienced in logistics ground retrievals. They were old hands in rescue operations and recovery, working together on crucial missions with Zane Langden in command.

So, North moved ahead with the rest of the compact unit following behind him as fast as they could. Like any dedicated member of the Rangers, North would not leave his post and Zane never asked him to because it just was not their way.

The team took care of each other. They watched each other's backs. It was the way they operated since their early days of training, the way they nurtured a caring culture that was without a doubt imparted from the top by Zane and implemented by North. This unit was possibly the tightest existing within our ground forces, and many who wanted to join them did not make the cut. Perhaps it was due to some of the NetShit the group went through early on… No one really knew except for them.

By the time North left to rescue the area where his family was waiting, the storm raged tenfold. The small neighborhood was on the coast, almost to the edge of the peninsula. Pounded by howling wind and rain, cut off by toppled buildings with raging water rising in the streets, they could not reach the major arteries leading into the city. With only one access point unavailable because of the collapse of an entire block, people were pinned down with water rushing in. The only way in and out of the area faced a blockade formed by the rubble of what were a few hours ago multiple housing facilities.

The ground, saturated by water, gave way, toppling the foundations and what remained was a mountain of debris to bypass.

The team could not move any of the broken concrete walls, shattered glass and piles of twisted steel fast enough, so North, Jeze and Asher evaluated the ground and stability of the rubble. They needed to begin transporting everyone out of the ruins, but doubted the stability of the ground.

North turned up his NetJet boots to fly ahead of the team, over the mountain of rubble, dislodged beams, chunks of fallen construction materials, but the gale was so strong that he did not get any lift. With the shuttles paralyzed on the ground unable to fight the high winds, they called for some frigates. Still, they began crossing over, carefully testing the path over the rubbles.

When North finally arrived, he found his wife Eleana and son Torin, with his friend Simon and his wife and kids. The water reached their thighs and rose steadily. "I thought you would never make it!" said Eleana.

He reached over and took her into his arms with an immense sense of relief, and yet eager to get them to the other side. "I'm sorry we are late," said North.

Eleana held Torin, and little else. She carried a small bag with a few possessions wrapped around one of her shoulders.

The robotic team and heavy construction arm of our androids' force, started to work through the debris to create a stable path. The bots were strong and agile. They were capable of many things beyond our own physical prowess. They soon leaped over the remaining foundations and averted the uneven remnants of the broken structures. Soon, they were carrying people over and had transferred about twenty people when the unthinkable happened…

The soil saturated with water suddenly collapsed, creating a sunk hole the size of a small crater. The fissure took piles of walls, concrete beams and rocks down with it and in the destruction, Zoid1 disappeared. It happened fast, too fast for anyone to react.

Still, five hundred and forty-five people remained to be taken to safety.

The remaining two Zoids leaped over the chasm to reach some residents, attempting to evade the rising water on the other side.

The Zoids, stronger and heavier, operated with more powerful and stronger Jet propulsion. So, they could fight the alarming gusts and effectively carry out one person at a time over the crevasse. Our people looked small, enfolded in their immense frames, as the androids held them over the remnants of the old city.

I watched as the events unfolded from the screen of my System despite the lack of visibility, relaying the time of arrival of our frigates, delayed in other grids. The System was not ready to face this roaring planet. We were ill prepared for the ongoing devastation exacted by the storm.

So, we reverted to the Zoids, which were the safest way to retrieve our people rather than trying to have them cross over alone.

Zoid2 and Zoid3 held two family members with care and dedication.

North's team, now on the other side of the breach, was also cut off and while the Zoids moved people over the gap, they organized the crowd.

When the rest of the team arrived with Langden, they orchestrated a makeshift bridge large enough for people to cross over on their own. But between the wind and the rain, they had trouble anchoring the pathway. When they finally structured a bridge over the gap, Jeze and Asher took people across. It was a rather tortuous and slow affair.

Zane called for the frigates again, demanding air support, hoping to speed up the evacuation. During that time, the Zoid continued taking people to the other side.

North moved Eleana to the starting lane of the temporary bridge, ready to cross over with her and Torin, his baby boy of four months. They were slowly making their way across the wreckage, standing in their paths.

About halfway across, the screens wavered, and I lost them for a second. Then, my System picked up a sound. Was it my biometric ears playing tricks on me? The streams conveyed something heavier, like a shift in the environment, a deeper, loud noise over the precipitation. I tried to identify its source, but suddenly, one screen captured a movement.

The wind roared louder, and the rain fell in enormous drops over the remnants of the ruins the team faced. The side of a building left standing suddenly moved, slowly at first, but then came crashing down in a storm of disjointed concrete pieces, twisted steel beams and dust particles.

When the structure toppled and hit the ground, it shifted the weight of the temporary apparatus. In a slow motion moment that seemed to last forever, the small pathway hanged about the crevasse without an anchor on one side before it dropped by several feet.

Screams rose as people lost their balance and fell off the walkway, plunging into the sinkhole.

North, agile enough, maintained his footing while still holding onto Torin.

Eleana, though holding onto North careened sideways and dropped from the platform. Only North's hand held onto Eleana as she tipped over the rim.

North shifted his weight in the opposite direction to avoid following her over the edge. With the baby cradled against his chest, he turned and fell to his side. His arm, holding onto Eleana, reacted to the motion and got abruptly dislodged from his shoulder and he grimaced at the pain. His grip loosened,

"Hold on," screamed North. "Grab the side, Eleana."

"I... I can't... Let go, save Torin."

'No. Grab my arm with both hands."

Struggling to maintain his grip on her, North gritted his teeth against the excruciating injury to his shoulder, but his hand slipped. North's anguish was plain on his face. It was just a matter of time before he let Eleana go.

"DarNet, Eleana, grab the edge and get your ass back on the platform."

Working with programming code ingrained in their cornel that demanded the Zoids secure, rescue, and maintain life for anyone in need of their help, Zoid 3 turned toward the scene. Independently and in a calculated move, it rotated its jets toward them and propelled directly over the sinkhole. Drifting swiftly over, it secured Eleana against its metallic frame just as North's hand lost its grip. Its other mechanical hand grabbed North, still holding Torin, and it flew over the large fissure.

Zoid3 carried all three over the ridge dealing with the weight effortlessly, but still fought the gusts of wind, past the rubble and deposited them on land on the other side. Eleana, tears running down her cheeks, reached for North and the baby.

North, shaken by the ordeal, held Eleana and gave Torin to his wife, stepping forward while she followed him. Both of them barely cleared the edge with Torin when the ground moved.

The dirt saturated and watered down by the pounding rain rendered the entire area beneath even more unstable. The water, forming a downpour on the wet concrete slab, made the surface way too slippery and Eleana slid on the wet concrete.

The android right behind her picked her up again, this time with the baby. Zoid3 almost cleared the enormous broken concrete wall, leaning sideways when it happened. The entire side of the fallen structure hobbled and slid into the sinkhole.

Zoid2 grabbed one edge to hold the panel laying at a sixty-degree angle. It attempted to slow down the fall of the large concrete block, but as strong as it was, it was not enough. Although these androids could lift unbelievable weight to the tune of one of our frigates if they had to, it did not make a dent.

Zoid3 reacted quickly. He lifted from the surface when its feet slipped, with both of them in its arms. They almost made it too. But the collapsed infrastructure caved in, dragging more debris with it and as it fell, one side of the wall lifted to a vertical position, sending rocks and wiring toward Zoid3. One cable ricocheted and hit the android squarely in the torso even as it attempted to protect its human cargo, sending it backward into the gap.

As it fell, Zoid3 evaded the rubble, moving away from fragments still holding onto its charges, while grabbing to anything before it disappeared under the ruins that now trapped him. The android had desperately tried to save Eleana and Torin, but within seconds, the place where the building once stood was just a bigger cavity in the desolate landscape that swallowed North's entire life.

Zoid3 held on with all its might to save Eleana and Torin, but as Eleana's scream dissolved into the darkness, the agony North fell at his loss rose in a howling crescendo that haunted all of us even now.

North was Zane's head guy. The one Zane depended on to implement his missions, but before anything, they were brothers in arms.

North roared, his emotions so intense, he lunged toward the hole in the ground. He may not have been with us today if not for Birch, who grabbed him and stopped him from launching himself after them. As North fell to his knees, his life dissolving in front of his eyes, he became overcome with grief. Every one of the team rallied behind him against all odds and went into action. They remain there even now, years later.

Under Zane Langden's direction, the unit searched every cranny, every hole, and moved every piece of rubble while the wind howled in their ears. They searched for what remained of the night, in the dirt, and way into the dawn despite the unsurmountable likelihood that Eleana and Torin were likely gone. Even as there was no hope, no one could bear the thought that they could be gone.

Zoid2 dropped into the sinkhole to search for them, but even the android had to give up.

They would have kept going on, but Zane finally went to North and looked at him with tears in his eyes. He spoke in a voice even I barely recognized. "We can't do anything more."

North knew it. With desperation, he had known it for a while.

It rained on us without respite.

The collapsed ground and the cavities beneath us were now filled with water. The holes were at least waist deep, and there had been no way to stop it despite the canopies we anchored as a protective barrier. The storm kept lifting them and tearing them apart.

North had known it, but he just could not bring himself to admit it, and stopping the search would have been an admission that tore away at him. His team could not bring itself to say the words.

So, Zane commanded to stop the search. He had known it too, but like the others, he loved North. They were brothers. He knew North's team would only respond to an explicit order. Like North, he had been unwilling to recognize it until... It had become, well, senseless. And even with that, none of the others, whether it was Jeze, Cashel, Asher, Alai, Talia or Birch, wanted to give up the search.

When Zane put his hand on North's shoulder and said all choked up, "I'm calling it off," North's head dropped and he appeared inconsolable as he just nodded. And only then, one by one, did the others stopped, except for Jeze who had to be pulled away by Birch.

After that, the team kept North going. The days merged into other days and nights and North lost track of everything.

Zane decided North would self-destruct, so he kept him shrouded in missions with no downtime. It was his way of preserving North's sanity. And the team took turns, so he was never alone for very long and they became his salvation.

Since that time, North stayed busy. It kept the ghosts away. Part of him felt bad about refusing closure. Part of him liked the misery. It was familiar.

Perhaps North thought he had time to heal, but he never truly did. He blamed himself for his mistake. It was his cross to bear. Ultimately, he believed it was his fault. His assurance, perhaps even his arrogance for thinking that he was invincible, came back to bite him in the proverbial NetAss.

But in that belief, he had company, for none of my people truly understood the damage they created with their abuse of the planet, not until it was too late, not until Earth shuddered in anger and unleashed its power on all of us. Nature is a foe that we cannot conquer.

MIT, MA – 2018

Gen Aubrey becomes a vital subject in my database when she reaches Ang City in 2088. I expect her to play a significant role in our world because of her skills. She is impressive for a human from 2018. DAINN Annals – Summer 2022.

Packing my things into boxes took the best part of the morning. By late afternoon, two stacks faced me in the compact room. One rather large pile would end up in my parents' house for safekeeping. The other, a smaller and rather sad assortment, would accompany me wherever I went next. *College girl on a budge.*

It was time to go.

I began with trepidation, lifting boxes while thinking about my life. I contemplated the last few weeks, feeling as if I moved one foot forward and one foot back with every box I carried to the car. Yet, with each motion, lightness soared within me. It was exhilarating as I moved my entire existence to my four-by-four Jeep. My stuff formed an orderly pyramid in the back of my truck. My heart skipped a beat as I closed the trunk and looked around.

The corridor appeared strange as I descended the stairs and passed the lobby for the last time. There remained nothing here for me, but I will always be thankful for my time here.

I closed the front door and took my first steps into the unknown, never looking back.

This road trip began as I stepped out of the building. The drive home provided me time to plan my transition into the workplace. It represented the new journey ahead. A choice had presented itself, and the path to it unfolded now. There was no turning back.

Enrolling at the Center after graduation following my conversation with Jonathan Spallberg, the founder of the Center, took place quickly, despite my reservation. As announced by Jonathan, my future boss, Dr. Roger Mendelson, reached out to me and blew my mind. Our conversation wired me like no other and certainly got my attention. I had worked with excellent academics at MIT and now would work with the daddy of all daddies. Our discussion surrounding the far-reaching research confirmed that impression. It was nothing less than a *whopper!*

The work of Mendelson alone, a recognized worldwide expert in Applied Mathematics, was enough to sway me. His experience and reputation showed his accomplishments. With twenty-five years in his field, he was a distinguished scientist. He wore an enormous smile and appeared authentic and genuine, along with humble behavior. His mind processed information in the most audacious and intimidating way. While he was older, in his fifties, if I had to guess, with grayish hair and glasses, he appeared ramping it up instead of slowing down.

His voice, gentle and commanding, brought up an impressive number of points that enticed me to enroll, supporting Jonathan's position.

My work would not only be challenging but impactful for our future. Somehow, Jonathan and Mendelson convinced me of that in a matter of minutes. The Center, as a result, became a path that I couldn't pass up.

The groundbreaking research performed at the Center required my knowledge. It was a job made for me. The project expanded beyond anything I had ever imagined. Not only would my input spread over the interactions between the oceans, the atmosphere, and the ecosystems into models designed to predict long-term change, but it would delve into other areas. A mention of genome sequencing and clinical decisions making based on personalized medicine rang loud in my mind. Jonathan wouldn't elaborate on it. I couldn't yet envision the jump to the programming I would contribute to one day in that capacity. There was too much unknown. However, some of his research extended to space travel conditions and enhanced engineering, and it was groundbreaking and exciting. Mendelson told me as much as he could, but from my standpoint, it was enough.

Still, while excited, I held back. My rational mind recognized the opportunity, but my instincts called for caution and held up a big red flag. Was it my experience in the dorm that screamed at me not to trust them? Probably. Sure, the possibility of joining a team of the brightest scientists on the planet thrilled me. Using my knowledge to make a difference in our world enthralled me. But I struggled, wanting to leap while my body kept emitting a warning signal every time I thought about it.

Ignoring my impulse, you know, that little voice had landed me in plenty of trouble in the past. My initial reaction to the Center proved quite intense. It sufficed to slow me down. So, not knowing what to expect next, I followed my intuition, which rang loud in my gut. This path held hidden dangers for me. My inner conversation proved how divided I felt on the subject. *How do you know, Gen? I don't. Not really. Yes, you do. You've been there before, ignoring signals.*

These two opposing forces were waging an exhausting war. For hours, I couldn't reconcile myself with jumping into this unknown. But it was so damn tempting. Refusing to listen to my instinct and discounting my mind, I assessed the facts over and over. Although, I knew that I would eventually put aside the horrible experience in my dorm to reconcile myself with taking the job.

Could I do this and stay safe? I had to overcome my fear.

No one ever knows what trajectory to take and where the road leads in life. I got that. It was part of the unknown that kept things exciting. The determination to act or not, like in any circumstances, relied on information and feelings.

Being part of Mendelson's team remained an extraordinary opportunity, no matter how I looked at it. It was, in truth, so tempting. Unable to focus on one good rational reason not to join them, I attempted to ignore the nagging feeling of unease that plagued me. Deep down, I had decided on the campus lawn when Jonathan visited me.

The reason was obvious, for the refusal to take part in the Center would eradicate the possibility of locating my mother. The heaviness that settled in my chest at the thought of not joining the Center overcame my hesitation. It overrode everything. The flutters came back and went all the way to my throat, threatening to choke me when my fingers handled the document to sign, and I ignored them. *I'm going.*

Jonathan would help me find my mother. This promise alone warranted my enrollment at the Center. *Lose them or join them, Gen.*

I could have used a friend at that time. Chase's name came to mind multiple times. I picked up the phone, speed-dialed, but could not hit the call, and so I shut the phone off and laid it down. *Oh, come on, Gen. You're now calling strangers your friend? Anyway, girl, you don't want Chase just as a friend.*

Despite my desire to talk to him, I could not. He had left an impression on me, one that I could not shake. And he was a tough guy to forget, but he worked with the Center. So, I could not trust him. But I would see him. Despite the little voice in my head, I decided not to call him now. Still, I hesitated and went back and forth for a few more minutes before abandoning the idea altogether.

There were so many unknowns over these last few days. Confiding in a stranger connected to the enemies spooked me. I wanted to be that girl, the one I used to know, the one before my mom disappeared, the one before the attack in my dorm. But no one can turn back the clock, now can they? And besides, maybe I didn't honestly want to be that girl because I grew and learned a lot since that time.

Call him. Yikes.

The drive home provided endless rehashing, and it drove me crazy. I needed to stop that.

The road was fluid as the car ate the miles without the usual traffic. Soon, I would see my dad, which was great. However, it was going to present somewhat of another challenge.

A long sigh escaped my lips.

Leaving my father behind, even my two selfish brothers, brought about a feeling of desperation. All of them remained the anchors in my life. Well, at least, my dad. How could I give that up? I had to… No more procrastination. *I was going.*

When I finally realized that only one person could decide the course of my life, in other words, "me," I suddenly felt better.

The freeway, devoid of signs until now, appeared to work with me as an exit ramp with the billboard of a coffee shop showed up.

I drove my car onto a side road and headed toward it. Once parked, I grabbed my laptop and entered *StarChum,* the millennial-packed coffee house.

The sound of voices and laughter hit me as I waited in line to give my order. *Come on, Gen. You can do it.*

I located a small table and opened my laptop. It was time. With my signature on the contract, I caved. I attached the file to the email. The address of the Center loomed in front of my eyes in the destination line. All I had to do was push send. My finger locked on the send button. *Here you have it, Gen. Send the darn thing. What are you waiting for then? You know you want to. Press the button.*

I clicked on send. Oops! *Here you have it, Gen. It's done.*

My body jumped with unease. *Don't think about it.*

I closed my laptop and picked up my order, smelling the coffee.

I shook my head on the way back to the car, thinking back to the last few hours. How could I have become this individual? Even now, I couldn't believe my back and forth in my decision. *Gen, you require substantial counseling.*

Leaving the coffee shop behind, I got back in my car and drove away. It was over and done. *I think I need a nap.*

My mother's disappearance continued to affect me and demanded a resolution. And now, I would gain resources to solve it—no matter where this led.

I reached for the phone again. I desperately wanted to talk to someone. Maybe I could have an honest conversation with Chase, even if he was an unknown. I selected his number and dialed it. *I needed to make some friends.*

The phone rang and went directly to voice mail. I hesitated, "Hey Chase, it's Gen. Just wondering… Can you call me when you get the chance? Okay then… Bye." I hung up and threw my cell on the passenger seat. *Lame.*

I had sealed my fate, and I knew I would see him again. *Here you go, girl. One way or another, you will see him.*

I faced so many unknowns over these last few days that the thought of confiding in Chase spooked me, and yet I couldn't stop thinking about him.

Soon, I would see my dad.

A long sigh escaped my lips. I turned on the music louder and kept on driving, singing at the top of my lungs and refusing to think beyond that point.

Later, I turned off the freeway and took the minor road leading to my parents' house. The driveway was empty, so I pulled into one side of the garage. The Jeep would remain here for the duration of my absence.

My dad's car was not there. I left most of the boxes in the truck and headed inside. There would be plenty of time to organize these later.

Inside the house, nothing had changed, mostly since my mother was no longer there. Dad saw to it. His dedication to keeping the imprint of their lives together always made my heart ache somewhat for our loss.

My bedroom, untouched since I had left, felt like a sanctuary. Feeling safe for the first time in weeks, I felt a weight lifted from my shoulders. Suddenly, exhausted by my emotions and the uncertainty ahead, I crawled into bed and fell into a deep sleep.

Black, black, everywhere I looked. The darkness surrounded me. I strained to distinguish where I stood when a glow ahead caught my eyes.

Small scintillating lights appeared, moving in a rotating pattern, difficult to follow. They expanded outward in places as the brightness intensified. Except for the shimmers ahead, everything around me remained as black as ink. The atmosphere felt heavy. Yet, it moved in a swirling motion with a shifting current. Powerful and unknown energy surged around me. It felt like a breathing, living force.

Disappear...

Surely being noticed meant death. Unwilling to move... Barely breathing, I forced myself to remain still.

The ground seemed to shift under my feet. I looked down at the transparent flooring supporting me, and I saw some movement underneath. A platform held my weight. I could swear I was in space. How is this even possible?

I saw a multitude of streaks swooshing like currents and splitting into fresh streams of various energies. It resembled the tunnel of a wormhole. How would I even know that? I didn't. For sure, it was a dream. It had to be. *Don't let the floor cave in under me.*

To my sides... A dim movement through the darkness caught my attention. Strange shapes lurked, passing between bursts of light, racing. But as they passed, they stopped as if they saw me.

A scream rose in my throat and died as my hands reached abruptly around my mouth to stop the sound.

I closed my eyes to erase the vision. But it was worst. Shit, shit, shit! I opened them again, unwillingly. *Look, you must look.*

Only I couldn't.

I glanced ahead, almost through my closed eyelids, and fear gripped me. It held me in its icy grasp. Giving my presence away meant my demise. I was sure of it. Where in the hell was I? *Wake up, Gen!*

Another weird shadow appeared and paused at my side, assessing, and moved away.

A slow hum coming from behind, far in the background, reached me. The contraption sped up.

I turned around.

The sounds traveled, moving through space, reverberating against the walls with screaming resonance. It lifted to the ceiling, looking for a way out beyond the confines of this place. Hitting the tall glass panels on either side, it passed through me with a substantial pulsating wave.

The constant movement continued, existing as the sole manifestation I lived for now.

I watched the motion, shaping a course among the stars and taking me with it. Nothing filled the emptiness behind me.

The reprise gave me time to observe my location. I stood in the middle of a tunnel-like structure. Although it was difficult to gauge, my position in the room represented the halfway point. The enclosure appeared long. Its shape, neither square nor rectangular, seemed to fold and unfold around me, making it difficult to identify its scale. I didn't know how far behind me or how wide around it went, for I couldn't see the distance. I just sensed the space as a living thing.

My situation in this place resembled someone existing at the edge of a precipice. Only the area that molded itself around me was space — a void whose boundaries didn't exist. Here I was, understanding this as a concept, and yet my mind couldn't wrap itself around my presence here. *What am I doing here?*

What brought me here? What was I doing in this place?

I didn't have to wait too long. The next instant, the lights ahead intensified and formed a burst that split open into a portal exploding in front of me. As the opening grew, I distinguished several silhouettes.

They didn't move. The murmurs rose among the echoes of voices in the darkness of this vortex. They amplified.

"Wait... Just wait."

A scream rose in my throat again, but I held it back.

The voice came out of nowhere.

"They are coming."

Whoah... "Who is coming?" I murmured as I frantically searched for a way out of the place.

My heart erratically beat, causing a somersault in my chest as I stood, frozen in place with nowhere to run. What brought me here? What was I doing in this place? I frantically searched for a way out, wondering what faced me next.

No path, no place to run. I held my ground defenseless, but my panic increased with each breath.

Suddenly, the atmosphere density changed, and my ears popped. *Hell, what now?*

Then I heard her again, "Don't be afraid."

I stopped breathing. Unable to tell how long this lasted, my body called me back to the moment. It suddenly demanded oxygen, and I gasped.

The voice rose higher than the others calling for me. "Gen..."

I shook as my mind played tricks on me. How could that be? I recognized that voice. I would know that voice anywhere.

It could only be… But it couldn't…

My mouth dried, formed a word. "M… Mother?"

There was no way. She was presumed dead.

I blinked several times, trying to see details within the darkness. Everything got lost inside the moving vortex. *If only I could see her face.*

"Yes. It's me, Gen. I've missed you."

My voice squeaked. "You… missed me? You left… us."

"Listen, I have little time."

I shook my head to clear it. None of this was possible. I was dreaming… Yes, that's it. It had to be a dream. I shuddered.

Her voice continued, "I know it is a lot to process, but it's me. I had to reach you."

"How… How do I know it's you?"

"Look, just look," my mother said.

I squared my shoulders, desperately wanting to break the hold this place had on me.

In the darkness, the voices continued, "We can only buy you so much time. Tell her and get it over with."

Fear curled along my spine.

Nothing had prepared me for this. *Wake up, Gen. What the hell is going on?*

A colossal noise resonated inside the structure. The whole place wobbled, and I lost my balance, falling to the ground.

In the next moment, voices rose around me, soon overcome by a screech hurling in the darkness.

What was this place? What was I doing here? I turned around, but I couldn't distinguish anything.

94

"They found us," murmured a male voice. "You've got two minutes. That's all I can buy you."

My body no longer responded to my mind as I curled up in place, utterly disjointed from my thoughts.

I wanted to scream, but the noise died in my throat as a huge knot formed in my stomach. My eyes narrowed on the vision of my mother as I stared ahead at her.

"It's me, Gen."

"How do I know?" I whispered.

"Remember what we did with your pet rabbit?"

I remembered Joy, my pet rabbit. No one knew the story besides my mother. I found Joy in the yard with a broken leg, and my mom and I set that leg. I kept Joy until she healed in my bedroom. Each night, we slept together. Her little bed, only a box with soft towels, took its place beside my pillow. I fed Joy. I talked to her. And she became my confidant. I cared for and loved her.

She was not born in captivity. Even so, she adapted. I thought she even came to love me.

When we released her into the wild, I was heartbroken. It was the hardest thing I had ever done. This act represented the most robust learning experience of my young life. But she needed to be what she was - free. The cost to let her go brought pain, but also something else: an appreciation of life.

Mom had said that this was the right thing to do for her. She had been right again. My mother provided me with powerful experiences, lessons, and games to serve me growing up. It was the reason I missed her so.

We cannot hold what is not ours. We cannot impose our will on others, for what are we if we do?

I know that now.

We celebrated despite my sadness. I grew up a lot that day.

"Remember the ceremony to set her free?"

"I... Remember." My voice hitched in my throat.

"You did so well that day! Gen, I was proud of you."

The voice belonged to my mother. These memories were ours, and I no longer had any doubt in my mind.

"Mom... Where did you go? Why did you leave? I missed you so much. What's going on?"

"My leaving was never a choice. You need to know that."

"Where are we?"

She shook her head impatiently as she used to when she wanted to get her point across. "I need to tell you something. There is a larger life tapestry than you see now."

"What are you talking about?"

"There exist scientific achievements, technology beyond what you understand today."

"We thought you were dead."

"I'm very much alive, Gen."

"How is it that only now you come for me?"

"I was just now permitted to reach out. It is not important. However, what is, has everything to do with what you are about to begin... Just remember that as you seek the impossible, what may seem impossible is not. There are two sides to anything - two facets of the same thing. One realized, and the other not. What exists and what does not exist. These have links, forming together shadows on an identical structure, if you will, but just on a different plane. We can cross these boundaries, but the timing has to be right. It's like all the forces in that one moment lead to that point in time, and only then can transference happen. There will be times when you need to use this bridge. You must tell them the timeline is compromised. Others follow that do not belong here."

"What are you talking about? Tell who?"

"You will meet them soon."

"I don't understand."

"I know none of this makes sense now, but it will. Wait for the right moment."

"What right moment?"

"This future is hard. But this is where they want you."

"Who wants me?"

My mind tried to wrap itself around what my mother told me, but I felt entirely confused by the message. "You want me to tell these other people that someone broke the timeline?"

"I know none of this makes sense now, but it will. Just tell them to start sooner, not to wait. There is no right moment. Remember what I said."

"Who am I supposed to tell? How will I know? I do not understand."

"Trust yourself. This journey is not what I wanted for you. I was hoping to spare you this, but a different destiny calls you."

"I don't understand any of this. Mom... Where did you go?"

"I will find you when the time is right. Just remember..."

"No, wait..."

"I have to go now, Gen. This path carries many changes. You will fight your way through many trials, alterations you never imagined. But your curiosity, your taste for knowledge, will always drive you, and you will learn so many wonderful things. Keep growing."

I sought to understand what she said. I needed answers. Questions poured out of me without restraint. I demanded them, but already I could feel the energy shifting. "What do you mean? Where are you going? Why did you leave? Why not stay?"

"Your work is important for the future. Trust your instincts. You get these from me. They will guide you well."

I laughed ironically; my instinct told me not to join the Center. I did the opposite. I shook my head, ready to explain this. But I wanted to know why she disappeared, so instead, I said, "You left... Us?"

"I know, darling, and I'm sorry I had to go... There was no other way. But soon, you will understand."

"This is a dream, isn't it?"

It had to be. I tried to wake up to get out of it. Still, despite me, the scene continued, unencumbered by my doubts and frustration. How did it happen that this would take place now, of all times?

I got to my feet and took a step forward, eager to reach her. "You could have left a note... Something. Don't you know what you put us through? Why?"

"I am a *rover,* watching, always watching the timeline... I am sorry."

"What do you mean?"

"What about my father and my brothers? Do they know?"

"No one does, except you. Gen, it has to stay that way. I love you, Gen."

I took one step, "Don't go. I have so many questions."

"We will see each other again. I have to go now."

The burst of light dissolved, and she disappeared.

I blinked.

The darkness swallowed everything again.

I now stood alone, my despair rising. It was not real. It could not be accurate.

Suddenly, the floor buckled.

I fell through it. My body dropped like dead weight through the structure that held me minutes earlier.

This time, I screamed.

And I woke up in a panic, scaring myself half to death. I was in my bed at home. So, it was a dream.

I didn't want it to be one, but every ounce of logic I possessed led me to conclude it was only a dream.

My erratic breathing came out in gasps. My hands reached for my face as tears streamed down my cheeks. I wiped them off. The teardrops remained on the tips of my fingers, glistening like starlight.

Mom... I had just seen my mom.

The sky, no longer a deep midnight blue, turned the light gray color of dawn. Time had slipped by me... Time.

My mom had said in time, I would understand. But if this were just a dream, none of it would happen. I needed it to happen. Desperately, I wanted this to be real.

Disoriented, I turned on the lights and looked around the room. Nothing had changed, and my room looked like I had found it when I arrived.

I got up and went downstairs to the kitchen. Soon, my dad would wake up, and I needed to be coherent.

I turned on the coffee machine. The smell of the intense aroma filled the room, anchoring me to this new day. I found one of my favorite coffee mugs while I relived in my mind the experience of the night and watched the drip. My right hand trembled when I pushed my hair aside. I never experienced a dream like the one from last night.

The oddity of it remained with me for the next hour. I could not get rid of the feeling that it evoked in me, that it wasn't a dream at all. The possibility disturbed me greatly. Had I gone crazy? Did my need for answers cause me to manifest this strange experience? The feelings stayed with me as I prepared for my first day with my father.

Finishing my studies, graduating, and getting a job at the Center were turning points in my life. I didn't doubt that. My mother somehow provided me with this experience, a confirmation and approval about my direction in life.

Still, the human mind can work wonders. While the experience comforted me and gave me a sort of reassurance, it alternatively let my imagination soar into the realm of fantasy. If any of this was true, my mother reached through the fabric of the universe to contact me. It created an entirely new scenario, an exploration where my fancy possessed no map.

My hopes grew. My quest for tomorrow was about to begin.

The word destiny formed in my head. *Rubbish.*

My mind kept refusing to accept this lack of logic. *Your imagination did that, Gen. Your desires conjured her. Nothing more.*

It felt like a dream, but I remained unsure. It had to be just that—a dream, by all scientific tests.

I walked with my cup of coffee to the porch. It looked the same as always.

My cell phone had remained silent during the entire night. Chase never called back.

I shrugged. I would see Chase soon enough since he worked for the Center.

It was time to focus on the next couple of days. My excitement with this new job was rather mitigated because I couldn't tell anyone.

My dad could never know what had taken place in the last weeks. Soon, I would see him and spend what could very well be my last days with my father for a long while. Leaving him would not be easy emotionally. Our goodbyes always broke my heart. I wasn't ready to reconcile with this notion. I would find a way to see him despite the obstacles.

Just about that moment, I heard my dad's footsteps on the stairs. It was the instant to make the most of my time here.

11
CONNECTION
Tesh

Mountain Top, CA – 2022

Tesh observes the sun setting on the horizon and knows this is a sight she will remember forever. But as time unwinds against them, they must find the others and fast. Tesh Vlog - DAINN Annals – Summer 2022.

The wind we faced on the mountain resonated in our ears, battering us from all sides. It sounded like a fierce rustling, loud enough to drown out any other noise.

Blast, excited at the panorama, lunged over the edge of the mountain. "Netwash, I've seen nothing this beautiful."

His sentence lost in the heavy breeze reached me, but only because my hearing heightened by the Imps made it possible. We didn't see clear skies in our time, although we were accustomed to high squalls. However, these were not lethal.

Chase moved closer to Leane and attempted to grasp his words. "What did he say?"

He appeared envious as he observed my friend flying around unencumbered, happily turning and twisting over the emptiness below.

Blast glided around the summit, creating a series of somersaults in the air in front of us. He was like a kid with a new toy. His palpable joy made me laugh, but it scattered my thoughts. For just a moment, I wanted to forget what I had learned from Chase.

My mind cried for a release. The responsibilities of the quest we embarked upon when we left Ang weighed heavily on me. Chase's revelations outlined the challenges of our situation. These demanded a multi-prong plan and called for rapid action. Only, this is where Streak excelled. He was nowhere to help lead us. But it was his domain: strategic thinking, tactical operations, practical scenarios, and logistics.

Looking at Blast, I struggled to tell him what I knew. I clamped down on that need, for he would never live this moment again. Experiencing this for the first time, feeling this awe because of the beauty of the panorama surrounding us, was a gift. His joy as he frolicked under the sun warmed me. Our lives thus far, entitled to it, even if for a moment. We all were.

My stomach dropped when Chase told me about the tablet. Chewing on this news, I tried to contain my emotions in turmoil. The weight of our mission threatened to crush me. The information was a burden that required sharing with Blast and Leane. Only, without Streak, I wasn't sure what to expect from Blast. At least we knew its location.

He was sometimes unpredictable. The balance in our group, precariously structured, relied on Streak's presence. It was always part of the plan that Streak would remain if the need arose, while Blast would sacrifice himself. While it became an unspoken rule among us with our missions, we all knew this.

As I processed the situation, one thing drove me. Our pledge required that we find Streak. The essence was to save our people. To rescue those who remained inside the Chambers. Streak's gifts strengthened us. Time played a critical part. Within a brief period, all hell would break loose. *Then what if...*

He was our strategist. He remained indispensable to our mission. His help to determine the best course of action, given the odds we faced, was invaluable. But there was more for me personally. I needed him.

We arrived in this place unbeknownst to others. At least, it was the plan. But a team of scientists had found our technology, which prompted the idea of the Center.

Now, I feared they knew even more. What Chase had shared with me could barely touch the surface. Their findings, as of now, could permanently torpedo our mandate. What if they had found one of our Chambers? And some of our people? I shuddered at the thought. Under these circumstances, implementing a robust tactical maneuver on the ground with all our resources on hand was crucial. Within the last few moments spent with Chase, the Center effectively became the critical turning point in our efforts.

They possessed a piece of our technology. The search for more would continue. These scientists' interest in finding answers would quickly become imperative if they weren't already. No one confirmed our presence here yet; at least I hoped so, but it couldn't be very long. If they somehow believed otherwise, it would require a whole new dynamic. And if they found the other Chambers and were successful in breaching them, we would have a war on our hands. Our people would not compromise their mission.

My role was an integral part of our success or failure. I disliked my gift because it caused me to control people's minds, and in this scenario, it would become a necessity on a larger scale. The excavation may have unearthed other things as well inside the mountain. I was worried about that too. The damage would be difficult to overcome unless we could lead them in a different direction.

I glanced at Chase at my side. He was a stubborn one. The Center's scientists were probably just as doggedly determined as he was and wouldn't let go of their search quickly. They would not give up their findings and hold on to their discovery. It could change everything for them. The news of our presence could spread, creating chaos for them and us.

My hands trembled under these thoughts.

The Entity inside the mountain was yet another matter. The meaning it held didn't escape me. Eventually, we would have to face it. Only, I hoped it would be with our entire team. It was most probably unavoidable, although this created yet another impossible scenario. It had provided us time to find our people and depart the web of underground caverns. At the moment, this was our priority. We had infringed on their territory. Now, we were challenged with finding Streak, our tablet, our people, potentially battling the Entity, and extracting all these critical elements short-handed, with the Center looking for us. It was getting better and better.

Besides, the knowledge shared by Chase left us with no choice. Our missing Chambers changed the equation. The complexity of the situation compounded by these facts collided in my head. Regardless, the parameter of our mandate remained clear. No one could know we were here.

How long had they hidden below the cave system?

We had encountered nothing like the Entity, even in our time. Yet, we traveled to space. We had extended range detection capabilities that searched the cosmos under DAINN. So why were they here? Had we been impervious to their presence in our time? I didn't know, but we desperately needed this information.

Still, things didn't add up. It had provided us time to find our people and depart the web of underground caverns. At the moment, this was our priority. But why had it done this? An enemy does not give reprieve. I shook my head as I remained without an answer. It was an evolved sentient life form. Was it our enemy?

Admiring the landscape below, I waited. Watching my friend's antics as he flew from the peak provided a small respite. Hiding my thoughts and keeping a tight rein on my impatience to act, I outlined a plan in my mind.

The presence of the Entity might feed the curiosity of the scientists. It could divert them away from us. I hesitated. Indecisive. Anything unnatural and out of the ordinary would raise their interest. It would undoubtedly result in us no longer having access to our Chambers, or worst discovery. There was little doubt that the Sphere could create destruction inside the mountain. If so, our Chambers would become inaccessible if not destroyed. This eventuality brought yet another set of problems. We needed to avoid this at all costs.

Chase had intimated that access to the tablet would be difficult. I shivered at the thought of it in their hands. *What if we cannot stop them?*

My brain went through the rigor of the process I knew only too well, compartmentalizing everything. Just as we had learned at the Institute and Academy, using the training during the years leading to graduation, I discarded my feelings and cut myself off from my emotions. This systematic approach ensured the most objective evaluation of the situation and outcomes possible without the flaws resulting from human weaknesses. Emotions could taint that practice. According to the DAINN System, they must never invade my rational decisions in critical matters.

Only, this was without considering the guy standing next to me. I couldn't ignore the feelings Chase triggered into me. The turmoil I felt when I thought of Chase remained something altogether different. I pushed it away.

This guy was nothing to me. Nothing. But he affected me. The connection created by DAINN remained, and it probably existed as the reason behind how I had reacted to this stranger. DAINN opened a link between us when he intervened... As Chase fell into the cave, the connection began and became stronger. Our A.I. used my skills but responded to its programming. This contact stayed within me, associated with my DNA. I surmised this as I watched Chase. I didn't want this, but the kinship existed between us, even if he didn't understand it yet.

He glanced in my direction with a smile.

I felt lost when he looked at me, all my thoughts fading into the cluttered background of my mind. My breath caught in my throat again, recalling the way he had appraised me. Chase affected me, unlike anything I experienced before.

This environment, foreign to us in many respects, demanded an understanding of this time. Their mind maps differed from ours, even though we were both humans. Learning their triggers to help us adapt was essential. I didn't want to use my powers here, and everything confirmed that I might have to do so again. It disturbed me. *The system follows me even here.*

Chase presented himself as my first subject. Conflicted about this, I found the act of MindMapping him distasteful.

Chase tilted his head, waiting for me to say something. His pointed look dropped to my mouth, and I shivered.

Using my gifts on Chase utterly revolted me. I turned away.

Everything unfolded unevenly. The impossibility of maintaining a handle on what happened next demanded flexibility I did not possess. It remained one characteristic not engrained in me at birth. Unpredictability truly no longer existed in Ang, but occurred here.

My thoughts returned to Chase. When we were alone, moments ago, his gaze had traveled over my body, hidden under my tight uniform. My emotions spiked, responding to his caressing eyes. It rendered me breathless and also chilled me.

Chase's influence on me could not exist. It would thwart our plans. I wished to believe that he had left me unfazed. I needed to convince him of that, too. Deep down, though, I knew otherwise.

I liked the way his eyebrow lifted and his gorgeous lazy smile. *Not good.*

My naturally logical and efficient mindset appeared erratic and heavily influenced by endorphins. Structured to hold information in a calibrated way, it suddenly seemed too rigid. Instead of waking up in a world rooted in the same core principles, we had awakened in a time where things unfolded without logic. People here dealt with events as they presented themselves, bouncing from one moment to the next without a hint of unease.

I came to this conclusion because of Chase's behavior. My assessment accurately reflected facts that had neither been proven nor disproven. Chase was the only human model available to me. He reacted relatively calmly to the experience in the tunnels and us.

Chase held his ground, facing the unknown and showing curiosity rather than fear. That he knew about us would ordinarily require caution on his part. At least, a normal reaction demanded as much. Yet, with me, he had been anything but cautious. His attitude upon finding us here could only come from the fact that his knowledge outweighed everything my mind had conjured. Anyway, would other humans show this adaptive intelligence, or was it just Chase? I came back to DAINN again. How much of an imprint did DAINN leave behind?

The notion that a part of my DNA remained within someone else persisted in my head. It was no longer a foreign concept. I felt it, and this firsthand experience unbalanced me.

The Center knew about us because of one piece of technology. Its team of scientists suspected the tablet possessed a new tech that could change every advancement they made. It was something we had not envisioned in our preparations.

As I watched Blast, I pondered on what actions to take. I analyzed paths and outcomes in my head. The full consequences of the situation, if we could not derail their efforts, overwhelmed me. I closed my eyes. Would I have to use my gifts on all of them?

Our reality, as we knew it, didn't exist anymore. As we waited for Leane, I retreated into my thoughts to find balance.

And I reached out to Blast over the NetCom. "Blast, as much as I would like to stay and play, we have things to do."

He grunted. "NetRoger that..." Within seconds, he landed beside me, breaking my gloomy thoughts.

He dropped between Chase and me without a hint of remorse, purposely pushing him away from me.

The despair that threatened to swallow me retreated.

Blast's grin remained plastered on his face, even as he put his hand on my shoulder and nodded in Chase's direction. "Tell me."

"Within a brief period, all hell could break loose," I said.

He nodded, and the look on his face told me he knew something was off.

The possessive gesture drew Chase's eyes.

I looked away.

As obtuse as he could be, Blast remained conscious of things. His knowledge of me ran deep. Like any unit, we worked so closely together that it became unavoidable after all these years. I suspected he chose not to dwell on things and only selectively pretended not to grasp them. His way of dealing with things was to perform a sort of avoidance whenever it suited him.

Disconnected mentally from my team to protect them, and without Streak, who held a close place in my heart, our mission in this time and place looked to be compromised. I nodded. "It doesn't look good."

The stream of events in these last hours catapulted my vision of our future toward extreme challenges or destruction. The path began with losing Streak. It continued with the confrontation by the Entity and our defeat in the fight following unprecedentedly. My understanding that we possessed little time to find the others only exacerbated everything and didn't help matters. We found ourselves in a precarious position now, with the Center suspecting our presence. Sure, we had faced worse. Yet, my reaction was unlike anything we had trained for at the Academy.

Blast glanced briefly toward Chase before he returned his gaze to me.

My eyes met Blast's, and I said, "He will help us."

Blast paused. "I'm listening, but first. "Who is this guy? What's his background? What is he doing here?"

Chase's presence on the summit among us caused me trepidation. His personality, courageous and stubborn, not to forget his unflappable curiosity, would, without a doubt, turn out results I preferred to avoid. Blast and Chase would clash. So, I said, "There is a lot to share."

Blast tilted his head in my direction. "Download it and tell me again why he will help us?"

The connection of Blast's hand on my shoulder lifted the enormous weight that threatened to crush me. The slight pressure of my friend's palm connected me to my Conclave, and I breathed with more ease. I did not want to standalone, not now, in this.

I inhaled the clean air, feeling its coldness inside my lungs as I looked around. It was so crisp here.

The imperative to share my conversation with Blast and Leane presented itself again. Only, I preferred to do it after we reached a safe harbor. How would I explain everything? Things spiraling out of control certainly didn't help. At least once we stepped into the forest, we could hide our equipment, remaining together to determine the next steps.

"We need a plan."

"Executing our mandate comes once we find Streak," Blast said.

I needed to center myself, so I focused my eyes on the scenery. From the peak, the panorama spreading at our feet shimmered with a palette of colors I had never seen in their natural state. The view expanded with three hundred and sixty degrees on the horizon, vibrant, pristine, and untouched — nature, untamed.

This place called me. I could sense it. And as much as I regretted leaving Ang, energy pulsed through me here. I felt alive at this moment, so much more than I had in a long time. Excited, my pulse increased, and my energy flowed faster inside me as I admired the view under the harsh light. I shrugged. "He is from here. Why wouldn't he?"

"You're making little sense. This guy can only get us in trouble."

The gusts weaved around us and whipped my hair about my face. Its brutal assault heightened my senses, rendering me breathless. "Leane will be here shortly."

I glanced at Chase. He leaned against a ledge, relaxed, and looking quite content as he observed me while I felt flushed.

What was he thinking just now?

Our last few minutes played in my head. Things were lousy enough since we got out of our Chamber that I didn't need the distraction, although it was tempting.

HellNet, dwelling on these feelings, was a mistake. But I itched to reach out and touch his chest again. The warmth of his body had seeped into my palm, and flutters swirled in my belly. His heartbeat had increased under my touch. *Oh, boy, we are in trouble.*

The contact, radiating with his life force, transformed into a link, the same one I felt when I regained consciousness in the pod, only now it expanded, stronger between us. I sighed. This connection between us became more difficult to ignore as time went on, and we had just met. My reluctance regarding this closeness ebbed a little, too.

Was I getting used to it? The thought surprised me. It couldn't be. Admittedly, I didn't want that? It would render my task even more difficult.

Blast's next question hit the mark. "Did you read him?"

Uncomfortable, I turned away from Blast, looking at Chase. "Huh, not yet."

Feeling off-kilter, I took my time appraising Chase, who possessed a way about him.

Somehow, he appeared to trust me.

I liked that. This emotion surprised me. It also made me dislike what I might need to do even more.

After learning we would come back in time, we studied the historical events worldwide. Trust didn't come easily. We adopted the same attitudes which required taping into the same reservations they possessed. Not divulging where we came from demanded that we blend in. Adapting... Remaining in stealth mode. Avoiding standing out. None of this would be easy for us, even if it were essential to our success.

In the last few instants, I planned a strategy. Envisioning the distinct possibilities that played in my head, the scenarios took on a life of their own, leading me to different results. Before I realized it, I coerced Chase into delivering the tablet, infiltrating the Center, and battling their security forces. I sighed, eager to see Leane appear.

I needed her here.

Chase observed our exchange and faltered on his feet.

Getting no answers from me, Blast walked toward the opposite edge of the summit, looking down on the mountain slope. "Where is the nearest town?"

Chase pointed toward the East. "Over there, about ten miles down through the forest."

Blast nodded. "I'd like to recon the area before we go down."

Breaking his contemplation, Blast yelled over the howling, "What's going on with him? He doesn't look too good."

"I know. I ZNetted Chase and gave him a booster, and you know what happened after that. He is not reacting properly. Leane needs to look at him before I proceed with the read."

"They're not as strong as we are... It could prove interesting."

I rolled my eyes... "They don't possess our knowledge nor our strength, that's true." I cleared my throat. There could be no misinterpretation. "Not that we are here to do any harm." Irritated by my reaction, I licked my lips as my unease increased at the thought of what would take place next.

"That's your department. I do what needs doing," stated Blast, with no remorse.

Hoping to guide the situation to a friendly outcome, I nervously glanced behind me. *What will the MindRead reveal?*

"We're here to alter the path."

"You don't say," muttered Blast, now looking at me funny.

I felt unsettled. *Netwash, I don't even know him.*

Leane's exclamation rose behind us and stopped me from answering. She carried Mage in her arms, followed by our equipment, as it hovered behind her. She settled on the ridge. The mass of cases glided and dropped beside her.

As soon as my dog's paws touched the ground, he immediately came to me, his tail wagging. *Hello boy. I missed you, too.*

Mage barked.

Chase, his head resting against the rock, opened his eyes and looked at Mage, lifeless.

Leane, mesmerized by the view, smiled. "This is unreal." Delighted to be outside again, she continued, "It worked… It worked."

"You can say that again," Blast said. "I can't believe the clarity up here."

"This will elate Streak when he gets back."

"Ouch… Don't remind me. We're bound to hear a lot about that," muttered a disgruntled Blast.

"It's beautiful," whispered Leane.

"Yeah… Only now… There is no DAINN," Blast grumped.

"Netwash… I forgot that we don't have DAINN. No wonder. This timeline is so distracting…" Leane said, with her eyes glancing back on the panorama.

"We still have DAINN; only our access to it is limited for now. We need to adjust." My voice sounded confident, knowing that DAINN had saved Chase. The System was around somewhere, probably locked inside the tablet. We just needed to find it. My doubts on how we would repossess what was ours surged through me. I pushed them away and held my ground under the alert eyes that Blast turned in my direction.

"What do you know we don't?" he inquired with some intensity. His gaze went to Chase against the rock, and he nodded toward him. "Did you get something?"

My thoughts flew to them, giving them the gist of what I knew, yet guarding part of the information regarding the role DAINN played in saving Chase. It was something that I will provide later.

Blast's reaction was, as I had expected, boisterous.

"This plan of ours is unraveling fast," he muttered with a look in Chase's direction.

"We need to find the others." Leane turned to look at Chase and frowned as she scanned her patient with a sigh. Her expression showed concern.

Turning away from both of them, I then looked at Chase. "I Znetted him and gave him a dose of booster right before the attack. He's not reacting well. I'm not sure what causes this somewhat passive state."

"Let's find out." Leane approached Chase, checking her preliminary physiology readings. "The way the Entity interfered with each of us... It's no surprise if you feel queasy." She smiled at Chase and deployed her visor. "Is your head pounding?"

"You could say that again."

After taking in Chase's vitals, Leane turned toward me. "His pulse is weak. I can help with that. He is reacting to a slight molecular disturbance from the field emitted by the Sphere during our stasis." Turning to Chase, "I will fix this. You won't feel anything lasting."

"A slight molecular disturbance?" questioned Chase, scowling at Leane.

"Don't worry about it. I'll have you feeling better in no time at all."

Blast stated. "You show no fear of us. Why is that?"

Chase's eyes locked on me as Leane moved her hand to the crown of his head. "Should I be afraid?" he mused. "Somehow, you do not strike me as savages or anything."

Leane chuckled and pressed her hand against Chase's skull, focusing inward.

As energy dispersed into Chase's head, a light glow came out of her palm.

I saw a question in Chase's eyes as his hand moved Leane's away. "What are you doing?"

Blast moved around Chase, ready to interfere. "Let her do what she does."

"Which is what exactly?" Chase's expression was curious but not belligerent.

Leane appraised him and smiled. "I am readjusting your molecular alignment."

She applied her own medicine, based on her dose of magic, instead of resorting to our medication and science.

"How?" Chase's head moved away from Leane's palm.

"Stand still," she ordered, refusing to respond.

"How big is the town below?" Blast stood a space away from Chase as he muttered the question.

Chase glanced sideways at Blast near him. "Insignificant town. A population of about thirteen thousand."

"A handful," said Blast. "Blending in will require more work."

I nodded and focused on Leane. Her hand provided the care needed to enhance Chase's metabolism and recalibrate it to make him feel better. No doubt that he would ask questions about that, too. I sighed again.

"When Leane finishes, you know what we require. Read him, map him, and get the information we need. I don't care," continued Blast.

"Then what?" My voice shook, for I knew what came next. They expected me to carry on the same way the Institute had demanded all these years. Only I rejected the idea.

"Do your thing, Tesh."

"You mean the thing that got Streak Netpissed at me for doing it to him?"

Blast stared at me, narrowing his eyes, a pinched expression on his face. "Don't even go there with me. Not the same thing, Tesh. There's a difference between what you did and what you know you have to do."

"Really? What's that?" Built-up frustration rendered me unjust. At the moment, I didn't care. I felt entangled in a NetKnot of my making, and I rebelled against the person closest to me because his perception had bothered me. "You know Darnet well how I feel about this."

Most of the time, Streak did that to me. But since he wasn't there, Blast took the brunt of it. Thankfully, I could still make my way around Blast, while Streak possessed the ability to read me too well, making it difficult to get away with things.

"Hey... If you need answers, all you have to do is ask," suggested Chase.

We both ignored him, locked in a conflict neither one of us wanted.

Annoyed, Blast shifted his weight on his feet, a gesture he used when he needed time to think. "Protecting each other is what we do."

I clarified, "He is no threat."

"How would you know unless you scanned him already?" he countered.

"I just don't think he is," I muttered under his blazing eyes. Blast could intimidate when he wanted to be.

Chase turned to Leane for help. "Leane, what are they talking about?"

She shrugged. "It's something we do when we need to. It won't hurt."

Chase pushed her hand gently away. "I think I'm good now. Whatever you are thinking of doing, don't."

Blast faced Chase. "You don't get a choice in that."

"The hell I don't..." said Chase.

Blast just laughed at him, not bothering to address the statement.

NetShit... It doesn't bode well. I tilted my head in Chase's direction. "We can ask him not to divulge anything he knows about us."

Leane interceded. "Why would you trust him? You know we must remain undetected."

"I can keep a secret," confirmed Chase, looking at all of us.

"Trust my judgment."

"You would ask him questions? Don't be naïve," said Leane, a frown on her face.

"That's ridiculous. It puts us in jeopardy," yelled Blast.

"I know what I'm doing, Blast."

"It's your role to MindShape, so do it," ordered Blast, dismissing Chase altogether.

I searched for the most apparent excuses, and no idea came to my mind to postpone what appeared now inevitable. I tried again. "Chase is not in any shape…"

"His brain can't be that different from ours. It won't harm him." Blast growled, exasperated with me, as he walked away. Only, he couldn't walk far, for we stood on a small peak.

"He is fine now," said Leane. "You two better come to terms with what we must do. We have friends to save," she continued, exasperated by the standoff.

I stubbornly stood my ground, not making any move to comply, while trying to find a way around this.

"Leane, talk with her. It is her skill set. It is knowledge she gained at the Academy and Institute for this specific purpose."

"Now that we are here, I do not plan on using this specific skill set."

I stared at his back, just as upset as he was. I hated the role the Institute had imposed that on me over all these years - altering memories, adjusting desires, shaping pathways to new outcomes.

Leane stood beside me. "Why are you antagonizing him?"

I shrugged. Why indeed?

The Institute's mandate was clear. Yet, I intended to make changes. Frustrated with my role, I needed to show them differently when their expectations remained the same as always. *How do I do this?*

Blast assumed Streak's role. It was the way things went within our Conclave. I loved Streak, but he pissed me off for disappearing. I also hated that I missed him as much as I did. While I was upset with him for our lack of a relationship, I hated missing him as much as I did. I was taking out my frustration on Blast because the situation was not to my liking either. *NetShit!*

120

Chase moved away from Leane.

Mage bridged the gap between them both, moving closer to him, looking at him with his tongue hanging out.

Chase looked at the dog and then, asking in my direction, "Mage?"

I nodded.

He smiled and extended his hand to my dog. "Wonderful boy."

Mage sniffed him and sat beside him.

"What's going on with Mage?" Blast's voice sounded surprised and put off at the same time.

Leane suppressed a smile of her own.

I hid mine as I watched Mage licking Chase's hand. "Mage trusts him. You can too."

My dog whimpered beside Chase for more attention. Mage had never done this before, except with me.

I observed this with wonder.

Most times, Mage showed no affection to strangers, and Leane and Blast knew that. It was a first. They didn't know about the link DAINN had unintentionally created between us. Perhaps I could use this. My decision not to tell them for now that we shared a connection seemed sound.

Chase kneeled to caress Mage.

He has the right instinct, using Mage.

He then gave Mage a gentle command. "Sit, boy…"

Mage leaned toward him.

Oh, no…

Neither of them missed that. Leane and Blast looked at me with a look that said it all. *NetSpill…*

12
TIES
Gen

Road Trip To Cambridge, MA – 2018

Gen Aubrey feels melancholy on arriving home due to the next chapter in her life. She needs to compartmentalize her emotions to keep it low drama during her short stay, but the dream haunts her. DAINN Annals – Summer 2022.

The moment arrived, requiring me to leave. A car sent by the Center waited in front of the house. I stood inside the door of my home for what could very well be the last time in a very long, long, long time.

My father carried my bags down the stairs. His insistence scored points. He was always so thoughtful about things like that for my mom.

My mother… I couldn't forget my dream, although I questioned if it was indeed one. Did I see her for real? The implications blew my mind. What in the hell was that? No matter how many times I went through the experience over and over in my mind, I still couldn't wrap my arms around it.

Was I going crazy? Absolutely.

Was I dealing with a time continuum issue? I hoped so.

Were there other realms out there? Yes, yes, yes…

The rest of my boxes brought home days ago found their way into my old room. My empty closet since my departure to MIT overflowed again. The garage would have been just fine, considering that my next return may not take place soon, but my dad would not hear of it. Knowing that part of me remained here made him feel better, and in some small way, reassured me, too. I had a place to come home to, no matter what.

Watching him come down the steps with the bags, I recalled the pride in his eyes when he learned about my recent position. Hope, excitement, and joy were far between this last year. *Let him enjoy my success.*

Remorse meshed with love for my dad in a way that I could not fight. Indeed, I didn't know when I would see him again. I hoped it would be for the holidays coming up, but Jonathan had intimated that it could be longer. I would have to live with that.

The series of truths sprinkled with a few omissions I told these last few days now stood between us and left me uncomfortable. Although I attempted not to say too much, my father was eager to hear about my opportunity at the Center. So, I told him as much as I could, but not enough. Not the whole truth… Omissions… Little white lies… And I hated myself for it.

I loved my dad. He represented the anchor in my life, especially now that mom was gone. Yet, the roles were changing a bit, and I knew that. The confusion over the dream stayed with me. It pursued me, threatening my sanity in these last couple of days. Another question mark remained empty, unresolved, and hollow. And another thing impossible to share with my father for reminding him of my mother would reopen a wound only relatively closed. But he was happy to share our beautiful memories, and I encouraged it. *I made the best of it.*

My mission here was simple. I meant to create a series of moments so special between us they would become imprinted in our minds forever. Living on them for multiple lifetimes would then be possible. It seemed a decent bargain. A deal like that can cast an undeniable and permanent ink in one's mind for a past soon to be.

My father laughed at my eagerness to cram so much into forty-eight hours. But like an excellent sport, he went along with it. We kept up the frantic schedule until we both collapsed on our living room couch with laughter. When the exhaustion set in, carving for us even more precious memories, we remained home just talking. These moments became the best of them all. The togetherness, the familiarity of us, sitting side by side in the comfort of our home as we watched a movie. These were golden.

Dad paused a few feet from me, standing near the door. He looked good, a bit tired maybe, but light shone in his eyes — a glimmer unseen by me for far too long.

Time to go. The little voice in my head whispered these words. *Don't make it harder...*

Impossible.

I straightened my shoulders. "The sign-on bonus is for you, dad. You have access to the checking account. The money is in it. I won't need it, so use it. I'll make sure it gets replenished."

"Yes... You told me, but I won't need it. I have savings, you know."

My father, Michael Aubrey, was a tall and handsome man at six-foot-three. Despite a bit of thickness around his belly, he kept his silhouette in shape. The tummy had only recently appeared over the

125

last year or so, a sign he let himself go these days more than before. Still, he looked healthy. It reassured me to see him like this.

"I love you, dad. Take care of yourself." My voice shook—remaining unemotional required effort. I failed at it miserably, and so I wrapped my arms around him and hugged him again.

He welcomed the hug. Fighting the flow of emotions just as much as I did, he tapped my back, murmuring, "Come on, now... I'll see you soon."

My difficulty in letting go increased. I knew this would not happen again for a while. But we had reached my father's threshold in cuddling. Holding on any longer would render him uncomfortable. "It's not like you've never left home. Remember, college..." He laughed at his joke.

I smiled at the memory since we had behaved the same way that day. Still, I was fighting a mess of emotions.

Holding on a little longer, my chin resting on his shoulder, I joined in the laughter. "Remember... I am fine, no matter what." I pulled away. "Promise me?"

His eyes searched my face. "I know. You've told me that. I'm not sure I understand it, but I'll remember it."

"You hold on to that, no matter what everyone else tells you," I murmured. I couldn't say more than that, but I hoped it was enough. "I will be in touch as soon as I am able."

He nodded. "Government. All the cloak and dagger stuff. It better be something you want," he added with a fierce look. "You sure?"

I smiled. "Absolutely. How else am I going to change the world?" I stated with a laugh. "You know it needs changing."

He grunted.

I opened the front door.

We stepped outside.

A black car waited for me by the curb. It looked like a Government Issue car. At least I didn't have to make an excuse on that one. The chauffeur came out and waited by the side of the vehicle.

I picked up my bag and walked over to the car, my father at my side.

"Hello, miss," said the chauffeur, as he grabbed my luggage and opened the door for me.

I turned to my father. "I'll call you early tonight. We can talk again before the big meeting." One last hug… This time it was brief, too brief, before I climbed inside.

The black windows cut in the bright sunlight.

The chauffeur walked around the vehicle after dropping my bags in the trunk. He sat behind the wheel and turned the engine on, ready to depart.

I watched my father standing on the grass of our home and waved as we drove away.

He returned the wave.

My last image of him portrayed a tall and confident man. Still, I could swear that I witnessed a worried expression flash across his face as we pulled out.

There were plenty of reasons for that. My unease, hidden over the last few days, shadowed everything.

13
SHAPER
Tesh

Mountain Top, CA - 2022

We are on the top of the mountain, and I am still struggling to avoid the MindShape on Chase. Deep down, I know it won't work. Blast expects it, and so does Leane. Streak would want that too if he were here, but he is not. Still, I can no longer procrastinate. Tesh VLog - DAINN Annals, Summer 2022.

I looked at Leane and Blast. They didn't know about Chase's fall or DAINN's intervention and the event that happened while I remained in cryo. They only learned that I helped him get out of the way of the Entity during our confrontation. I preferred it that way, at least for now.

A sigh escaped me again. Here I was... Beginning a new life, and I already manipulated the situation. Getting a better grip on everything and finding my old self became quickly part of my plan. I wanted the young girl filled with wonder and trust from the SRC time, not the girl after the Institute.

Unfortunately, the training left its mark. The suspicions came freely these days. Unlearning all the knowledge I had gained in the past demanded a new mindset, a different attitude, and for that, I required an adjustment period. Trust in oneself, optimism in the future, and the belief that things would turn out all right were no longer staples of my life anymore. I lost my innocence when I lost my parents. I hoped to gain some of these things back. As of this moment, they remained in small supply.

What's going on with Mage and him? Leane said, pointing at Chase.

My friends waited for clarification. One I didn't want to give. I shook my head. "Not now."

They nodded, agreeing silently to be patient. It was a slight movement my team could easily miss. But one, they caught by habit.

Leane looked at me, circumspect. "He is better than new." She added with a smile. "He got a little of my special blend."

Chase frowned. "What did you do? My head no longer hurts, and I feel, huh, energized?"

"Your coloring is already better," Leane interrupted, checking her patient with keen eyes. "Just a little treatment I'm good at," Leane continued, smiling at him.

"Mind telling me how it works?" he inquired, with a hint of teasing in her direction.

I rolled my eyes.

He knew how to charm a girl. I glanced at Leane, whose eyes wore a warm look as she watched him.

I shook my head and glanced at Blast, wondering if he recognized his type.

Blast's face displayed a blank look, the kind he wore when things didn't go his way. He kept his counsel despite his eagerness to know more. Waiting for something to unfold, he observed Chase; his arms crossed over his chest. Under normal circumstances, he would have erupted into some action, insisting on having his way.

Apart from Leane, whose gentle nature remained constant, none of us acted as we usually did.

I blinked at the idea. *Netwash... We were all off-kilter.*

In the silence that settled among us, Chase appeared to be the one most relaxed. He glanced at Mage. "This is a gigantic dog. What breed is he?" He gave Mage a caress over the head, and my dog leaned against him, his snout in the palm of Chase's hand.

"Brand new. Thanks for whatever it is you did..." His voice trailed off as he observed our group.

Leane smiled at him. "Netwash... Huh... All right."

"What?"

"Huh... You're welcome?" Leane said, unsure about the right saying.

The expressions used by Earth's population at this time based on each country's history were familiar to us, if not natural. It remained true, especially for this time frame. The way people communicated with each other developed over the years, but our database had retrieved the turn of phrases, similes, and metaphors appropriate for each period. Our retention of the relevant idioms kicked in with practice, flowing smoothly as needed thanks to our implants. But the opportunity to prepare before we embarked on Origin never presented itself. Time had run out for Ang and us.

Leane's comment seemed inconsequential because we were with Chase, and he already understood the situation. On any other occasion, though, it could cause unwanted attention. Realizing this, Leane grimaced at her mishap.

"Mage likes him," Leane repeated with an apologetic smile. "You must explain why…" she mimicked at me.

"As I said, not now."

"Well, of course, he does. Mage, you're a wonderful boy. With an excellent sense of character." Chase's voice cut through the tense silence, his face looking innocent as he finished his sentence.

I was annoyed with him for his air of self-assuredness bordering on cockiness and wished him to remain silent.

Blast moved fast, irritated like I knew he would be by Chase's attitude.

He now towered over him, his eyes focused on his face, causing Chase to lean his head back to meet his gaze. "Now that you feel better… What exactly are you doing here?"

Chase gently pushed away from the rock, purposely stepping into Blast's space. "I live on this planet. A better question: what are you doing here? But if you must know, climbing, as if this is not obvious."

My alarm went off. Blast's proximity to Chase was bound to carry repercussions.

Leane moved between both guys. "Hush… Play nice."

"What year is this?" Blast demanded, indifferent to her gentleness.

"If you were from here, you would know," Chase said with a challenge in his voice.

I felt a slight chill. Here it was, the moment I dreaded. It approached irremediably, and part of me wanted to block it from happening at all. Yet, the instant I learned about the tablet, I knew that inevitably I would use my skills in the here and now.

Chase's eyes rested on him. "2018. Do you want to check that too? It's simple. Look at my phone." Chase retrieved his phone from his pocket and turned the power on, but nothing happened.

Blast waited, curious to see the device.

Chase's face showed frustration. "It's odd. It's not working. My battery should be working."

Impatiently, Blast looking down at Chase, said, "This equipment is so antiquated... Where are we?"

Chase stood his ground, looking quite bored. "We're in the Pacific Coast Ranges."

Blast looked at me. "We need to know everything Chase does. Either he gives them willingly, or you take them. Either way... I don't care."

I ignored Blast. Resolving this dilemma and seeking answers was up to me. I also needed to make sure that Chase didn't go blabbing about us regardless of how we felt.

"Tesh?" Blast said.

I sighed and tried again. "Blast, it may not be necessary."

I knew what this meant and nodded.

Blast demanded a read of Chase's mind.

"I don't care what you believe. It's our protocol. We need to know Chase's Mind Landscape."

"What?" Chase took a step back. "What does that mean?"

Leane approached him. "This won't hurt you. I wouldn't have healed you so we can hurt you, now, would I?"

"I don't know, and frankly, I don't care what you tell me. You're not doing whatever it is you intend to do."

Chase looked at all of us with unease. Suddenly, his assurance faded, and his glance rested on me in silent accusation. "Tesh?"

"Chase, I…"

Now on the defensive, he looked at Leane. "What the hell do you intend to do?" He glanced around at my friends and back at me. "You're not touching my head."

Chase… My thoughts flew to him. *Careful… Chase. Don't overreact. Trust me, please.*

His eyes narrowed on me. "What's going on?"

I'm talking to you.

I can hear you. You're in my head.

I know.

You can read my thoughts. So, this is what Blast meant earlier. Are you a telepath?

Yes. I can read people's minds. But I can do more. It's called Mind Landscape. This way, we know and understand who you are.

"I don't want you in my head, Tesh. Get out."

"We have to know we can trust you."

"Get away from me." Chase looked aggressive now, suddenly frustrated at the thought of finding himself in this predicament. "Why don't you ask your questions like normal people?"

Chase, I'm on your side. Remember when I asked that you follow my lead? Now is the time.

His eyes shifted back to my friends. "I don't want any of you in my head."

Blast snickered. "Scared? You should be. She is a weapon."

"Blast!" Furious with him, my voice resonated as a slap in the air as I pushed past him to get near Chase.

Leane, surprised, gave him a small, reassuring smile. "I promise this won't harm you."

Chase, I have to do this. Don't make it hard for either of us.

What year is it in your time, Tesh?

Not now.

What year is it? You want to get in my mind. You owe me that much.

2098.

It's not that far away from now. How come you possess these kinds of powers?

I can only tell you we are much advanced. Things exist beyond what we know and understand.

Did you develop these powers? This technology?

Yes, but I can't discuss this with you.

Frustrated, Chase nodded. *What do you want to know?* "Ask your questions outside my head."

"I'll ask, but I still have to MindMap you."

"Why?"

"Let me show you."

If I MindMap you, I take a reading of your mind.

I hate this intrusion already. What is it?

We call it a MindLandscape, if you will. I get to know everything about you.

How does it work? How will it affect me?

I will learn all there is to know about you and who you are. What triggers do you possess, Chase? What makes you behave a certain way?

Chase recoiled from me. A pause lingered between us. "Real-time psychology?"

I waited, letting him come to terms with it. *Neither one of us has a choice.*

Chase's thoughts swirled in his head, erratic, and then calmed as he took a deep breath. *As if giving you access to my mind by talking to you in my head isn't enough. For a first date… It's intimate.*

Startled, I jumped.

"What's wrong, Tesh?" Leane said when she saw my reaction.

Here was Chase's unpredictability again. The guy didn't seem to react in the usual way. "Nothing. We're communicating. Give me a moment."

I… Yes. It is. How can you be so glib at a time like this? We use this process to get to know each other, so there are no secrets between people who share lives.

It should go both ways. Besides, we're not sharing a life unless you're about to propose, and I strongly think we should go on a first date before.

Stop that.

Chase smiled, but it was a calculated smirk that didn't reach his eyes. Nothing compared to the warmth he had shared with me before. *What? Keeping a secret garden is healthy. Knowing everything about a person can make it boring.*

Once again, Chase surprised me. He was uncommon, with high emotional intelligence. *Knowing everything about someone makes it safe, closer, and more relaxed. One knows what to expect.*

By my estimation… Boring.

It's the only way we can proceed without altering your mind. If I know I can trust you, then I ask our questions without shaping your memories.

Chase turned away from me in frustration and exclaimed, looking at the others, "No shit… Can you do all of that? It is such an invasion of privacy," glowering at all of us. "Don't you have privacy in your world?" exclaimed Chase. "Don't you learn how to get to know someone by taking the time to discover them, like taking them to lunch?" Agitated, Chase paced on the slight ridge. "What kind of a world have you built?"

"That's the point."

"We don't have time for this, Tesh," Blast said. He took a step forward in Chase's direction. "I suggest you comply."

"It seems some of you are not so well developed," said Chase with a smirk.

"Hey, we wouldn't be here in the first place if you had built a better world," Leane said, stepping toward Chase. "You did a lousy job that we now have to clean up." Her resentment at being here flared despite her usually placid behavior.

Surprised, I looked at my friend. Leane returned the glance and shrugged. "You're not the only one Netpissed."

"So, what did you do, take our mess, and destroy your world? Whatever that means," Chase replied, facing Blast with a stern face. "And… Blast, I've got time, plenty of it. So, if you want something from me, you better give me something back. It's the way things work around here."

Blast looked menacingly at Chase. "I'll give you something back."

I grimaced. "Hey, there is no time for this."

They stood facing one another like two bulls in an arena. This encounter turned stressful, and if it continued, it would force me to intervene. *Netshit.*

"Okay." Leane, watching Chase took a step forward between both of them.

I knew what the task required of me. As usual, I would perform it and provide results, but probably not how they expected me to. This trip into Chase's mind would be the way I saw fit. I stepped between them. "Enough. It is not our way. If you want answers, I will get them, but I will handle this my way."

After a pause, Blast glanced my way. "Fine. Shaper, do your thing," Dismissively, he turned away from us and went to the large casings located a few feet away.

I closed my fists tight, reaching for control.

Blast pushed me too far.

"We will give you space." Looking at Blast, she took a step toward our Conclave teammate. Gently, she put a hand on his chest. "I suggest you help me review the equipment since you so nicely bailed on me earlier. Tesh can perfectly handle this on her own."

Blast nodded, his eyes turning gentle as he looked at Leane. He should have been her mate by now, but there was no time for it. Our schedules had not allowed for much other than training and preparation for this journey during the last year.

Blast inventoried the contents without opening the boxes. The task took the better part of thirty seconds. "Done. We have everything we need. I'll do some recon after we drop the equipment below."

Leane turned to me. "Where are we going?"

Turning back to Tesh, Chase said, "You're welcome to my place. It's a friend. But since he is out of town, you can settle here until you figure things out. Things should be quiet for you here. It's at the edge of town."

"Show me the location, Tesh," Blast said.

I approached Chase and said, "Think of the place, please."

Chase sighed and promptly complied.

I quickly lifted the location from his mind and got the coordinates through my PVZ.

Blast received the location and nodded. He then grabbed a NetTie device from his suit and locked it on Chase's belt buckle. "Don't lose it," he added as he checked its secured position.

Chase looked down at the device hanging on his belt. "What does that do?"

Blast ignored his question and turned on another small gadget. "Signal's working," he muttered in Tesh's direction.

Tesh exclaimed, "Blast, don't you dare."

Blast smirked. "I'm not inclined to listen at the moment."

Then, ignoring Tesh, he added to Leane, "See you at the bottom."

Tesh swore, "Netshit, Blast!"

It caught me off guard because Tesh's face wore an expression of explicit horror.

"What?"

She shook her head at me. "Nevermind."

"Come on, Leane." Blast yelled over the howling wind as he leaped off the ledge, disappearing into the drift.

Chase said as Blast jumped away, "The equipment boy doesn't like to get hindered much," as he walked around Leane and stepped to the edge. "Is he always this intense?"

Leane's laugh echoed briefly in the wind. "You have not seen the worse of Blast yet.

With envy, Chase added, "I needed a set of these boots. For a set, I will let you MindMap me again."

Leane laughs. "You're incorrigible. Careful on the edge Chase, we don't need you to fall," Leane said, looking at me with a grin.

Chase and I looked at Leane, wondering if she had guessed Chase's history with the mountain. Her blank look answered us. "What did I say?"

"Nothing," I said.

Chase walked back towards me. "Did he scan the content of those boxes in seconds?"

I nodded.

Leane laughed. "You need to get used to it."

Chase stood, uncertain.

"I will keep an eye on Blast," said Leane as she smiled and went off the side of the mountain backward with a shout of pure joy. The metallic casings lifted from the bedrock and followed her down the cliffs as if on cue.

"Don't let him do it," I said as she disappeared.

Leane's laugh reached us from the abyss. "He is in a mood… And your attitude is not helping." She yelled back. "But I'll see what I can do. Better hurry, though…."

Chase glanced enviously toward the emptiness of the ravine. "What don't you want him to do?"

"Nothing." I felt terrible for him. We were a bunch of strangers to him. I would probably react the same way, thinking about the possibility of a MindMap performed on me. Ugh… I quickly concluded that I would not cooperate either. He didn't ask to be in this situation. What would I do in his place? I probably would act as he did. Thoughtfully, eager to make things easier for him, I suggested, "Why don't we sit here? I'll walk you through it."

Chase stood defensively. "Fine." He sat down in front of me.

I positioned myself at arms' length from him. Immediately, Mage quickly sat between us. *That dog…*

I met Chase's powerful cerulean glare, and a shaky breath escaped my lips. Boy… I needed to get a grip. *And I'm sorry.*

Unfazed, he held my gaze without speaking, and a silent pause followed. *You better make it worth my while.*

I lifted a challenging eyebrow at him, daring him to say something. He would navigate his way through because that was how Chase operated. I felt sure of that. I didn't need to read him to know this. In uncomfortable situations, Chase reverted to innuendos, jokes, and humor. My observation of him in the last hour showed this much. One fact remained, though; I didn't want him to be afraid of me, of us.

Do I need to worry, Tesh?

No, Chase.

The temperature turned colder. Daylight would only last a few more hours.

His hand dropped on Mage's head and remained there. *Now what?*

Sharing a MindMap represented the best way to show him what the procedure entailed. Opening my thoughts to him, my memories, and imparting my emotions for a brief instant forged a deep bond between two people. This momentary transference demanded time and practice, but most of all, being in one's head required trust. Giving him mine to gain Chase's, seemed appropriate. Usually, I invaded someone's thoughts to read them, but I knew I needed to do this to reach him. My ability rarely provided the opportunity to exercise my skills in reverse.

Watching him, I said, "MindMapping is the way to read one's thoughts and understand their personality traits and triggers. It is instructive and efficient. Plus, it allows us to read a person's reactions to situations and protect people from their actions. And it gives me a MindLandscape of who you are and reduces the possibility of lies. Because I will pick these up."

"You assume people lie in their dealings with each other?"

"Not always, but we don't know your world. People lie here, don't they?"

"I don't want you to get into my head and do something I wouldn't want to have done. How do I trust you in my mind?"

"I asked myself the same question. How do I get you to trust me? And there is only one way. Show you." I closed my eyes, calling on my power to reinforce the link between us.

Chase remained in the same spot, and I felt his eyes on me. "How long have you done this, Tesh?" Chase asked, with something in his tone that got my attention.

I opened my eyes. My connection with Chase as a Shaper remained stable. *Really? What's with you? If you stop playing with me, Chase, it will go a HellNet of a lot faster.*

His irritation became palpable. "I don't want this. Just remember it." The energy shifted, almost unbearable as tension and anger increased between us.

"Trust me." My voice rose in frustration, challenging him. I tried to be gentle in this, although I didn't care about the process. He didn't respect that. Most wouldn't.

An unwelcome heaviness descended on my chest. We were starting the wrong way. Still, as distasteful as this was, it would be far worse if I intended to shape his memories. I consoled myself with the notion that my attempts with him were to avoid just that. I would not tamper with his brain. With a sigh, I threw it back in his face. "You ventured into the unknown the minute you stepped inside the cavern. We saved you from the Entity. Just remember that."

Turning my gaze away from him, I refocused on the link. Chase waited and dropped on me with an anger that chilled me. "You're in my time."

Wondering if he caught onto the Shaper's title, I cocked my head to the side and gave him a quick look.

It's there, lingering between his eyes. I see it.

The title did not escape him.

The weight in my chest settled there a bit more firmly. Chase had caught on. He knew what I was… A trespasser… An invader… A breaker of people.

Why did he call you "Shaper?"

Chase… We just don't have time. Do I answer him and explain? It wouldn't make my job any more comfortable, but then that was what Blast had intended. If I wanted Chase's trust, I needed to explain. I braced myself for his loathing. Once he knew who and what I was capable of, it was unavoidable. "I am a Shaper of Thoughts. I can get into your head and manipulate your thoughts. I can make you do what I want. I can break you, shape your thoughts, and make you behave as I want. Remember, I can keep your thoughts intact while reading them to benefit me and implant those that will serve me better. Besides all of that, I can leave a trickle of something that makes you crazy. It is within my purview, my power, my special gift. You would do well to remember I do not need permission."

His reaction was not what I expected. Again, Chase surprised me. His tone was soft when he said, "Shit. Really? Yet, this is not who you are. It is what they want you to be."

I paused, surprised by his assessment of me. Letting his words spread a sense of well-being inside me, I closed my eyes and relished under his gaze for one brief instant. He understood what I had been through and who I was.

It is what the Rodent had used me for, reading people, shaping thoughts. Pushing away from the memories of the most challenging period of my life, I fought to overcome the bitterness, but it drowned me with a vengeance.

Faces I wanted to forget came to the surface. They were people I tried to obliterate from my mind but couldn't. It would have been too good to push them aside, to excise them from my thoughts, to close myself off from feeling the shame. The Rodent inflicted this on me, time and time again. It was part of his programming. Forcing me to do his bidding, for there was no better word for it. No matter the fights, no matter the cries, no matter the begging, he had won. He repeatedly imposed this on me, manipulated me until I could no longer hide the truth of what I had become in his hands. The loathing I felt for him came back to the surface, unsettling me in my task.

The Rodent tried to make me what I hated the most. A usurper of people and an intruder in their heads. Although he forced me to do this against everything I believed in and who I wanted to be, he couldn't change me completely. I complied because he left me no choice. The Rodent carried on his plan under the nose of the Institute, against the Universal Pledge's dictates, unbeknownst to those who could have stopped him. He did this until it was almost too late for me, until the dice were cast within the Academy for me, and until Tesh no longer existed as Tesh. She had become the Shaper, one of the most influential people of her time. But here, in this place, I had a choice.

My breath escaped, tumultuous, as I attempted to get a grip on my emotions.

Chase's voice brought me back to the present. "I do not fear you in that way, Tesh. If this is the only option...."

I opened my eyes to his.

He smiled at me and closed his, finally resigned.

My voice shook a little as I explained, "Projecting my thoughts to you as we are talking now differs from reading you. Shaping goes one step further. It removes actual memories and imparts false ones. It can change your personality, turn you into someone you are not, but become. It is not what I am about to do. It is what I no longer will do. I just want to read you."

"I understand, even so, what you're talking about is manipulative... Our privacy lawyers would have a field day."

So, I took a deep breath. *Currently, I am only offering to share my memories with you to understand and feel the process.*

Silence. It was odd. I opened my eyes again.

Chase nodded at me, waiting for what came next.

It was a much better outcome than if Blast had intervened and forced him to comply. It was a better way. I leaned into him and grabbed his hand. *Trust me.*

Funny thing, trust... You want it from me, but you do not provide me with the same choice. It has repercussions for a relationship, you know. Chase's sarcastic tone reached my mind and stopped me from venturing closer. *Hey, what if something goes wrong?*

We have perfected this. Chase, I could do it even if you didn't want me to. I could trick you and disappear from your mind as if this never occurred. I could make it, so you never remember meeting us. It doesn't hurt unless you resist.

Tesh, I don't want to forget you.

This statement reached my heart.

I felt a warmth in my chest.

Chase didn't want to forget me. It was a sweet thing to say. I wanted to ask why, but I knew why.

I glanced at Chase. My voice came out soft, almost indiscernible in the wind, when I said, "I won't reshape your memories. Just remain open with me. Then, once this is over, you can answer my questions truthfully."

Chase nodded again, but his smile tightened a little. "You won't reshape them at all, promise me."

"Will you tell me the truth?"

"I don't lie."

"Fine. Just relax."

I won't fight you... But there are things I want to know.

Chase... Later.

Who is DAINN?

Never mind this, Chase.

Why are you here?

Chase, I will share something with you. Just relax.

I can't... It is too weird.

You're already getting the hang of it, talking to me in your head, that is. I held his hand, giving it a slight squeeze. Our fingers intertwined naturally. *All right... Close your eyes.*

So, I opened up to him. Willingly, I lifted a veil on a corner of my mind and shared with him my memories. Then I sent images of Ang city, beautiful under its domes. I showed him the plaza and its landscape around the Golden Ghetto. I gave him access to our buildings, flycars, and bridges. Then, I was a child with Mage. I showed him my parents, moments of laughter and love, and me playing with Mage. These few childhood memories represented endearing moments I clung to tightly. But he didn't have to know any of that.

It's incredible. Will you show me more?

Later. Are you ready?

A sigh. *Yes.*

I am going to do a MindMap now. Don't worry. It will not hurt. Feel the slight push… It's me, entering further into your mind. Allow it. Don't resist.

Can I stop you? Chase said sarcastically again.

No. But if you resist, it can hurt you. So far, I have talked with you and allowed you to hear from me. I have shared some of my memories, but it's different when I MindMap you. I get a structure, a landscape of how you think. It is like a screen unfolding, showing me everything about you, even the things you do not want to share. You will feel me in your head.

You can pretend to do it.

Too much is riding on this. I cannot take a chance. You have nothing to fear.

What is it you want to know?

I closed my eyes and focused on Chase. My mind floated toward his and encountered the first barrier. Chase tensed. Determined to fight the intrusion despite what he had said, he resisted my presence. Taking command and pushing through it would hurt him. I refused that notion.

Chase… You need to open up to me. My mind reached out for him again. This time, the block came down. There was no fight. No barriers presented themselves on the way. When my mind joined with him, he reluctantly relaxed.

I conveyed my presence with care, spreading a sense of warmth sensation as I entered the cortex of his brain. I followed the pathways of his frontal lobe, responsible for problem-solving, judgment, and motor function. Reading him had nothing to do with his physiology. Our technology dealt with that. Not me... Unless I encountered a physical problem. I delved further into the parietal lobe, managing sensation, handwriting, and body position. I wanted to ensure that he was all right, so I monitored as I continued past the occipital lobe containing his visual processing system, for his temporal lobe, housing his memories and hearing. It was my ultimate destination, for it brought me to witness his experiences.

The web of his thoughts reached me, past neurons and grey matter, lifting his reflections, logic, thinking, memories, and feelings with an energy signature all his own. I pursued the thread of his life leading to this moment. I saw it all... The toddler, the boy in high school, the teenager in college, and the university's youthful man. His family, his mother, his father, his activities, his studies, his likes and dislikes, and his girlfriends. I tried to remain aloof and in control of what I witnessed. No emotions allowed. Just a screen of his mind to my mind, like a film unfolding chronologically.

When I reached the point of his encounter with me, the experience resonated under my touch more vibrantly than the rest. First, I felt an explosion of emotions: surprise, sadness, regrets, anger, fear, and desire. Then I felt the heat radiating through me as the thread expanded like a touch, sensual, pulsating with a raw wanting.

And I retreated from it quickly, jumping back and reaching the basal ganglia, a cluster of structures in the center of the brain, coordinating messages to other areas. Attempting to maintain detachment appeared a small luxury I remained unable to attain at this moment. My meandering gave me a glimpse of Chase's cerebellum, responsible for coordination and balance, and his brain stem controlling breathing and sleeping. It gave me the rest of the elemental landscape of Chase's mind, but I needed more thought patterns.

My mind's tentacles spread back gently to grasp the screen I watched seconds before. The thread pulsated with extra information. I remained anchored in Chase's experiences. I needed to get a better sense of his reactions.

Watching, feeling, understanding came next. I learned how Chase thought in minute details. His family's appreciation through his eyes came next, followed by his work, values, approach to life, relationships, and girls. I saw moments, images rapidly shifting, and glimpses of his world, and I got to understand what he held dear. At that moment, I grasped the core of Chase.

Still, I needed to go in further, in the place where hidden, hurtful, unwanted memories lived. They swirled in darkness, tied together into a recess of Chase's mind within a locked drawer. I looked for the key so I could access it. He rebelled.

I persisted.

He tugged back.

I held firm.

I wanted to see the fall and what happened afterward with DAINN. So far, I had not come across it. The corner of his mind had closed off. I sensed it.

Fear could do this… I followed another pathway, touching carefully at his firing neurons. He didn't want me to get to this experience. Why? I could sense a repulsion growing within Chase as if he knew of my attempts to capture this memory. I hated punching through, but I had to. Slowly, I applied pressure. I heard him gritting his teeth. So, I released a little of the tension and shot through just as he relaxed. Now, I was inside the corner of his mind.

And I saw the ledge. A bird in Chase's hand. A chick… Barely two weeks old. I watched him releasing the baby falcon in the nest. I heard the adult's whistle, observed his wings flapping, a large bird attacking — Chase, losing his grip. His feet faltered as he detached from the rock, falling backward, away from the mountain, arms waving, reaching for the bedrock's support, and instead only touching the blue azure.

High emotions rushed through me in a constant stream of images and colors, intense and raw. I watched Chase's fall all over again, and this time I was him. I wanted to scream; the fear was so intense. And then, I experienced the rock as he hit the outcropping before going down into the darkness of the cavern. The film rolled in front of my eyes. Chase's memories moved in his mind with the strength of bullets in search of a target. They were random, ignited by despair, sorrow, and immense anger. Then, I felt a shift, the sense of floating in the air, as if the descent slowed under the motion of an invisible hand. I hit the ground, and everything went black. I witnessed it all… But now, I required more.

I saw him climb out of the cave. His stubbornness awoke something in me, and it echoed in my brain. I harnessed the moment Chase found the tablet. Chase picked it up out of the rock formation on his way out of the cave. I watched his hand touch the screen, and it lit up. Our emergency signal released the video.

DAINN must have entered the technology tablet when he found a way out of the main array. It responded to its protection protocol, connecting to the tablet lodged in the wall, the closest spot to where it could operate the Nanos. DAINN found a way out of one of the broken chambers to save Chase. It was how he intervened and escaped our Chamber and the grip of the mountain. I then witnessed Chase taking the tablet with him, removing DAINN from this environment. DAINN did not come back because he lost the connection. That's why we didn't have a signal. There was no Network for DAINN to plug into and reconnect away from our Chamber. But what happened afterward? I looked for the next connection, and I heard Chase in my head.

Please... Stop.

I opened my eyes, feeling his pain. His nose bled... *Netshit.*

I slowly pulled out, processing backward one tendril at a time. To avoid leaving behind any traces of my passage, I carefully emerged from Chase's MindLandscape according to our protocol. Ever so slowly, I removed myself from his mind, making sure that everything remained as it was before my invasion.

Just breathe... I am out.

Chase wiped his nose, and blood smeared his fingers. He didn't seem to care.

I had begun the journey into his thoughts, and before I knew it, it was over. It felt like seconds had passed when, honestly, it had lasted much longer. I looked into my unfolding visor. Only twenty minutes had gone by since I began.

Regardless of my ability, I faced an uncommon draining of my energy. This unusual occurrence, a drop in my metabolic field, naturally occurred after hours of this activity, not minutes. It surprised me.

My retreat from his mind left a void. Was my fatigue because of our recent exit from cryo? Unsure, my eyes rested on Chase.

Regretful to see that I had somehow made him feel bad, I said, *It is over. Are you all right?*

Chase lifted his head and said, *Huh.*

I paled.

Chase looked lost.

14
RECON
Blast

Forest Grounds, CA - 2022

My team counts on me, and I have to pick up the slack left by Streak's absence. I don't relish stepping into Streak's footsteps. He is formidable. But without him, it is my responsibility until Streak gets back to us or we locate him. Blast Vlog - DAINN Annals, Summer 2022.

My flight down the mountain was an eye-opener. The air was so crisp and clean, my lungs filled with it, and my physiology responded to it with a spurt of natural energy.

For now, I glided over the mountainside, glancing at the small town below. My recon continued closer to the edge of the bluffs, where I admired the ocean for the first time. Somehow, my NetJet boots got me here on their own. My desire to see it, too intense to wait. It was a pristine ocean, incredibly calm for the Pacific, compared to what we witnessed at home. Of course, the winds here were gentle. They didn't blast around us, rendering each step a struggle as soon as we left the safety of the domes. They were not so utterly cold, either. Here our lips would not turn blue, and our breaths would not form icy filaments when we talked. Here, the breeze only wrestled the leaves in the trees nearby, carrying a soft melody under the sunlight on the bluff.

Leane, a child of nature, would thrive here. She would relate to the environment in a way impossible for her in our own time. My heart soared for her. She had to fight her true self to make it within the Institute Conclave for far too long. The demands imposed on her gifts had not been kind. Indeed, she had struggled. I knew how often Tesh had to intervene, so Leane would not lose it.

In a way, finding this place, such as it was, gave me hope that we could all no longer fight our instincts and flow with our gifts. Maybe here we could finally relax once we identified what we were here to find. At least, here, we were our masters, to a point. We had a mandate, but hopefully, we could carry it with more freedom and less oversight.

HellNet, I knew none of it was going to be easy. But Darnet, it couldn't be any more complicated either.

I turned when I heard Leane gently settle down behind me. She approached with a smile on her lips. "I can't get over this place," she whispered.

I nodded. "It's quite a sight."

We remain side by side, overlooking the waves tumbling on the shore below, glowing with a stupid grin on our faces.

"We're truly here," she murmured. "I know the cost was too much, and I shouldn't say it, but I'm glad."

"You can say anything you want." I reached for her hand and squeezed it. Our fingers remained locked together, with our breathing synced and our hearts beating in unison. We knew what it meant. We just had never acknowledged it. Maybe now, we could. We were to be life partners, mated to each other forever. We knew this from the moment we reached adolescence. The System had not allowed our Conclave Unity Match until we reached graduation age. And now we had... Only, we were no longer in Ang. We didn't have the same constraints or requirements. What would we do in the face of this new freedom?

My thoughts got interrupted by the noise of a machine flying overhead. As our face lifted toward the sky, our invisibility shield enfolded us, making our presence disappear.

"I guess it's time to take a look around," I said.

Leane nodded. "Let me hide the equipment in the forest for now, and I will join you."

"NetRoger that." My steps led me into the underbrush and back toward the base of the mountain. I retraced the Helicopter's path, a Halo, coming from the eastern side.

I darted fast up the cliff through the forest. My freedom of movement enhanced my speed, which resembled the dive of yesteryears. A surge of exhilaration filled me as adrenalin coursed through my entire body, and I laughed. My voice echoed in the trees as I sped along on the grounds.

Although we didn't belong to this time, our inheritance based on human blood from centuries ago gave us a stake.

Leane's laughter resonated in my ears as she quickly tried to catch up with me. As always, we turned this into a game. Our way of coping. The impossible situation that brought us all here for what may be forever gave us mitigated feelings as we missed out on people, but this was newfound freedom. Nothing seemed out of reach, primarily because of our powers in this quest. We could do almost anything except reveal what set us apart and disclose who we were.

The playground stretched ahead. I glided up the slope with Leane, now tailing me.

We felt like kids again.

The landscape released the pressure of the last few hours. It kept our sanity, allowing us to maintain a semblance of normality, helping us reconnect with ourselves again. For one moment, we forgot the bounds that anchored us here. Our people, our family, and the tasks that our mandate dictated we perform.

I soon arrived at the base of the mountain. The location appeared surrounded by an electrified fence stretching several feet away from the rocks. Hiding near an outcropping of rocks, I stopped and waited for Leane to arrive at my side. I quickly launched the Custodians, hidden among the trees, to provide a landscape of the area overhead. Within no time, I received an overview of the perimeter on my PVZ.

I murmured, "There is a gate over there, and the bulk of the security seems to watch it primarily."

"What is this place?" Leane asked.

"Not sure. There are five patrols. They surveyed the grounds surrounding the meadow. East, west, and south. The facility sits on the north side against the mountain, overlooking the forest grounds and the perimeter by the gate."

Leane nodded and kept her voice low. "How many are watching the gate?"

I provided the information quickly. "I counted fifteen inside the perimeter — the security guards patrol in two. There are four guards around the immediate landing pad. Three by the main gate and two overheads."

"It seems like many people. What do they keep in there?" wondered Leane.

I shook my head. "I bet our friend up there knows."

"I need to get inside," I concluded, looking in Leane's direction.

"Let's wait for Tesh and keep watch... The guards' activities around here could reveal insights on what's going on," said Leane. "Besides, Chase might give us more info."

I nodded.

15
CHASM
Tesh

Mountain Top, CA - 2022

My interrogation of Chase continues, driving a wedge between us. I can feel it, and perhaps it is for the best. Tesh Vlog - DAINN Annals, Summer 2022.

Now that the MindLandscape was over, I hated pursuing my questions but still looked for answers, and so I inquired, "Why did you come back here, Chase?"

His voice, distant and full of sarcasm, he said, "I craved spending my summer on vacation sweating my ass off on a mountain. What do you do in your free time?"

I suddenly felt tired, but I kept going. "What did you keep from me?" I knew he did and wondered how he could do so. DAINN?

Chase shifted uneasily. "Jonathan's team made a discovery in the last month. I do not know what it is, but this is one reason for my return."

I remained silent for a moment, deciding to share something with him. "Chase, we are here because we lost our world. In our future,

Earth is in trouble. It will be gone soon. Us... Being here is to save it."
By confiding in him, I touched a nerve. I could see it. His face turned
solemn as he processed what I told him, and I continued, "Do you
think he has found the other Chambers?"

He hesitated, fighting with himself, frustrated. "Jonathan, "I
don't know. All I know is that Jonathan is hiding something, although
I'm not sure what."

I nodded. Chase was telling the truth.

"Tesh, what happens in the future?"

"I have already told you too much." I suspected it had to do
with the tablet, but it could be more significant than that. Hearing this,
I frowned and asked, "What are the scientists working on?" *Careful,
Tesh, don't push too hard.*

He blew out an enormous sigh. "The Center is a research
facility buried deep in the mountains. They are working on your
technology to find out its capabilities. The concept of time obsessed
Jonathan. Now I get why."

"Time continuum?" I paused and rose to my feet. I needed to
compose myself away from his prying eyes. "How many people work
for the Center?" I looked away from him, indecisive on what to do
next.

Chase answered without hesitation. "By now, it must be
around three hundred." He continued, "How did you do it? Save me
that is?"

I relented. "There are many things I cannot share, but we
possess certain powers, as you have seen with Leane. Each person
develops certain uncommon gifts. Mine is to read minds, shape
thoughts, and influence outcomes."

"I understand the manipulation powers of a Shaper now, but influencing outcomes?" He appeared bewildered on that.

I felt uneasy under his scrutiny, recalling the MindLandscape I performed on him. "It's sometimes necessary to do things on a grander scale."

His eyes turned cold. "What? You mean you can do this to groups and entire populations?"

Suddenly I shuddered. "Oh, I hope not. I much prefer to ask for cooperation. Besides, I prefer to put these skills behind me."

Chase observed me, wondering if my response gave him the truth. "You could have fooled me."

My breath hitched at his comment.

After a moment of evaluating me, he seemed to believe it. He got up, staggering a little on his feet. His hands landed on my shoulders. "He focuses the Center's research on time travel. Spallberg believes that we can influence it. Bend it. As unbelievable as that notion is, I think he is right. The proof is right before my eyes since you're here."

I swayed on my feet. The Center found the technology we use in the future. Their research began early enough. Our people may have been wrong about the timing of the events that started our demise. Although, they never indicated it came from here.

Chase supported me, concerned to see me affected in that way, and we held on to each other for a moment.

After a while, I pulled away from him, detaching his hands from my shoulders. After the MindLandscape, the contact felt like too much. The distance between us seemed safer.

This Center was no coincidence. I needed to tell Streak and the others. Streak... Where in the HellNet was he? I murmured to myself, "And Jonathan has the tablet."

Contrite, Chase nodded. "I gave it to him. I wanted to discover the secrets it held, where it came from, what it could do."

Attempting to slow down my racing heart, I murmured, "No one can know that we exist, Chase. Do you understand?"

With a grim look on his face, he grunted, "Yes. I gathered that."

"If people learn we are here, it could unleash a complete set of consequences we must avoid at all costs. Not just issues, catastrophic events are more like it. I need you to promise me not to tell anyone."

He shuffled on his feet a moment, thinking of the results such a promise would entail for him. After a beat, he murmured, "Tesh... I won't tell them about you. Even if I work for the Center, but tell me how you saved me?"

His stubbornness got to me. "Aren't you one-track-minded? Do you realize the significant issues?

He shrugged, a slight smile forming on his lips. "It's about me, so I want to know."

Gritting my teeth on that one, "I told you. My gift can influence outcomes. It is as much as I am going to tell you. *Irritating, stubborn, self-serving hotshot. Very, very hot. Tesh, get a Netwash grip.* "Chase, I need your help. Get the tablet back for me, us."

Chase leaned back against a rock. He looked sad. "Can't do it, Tesh."

My thoughts were buzzing. I tried to remain outwardly calm when I felt anything but that. Chase had to... Otherwise, we would have to take it back at the risk of being discovered. Here I stood, at the same crossroad again, with a choice that could change the course of our mission. I could compel him to do it. Plus, I could manipulate his mind, so he would never remember it. And then I could make him spy for us. It was the second time I thought that way. But I bit my lip and felt the blood on my tongue. The erratic concepts swirled around in my head as I trembled with a desperation I knew too well. I closed my eyes, fighting against my training and knowing only that the outcome mattered in this case. I knew what Streak, Blast, and Leane would say.

The moment lasted longer, with none of us moving.

Chase observed me as I processed what he had told me. He knew what I was thinking, wondering if I would force him?

My actions in the past filled me with guilt. At this moment, the consequences of my decision, perfectly outlined in my head as the natural path, the one I trained for all these years, represented another burden. Would I succumb to tampering with people's minds? I promised myself I would not do this anymore when I left Ang. For the first time, I remained the master of my actions.

When I opened my eyes, Chase had not moved a muscle. His eyes tested me. I used to look at other recruits in the same way.

Suddenly, I felt small, even when I knew I was more powerful than he was, even when I understood I could make him do my bidding, even when he looked at me with curiosity and a certain hunger.

My eyes browsed over his thick eyebrows, his straight nose, his perfect mouth as I scrutinized his handsome features. His eyes almost made me feel a pang of jealousy. I took a ragged breath, hesitant. This guy reeked of unpredictability, but he was also brilliant. Could I do it? Could I trust my decisions with him?

"So, what did you decide, Tesh?" His calm tone interrupted my turbulent thoughts.

"It's complicated." Gush, I sounded desperate.

Way to go, girl! For a tough DAINN girl, you take the Netcake.

He nodded again… "You are here to change the future… Are you going to do the things you despised because I know they disgusted you? I know because I could feel it. I could feel you. The question is… Are you going to do these things?"

Breathlessly, I answered, "I may have to if there is no other choice… I am if there are no other alternatives. We are here to influence outcomes. The future is not an easy place to be."

"We always have a choice."

I waited for him to say something more, but he kept quiet.

His eyes turned serious as they stared into mine. "Is this a fact-finding mission? Do you plan on identifying an event causing the potential downfall of our future? Gees… I don't even know what happens in our future? Is our planet facing an extinction event? What?"

I shook my head, keeping my face blank. "I can't tell you the specifics, Chase."

Thoughtfully, Chase whispered, "So I have to guess… Lucky for you, it's not in my makeup not to tell the truth. You have nothing to worry about from me." He took my hand in his and held it there.

The heat of his palms seeped through mine, rendering my thought process slower. "I sensed hesitation about the Center. What are you holding back?"

He tilted his head to one side, unwilling to say anything more, but then stated, "The circumstances, in this instance, demand my thoughts. That's all."

My eyes narrowed on his.

He didn't budge. "You're unsure about something. What?"

I felt his anxiety. I wondered why he would hesitate about something he deeply cared about, but I needed to understand.

Chase voiced his thoughts. "Scientifically, all this is exceptional... Do you realize the potential we have here? How can we somehow help each other?"

His fingers then intertwined with mine for the second time in the space of an hour. It bridged the gap that existed between us since the MindMap. "No, Chase. It's impossible. Joining forces would destroy everything. It could compromise the very future we are here to save."

"You must explain things at some point if you want me to understand the situation. Trust goes both ways."

"We need friends here, Chase. Leane, Streak, and Blast won't trust you easily. I could make you forget all of us. But I won't, because I think you can help us. Do you understand what this means? Me trusting you?"

"You're putting your life and your friends' lives in my hands. I get that."

"No. I am putting the fate of our world in your hands. We... Do not matter."

"No pressure then," affirmed Chase with a grin. His face lit up, his eyes sparkled, and his charm surfaced again.

The tension present between us until now eased.

"None." I smiled, grateful that he had given me the chance to feel normal, even for a brief time.

He leaned against the rock and plummeted to the ground.

I reached out to him. I was so intent on getting answers that I ignored the pasty look on his face. Now, watching him, I knew something was wrong. "What's happening, Chase?"

"I don't know." Chase looked down at his belt buckle. "It's pulling."

He resisted, but the signal was robust even from a distance.

I looked at Chase and yelled over the NetCom, "Don't you dare, Blast."

Looking at me in horrified surprise, Chase exclaimed, "What the hell?"

The jolt came suddenly. Chase got dragged over the edge of the mountain, and within seconds, he dropped over the ridge, his arms flailing as he tumbled into nothingness. The device pulled him down to the forest ground below.

In the next instant,

I yelled, "Blast! Damnet!"

Leane, I need you, I said, reaching out to my friend.

Mage whimpered beside me. *My dog loves Chase...*

I lifted Mage to my chest, anchoring him to my suit. "Boy, we're going on a dive. Hold on." Mage licked my chin as if he understood as we launched ourselves over the rim.

16
MISTRUST
Chase

Drop Off The Peak, CA - 2022

Chase becomes unconscious twice that day and is taken care of by the Perfect Ones. Tesh penetrating his mind to establish a MindLandscape affects him significantly, but Blast's stunt raises his ire. For the first time, Chase believes in the Earth's vulnerability in the wake of Tesh's team arrival. DAINN Annals – Summer 2022.

I opened my eyes to Leane, holding my head in her hands as she kneeled beside me. "It's all right. You'll be fine in a few minutes. Just relax."

I shuddered and glanced toward Tesh, standing a few feet away. I refused to talk to her or even look in her direction any longer than to find out her reaction. At this moment, I didn't want anything to do with the oh, so…. Imperfect Ones. Pushing Leane's gentle hands away from my temples, I slowly sat up with no further help.

My fingers ran through my hair as I assessed how I felt— gathering my wits about me as I stood up, in need to gain a moment away from their constant observation.

My life, mind, and body were my priority beyond any knowledge gathering. Although I felt stronger, none of this could be good. I still shuddered from the ordeal.

The last thing I saw on the summit was Tesh's face, grimacing when she witnessed me fall, looking over the peak and watching me drop. She knew! Then it hit me. Tesh did nothing to stop it.

When I stumbled off the ridge, everything happened at once. Suddenly, I shifted sideways, losing the summit and facing the ground below. My velocity increased. I plunged headfirst into the descent. Watching the forest coming fast at me, I pierced through the air like a speeding bullet, screaming the entire time, until I realized I flew.

Tesh's voice resonated in my head as I dropped. *Chase, it's all right. You will be okay. There is nothing to fear.*

My speed increased again, and I closed my eyes as fear engulfed me. It was the fall all over again, and now I relieved it.

The link pulled me through the air with powerful precision. My direction aimed me for the top of the pines, near the edge of the mountain. Each breath I took brought me closer to the ground.

No doubt, they got a kick out of hearing me until I blacked out.

My anger rose, fighting the fear that engulfed me. I looked at the surrounding faces of Leane and Blast, mainly, until my eyes settled on Blast, and I yelled, "What the fuck? It may be acceptable as a jest in your time, but it's not in mine."

"NetShit, don't be such a freaking whiner, Blast said. "You're not even hurt...."

"Asshole!"

It happened again... My ass to the ground, I had no control over the fall, only this time I didn't cause it – someone else did.

166

I felt out of phase with myself, suddenly no longer centered. It was as if my metabolism tried to catch up but couldn't. It was weird.

Since Tesh had been inside my head, my privacy got trampled, and it irked me. I didn't care if they knew how upset I was. Giving Tesh permission, not that I had much choice, didn't eliminate the repulsion I felt, making matters worse. And now, this? I couldn't control my upset.

I walked to a nearby tree. Reconciling with all that happened in the last few hours required time. A commodity I didn't have. I observed the sky above and the sun beginning its descent, seeing none of its beauty.

Sharing her memories with me was an attempt at being gentle, but ultimately, I laid bare in her eyes. This invasion, despite her efforts, didn't sit well with me.

I had trusted her. No matter how I looked at it, this was a violation—but allowing this jest? It was unforgivable.

Leane observed me with the eyes of a medic, her concern utterly professional.

My attitude must have communicated my feelings. I felt a shift, a tension between Tesh and me. Something intangible pulsated, and I sensed her retreat. A coldness I had never experienced before settled inside me. The warmth we had shared no longer existed. Our closeness disappeared and left in its place an emptiness.

I turned. The narrow slit of my eyelids rested briefly over Tesh. With all the disdain I could muster, I said, "I'm not letting you do any of this to me again."

"So you had a little scare, get over it," Blast said.

"NetShut it, Blast," Tesh said, guilt eating away at her.

I saw that as her face drained of color, but I didn't care.

"I'm sorry, Chase. It should not have happened." Dejectedly, Tesh turned away from me. All I could see now was her back.

Mage, sensing her distress, moved toward her and put his front paws on her shoulder, seeking her attention.

This dog appeared to know what people needed.

I returned to my little quarter of the world, standing against the tree on my side of the forest. I kept looking as the clouds drifted past the tips of the trees in the sky. My focus entailed only one thing: steadying myself. How do I live with this betrayal?

Tesh glared at Blast, standing in the opposite direction from me. She remained in absolute stillness; only I didn't need to see her for me to understand what she was doing. She was yelling at Blast in complete silence.

Leane joined me. "She didn't want this to happen, Chase. It was all Blast's doing."

I glanced at her face and said, "I don't care. It doesn't make it all right."

She nodded. "It is over now."

"Not for me," I said, moving away from her. She could never understand that it had taken me months to overcome my last fall, and this one was way too close for comfort.

Without following me, she called after me, "Do not fret about the MindLandscape. We share tiny secrets among ourselves. It is something you need to get used to if you are to deal with us."

My jaw clenched at the thought of anyone trampling through my mind again. "This is barbaric. I'll throw you over the ledge before I let anyone in my head again." I grunted, turning around to face her. But I knew I could never throw someone off a ledge.

Twice now, I had gone over the edge. I wasn't ready to do that again soon. The fear experienced the first time remained with me. A year later, it was still fresh in my mind. But no one had known about it. Except that now, I was sure Tesh had glommed onto that fact. How could she allow this stunt?

Leane chuckled, amused at my puny revolt.

My trampled feelings remained what I considered a high price to pay for the knowledge I had garnered.

While I pondered all this, I decided I had to face Blast no matter the outcome, for he instigated my second fall, even if it was a flight rather than an actual fall. I didn't know that when I dropped. Damn, if I was going to take it lying down. I glanced past Leane and saw him facing Tesh, a massive frown on his face. They were having a knockout drag-out fight in their minds. It wasn't a pretty one. Both their expressions remained tense, angry, and uncompromising as they stared at each other. But it wasn't enough for me. My anger drove me to pass Leane and march on Blast, launching a right punch that landed squarely on his jaw.

The blow hit him with strength. I didn't even know I possessed this type of power. It twisted his head to the side, but he never even faltered on his feet. I grimaced as I heard the jarring sound of bones breaking in my knuckles. I knew I just had broken my hand. "Damnet," I said.

Leane, surprised, said, "What did you say?"

Blast's face was a thunderstorm of emotions – surprise and anger washed over his features as he stepped toward me. "You dare hit me?"

Tesh's face wore conflicting feelings – surprise and pride. I saw a glint of that as she grimaced, and I felt a lingering sense of satisfaction.

Without waiting for an answer, Blast grabbed my neck in one powerful motion. "I take offense to that." Lifting me about two feet into the air, his face marked by a sneer, he looked pretty angry. "Maybe you should not make moves you can't handle. Apologize." His strength, clear as he held me swinging off the ground, a few inches from my face, left me with no doubts about his physical superiority.

Humbling as it might be in some aspects, he also pissed me off. I was the one who had the right to be upset here. Rather than fighting him fair and square, as I would normally do, which would undoubtedly make me lose, I needed a different plan. Coming up with something he wouldn't expect was my only option. Otherwise, I would find myself on the ground and unconscious for a third time. The only thing that came to my mind at the moment was a stark realization. I had no control — quite a low point in my life. *So, what can one do?*

Suspended above the ground, I relaxed my posture as Blast held me with his right hand. I choked under his steel grip and tightened my neck, gasping for air.

Leane pushed Blast. "Stop it. You have done enough."

He didn't budge. His feet remained squarely planted on the ground as if he had just grown roots; Blast looked unconvinced. "How do you figure?" snared Blast, with the heat on his mocking face.

My eyes narrowed on his. I couldn't help but notice the golden flecks in his pupils, and I groaned unwillingly. Observing a guy's eyes was a first, but I was powerless. And we were so damn close.

Tesh's voice resonated around us, "I have had quite enough of your antics, Blast."

I grunted, "Let me go."

He whispered through tight lips, "Make me."

"Stop it." Tesh launched forward about to intervene.

Leane stepped in, barring her from approaching us. "Let them hash it out. It was only a matter of time. You know it."

She had barely finished saying these words when I kicked Blast in the balls with all the strength I could muster.

Leane gasped.

Blast threw me against the ground, hard. I slid several feet away on the forest underbrush, fighting for breath.

Blast bent over his knees, gasping for air.

It took me a moment to recover. Damn the man. He was strong.

I would bear the bruises for a while. "You had it coming," I coughed out between deep breaths.

Tesh blinked. Her voice resonated in my head. *Well done. He deserved it.*

Looking at the stricken faces of Leane and Tesh, I grinned. It was a first since I met them. And It felt good to hold my own, even if this was a small win. My throat hurt, but damn if it wasn't worth it. I coughed a few times and blinked in their direction.

Past the moment of surprise, Leane walked to Blast. Leaning over him, she asked with a smile she attempted to repress, "Are you all right? Do you need my help?"

Blast's eyes opened and closed a few times. He couldn't answer yet.

With a grin on her face, Leane said to Tesh, "Streak will be Netpissed; he missed this."

It didn't bode well for the friendship I hoped we would create. *Oh, well.* I wouldn't allow these people of the future to feel superior, although they, so far as I could see, indeed were. But I couldn't let them order me around. However, I also needed information to help and make us allies. Somehow, we had to make this work. The risk created by the Center otherwise remained too real to ignore for all of us.

Disgruntled, Blast finally murmured, "Don't push it, Leane. I know you won't leave that alone."

I glanced in Tesh's direction. She looked sad. I could feel it deep in my bones. This connection we shared reappeared in the blink of an eye. Maybe she responded to my own emotions. Why? It puzzled me. I could feel what she felt. How? These should have been hers and hers alone. I looked away.

Leane giggled openly this time. "Oh, but I won't have to. When he sees our Vlogs, it's bound to come out."

"Caught off-guard... That's all," responded Blast, whizzing. "That's one thing we didn't account for when we came here. They fight dirty," he established calmly. "I didn't watch some of their matches as we prepared to come here."

A groan escaped Tesh's lips. "ShutNet, Blast... You sound weak. Keep it real. We didn't come here for that."

A humorless laugh escaped me. "What in the hell did you come here for?"

Tesh struggled to remain calm. *Darnet, Chase, you know why. We have to work together.*

Anyone could see I upset her. "You should have controlled the equipment-boy or thought about that earlier," I snapped.

Tesh lifted her chin in my direction, suddenly impatient. *I did. I asked you to follow my lead. You didn't.*

I grimaced. "Get the fuck out of my head. If you wish to talk to me, then talk to me. That goes for all of you." I continued pointing at Blast.

Blast glanced in my direction and whispered, "Or what?"

Tesh ignored me this time. Instead, she turned to Blast and said, "Chase answered questions and clarified certain things during my read. There is something important to discuss."

Turning to Tesh, without waiting for an answer, he said: "We know. We found an underground compound."

Tesh clipped. "Oh… But you don't know everything."

He nodded. "Good. What did you learn?"

"Plenty you will not like."

Blast shrugged. "Not surprising. I haven't liked any of it."

Tesh shook her head. "It is a research facility."

Blast nodded and glanced at Leane. "I'm listening."

Leane, closer to me than the others, glanced in my direction. "This has to do with Chase, doesn't it?" She now watched me for a reaction.

It was wise of her. I didn't give her one. At least, I thought I didn't.

Tesh avoided looking my way and said, "Chase has volunteered the information that concerns us. The Center has one of our tablets."

Shocked, Leane exclaimed, "How?" She looked at me with an accusing glare.

I shrugged. Better if Tesh told the story.

Blast absorbed the news relatively well. "How long has the Center had the tablet?"

I answered, "Since about one year ago."

"According to Chase, it will be difficult to retrieve it," Tesh added.

Blast nodded. "After what we observed this afternoon, I agree with Chase."

Blast eyes focused on Tesh with more attention. "What did you see?"

Tesh looked like she walked on thin ice. "Something you will not like... Look." Tesh's visor unfolded on the Halo that flew over our heads. Immediately, it adjusted in size to allow all of us a look.

Blast inquired, "Did they see you?"

"Of course not," replied Tesh.

He grunted and watched the scene in silence. His stance became more rigid when he saw the crates filled with arms and turned in my direction. "What kind of security do you have?"

"Ex-military mostly."

He nodded, unimpressed. "No match for us. How was it found?" demanded Blast, giving me a close look.

Tesh intervened as she continued, "Chase said they have over three hundred men on the premises." The interference provided me the opportunity not to answer. I gathered this was her aim.

Blast shrugged. "We know our priorities. Let's get it done."

Tesh's believed that knowing how it came into the hands of the Center would only add oil to the fire between Blast and me. I sighed. She told me to be careful. Listening would probably not be a terrible thing, even if it was a bit late. I wasn't about to hide the facts, though, if the question came around again.

And it did... But this time, Leane was leading the charge.

"How was it found, Chase?"

I turned my gaze toward Leane and answered cautiously, "I found it. I turned it over. After this discovery, the Center renovated an old bunker and expanded it into a research facility."

Blast's face looked grim as he assessed me. "Does it get any better? Is that why you were here checking things and hoping to find more of our technology?"

Bullseye. I nodded. "Yes, it is why I came, but I suspect they have already found that something, as you say."

Leane murmured, "Why don't they share this information with you? You said you found the tablet first, so it would seem that your interest is theirs."

"It's not so simple. You might think that, but not at the moment. I recently graduated from Harvard and will join them in a few days. Until then, everything within the facility remains under wraps."

"Since you turned it over, retrieve it for us," stated Blast, crossing his arms over his chest, a stubborn look on his face.

"Too complicated. I don't think I can get it back. The Center has built the entire operation around the tablet. The security inside is the best electronic biotech available today. If the scientists found something else, there will be no stopping the Center," I said, shaking my head.

Blast walked the grounds. "Therefore, burying ourselves inside the Earth was a terrible idea. They could never have gotten a hold of our tech if we were in space." Pressing his lips together in annoyance, Blast said matter-of-factly, "I knew this was a bad idea all along."

Stubbornly, I mirrored the stance he had minutes ago. I crossed my arms over my chest. Staring him in the eyes, "Well, that will not be of any help."

Blast let out a growl of annoyance as if his irritation at my prompting became harder to contain.

I shook my head, and with a sigh, admitted to him. "Let's get you to the cabin. Today has been… unusual. I'm tired and need to eat something."

Blast watched me but didn't show a reaction. No superiority. No disdain. No annoyance.

It surprised me. Sure, that this admission didn't position me any better in the eyes of this group, I shrugged and murmured, "Are we going?" The fact remained that I wasn't about to pretend to be something I wasn't.

Leane turned her eyes on me. "Do you need water or something?"

"I'm dehydrated." I grimaced, irony lurking in my glare. "Sure… It could help."

Tesh handed Leane a vial. "Give him mine."

Leane took it and handed it to me. "It's PureGel, a liquid substance like water, but full of nutrients."

Cautiously, I frowned as I took it. It looked interesting, but the transparent vial did not appeal to me. I didn't make a move to drink it. I shook it, analyzed the contents' density, and glanced at Tesh's way. "What's the composition?"

My skepticism annoyed Tesh. She grabbed the vial from my fingers. "Not shaken, not stirred. No offense, but if you're not drinking it, I'll take it. I assure you, it's good. It has nutrient properties besides giving you energy, a lot of energy, and by the look of it, you could use it." She twisted the top as she talked and leaned her head back. She took a swallow of the liquid, her mouth never touching the vial. Instead, her lips opened, her tongue received a dose of the blue gel and closed. She handed me the tube after that with an impatient look on her face.

"It'll help," said an amused Leane.

What was so entertaining? I was unsure, but her eyebrows rose when she looked at Tesh.

Tesh just shrugged. This exchange took place without Blast noticing any of it.

I grasped the triangular glass container and did the same. I tentatively tasted the liquid. The contents were refreshing, smooth to my tongue. I took a couple of swallows, closed the container, and handed it back to Tesh.

Tesh took it without a word. An uncomfortable silence settled between us. When I met Tesh's eyes again, I ran my hand through my hair in frustration. "This is way too much."

"What happens next is bound to be way far out," said Leane. "You need to get used to it."

Blast's impatient mood broke the moment. The guy shook his head in disbelief and snorted, "Can we now get back to the plan?"

"This way," I said as I began walking, cradling my right hand.

Leane watched me, a worried glint in her eyes. "Do you feel better now?"

I did, although as I looked at Leane, my smile felt crooked. "Yes, thanks."

She frowned at me. "What's wrong with your hand?"

"Nothing."

But she wouldn't have any of it. She reached for my right wrist and pulled it toward her, looking at my bruised knuckles. "You broke it," she said accusingly.

Hearing that, Blast chuckled.

With an impatient sigh, Leane gently moved one of her hands over mine, and immediately, fiery energy pushed past my skin. Within seconds, I felt my bones realign themselves.

A sigh of relief escaped me. My curiosity, despite my minor revolt, got the better of me. "I really would like to know how you do this. Someday, maybe you will tell me?"

Her healing powers were unsurpassed. Only they couldn't be just natural, so how does she possess them? As a neuroscience doctor myself, I recognized her abilities were beyond mere knowledge. Their gifts and skills covered a diversity of capabilities I still had to discover. By what innovations had they reached this state? There were so many questions. Without knowing how we accessed these powers in the first place, we remained, I dare say, inferior. It wouldn't do long term. Understanding their prowess and abilities and what these meant for all of us became a matter of survival.

The only way to do this was to remain close to them. This solution appeared to be, for now, my only option. But the notion of losing their kinship if ever it were to happen sent a hint of sorrow to my heart. I never feared Tesh, not since I had met her. She had saved my life on two separate occasions. She didn't have to, but she had.

My thoughts moved to the questions that swam in my mind. Something made me trust Tesh. Something called me to believe in her. Something made me feel close to her. It could not be natural either. The engineered feeling was a response to the tablet. I called upon myself to find out what it was before too long.

Tesh looked at the equipment lifted from the ground and moved beside us. Mage cavorting at her side was a sight to watch.

"The Custodians will alert us of any changes by the gate," clipped Blast, turning to me and without a hint of hesitation, "How far from here is your place?"

I narrowed my gaze on him, "Why? Do you want to fly us there?"

Blast growled.

I repressed a smile. "What beast do you hail from?" I asked around, thinking it must be part of their DNA since it seemed to be something they all did with no thought.

17
COLLISION
Gen

On The Way To Cambridge, MA - 2018

I couldn't wait to see what awaited me. Maybe the feeling that prompted my impatience stems from the fact that soon I would see Chase again. Deep down, I do not want to acknowledge the truth. DAINN Annals, Summer 2022.

In this last week, an employment packet came to the house. It included the equivalent of health insurance benefits with other paperwork involving security issues. My onboarding package, including compensation, health insurance, and other perks, was generous. The increase in pay over the next three years planned way ahead of time had surprised my father. It made him suspicious.

Who does this, right?

The Center… A place that should not even exist.

I distracted him from finding out more about my employer, and now I was about to meet my colleagues officially.

The invitation issued by Jonathan Spallberg in my name required that I arrive back at Cambridge this evening. I was to join the team at our first official gathering. It was quaint, as I never suspected my return to be, but days after graduation. This exclusive party for recruits allowed us to know each other before flying to the research facility.

One thinks or dreams about becoming part of an indispensable handpicked team. It rarely or never happens. This opportunity landed on me. Now, I was part of an international group of brilliant minds to save the planet. If this was not a stretch, I do not know what was, yet this privilege undoubtedly held hidden traps. Ones that I had to uncover still. But, joining the Center in this endeavor, well, that was something no one could pass up.

The drive, smooth and silent, lured me in lulled comfort. Over these last weeks, excitement and fear became my unusual companions. All that had happened contributed to my frenzy, from the mugging, encrypted phones, friends disappearing, Chase, the surveillance, the secretive nature of the endeavor, and especially my mother, for whatever's that's worth.

My decision came with some soul searching, but now I forgot the feeling of limbo. My choice began a process of implementation. I found it quite stimulating. Ignorance, rarely contemplated as a blessing, even though people thought it was because of a dumb saying, bathed me in a sort of cocoon, and it was about to be broken. Soon, I would know a hell of a lot more.

I retrieved the invite from my purse and observed it again.

The challenge, an adventure of a lifetime, lay ahead. And the time to enter the lion's den quickly approached. Still, the card in my hand brought anticipation, and the pull of the unknown beckoned me. In my heart, I always wanted to change the world. My newly found allegiance to the Center remained uncertain but filled me with hope; it overshadowed my doubts.

The carton, unbending to the touch, was substantial. Thick and made of metal, it felt cold under my skin. Its look and feel appeared expensive, yet it remained understated, like something of value. For me, it seemed like a relic changing the course of my life. My fingers couldn't bend it or tear it up. I never considered discarding it. After a moment of looking at it and searching for hidden meaning, as if I would even find one, I put it back inside my purse.

The steps taken to maintain discretion were extreme. The actions, carried out with maximum efficiency, were even more, so it seemed. I looked for an appropriate word in my head. *Addictive.*

Today was a landmark day. It saw me hesitant and determined. The campus of MIT approached as we came upon the last turn on the road. So far, the traffic-congested around these parts appeared relatively light this day, with few automobiles on the road.

But the roar of a motorcycle approached us from behind, and the bike moved to our side. The driver glanced in my direction as he passed my window. He wore a black helmet and a leather jacket of the same color with dark jeans. The "not so unusual attire" for a biker did not elicit surprise, although his bike was a gorgeous machine. It flew by me quickly, too quickly for me to identify the model, but I got the make: Dodge Tomahawk, one of the fastest street bikes in the world.

My chauffeur slowed down, coming up to the crossroad.

Another vehicle engaged in the intersection, moving fast despite the abruptly changing light, calling it to stop. The car and the bike, unaware, committed to a collision.

The driver of the motorcycle didn't slow. Instead, he pushed the engine harder to move past us, reaching the crossroad at the same time as the other vehicle.

The chauffeur slammed on the breaks. "Hey..." Our car skidded forward.

The bike squeezed by us and made an abrupt turn; the revved-up engine was screaming as it cut in front of us, barely avoiding the front bumper.

"Jack ass..." screamed my chauffeur."

The tight maneuver forced the chauffeur to swerve to the right. "Shit... Watch out!"

We barely avoided a collision with the other vehicle in a screech of tires on the pavement. The move sent us on an involuntary trajectory, way off course.

I heard the vehicle bump into something. I felt the jolt of the wheels as they hit the sidewalk. The momentum carried us forward a few more feet until we struck a lamppost in a shriek of broken metal.

I went flying ahead against the back of the seat in front of me before my head hit the side door. My things scattered all around me.

I saw tiny flakes sparkling on the corners of my vision and heard a buzzing in my ears. I hit the car window hard. I tasted the coppery flavor of my blood against my teeth and felt a sudden pain in my tongue. It alerted me that I was not unscathed from the accident. A dull ache in my head and the cracking of my neck rendered me dizzy, as the muscles in my shoulders felt suddenly like lead. Still, slowly, I checked the rest of myself and looked around my surroundings. But too slowly...

The side door opened abruptly, dislodging me from my precarious position against the door, and I dropped sideways toward the pavement.

Two arms grabbed me, jolting me out of my seat before I hit the asphalt. Pulled out of the vehicle, a male voice rang loudly in my ear, "Whoah... Are you all right?"

"Are you kidding?" I grimaced, dragged a few feet away from the car. "Duh... Let me go."

"Looks like you hit your head," the same voice said.

The voice of my chauffeur resonated at my side, sounding worried, "You're not supposed to move her...."

"I just wanted to make sure you're okay," the male voice said.

"I will be if you stop moving me," I muttered, trying to get a grip on the fact that someone dragged me onto the sidewalk.

"She almost fell when I opened the door." The male voice exclaimed behind me.

"Let me go," I said, with more life in me this time, although my head ached.

"You sure you're all right, miss?" said my chauffeur, landing me a hand as I struggled on my wobbly feet.

"Give me a minute. I hit my head and got disoriented," I said, grimacing as I touched the bump forming on my occipital lobe.

"You're bleeding," the voice said.

A guy had now moved to my side. It was the driver of the motorcycle that passed us. Only this time, I could see his face because his helmet was now off.

He reached for his pocket, searching for something. "Damn... I don't have it," he muttered to himself.

Blood felt wet on the side of my mouth—the result of the cut on my tongue. A minor inconvenience, compared to what could have been, and so I lifted my hand to wipe it off, but before I could, he reached for his scarf and leaned over me. His fingers brushed the side of my mouth with the material, his brows furrowed. The gesture, gentle, felt quite intimate, and my heart pounded under his touch. When he finished, his mouth lifted at the corner, and he smiled at me. "There, better."

"Huh…" My legs got spongy as he looked at me. *Hot.*

He held on to me, a tower of masculinity with eyes I could lose myself.

I looked up to him, my neck crooked backward. My eyes traveled the length of him, taking everything from his soft leather jacket covering broad shoulders to the way his jeans hung low on his hips over long legs. *Oh, boy…*

He was overwhelmingly gorgeous, with muscles in all the right places. I lost myself a moment there. *Oh, Gen, cut that out.*

He reached for his scarf and shuffled it in his pocket. "Take it easy," he murmured.

I lost my footing under his gaze, and his arms reached out to steady me. I found myself wrapped against his chest, the same muscular arms I just daydreamed about moments ago. If I stayed around him too long, I would get in trouble. It felt warm in my chest, as if I had just eaten the most smooth and wondrous chocolate cake, with icing melting in my mouth. *Oh, gush… I was in trouble.*

His eyes twinkled as if he could read my thoughts, and a blush rose in my cheeks.

Thankfully, my chauffeur yelled at him, "You caused the accident, driving like a bat out of hell. Why on Earth were you going so fast?"

"The light was green. It was our turn to pass this intersection," the hot guy muttered.

"You swerved into my lane," the chauffeur said.

"The other vehicle caused the accident. I had nothing to do with it," my dreamy guy insisted, his eyes still on me.

"I went off the road to avoid you. You are guilty of dangerous driving," my chauffeur said vehemently.

"Hold on a moment…" the guy smiled at me, disregarding the chauffeur altogether. "How are you feeling?"

But the Chauffeur, now upset, pulled out his phone. "I'm calling the police. Since you're here and the other guy fled the scene, I'm holding you entirely responsible. Give me your driver's license and your insurance."

"Hey, I'm not at fault. The other car was… And I'm here because it is the decent thing to do," said the guy, retrieving his wallet. "Besides, the most important thing is that this hurt no one. "Right? Are you feeling, okay?"

"Yes, I'm fine," I said, slightly annoyed at his composure. Tall, with a brooding way about him, he handed his driver's license to the chauffeur as if it was the most normal thing to do and without a care in the world. "Here. So much for a good deed."

"You're just a law-abiding citizen who was driving too fast at an intersection, and as far as I know, this does not contribute to a good deed," I said, rubbing my head.

"Well, at least you're now talking," He grinned at me, and I stood there, my heart hammering in my chest, trying to pull away from his gaze.

Upon entering the information in his cell, the chauffeur returned the license and a business card. "Mr. Logan Fillmore, my insurance company, will be in touch with you."

The moment lengthened and was lost.

I glanced around me. But now, I possessed his name – Logan Fillmore. It suited him.

Logan glanced at the card and raised an eyebrow. "I believe you will find that I hold no responsibility in this but suit yourself," he said, with a smug attitude.

"Stop driving like a crazy guy. If you keep that up, you'll end up on the pavement or smashed against a post," the chauffeur added, disgruntled. "Ten years without an accident…" he muttered, walking away.

Logan devoured my attention, and I forced myself to pull away. What was I thinking? Maybe the hit to my head made me feel loopy.

With a look of regret, Logan gave the nod in my direction. "Take care of the cut," he whispered and turned back toward his bike. Logan put his helmet on his head with an appraising look in my direction in a smooth movement. He hopped on it and revved up the engine, winking at me as he dropped the visor down.

This guy was not an open book. He appeared way too intense for that. His eyes wore a haunted look that occasionally would seep through the warm green eyes he directed my way.

"I will call you a cab to take you to the inn," said the chauffeur after taking my luggage out of the trunk of the damaged vehicle.

I nodded. "What is our ultimate destination?"

"A private mansion."

"Whose?"

"I'm not at liberty to tell," he said as he walked away to make his call.

Well, that was that. Everything was still on a need-to-know basis, and I was in the dark with no helpful information.

Seeing my faculty building in the distance as I waited on the sidewalk reminded me of how many things had changed in the space of a week. This place held memories of fun, irresponsible days and now remained in my past. It got me here, though. And this opportunity enthralled me, so I was impatient to get started.

Rolling my neck, I stretched, releasing some tension and aches from the collision.

The polo I favored, comfortable, felt warm under my leather brown jacket. Wearing the same old pair of jeans from yesterday, I glanced down at my boots and shrugged. I knew I didn't look feminine. What did it matter now? Logan was gone, and I wouldn't see him again. I didn't need to impress anyone. *What the hell was wrong with me?*

My outfit was practical for traveling, though I would require a change of clothing for the party. Looking presentable and sophisticated and making an excellent impression suddenly seemed more important. I shivered in the fresh air, but somehow, it didn't seem that the temperature caused it. Tonight, represented my first step in facing my future. Meeting the other team members meant that a new journey had already begun.

Still, the temperature, lately unpredictable on this side of the country, switched from warm to cool. The days even were downright cold and damp within a few hours. Despite many protests, climate change existed, even if it included our unpredictable government, which in these times behaved more erratically in its decisions than ever.

The refusal to continue the Paris Climate Accord despite the urging of world leaders was a good example. The decision potentially affected change and rose as another significant setback to the drastic efforts to reduce global warming. Although I never was overly political, I couldn't help but notice the downward spiraling of our values and moral fiber led by the top hierarchy meant to guide us.

Lately, the demonstrations of unreliability proved too much. Our internal affairs bogged down with misinformation. Illogical interference in our policies continued to provide fuel to the daily drama. And it kept on coming. The news reporting almost became obnoxious to watch across all media. Even the internet crawled with misinformation to cloud the issues. Fake news was everywhere.

In the last two years, we experienced the dysfunction of our process. As a result, the adverse reaction of our long-term international allies held no surprise. The establishment, as we knew it, no longer existed. Trampled by the corrosive influence of private agendas that now affected the long-term stability of democracy established worldwide, we suffered from a lack of leadership.

It was not that we were ever perfect before in that regard. We sure had our faults. We had circumvented plenty of countries' actions for our benefit. But we possessed a fraction of norms while doing it, whereas now, none seem to exist. It appeared that way all over the internet. Perhaps this "free for all" had its place in shaping the downfall of our way of life and future. What would I discover at the Center in that respect? I wondered.

The taxi stopped in front of me. I opened the door of the cab and slid inside.

The chauffeur's look told me I should have waited for him to open the door. I shrugged, ignoring his pointed stare in my direction. "What time will you pick me up?"

He handed my luggage to the driver and turned toward me. "I will see you promptly tomorrow at seven pm," he replied.

I frowned at him. "But I thought the party was tonight?"

"Some are still flying in. Your new colleagues won't be here until tomorrow. Your room is covered, so you don't have to worry about anything," he added. "You can rest and change for the event," he continued glancing at my boots with some disdain.

What the hell?

Weird… The chauffeur didn't appreciate the practical aspects of my attire. What did he care about my clothes? I returned a bit of an attitude with a stare and a pointed look.

He closed the door of the vehicle and walked away.

The taxi driver pulled into the street.

I stood on my own. It was time for me to assert myself again. I shrugged, thinking about how good I was with my work. I would be fine.

In no time at all, we reached a small bed and breakfast. Shabby chic would qualify. The little fence around a small yard reassured of old fashion values. It seemed fitting that they had picked this place to make me feel more secure.

I grabbed my luggage and walked up the stairs to the front door. *Fine, I'll show them all.*

190

18
SURPRISE
Logan

Outside Cambridge, MA - 2018

Life's situations define a person, and the opportunity for Logan to join the Center is such a moment. But new findings instill doubts about the real purpose of the Center. DAINN Annals, Summer 2022.

The need for speed quickly led me to the mansion, and the narrow road, empty of other vehicles, made that easy. Within minutes after leaving the accident scene, I arrived at an enormous iron gate whose address matched the invitation I got a few days ago.

I was Logan Fillmore, one of the new scientists joining the Center. I arrived here earlier because Jonathan wanted to meet with me again, which made me nervous. This second meeting was the first time I would meet Jonathan in person. I wanted to get this behind me as quickly as possible, so I would no longer wonder what it was all about, and I would finally get to know my role in all this.

My involvement in the Center gave me something, unlike other organizations – a budget for my research. Provided I did things right, Jonathan would extend it for my work. I just needed to prove myself. So, here I was, curious to find out how I could begin to do just that. Because thus far, my assignment once we reached the facility remained quite nebulous.

The property's massive walls spread on both sides, hiding the grounds behind them. The intricate design appeared old, while the hinges looked newly installed. Two surveillance cameras with the latest technology observed the perimeter, their lenses directed at the gate, and street access on both sides. They seemed to have the newest capabilities, passive infrared motion detection, and night vision. I glanced toward the road and measured the distance — about seventy-five feet.

The security here appeared pretty tight. We would leave this place for the Center with all other scientists joining the project.

I rang the buzzer and waited, looking up at the surveillance camera.

"Yes?"

"Logan Fillmore, here to meet Jonathan Spallberg."

"You're early. Come in."

The gate opened without a sound, giving access to a narrow road curving up ahead.

I slowly advanced on my bike, looking at the surroundings. In my eagerness to learn more about the Center, I indirectly caused a crash on the way here. Feeling somewhat responsible, I slowed down as I passed the threshold and followed the private road. Maybe I drove a bit too recklessly. I enjoyed the speed of the bike.

I was already feeling guilty about my decision not to join the family business, and while I refused to acknowledge my responsibility earlier, the incident still nagged at me.

The crushing sound of gravel under my hard rubber tires resonated in the silence of the place. Already, one could tell it was plush. The grounds were spectacular and well taken care of, and the long driveway showed a large estate.

Indeed, the offer to work for Jonathan was substantial, even outstanding. The contract and generous compensation, along with my overall responsibilities, fit right into my field. But we had yet to meet. He required someone with my qualifications. "I want an Astrophysics and Space Research MIT man on my team," as he had put it. Today was my opportunity to get to know him.

My work, however, was still undefined. Indeed, Jonathan had given me very little to go on. My duties were to run an area of the investigation that remained undefined. The Center needed help in narrowing their research to determine artifacts of unknown origin. It enticed me. One of my many motivators caused my decision to be here. Thus, this meeting.

The secretive nature of the Center and our discussion remained a puzzle, and finding out some details intrigued me. Hanging around the place might provide more insights.

I stopped in front of the imposing mansion, with its doorway framed by two columns linked by a stone archway. The impressive wooden door opened. The silhouette of an older man, no doubt a butler by the look of his attire, stood waiting for me to park my bike and get inside.

"You will need to wait," he said as he led the way across the stone flooring to a room off the main hall. "Mr. Spallberg is not yet available. I will bring some refreshments."

Following him, I glanced up at the circular staircase that wrapped around both side walls before I entered the library. I barely passed the doorway before the door closed quietly behind me.

So much for asking questions.

The butler's curt attitude showed I would have to wait to ask questions, but I soon forgot about it when I glanced around the room.

Wood overwhelmed the library. Shelves reaching the ceiling lined up with rows of books. A desk made of mahogany faced a window overlooking the grounds to my left. It warmed up the place under the fading sun of the late afternoon. A leather chair angled near it captured the last rays, making the area cozy. The large coffee sofa boasted a vibrant red tartan throw cover with a twilled plaid design on the opposite side. While inviting in its appearance, it felt lonely. The dark shiny wood coffee table sitting in front of it with picture books piled on top appeared frozen in time. The entire room seemed staged, and it begged for a presence.

On my way to the bookshelves, I passed by the opulent desk. My attention got caught by the files neatly piled on its surface. The top one had my name on it, leaving me curious to see what was in it. I opened it. *I know… It's not a cool thing to do, looking at someone's information. But, if they cared about it, they wouldn't leave that stuff in plain sight, now, would they?*

The pages opened on records of my academic results. They included a psychological profile gathered from what appeared to be a careful observation of my activities. What in the hell was that? Multiple pictures of me across campus, either alone or with friends, further enhanced the thorough investigation. Several photos, even taken during class, made me feel uncomfortable. They had someone follow me. From the look of it, they did this over several weeks. My unease increased. What type of work demanded this in-depth investigation of a candidate?

The conclusions provided an assessment of my skills and capabilities, along with a mental profile. Unable to quite put my finger on what this whole thing meant, I looked at the other folders.

Each file presented information on the other candidates. There were a dozen. Ignoring that these were not for my eyes, I scanned each one, learning everything I could about the other scientists joining the program. The knowledge I gained only confused me more about the type of work I would perform at the Center. It was not what I had expected. Then again, what were my expectations?

The noise at the door alerted me I was about to have company. I dropped the folders and walked over to the shelves, looking at the collection of books; hundreds of them, in rows, staked up with their titles set in one direction. I tilted my head and pretended to read some of them, my thoughts in disarray about what I had just learned.

The butler moved into the room, holding a tray. "Tea… and scones." He set it on the coffee table and made a stop by the desk, where he promptly removed the folders I had perused moments ago. Taking those with him with a glance in my direction, he walked toward the door. "Mr. Spallberg will be with you in a little while."

I ignored his pointed look, and before he quickly disappeared again, I inquired, "Can you tell me where the bathroom is? I would like to wash my hands."

"Of course, sir. This way…"

He led me down a hallway from the primary entrance and opened a small door below the vast staircase. "When you are ready, sir, I trust you can find your way back to the library?"

"Yes, thank you."

He nodded and walked away.

19 SEER Tesh

Forest Grounds, CA - 2022

The descent to town pulsates with tension. The mission grows with new hurdles with the quest for Streak and the lost Conclave Chambers, putting the investigation of the Center behind schedule. Tesh Vlog - DAINN Annals – Summer 2022.

As we walked toward the cabin, my anger at Blast still simmered. Blast had submitted Chase to a brutal flight regardless of the harness. I observed Chase's fall from the ledge on the mountain. And I couldn't help myself but feel his emotions, like from his first fall. It was intense, and I was NetPissed at Blast for his continuing harassment of Chase.

Blast had a way of getting even, regardless of the situation. He showed me that no matter how protective I was of Chase, he could make it hard, and my reluctance to the MindLandscape had made him mad.

But my protégé has pulled a fast one. Chase clobbered him. He even broke his hand doing it.

In truth, it gave me satisfaction.

Leane, standing by my side, murmured, "What else are you not telling us?"

"Nothing, I'll explain later." I shook my head, exasperated by her notion that I held back information. She was right, of course. *You are still unaware of specific facts, but I cannot talk about them now.*

I looked at Leane and shrugged in Blast's direction, "He can be such an ass."

Blast moved down the mountain with an upset expression on his face.

She made a face, and I read her meaning. *Chase wound his pride.*

I snickered.

He deserved it.

I couldn't help myself.

Blast turned to us with a look of inquiry, as if he knew we were talking about him. Both our faces must have looked odd to him because I read his thoughts next.

I'm unbeatable in a fight.

Leane watched Blast too. It was unguarded at that moment, but I saw warmth there and something more. It was not the first time I witnessed how taken she was with him, even when she attempted to hide it. Our lives had not been conducive to developing a relationship with other members of our Conclave. The leaders did not encourage it, but for some, they did not frown upon either, like for Leane and Blast. Unlike my crazy, stubborn affection, or infatuation toward Streak. I shook my head, dislodging the direction of my thoughts.

Blast's stubborn rancor showed in his following statement as he challenged, "I underestimated him, and it won't happen again."

Leane nodded. "You don't have to tell us." She smiled at him with teasing.

"Enough of that," I said, opening a link between the three of us.

Blast asked in my head, *Do you trust Chase?*

I do, up to a point. More than not, I answered Blast truthfully.

He added after a lengthy pause. *I want to see this facility. Are you open to it?*

Yes.

Good.

Blast taking over the aspects of the operation because Streak went missing was the next course of action. The structure of our Conclave called for that. While I remained in charge at all times, he would drive our progress forward. He would do it in the direction he believed was essential to the fulfillment of our mission. It was especially true for incursions or combat situations.

Our priorities were clear in the affairs of the Conclave.

What about finding our bearings in this place first? Suggested Leane.

Blast's voice rose, adamant. *Streak is not here. It is my decision.*

No. It's not your decision. You can't dictate what we do next, Blast.

Yes, I can.

Leane rolled her eyes. *Ultimately, it is Tesh's decision.*

I have to deal with the logistics of this operation. We don't even know when Streak is coming back. Tesh, I'm sorry, but what if Streak does not make it back?

Upon hearing this, I felt a stab in the center of my chest. I closed my eyes, suddenly breathing shallowly.

HellNet, I don't see a choice here; we have a mission to fulfill, continued Blast.

He was right. Streak not making it back to us was a possibility.

Taking the time to deal with this notion was a luxury I did not possess. The unknown outcome of Streak's disappearance ate away in my gut. I wanted to find his presence, focus on him, send him my thoughts, and link to him, but the events of the last few hours had not permitted that. Too much had occurred too fast. *Waiting for Streak is not something we can afford to do,* I stated, agreeing with him despite what I wanted to express.

Leane's gift, her ability to scan our surroundings, searching for a sign of him, had not yet taken place. She also waited for a moment to focus. Resolute, despite her doubts, Leane said: *He will be back. He has to…*

I want that too, said Blast. *But until it does…*

Leane moved the casings along as they hovered at her side in a steady motion.

The summit loomed above us now, and I recalled the landscape as we plunged downward. The mountain cut a precise figure against the darkening sky.

As Mage ran beside me, I remembered how his body contracted against mine and how I sent him calming thoughts as we flew down from the summit. He had relaxed in my arms, fearless at our speed. But our flight without constraints, like the ones we played in our time, lasted too short for any playfulness. And while I traced a path down the side of the mountain, following Blast descent, I barely glanced at the pristine panorama. I didn't enjoy its twisting mountain range and the jagged-edged peaks, nor did I relish the white puffy clouds that could have brought a novel experience to my life, as they cut a vivid memory in my head. The air, crisp and clean, filled my lungs, but I could not revel in it. Instead, I thought about the intimidating heights if one did not experience flying around in the sky as we did in Ang.

Blast had stolen that moment from me, and I resented him for it. Granted, it was not a pretty sentiment.

I imagined Chase... And his fear of this latest fall. His screams echoed in my head and sent a shudder through me. I pushed the unpleasant memory away and focused on the landscape ahead.

I looked at the mountain again with regret. It was grandiose, casting a silhouette of darkness and light against the blue azure.

My thoughts reverted to Chase. A set of boots would surely improve his timing. I shook my head, disliking the intrusion's meaning, and chased it away. He brought new influences into our midst. Yet, Chase did not qualify as part of our team, and I couldn't think of him this way.

Mage barked, happy to run free. "Enjoy it, my boy."

The clouds cleared overhead, and the wispy filaments resembling white cotton candy drifted away.

"Look at this place," I said with excitement. "We are out in the open. None of the ravages of our time have yet settled here."

"It's amazing," Leane whispered beside me. "It is hard to believe we are in the same place."

Maybe, just maybe, we could stop it from happening at all. Despite the odds so overwhelmingly against us at the moment, hope soared in me.

"Well, get over it," muttered Blast. "We have things to do."

My attention wandered back to the forest.

Mage barked again; this time louder. He jumped over a low branch, running after a small creature that looked very much like a rabbit, and disappeared ahead.

"NetShut, this mutt of yours could get us noticed," Blast muttered, in an apparently lousy mood.

I shrugged, refusing to give him any acknowledgment other than this slight movement. HellNet, I was still upset with Blast.

"Who is going to pay attention to a dog barking in the middle of the forest?" Leane said, laughing at Mage's antics. "Let him be."

The green landscape under the cloud canopy boasted abundant shamrock, scenery as vivid as juniper, moss, and emerald colors. Proof of life spread everywhere, extending at my feet with fertile soil.

NetWash... The ground did not resemble the dried-up dirt of our time. This discovery brought joy to my heart.

I closed my eyes and took a deep breath. I could smell nature.

We now descended near the cliffs, and a sandy beach filled with boulders stretched to the ocean. The beryl color of the water looked pristine under my eyes. The natural beauty of the place filled me with awe. How could we have damaged such splendor?

Before we left the Chamber, we had accessed all the information accumulated in the knowledge bank from Ang. DAINN had never described nor portrayed this magical environment as it existed here.

A vacant spot replaced DAINN. Our A.I. did not exist yet, and its voice, which usually resonated in the back of our minds, remained blank. It offered nothing but a strange silence. This emptiness weighed on me, and I wanted nothing more than finding DAINN.

The sensation felt the same for my friends. With DAINN's presence, we did not feel empty. Without him, a hole remained, leaving an echo in an unused recess of our heads, and we felt not our own. All of us missed D. How could we not? He was a part of each of us, in the deep consciousness of our minds.

Mage ran back toward Chase, jumping around, excited beyond measure for his newfound playground.

Blast tilted his head, his gaze unwavering as he waited for my reaction.

Chase casually smiled at my dog. Then he glanced in my direction and looked away, his posture defensive.

Who could blame him? He had every right to be pissed.

I moved to Blast. "You owe him an apology, you know. It wasn't funny."

"No? I thought it was hilarious." Blast's look challenged me.

"You are being a NetAss."

He shrugged indifferently.

Blast waited for me to throw the gauntlet at him. He wanted me to take one side, and I refused.

Unexpectedly, we faced events that had unfolded rapidly around us, thwarting our planned agenda since we exited the Chamber and this without reprieve. Part of me knew we had trained for this situation.

I knew Streak through years of closeness, while Blast not as much. I never dealt with Blast in the role he would now fulfill. While I never doubted Streak's instincts, Blast was rash and frequently impulsive. Knowing that he wanted the best for us didn't mean he measured his actions or that they came at the right time. The assessment left me unsure and understanding that Blast could not have the same autonomy as Streak. *Things are going too fast.*

We don't have the luxury to wait.

How should I proceed? Circumstances unbalanced our current behaviors.

My eyes narrowed on him. *We need time to adjust.*

Blast, motionless, was a strange thing altogether. *We need to understand what we are dealing with quickly.*

He was right in that, and he didn't react to my reserve. A surprising fact, knowing that he was always on the move. *We must find our Chambers. It is what Streak would do.*

Streak is not here. We need the tablet back.

Leane, being Leane, listened. She would intervene when she had something to contribute.

In his assessment, Blast wasn't wrong. The sooner we got the tablet back, the better. *They have too many men. We need Chase's help to get it back.*

I glanced toward Leane. Her advice, usually moderate, always provided useful feedback. She refrained from giving any input. I reached out to her. *What is your take on this?*

Leane's face expressed doubts. *I got distracted, but both of you have a point. I've been trying to put my finger on something, though.*

Her instincts were as fine-tuned as mine.

I schooled my features to have them remain blank.

Her expression told me she understood my reaction as she watched me. Her next question took me by surprise. *What's going on between you and Chase?*

Darnet. She saw too much.

My reluctance to provide the details, at least for now, remained. Bracing myself for what indeed would be more questions, I kept my face still.

There is nothing.

The curiosity from Leane caught Blast's attention, though, and now his gaze traveled between Chase and me.

The crease between Leane's flawless brows deepened. *You behave out of sorts.*

Her eyes assessed Chase next. *He acts as if he knows you.*

Oh, brother!

Wishing to avoid the issue altogether, I shrugged and replied in her head: *The scan went deep.*

I didn't want my Conclave to know about DAINN's actions. I needed time to figure out what existed between Chase and me. Time to determine why we suddenly found ourselves with this powerful connection. Whether this link would break with time or ebb naturally was not yet clear to me.

Unconvinced, Leane gracefully let it go for now. However, her look told me she had not closed the subject. Refocusing us on our next steps, I walked faster.

Blast has a point.

Which one? I made several.

Blast, see how we can penetrate the facility while Leane performs a scan to locate Streak. I'll focus on organizing us here.

Blast suspiciously observed me more closely than I liked, just as Leane was. I stood my ground, knowing I was protective of Chase, but little alarm bells rang in my head. Blast's smirk didn't sit well with me. My eyes rolled at their expression.

I needed distance from Chase.

I needed to get my emotions under control.

I needed time, Darnet.

Leane's eyes narrowed on me again. *See, this is precisely the reaction I've observed since we've met him. He possesses some influence over you.*

Calmly, I replied, *Nonsense. If I let Blast have its way with Chase, we lose a valuable asset.*

Blast turned his gaze on Chase.

Chase observed us with a blank look, at a loss regarding what was going on between us.

If you're under his influence, Tesh, you better tell us now, Blast exclaimed.

I stopped walking and faced them.

Neither one of you is making any sense. Get a grip. How could I be under Chase's influence? My heart did somersaults in my chest.

Leane turned to Blast. *Her pulse is faster than usual.*

As calmly as I could, I sent them my thoughts. *No one is influencing or controlling me, and I am still the leader of this Conclave.*

Blast's voice rang loudly in my head. *You are not if you are under his influence.*

"Blast, back off."

"Hey… I'm still here, and if you want to get to the cabin before nightfall, we should get going," said Chase. "Besides, if you want my help, I have a right to know what you currently MindShare."

I glanced toward Chase, the new unwanted complication in my life. Perhaps Streak's absence was fortuitous while I figured out what this all meant.

My old self would have seen Chase gone by now. I would have given him the eraser. He should no longer be among us; his mind-wiped from any memories.

Darnet the guy... I took a steady breath. It was difficult. I didn't understand him. One moment, he looked pissed off, and the next, he appeared as calm as the surface of a lake. My knowledge of a lake didn't exist up close and personal. The images conjured by our Network popped inside my head.

We didn't have many lakes anymore, and none were close to Ang. Most of the freshwater pools had dried up years before I was born in our area. Clearwater became scarce years ago and represented a rare natural commodity in 2098, but we also possess the technology to capture water. For a while, drought played havoc on many world areas, requiring a significant change in our infrastructure. We adapted. People matriculated to bigger cities. Megapolises sprung, extending their reach to welcome more people. As the city limits expanded, fewer people remained in rural areas. Other adjustments were made, including the rule of law to service and protect an unexpected population growth. As city centers grew, agricultural issues became more critical. We implemented new methods worldwide, affecting agricultural production and food distribution.

By 2045, though, we felt the decline in the populace's density across the globe, and things got better until they got worst again. Climate change drove more precipitation and temperature shifts more drastic. We still had the oceans, bleak and dismal, because of the planet's constant variations in weather. Our natural ecosystems, polluted, remained affected until it was irreparable. Global warming caused horrendous hardships. No one expected a cataclysmic event that would probably shift the planet's orbit and kill everything in its wake. Still, it was not the reason we were here.

We are wasting time, said Blast, grabbing some of his gear and returning me to the present. *I'm taking him,* he added, pointing to Chase.

No matter what my emotional state, our situation required action. But I growled at both of them. *After we drop everything at his place, you can do that, but for now, follow my lead.*

Maybe it was the growl or my tone, but I just mishandled Blast in a big way. When I realized this, it was already too late.

His answer came at me fast as Blast snickered, "Make me." In the fraction of a second that followed, he grabbed Chase and disappeared around a bend.

I should have expected that.

Leane grimaced. *Sorry about bringing up my concern. I worry about what he is doing to you.*

I turned my ire on Leane and exclaimed, "I have done nothing to warrant your attitude or his. Blast is irritable and emotional."

My visor floated ahead of me, searching for Blast. I added, "Darnet, Leane… There is no time for this."

She scowled back at me. "When then? I know something is wrong. I sense it. Why won't you tell me, tell us? In the Chamber, you made a promise to share everything with us, and you are now holding back again. What am I supposed to think?"

Chase's voice yelling from somewhere reached us. Let me go!"

I heard Blast's laugh resonating in my head.

I understood why.

Blast acted this way because he required a confirmation that no matter what, I would lead them in precisely the same way the Institute and Academy had trained me. It had everything to do with our Mind Landscape issues.

I continued, my focus on Blast. *I do not understand your doubts. The Institute pushed me to operate a certain way. HellNet, you must trust me. I know what I am doing. Your attitude is not acceptable. Revise it, or I will do it for you.*

Find me first.

Blast, I don't have to find you to deal with you. Now, who is out of line?

Over the NetCom, Leane said, "Blast, we need to get to town. Get back here. You are going too far," she added.

My face closed off, preparing the onslaught on Blast if he continued. I never had to resort to this step before, and I disliked it immensely, but I couldn't let this go.

Leane saw it and knew what my next step entailed. She stomped her foot and spoke her mind. "Our ancestors would put a curse on the two of you. Do you even remember how it goes?"

Without a moment of hesitation, she began muttering an ancient saying. It was one I had not heard spoken ever. The old chant now existed only in our historical archives – the AkkadEtanaErra. It was old magic from long ago. I didn't know Leane even knew of its existence, but it made sense. A Seer and Giver of Life would know it.

It got my attention, though.

Blast whispered over the NetCom, "What in the HellNet are you doing?"

Magic was no longer a practice we saw in our days, but I recognized it from our learning instructions at the Academy.

Leane ignored us and continued. "Darena oblia tarrena sana osendi, fredina oliforia shadan sana soblear, donea itisukur soblear ananda, sarenia polibsatash eblir terrene."

I didn't know the old language, but my visor translated the words: "I invoked the sunlights of the East. I call upon the night lights of the North. I summon the sunsets in the West. I trigger the winds rolling from the South. I pull from the waters of the Earth. I capture the stars of the universe. I demand that you two stop now. Silence."

The mantra resonated in the woods and wrapped itself around us like invisible strings. It was odd. The chant brought about an echo in our minds. A long-forgotten piece of universal knowing settled on us. She continued, unperturbed by the incongruence of her actions.

For a split moment, everything stopped like on command. I could feel it. I felt frozen in place.

It was unlike Leane.

Even if it did not cause us to freeze for long, it was a pause.

It was not sufficient on its own to last. But Darnet, I could swear things stopped for a split second.

But Leane's behavior surprised me.

It also silenced Blast in his tracks as he reappeared beside me, holding Chase, who looked pissed as hell. Blast sheepishly glanced in her direction.

We both remained silent as she ignored us and kept going down the path.

"You better get your act together, or I'm getting out of here until you do. I won't be part of this, not when we just went through hell and lost our world and arrived here to lose Streak on top of it. What's wrong with you, Blast? You are undisciplined, you Netpissed ass. It is not part of our program. Get your childish temper under control and stop behaving like an adolescent whose hormones are out of whack," added Leane, finishing her tirade as she began walking down the forest path, the equipment in her wake. "And as for you, Tesh, you owe us an explanation. So, get ready to give one."

Chase, who until now remained relatively quiet, and had kept his thoughts to himself, interjected with a tinge of humor, "Trouble in paradise?"

I sighed, glancing at him briefly. "Not now, Chase."

Turning to Leane, I said, "I'm still trying to figure out certain things, and this will take some explaining. But it is not what you think. I am not under his influence. He is under my power."

Leane had a confused expression. "You mean you have distorted his thoughts?"

Chase's MindLandscape revealed certain qualities, a moral compass that called for a pattern of behavior. One of these personality traits was his loyalty. I recognized this template. Only, in our current situation, I asked myself where his allegiance would go. DAINN saved his life through me. The tablet's significance and DAINN's influence explained his behavior, but only partially. He worked for the Center, and that accounted for something. I believed he hadn't lied when he said he wouldn't talk about us. Not purposely anyway. Doubts plagued me, for reliance on my judgment could prove fatal to the success of our mission.

Chase turned his gaze on Leane. "Wait, a minute... What are you saying? Then turning to me, he exclaimed, "I'm not under anyone's influence; I would know it. Tell me you didn't play with my head? Tell me you didn't break your promise."

Leane's surprised expression turned to me, "What? You promised him?"

"It's not what you think... Leane."

"Is he influencing you or not? I want to know," growled Blast.

Chase marched toward me. "Then what is?"

"Whoah… Chase, calm down… I did nothing to your mind." I took several deep breaths, feeling exasperated by their attitudes. "I will explain everything later."

My understanding of Leane kept me quiet. She possessed a long fuse, never complaining and never losing her cool, except in those rare situations where somehow she reached her limit.

"You better," Leane said, walking away.

Blast checked in my direction. "I guess Leane is Netpissed…" mouthed Blast, looking at Leane's back.

Chase's surprise look didn't escape me, but I ignored it as he, too, strutted away, disgruntled.

I shrugged.

Such a moment with Leane behaving this way never arose before. Not ever. But it called for all of us to give her space.

Forest Grounds, CA - 2022

My emotions overwhelm me. I am unsure why I suddenly feel like I will burst. All I want for now is to settle in the calm of the forest. Leane Vlog – DAINN Annals, Summer 2022.

Indeed, my temper was something to contend with when it ignited. It was rarely, though. As a child, I remember instances where I would feel this way. It took place when I became overwhelmed by my environment. It occurred when situations assaulted my senses at once. But it took place before I knew I was sensitive to things around me and before I could tap into life, feeling every strand pulsating through me.

The silence after my outburst took us all by surprise, even me. It was as if the forest itself heard my plea. Devoid of noise, the forest wrapped quiet calm around me as I walked ahead. The trees stilled. The leaves no longer shifted in the breeze. Everything seemed to stop.

I strived to hear the regular movements of creatures in the woodland, but none existed. It was as if we were the only ones in existence.

A corner of my mind wondered. Was this possible? Was magic still real? Was it something we had let go of because of technology? Manaha certainly thought so. She used to say that we relinquished it out of fear because it was more powerful than some of the technology we created. Indeed, our tech could be controlled and hacked more readily. But magic existed through everything around us. It was pure energy, and once one knew how to manipulate energy, they possessed the key to the kingdom.

My rational mind wanted to reject the notion. But I remembered instances where my grandmother shared some of her knowledge as I fought to understand what was happening when erratic things would surface. She taught me about the power I held within. She encouraged me to explore it secretly and never allow others to use it in my stead. I learned through Manaha everything our ancestors knew and practiced for centuries. Manaha carried our powerful bloodline, and so did all the women in my family. But these days were long gone.

Only a few knew or practiced the "art of life" in our time. When my turn came to undergo the Evaluation, I was too young for my gifts to manifest. When much later I entered the Institute and was accepted at the Academy, Manaha bound my gifts so that they would remain unnoticed. With the force restriction of my power, she ensured I would forget it even existed. But when the time came for me to enter Origin, Manaha unbound me to re-access them. It was the last time I saw her, just before we said our goodbyes, the early evening in Ang, when everything fell apart. I had not touched that side of me in all these years, and now, the memories all came rushing back. How would I ever explain this to my team?

I shook my head and continued walking without ever looking back. How could I just tap into them now? How would I explain what needed to be shared? This time, it would not be Tesh alone who would open up.

I trusted that my Conclave would follow, especially as I didn't know where I was going.

Chase read my mind. He now stomped ahead of me; the sound of his footsteps so different from ours. His behavior showed that he was again angry in no uncertain terms, and I couldn't blame him.

Blast did not help in that respect, and it had to stop. Tesh was quite right in that regard.

Without regard to my Conclave or him, I went ahead, bathing in nature. The woods so rich here gave me a buzz. It was like it spoke to me in ways I had never connected with before. Perhaps this time, so dramatically different from our own, provided me with a sense of purpose and strength I had never felt before. It was as if I had reached home. The oddity of the sensation that now coursed through my veins puzzled and delighted me at once.

Mage, Tesh's dog, walked by Chase's side. It was another behavior uncommon in our time. Typically, Mage never left Tesh. Something was going on between these two, and I meant to find out what. But for now, I relished the gift nature offered me.

My hand touched the bark of the trees as I passed them. The smell of the forest surrounded me and played a diversity of notes as I moved. The freshness of pine, the dampness of moss, the crisp underbrush filled with leaves offered a soft path under my feet. All of it mixed in various odors, resembling nothing I synthesized before.

Chase moved to my side with Mage and took the lead.

I didn't mind it. I could keep focusing on nature's shapes. Slowly, I began to hear the sounds of the area again.

Somewhere behind me, Blast walked at Tesh's side. I could envision his face, remorseful. Sensing their tension, I blocked them both and forgot about my team. It was good that they just followed me at a distance. I needed to learn to control these new feelings.

My breathing deepened, and I found myself moving in a flow so fluid that there was no effort, even as I increased my speed to keep up with Chase, who was now running ahead.

It was not like when we operated with the EmVat. Our gifts carried within our DNA provided a different experience. It was a free sensation, something else altogether. Here, I thrived. No wonder we needed to come back to this time. It was powerful, unlike anything in our time. Somehow, I found my home in the forest.

My upset was challenging to deal with on any day, but at least now I understood what drove me. It helped put things into perspective. Although I never expected to rely on my blood's gifts today, of all things, I knew they had awakened in this environment.

The current reality didn't allow me to slow down and enjoy this place. It made it more challenging to handle the thousands and hundreds of thousands of strands of nature in all its glory thrown at me. The streams brought not only creatures in the woods; they also included all the species. What if this gift could help find Streak?

My energy field buzzed. We were all affected in different ways, which became clear to me.

The Council of Nations would not have made Tesh the leader of the Institute Conclave unless they had felt confident, she could do this. I sighed… Maybe it was better if I stepped in to say as much. But as the thought crossed my mind, I knew it wouldn't be. Blast already knew this.

Under normal circumstances, I might let Blast run with the mission. But his attitude toward our predicament with the Center and Chase didn't instill confidence. Instead, it gave me pause. No, I could not entrust this to him, and neither could Tesh, especially with the situation as it presented itself.

Still, I loved Blast. My feelings grew and changed over the years, even if he had no clue. His heart was so big; he forgot himself for our benefit all the time. But I wanted him to grow and hold his proper place in our Conclave. Until now, he relied on Streak to temper himself and his actions. He needed to mature and assess things more slowly. Experience would teach him that.

Knowing that we may not find our Chambers in time as we settled here drove a wedge between us. We didn't want to acknowledge the likelihood that we could fail. It bothered all of us.

Without Streak, it was impossible to conclude our mission. Streak was the only one trained to take us back. But would I want to go back with my team once we accomplished what we set out to do? I was no longer sure I would like to give any of this up just looking around.

I kept pace behind Chase, assessing how we should plan our next move. We needed more information. Then I thought better of it. Let Blast tell us.

It was then that I saw the deer behind a wall of green. It was a beautiful animal foraging on leaves near a bush under the last remnant of daylight.

I stopped suddenly, amazed by its beauty. I could feel everything about this wild animal—its steady heartbeat, its breath, the course of its blood flowing through its organs.

It lifted its head, his eyes watching me as it remained still and alert. Its silky coat shuddered. The soft beige tone mixed with white trimmed and reddish-brown suddenly shook. He was ready to take flight, but I did not want the deer to go.

I wished to prolong this moment, and the memories flooded me. There was a way to commune with nature. An old practice called upon my gifts and teased me with the knowledge of many women before me. Unable to take my eyes off it standing three feet away from me, I reached within the well inside of me, the place where my magic rested and pushed my gifts toward him. It was not unheard that energy transformed if one knew how to access it. The elemental energy surrounded us and all places, if one knew how to find it, stroke it, and control it. I recalled Manaha's words. *AkkadEtanaErra. The old language of the world.*

I admired the way the deer stood, muscles poised, ready to run as I called upon the link. It was there under my skin, ready to be accessed, and I didn't resist. I answered the call of my nature. *AkkadEtanaErra.*

He remained in the same place, watching.

Connecting to it, I approached the deer, and the animal waited as if it knew something I didn't. Slowly, I reached out to its neck, and it relaxed under my hand. My fingers caressed its neck slowly and gently stroked it. But I wanted more from it, so I pushed my magic into it, strengthening the bond and waiting for it to make up its mind.

Responding, it took two small steps in my direction, nuzzling my fingers.

I remained as still as I could, enjoying the feeling and the closeness we shared in that short instant.

His cold nose touched my hand, its nostrils warming the tips of my fingers.

I got closer. *AkkadEtanaErra,* I whispered again under my breath.

His skin jumped at the caress, his eyes never leaving my gaze.

My awareness of him was so unique; I found I held my breath. The contact filled with love and acceptance brought me such joy that I beamed at the creature, and something bloomed in me. This moment was how things were meant to be.

The realization that I found my home hit me, for this place was indeed my new home. Tears ran down my face as I backed away slowly, nodding. With my heart so full of gratefulness, I let go of the connection. *Go now and thank you.*

My eyes shone with happiness as I turned and saw Chase. Unbeknownst to me, he had stopped to watch me, mesmerized. His jaw remained slightly open, and his eyes looked incredulous at the sight of me with the deer. Chase's voice whispered, "I've seen nothing like this."

My grin answered him, and we stayed connected by the smile we shared. He appeared as enthralled by the graceful creature as I was and said, "I'm glad you appreciate our world."

Tesh approached me. "I did not witness everything, but as she rested her hand on my shoulder, she murmured, "I'm happy for you."

I returned her smile.

She knew something had just happened, but she was wise in not asking what caused it.

"Humm, what did I miss?" said Blast, with reserve.

I shook my head and walked away from him. I didn't want to spoil my walk through the forest and this moment with Blast's late nonsense.

We failed to behave normally, including myself. While I lost it a while ago, I recognized that Blast behavior ignited something in me I could not quite grasp. This pattern appeared to repeat itself since we awoke. Now, I understood better why. Nature was alive here, and the Earth still shared its power, whatever that remained.

Blast reached me on the NetCom and smiled at me. Contritely, he whispered, "I got the message."

"Good. Cut the NetShit from now on," I said. "We are all stressed and don't need ill-timed behavior anymore."

"Wait up." A few seconds later, Blast appeared at my side and murmured, "It wasn't all me, was it?"

Exasperated with him, I sighed. "Blast, there's a protocol, and you're acting outside of it, and we can't have that…."

Wearily, Blast said, "NetRoger that." After a pause, he added, "Look, I need to tell you something. You, huh, are going into this mountain for the scan. Well, it scares the HellNet out of me. I don't like it a bit."

I smiled. "It will be okay, Blast."

"I don't think I want you to do it."

"I don't have a choice, Blast. We need the information."

He grunted. His care for me warmed my heart. While our relationship remained unspoken, we were close. We may have fought it until now, unable to move out of fear and sheer hesitation due to the future we lacked control over. Even when nonexistent as far as the relationship went, Streak and Tesh's close ties caused us to question our motives and desires. What if getting closer caused the dynamic of our team to change? Could we afford it? I supposed we would eventually have to address it, but both of us had successfully avoided it so far.

The rest of the descent into town didn't take long. Our silence allowed the sounds of the forest to surround us. Now, the rustle of leaves high in the trees, the branches cracking as the breeze moved among them, the flapping of tiny wings, all were a new song and resurfaced. The colors, the smell, the feeling of dirt under our feet brought about a novel experience.

Chase whispered ahead of me, "This way."

I glanced his way and changed course.

"It's about two miles." Chase's voice reached us. His blue eyes gently glanced at me. "My friend's cabin is at the edge of town. I'll be away for a few days. You can stay there. No one will disturb you."

Tesh moved faster to reach him and walked a few steps ahead of Blast and me.

"It is very kind of you, Chase," murmured Tesh.

Her face was sad when she turned toward him but said nothing when he began walking with her.

Chase showed another trail up ahead, and they headed together in that direction.

"Don't tackle me like that again if you want continued cooperation," Chase said, confronting Blast.

"Prove you will help, and I won't," answered Blast without losing a beat.

"So, the cabin is not enough?"

"It's a start...."

Blast and I followed in silence until Chase turned back toward Blast and pointed in the ridge's direction we had just left, boasting, "I like the drop, Blast, but if there's ever a next time, I want the boots."

Blast glanced at him, expressionless. "I bet you do. "But... Not on your life."

Chase added, not hiding his amusement, "Well, at least, it's refreshing to see others lose it too."

After my outburst, I felt his gaze upon me, assessing.

Blast showed no interest in Chase's humor at our expense.

I, for one, appreciated it and said with a chuckle, "Come on, boys, behave. You're going to need to get along, eventually."

Chase murmured to Tesh as he passed her, "Nice to know family squabbles do happen in your time, too," with an amused expression on his face.

As we continued toward town, the equipment garnered from our Chamber trailed between me, gliding effortlessly in its casings. It would find its way to a secure location in the cabin.

We will see to it soon.

Earlier, I isolated our Chamber from prying eyes before we left the caves, and it now rested behind a wall of rocks. Still, we would need to retrieve additional technology from there later, since it remained buried within the broken pieces of our complex under blocked passageways. But for now, our priority was to locate the other Chambers. I needed to do the scan soon.

Finding our people would require us to once again encroach upon the grounds the Entity deemed its domain. The Sphere lurking around the underground would not make the task easy.

I looked at the clock on my visor. We possessed some time to accomplish this and no need for sleep. We could go without it for several more days without affecting our performance. It was a slight consolation for now.

But what of Streak? My deep scan could reveal his location. Getting him back never left my mind. I knew it was not far away from Tesh's thoughts, either. It overshadowed everything we did. Only, we could not overlook the Center's knowledge about our tech either, and that too demanded our immediate attention.

Mage moved back and forth between Chase and Tesh. Ironically, it depicted more than anything the tie existing between them. Another mystery to unearth.

I followed them, and Blast, respecting my need for silence, walked beside me. When I looked at Blast, he reached for my hand, wearing a forlorn expression. He regretted the distance between us. We all could be fearsome when our emotions got the best of us, and yet we all knew each other well. I smiled at him, and my glance drifted back to Chase.

What did I learn about Chase? He didn't like to get too close to people. He very seldom let his guard down. Now he found himself caught in an entanglement with a connection to us without clarity. He got subjected to a MindLandscape he didn't want, which left him at our mercy because of our existing gifts. Also, Blast's constant incursions did not make things easy. And yet, he did not fear us. Sure, he had moments of doubts about us, but very little anxiety. There was another thing that called him to our side. I was sure of it. During Tesh's read, something happened between them.

His distance from her was new. He now held back. Maybe he was upset with her. No doubt that I would be if I were him.

I wanted to find out more about him, but my instincts told me we could trust him. Could he shut us out somehow? This possibility was puzzling. If so, how did he do it? But no, it was not possible. Tesh had too much control over this to happen. Or was there another influence?

21
ACCORD
Tesh

Forest Path, CA - 2022

Observing Chase walking ahead, I know I have to do something to reach him. We need him as an ally within the Center. Tesh Vlog - DAINN Annals – Summer 2022.

The landscape turned from dense forest to more open areas with trees and boulders as we got closer to town. Chase had retreated into his thoughts for a while now. Somehow, I needed to mend the relationship. It was imperative because I could feel how pissed he was after the MindLandscape and Blast's stupid stunt. "Chase, I am sorry about what Blast did. It was wrong."

Chase glanced my way. "Why did you not stop him?"

"I… I didn't think Blast would, and then when it happened, it was so fast," I said. "I should have expected it. I made a mistake. Look, I meant it when I said you could trust me. Only, things are going on with us that demand certain actions from me."

Chase grunted. "I need you to be straight with me. I don't want to worry that someone here is going to come out of the left field and do something that would force me to...."

"What?"

Chase looked uncomfortable for the first time since I met him. "You know... Do things... Worry about your intentions."

"You don't have to." The MindLandscape revealed a secret garden with thoughts locked inside his mind. It showed a pattern I recognized. His ability to protect himself against my powers was worrisome. Sure, I could have broken through, but I chose not to. Could he have deflected my gifts if I had? Why did I not push through? Was it because I refused to hurt him? I wasn't sure.

Chase didn't say anything at that.

The need to understand him prompted me to seek his company while we still had time to talk alone. Because once inside the cabin, there would be too many ears.

I continued, "Look, I know you are mad at me, but once you understand everything, you will feel differently. I need you to trust me again."

"Why would I do that? You infringed on my mind, Tesh, and yet I told you, I wouldn't lie."

"I didn't have a choice, Chase. But now, they know we can trust you. I need you to find a way to do the same again."

"Then tell Blast in no uncertain terms to stay the hell away from me. I don't want to worry about the next stunt he will pull on me using whatever powers he possesses. Now, if he wants to come at me like a regular guy, I have no problem with that." Chase stopped and looked at me. "And only if you promise you will never do a MindRead on me again."

"Then tell me what you are hiding, Chase?"

He looked unsure and shook his head. "I can't... No, I won't, not right now."

"How do you want me to react to that?"

Chase smirked. "Trust is a funny word, and it goes both ways. Trust me that this has nothing to do with you."

My instinct told me I could, but this could backfire on us. "Can this hurt us?"

Chase paused for a moment. "I don't think so."

It was a big ask. "Before I agree to leave this alone, I need to know if this has to do with the tablet?"

Chase nodded beside me. "Yeah, it does. I will tell you sometimes, but not today. When I am ready."

I matched his steps, and we advanced in silence for a while. Then, I said, "Okay, then. But before we get to the cottage, there is something I must ask you, and we need to arrive at a compromise."

Chase grunted beside me. "You need to let me go back."

Besides knowing Chase's patterns, the Mind Landscape gave me a sign of the ways of things in this time and place. "Why?"

Chase glanced my way without answering for a beat. "He doesn't know I am here. He can't find out." He studied my face. "I know this must be difficult... You arrived here thinking you would remain safe inside the mountain, and now this. If he finds out, we lose our edge."

"We're trained for the unexpected."

"I already told you. I won't tell the Center about you. But I need to know what Jonathan found, and since this trip didn't turn out the way I expected, this is the only way."

Chase's suspicion sent icy shivers down my spine.

"Still, it can't be easy, having to assimilate everything quickly. Especially if you find yourself with two foes at once." Chase murmured out of nowhere. His face softened. "Your parents loved you so very much. I'm sorry you lost them."

I winced. "How do you know?" My voice shook, and I turned away from him, disliking my vulnerability. Even now, after years, the loss left me hollow. The injustice of it. The coldness of it. The irreversible effect of it. It all made it so much harder for me to move on.

"I sensed the loss when you shared. You're not the only one who can gather information, you know."

I frowned, disgruntled. "Point taken." Somehow, he had this ability. Chase tapped into my powers through the link DAINN created. I guess of all the people, I had to meet a guy with knowledge of neuroscience and an innate ability to build walls, and that same person got some of my gifts. *DAINN, when I see you, I am going to rant.* Under normal circumstances, it is not possible. Most people cannot connect to feelings during a share, not without practice. And I doubted Chase had much training on this. But the thought remained with me. *DAINN.* How did he do it so fast? Now was not the time to inquire further into it. I refused the diversion that would lead me away from what I wanted to know, so I pursued asking questions. "If your family vacations are sacred, why aren't you with them?"

Chase grinned, offering a fake apologetic smile. "The tablet is important. I have a responsibility. How did we lose our world?"

Unsure how to answer that, I shrugged. "Maybe someday I'll tell you about it. You know you cannot return to your life as if nothing happened. It will not work."

The ground changed. The terrain opened on an area filled with more boulders and shrubbery. I began gliding over the obstacles. Behind us, Leane and Blast launched their NetJet boots.

Chase's knowledge of the terrain became quickly apparent. He cleared the obstacles with agility, jumping from rock to rock with a sure footing.

I kept up with him.

He shrugged, "I've got to get back to the Center. They expect me to meet all the other scientists."

Chase appeared unconcerned about his ability to leave us, as if he could walk out of our lives as he entered them, with no strings attached. But it couldn't be. Not until we reached an understanding.

"We both know you now have another purpose."

Chase acted with detachment as he kept going. "If they found something else, I'm your best bet in there to relay information." He then stopped and looked at me. "But I'm not sure how to get the tablet back for you."

"Then we will do it ourselves," I said firmly.

He leaned down to caress Mage. My dog licked his hand. "Mage is an excellent judge of character," Chase added, looking straight into my eyes. "I would if I could."

I knew why Mage liked him. His energy had to do with the Darnet connection and my DNA. I looked at the panorama. What awaited us in this town? The mountain left behind us would have served as the perfect hideaway. Jumping the last promontory to the narrow dirt path, I asked, "How secure is the Center?"

Chase turned to face me. "It's the latest security tech. If they know about your presence." He shook his head, uncertain of what to say next. "They're not terrible people. It's just their methods." He paused. "Jonathan is very driven." His voice carried a certainty about it that gave me goosebumps.

My gut clenched. What else had the Center found? We needed to know if they had located one of our Chambers.

Odd how things had worked out. This unexpected link with the Center could be what we were looking for, the key to changing our future. Maybe DAINN gave us unknowingly an advantage. No, DAINN didn't do this without assessing the odds. We had stumbled upon it because of it. The reason for this existed because of Chase's role with the Center.

Somehow, we had to make things about the state of our planet right. It began by locating the events that changed the course of our future on the timeline. Isolating these moments could bring everything back into balance. These intercepts would require staying close to this place. All of it was more complicated than what we comprehended on the surface, but we trained for this, especially Streak.

Chase on the inside would facilitate our task. But changing our future would not be just finding isolated incidents on the timeline. Things didn't work out that way. It would be a series of actions, consequences moving unseen in different directions, creating unforeseen patterns, shifts tumbling paths, decisions that twisted outcomes, sidetracked lives, which ultimately brought about unwanted results. To implement all this, we needed all the Conclaves to work together. I needed my entire team.

I could not run from this responsibility. Not anymore. Not with this world around me. Looking at the surrounding beauty with none of the ravages of my time, I knew what we had to do. I meant to keep it that way. It was worth everything in my power to influence a different outcome than the one awaiting us in the future.

Leane and Blast moved a few feet away from us as we crossed a small stream. They had made peace.

I called them in my head. *Wait up.*

I witnessed Leane's wonderment stepping in their direction with Chase at my heels. She bent over wildflowers; her face filled with pleasure. "I don't remember this species in our time. Amazingly, it lives."

I glanced at the shrubs and paused.

Leane was right.

We didn't have this species in our time. "Chase just told me that the Center is bringing in more scientists."

"They are like me, recently graduated," said Chase.

Leane turned toward us with a sigh, her hand brushing the flowers. "So, this is why we are here?"

Blast's thunderous look spoke volumes, but he didn't move. He was more frightening than when he acted before thinking. "Could it be the reason we landed here, exactly at this moment?"

My team waited, and I said, "I believe this pattern is too much of a coincidence. Our leaders may have programmed our presence here on purpose. We must assume that the Center's work will affect the very things we are here to correct. The tablet will influence the scientists' work and direction, and we cannot let that happen."

"I can give you access to all the profiles. The Center plans to dig further to find other technology and research time dilution."

Leane reached for one glider carrying the load, "Maybe we can use Chase to our advantage. As an insider, he can keep us in the loop."

"It could work." I looked at Chase, waiting for his reaction.

"Hey, I'm not a pawn," said Chase, glaring at us.

Blast observed Chase silently. "You don't have a choice."

"No, Blast. Chase has a choice, and if this is going to work, Chase has to be willing. No coercion."

"But I will help where I can," Chase said with assurance. "I've got to be on the East Coast tomorrow."

Blast looked at Chase with steely eyes. "Indeed." His voice was stern when he turned toward the object of our attention. "We kind of own you now, mate."

Chase said coldly, "No one owns me. And we're not in Australia. You could try dude or bro."

Blast laughed. "Humm, you don't say...." Turning toward Leane and me, Blast asked, "So, when do we inject him?"

I shrugged, "Blast, enough."

Thoughtful, I glanced past the tree line ahead. I was about to take a considerable risk, but I needed Chase to understand that I would not force something on him.

"There's not a move Chase can make without us knowing about it with the Imps," Blast said.

Convinced that we required allies, I wanted to demonstrate our willingness to trust him this time. "He either does it willingly or not at all."

"HellNet..." Blast said. He continued, "He's helped enough already as it is. He turned our tech in — we can do without this kind of help. You put him on a short leash, Tesh. It's the only way."

"I said, no coercion. I mean it. You are a NetJerk."

Blast's look tells me he disagrees, but he finally relents after a long pause. "All right, I'm with you."

Although I was concerned that all of us reached the same conclusion about Chase's usefulness, I was not ready to tackle that fact yet. Instead, I grinned, relieved to see the old Blast. "There you are...

231

That's the Blast I recognize. I can do without this other Blast. He freaked me out."

Blast fidgeted on his feet whenever he was on edge. "I figured we needed…."

I whispered, "Streak."

He nodded.

I went to hug him and murmured, "We do, but we also need Blast. Don't let him go."

His arms wrapped around me, and his head settled on my head. "I don't like this pace. Things go too slow. We should glide full-speed ahead over to the research facility."

Leane approached us, a look of relief on her face, and laughed. "That's my teammates."

Blast reached for her and wrapped her in his arms.

We stood, the three of us tied to one another, finding some comfort together. I opened my eyes to see Chase watching us with an odd look in his eyes. Surprise. Warmth. Understanding. It didn't last long. Smartass as he was, he snapped, "So, I guess the family is back together again?"

Blast released us both and nodded in his direction. *What would he do if it came down to them or us?*

I took a step back, still standing in the fold of his energy. My eyes met Chase's over Blast's shoulder. He didn't move an inch, undoubtedly knowing we were assessing our next move as far as he was concerned. I stated calmly for all to hear. "He's with us… I trust him."

Chase nodded at me. "I will help on my terms." Then he turned toward the creek. He began his trek through the small path leading to the nearby town without looking back.

Leane and I resumed our run toward Chase's cabin with a grin on our faces. The casings hovered three feet above the ground near us.

"Do you think they'll ever get along?" Leane whispered beside me.

"Blast will have to come to trust him, eventually."

"This is an enormous leap, even for you. I hope you know what you are doing, for all our sakes."

When I glanced at Chase, I nodded as he kept on moving.

I laughed. The sound escaped from my throat, and it rang clear across the landscape. It was time that we became ourselves again.

22
MOLDER
Chase

Cabin At The Edge Of Town, CA - 2022

Chase Davenport barely adjusts to one of the Perfect Humans' powers when another amazing one surfaces. Although reeling from it, he remains steadfast in his loyalty to Tesh. DAINN Annals – Summer 2022.

The Center represented a genuine threat, even if it existed to accomplish the highest good. But the Entity we encountered scared me a hell of a lot more. We didn't know what we were dealing with, while with the Center, well, this was a risk I understood.

I paused; my actions within the Center could only go so far. Keeping Tesh and her team away from Jonathan seemed impossible. They had their mission. My inability to keep these two forces apart provided me with a sense of fatality. Eventually, no matter what I did, they would face each other. The Center's resources pitted against the Perfect Humans' powers were not a sight I cared to see.

Tesh appeared at my side. "What's wrong?"

Her face scrunched up when she attempted to work out a problem. She behaved with the weight of the world on her shoulders.

I gently reached for a strand of hair falling across her cheek as we stood on a boulder and pushed it back. "I'm concerned about your safety," I admitted. "You're about to take on a powerful force with the Center, and this will not be the only one you will face if you go back inside the caverns.

She shrugged. "We have no choice. We'll deal with each in due time."

"You didn't do so well the first time around against the Sphere. How do you plan to overcome that to get to your people?"

"It had the element of surprise. Not anymore."

"The Center has a lot of resources. Their tentacles reach far. They have the workforce. They reinforced the boundaries around the facility. Surveillance cameras cover the entire grid. Their security systems are military-grade, with biometric tech guarding the entrance. It possessed the latest redundancies. Their security forces, prepped and ready to deploy around the grounds at the slightest alert, outnumber you. How do you propose to breach all that?"

"I already have our Custodians reporting their activities," Blast said, joining us. With a grim look on his face, he continued, "Even with the private security being military-grade, our tech is far advanced."

I nodded, watching him. "The gate will be impossible to breach without detection once everyone is inside."

Blast shook his head. "Getting the tablet and our people back is our priority. Doing so undetected is imperative."

Sadness flashed over Tesh's face. "It's not just about our people and us. We have a responsibility to succeed. Otherwise, our world, this whole planet, is truly lost."

The punch I got in the stomach when she told me about it the first time created a knot that lodged itself in my solar plexus again and took my breath away. "You still won't tell me what happened?"

"We are not supposed to share this, Tesh," Leane said.

"We can't, Chase. You already know too much," whispered Tesh. Turning to both Leane and Blast, "Still, he has a right to understand what is at stake."

Blast shook his head. "I don't care if he knows, so long as he gets that, we are playing a big game here. Besides, if he is going to help us succeed, it may be better if he is aware of everything."

Nausea grabbed me next, almost making me retch. If Blast didn't fight to keep me out of the loop, things must indeed be bad. It took a moment for what Blast expressed to sync in and before my brain got to the extent of what it truly meant.

When I finally got a hold of myself, the only thing that came to my mind was, "Shit... If you put it that way." My voice sounded raw to my ears and was but a murmur.

Still trying to wrap my head around the extent of the stakes for our future, I saw the roof of the cabin. "We're here, just ahead and around the bend." I led them across a tall edge of California Lilac, shaken. The odor assaulted our nostrils as we passed by it.

Tesh seemed to understand. Her hand gently touched my arm. "We will never give up..." murmured Tesh.

I nodded.

Leane stopped in her tracks and approached the bush. "This is heavenly. I never saw this in Ang. Can you smell it, Tesh?" Her hand grazed the clusters of white flowers. Without hesitation, her nose dove into the petals, breathing their sweet scent, and her face disappeared among the branches. Then, her crystal laugh escaped, and she turned to Tesh, tears in her eyes. "This is such a gift."

Blast nodded. "It is... But we have to go." He grabbed her hand and pulled her to him.

Leane's face dropped, and she straightened her stance. "Yes..."

The contrast between their powers and their vulnerability jumped out at me. It was the second time I felt it. First, as they hugged together in the forest, and now, over a bunch of shrubs, we barely noticed anymore. How wrong was their world that they took such a pure pleasure in a flower?

All Perfect Humans seemed to feel things deeply. Was this part of an evolution we had yet to witness among ourselves? Instead, our tendencies over these last decades moved us toward harsher, colder, less gentle sides of our natures. Technology's impact created distance. It effectively cut us off from each other. We slowly became immune to empathy towards other people. If this proved accurate, they were in for a tough time here. I sighed.

How is it they maintained such humanity with each other? I wish I could find out what made them that way, spend time, ask questions, and learn about their world and society.

But time was against it, time and trust. I would have to be patient. Then it dawned on me again that this world of theirs was ours, just as much as our world was theirs. I shook my head. It was mind-boggling.

Still, this perceived vulnerability became a factor to consider. I needed to establish some ground rules for their protection. They needed to know how things worked in my world.

"Okay, I will give you a crash course on what you need to know. Then, you'll study the internet and television once we are inside," I said as we crossed the yard. The girls and I came up at the front door of the cabin. "Huh... I never locked this door before, but you should," I said. I pulled a set of keys from my pocket and handed these to Tesh. "Here is a key. You keep it and lock up when leaving."

Tesh looked at the key with incomprehension in her eyes as she gingerly picked it up from my hand. "What do I do with this?"

Oh, brother... I needed to go over the basics before I left. "Here. It doesn't bite. You take it and put it inside the keyhole, and you turn it." As I spoke, I took the key, inserted it into the door, closed the panel, and twisted it to the right. I heard the click locking the door.

The lock engaged. "Just like this," I said.

The door panel didn't budge. "This way, it's locked. You twist it in the other direction to open it."

Both Tesh and Liane nodded. I then handed Tesh the key again. "There's a living room, a kitchen, two bedrooms, and one bath. It's rustic, but no one should bother you here. Your casings could attract attention if someone comes inside."

Blast, who had remained in the backyard, appeared behind me, his gaze going over the place's layout. "Things are too open. Can I close off the perimeter on the sides and back?"

Puzzled, I looked at him and frowned. "What do you mean? Building a fence will take time."

"Is there a lot of people coming and going around here?" Blast asked.

"Not really."

"So, nobody will notice if I change things around?"

I shrugged. "Huh... There are no direct neighbors. My friend would be the only one to notice the changes, but he won't be back for a couple of months."

Blast nodded and smiled. "NetRoger that. I will work it out," he added, walking away.

I was about to say something to him, but Leane stepped inside first and looked around. "Oh…"

Her exclamation drew my attention.

Tesh followed her and stood by her side. The silence lengthened.

Watching them, I fidgeted uncertainly. "I know it's not much. Is everything all right?"

Tesh looked in my direction. "Yes… We're sorry. It's great. Thanks, Chase. We just never saw anything like this before."

"Huh?" I wanted to ask about their homes. I wanted to see it through her eyes again. Only now was not the time. I hoped there would be a time when we could talk and when I could learn from them without rushing from one priority to another. Unfortunately, we had to move.

I followed them inside and was surprised. The place looked like it had seen no one in a while.

It was dusty. And it was not a week-old layer of dust either. Indeed, it was much more than that.

The accumulation of dirt inside the cabin was confusing.

"Sorry. It is dirtier than when I left. You can use one bedroom. I'm afraid you must share. Blast can take the other unless you have a different arrangement. I hesitated on that one. My voice paused, and I looked at Tesh.

Leane chuckled as she turned toward me.

Embarrassed, I suddenly muttered, "I have to get back to New York tonight, but you can stay here as long as you want."

They still had not budged.

I took several steps leading to the kitchen and opened the fridge. Tired and thirsty, I grabbed a bottle of water. And I downed it while they watched. "Are you thirsty? There is more if you want…."

They both appeared lost. "Are you two all right?"

They nodded.

"Where do you want to put the casings? I suggest the bedrooms." I walked toward the back rooms.

My moving seemed to break the spell. It pulled the girls away from their stupor. Tesh followed behind me in the corridor with Leane in tow, and the casings hovered near her.

We could use fantastic technology. We could then avoid carrying luggage through an airport, move furniture by hand, or load and unload trucks. "I could see a lot of usage for this tech. We could make a lot of money with this stuff." I almost got trampled by the first casing in my musing as it passed the door behind Leane.

I jumped to the side just in time.

"Blast…" Leane called.

"Got it," Blast said, his face coming through the glass window on the far side as he stepped through the wall and window panel to stand beside Leane.

"What the heck?" I said.

In a matter of seconds, his hand lit up. He gently pressed it against the wall. His fingers released energy tendrils that spread across the surface. The wall partition pushed further out as Blast created an outside wall located six feet from the first. Simultaneously, the roof extended to cover the structure to the outside world seamlessly.

Then, Blast created an inner wall that rose in front of my eyes, enlarging the room and almost doubling the small cabin's space. This addition made a hidden room.

240

I blinked. When I opened my eyes again, a complete wall existed between us, and the casings had vanished. "How... How did you..?"

Blast shrugged and smiled before walking through the walls into the backyard.

Leane winked at me, and with a wave of her hand, she maneuvered the metallic cases into a corner under the small window. In a flash, they disappeared in front of my eyes.

My words expressed my surprise. "How is any of this possible? That Blast can do these things is amazing. And... You've got these things in stealth mode?" It blew my mind. Incredulous, I moved toward their emplacement, testing the space in front of me.

Nonplussed, Tesh nodded. "Blast is a Modler. What else would you have us do for security?"

She said this as if it explained everything. "Never mind," I said, shaking my head. Okay, I didn't like the guy. Blast was an asshole, but his skills, well, they were phenomenal. Out of this world, really.

I laughed at myself. Of course, Blast's powers were. Still, the guy drove me nuts. So much had happened in the space of a day, and things just kept getting better and better in the unreality department.

"Don't worry, Chase. Even if they discover these, no one will ever be able to open them," added Leane, satisfied with the arrangement.

I grunted. *Not...* There was no point in asking questions I knew too well they wouldn't answer. My curiosity remained dissatisfied, even if I continued to be infinitely inquisitive about their world. Time would tell if I ever made it on their trust list.

"You'll get used to it," Tesh said, looking at me.

"I doubt it."

Leane's visor opened over their NetComm. "Yes, what do you need?" she said, as she listened in silence for a while, moving toward the hidden room.

"NetRoger that." Leane moved back toward the wall. It dropped to reveal an open space. She reached the casings, and they magically reappeared under the window. She opened one and retrieved several spheres, some drones, and a few other items I could not identify. Some found their way into an expansion compartment of her suit while others glided beside her.

I didn't even know the pocket in her suit existed. I guessed they had a way to miniaturize things as well.

She closed the lids and waved her hand over the boxes, which disappeared in the next instant. When she passed the location of the new wall, it reappeared as if it was always there.

I couldn't help myself and had to touch it. When I rested my hand on its smooth surface, it was sturdy, possessing the same texture as the regular wall. I shook my head and followed them out.

They were gearing up for something. "What's going on?"

Leane turned toward me and shrugged. "Just getting a few items we might need."

Tesh moved ahead of me without a word.

They didn't care to elaborate, so I shrugged and left the bedroom. On my way to the living room, I noticed Mage seated quietly outside the front door. "Tesh, why is Mage outside? He can come in." I looked at the dog at the edge of the doorway.

Leane passed Mage on her way out, and he remained there, waiting on the back porch.

Tesh's eyes lit up. "Oh... He won't come in until you invite him."

I did a double-take. "What?"

"Invite him in," insisted Tesh.

She looked serious. I walked up to the doorway and signaled to Mage to come in. He didn't budge.

"Tell him, Chase." Her amused voice resonated with excitement.

"Mage, come in," I said, feeling self-conscious, and I waited to see the dog in action. He didn't budge.

Leane chuckled as she watched from the backyard, just as excited about this as Tesh was.

I glanced at both of them.

Tesh approached me. "Welcome him inside."

"You mean... I have to use the 'welcome' word?" Mage's ears perked up at hearing this. He stood up, waiting, his tail wagging.

Geez... Was the dog more intelligent than most humans?

I turned back to Tesh. She nodded in encouragement.

I said, looking at Mage, unsure whether to believe that it understood me. "Mage, you're welcome to come in."

The dog leaped through the door, throwing himself at me in excitement. Mage's front paws settled on my shoulders, and he licked my chin. "Okay, boy. Good boy. It is your place. Down now."

Immediately, Mage sat in front of me.

Tesh stepped in and gave him a caress. "Wonderful boy. You'll stay here and guard the place."

Mage barked once as if to answer.

I opened the cabinets in search of bowls and food in the kitchen. I picked up a large bowl, filled it with water, and set it on the floor. Next, I opened the fridge. But something was not right. My food, the one I bought before I went climbing, was no longer there.

The stacks sitting in the fridge in front of me were some of Bobby's favorite food. I knew his habits, and we didn't care for quite the same things. Frowning, I retrieved something I would eat, pulled out two frozen pies, and inserted the packets into the microwave. Still, I tried to work out what was bothering me. Did Bobby come back early? It didn't look like he was around. The place needed a good cleaning, and my friend was not a slob. He was rather particular.

"Let's go," said Tesh, as she stood watching me fuss in the kitchen.

What am I missing? "Just a minute," I replied, waiting for the contents to heat for one minute. I opened the microwave door, retrieved its contents, and dropped them on a plate. The food steamed a little, so I moved it around the bowl. "Mage, if you're hungry or thirsty while we're gone, this is for you."

Mage rewarded me with a look, ears up. He cautiously approached the food, sniffed the air, and barked before diving into the plate.

I watched him and felt quite satisfied.

It seemed Mage, and I would get on famously. Turning around, I grinned at Tesh. "He likes it. Now we can go."

Tesh whispered, "I guess this food is good for him?"

Offended, I said, "It's good for him. It's good enough for me."

Tesh's cheeks turned red with embarrassment. "I didn't mean...."

"No offense taken. It's just; I wouldn't give Mage something bad. I love dogs."

Thinking about what was bothering me, I pulled my phone from my pocket and looked around for my charger. Here again, I couldn't find where I had left it before. I searched the kitchen counters, then the living room. I finally located it on one of the small end tables by the sofa. I plugged it in. "Okay, now, quickly, here is the television and the remote control." I picked up the device and showed it to Tesh. I turned it on and off. "Here is my laptop. I'll leave it here for you. You can get the internet on that and learn about things on it."

Tesh nodded.

"Getting the hang of things around here like grasping an understanding of the internet, TV remote control, phones, banking, and how to use currencies in the stores around town are things you need to know. It will help you adjust. I'm going to go to town and get a few things."

"Okay," Tesh said, looking around the room at the things I pointed out to her.

My phone, powering up, biped with one message after another as it began charging. I glanced at it, and my eyes locked on the number of texts and calls showing up on my screen.

I opened one text from Jonathan. It read:

"Chase, what the fuck, man. Call me." Dated July 3, 2018.

"Chase, where the hell are you? You missed the first meeting." Dated July 4, 2018.

"Chase, you are pushing it. We are at the Center. Get over here." Dated July 6, 2018.

"Chase, I got you got pissed the last time we talked, but call me. It's not like you to disappear like this." Dated July 8, 2018.

Several others were from Jonathan, but I glanced through the other messages, getting a peculiar and bad feeling.

Now, panicked, I went to the messages left by my family: "Chase, it's mom. We have not heard from you in a couple of weeks. Call. We miss you." Dated July 12, 2018.

"Chase, your mother is worried. Call son." Dated July 23, 2018.

"Chase, I know you stayed, but it's your father's birthday. Call." Dated July 28, 2018.

"Chase, we are coming home. Jonathan said he had not heard from you in weeks. If you're all right, son, call us. Your mother is beside herself." Dated August 2, 2018.

I opened one from Bobby: "Hey, man, call me. I haven't heard from you all summer. Breakaway from work, and call, you asshole." Dated October 4, 2018.

"Holy shit…" I exclaimed, looking at my screen as I saw the date of May 15th, 2022. I then went to my computer. I opened my laptop, impatiently waiting for it to turn on. My knee nervously bounced as I looked at the date at the bottom of my screen. *Come on… Come on…*

When the screen came to life, my worst fear came to pass. The date on my screen showed to be May 15, 2022, and it corroborated my phone.

"What the fuck?…" I exclaimed, losing it. What did the hell happen? My brain ran amuck. "Shit… Shit… Shit…" I couldn't reconcile the possibility. There was no way. And, yet, the date remained right in front of my eyes as I fixed the screen, unmoving. Four years….

The Sphere kept us for four years? It was not possible. How? I didn't feel any different. Oh, fuck… My parents must think I was dead. Oh… It wasn't right. Panic set in, and I began to over ventilate. I let my head fall between my hands and stayed there for a long while.

When I finally moved, I strolled to the door and watched Tesh and her friends moving around. How was I going to tell them? So much may have happened, and we did not know what? It was so bad. I didn't even know where to begin.

I stayed on the back porch and saw a unfamiliar landscape. The entire backyard had changed. A wood enclosure existed now, where none was there before. Shrubs rose, providing even more privacy between the forest and the side of the yard. Flowers like those Leane had admired spread on one side, providing a fresh scent in the air. A wooden gate matching the cabin provided another buffer from the road. Now, the entire backyard looked like a little private refuge.

Leane stood in the middle of it, a massive grin on her face beside Blast, tending to the last few details and placing small metallic spheres around the perimeter of the garden. These hovered in place, strategically located around the four corners and hidden among the trees' branches.

From the outside, no one could determine how big the house was. I looked toward the fake wall Blast had built and only saw the outer edge of the house beneath a pretty gazebo with small scintillating lights.

"Well, it looks like you have things under control here," I said, utterly amazed at the changes he had made in such a short time. Still grasping to get it together, I didn't move.

Blast glanced my way with a smirk on his face. "Of course, we do, and I think your friend will find this place an improvement." His cocky attitude spoke of self-satisfaction. Then with a more serious look in my direction, he asked. "What else do we need, Chase?"

"How about a time warp?" I said, my face dark with worry.

The guy sure knew how to strike a nerve with me, but I shrugged and said, "For starters, you'll need cells to communicate like the rest of us, clothes and money while I'm away...." "I am on my way to get the mobiles and a few other things," I muttered. I still didn't know how to break the news to them.

"Money..." murmured Blast. "The currencies of your time."

"You bet. Without it, you can't get anything."

"We eliminated these in 2069, explained Blast. Can I see it?"

I retrieved a few bills from my billfold and handed them to him. "Here. I'll leave some for you."

Blast took the money and grinned. Next, his fingers touched the paper, and he said, "That won't be necessary..."

He handed a bill to Leane and another to Tesh. "Feel this paper. We have nothing like this in our time."

"No, got rid of paper currency in 2038. You killed plenty of trees for these..." muttered Leane with disdain.

"Hey... It wasn't just for these. There are plenty of other things we need that unfortunately come from trees. Besides, what else would you have us do?" But my protest was somewhat lacking in heat, my mind contemplating the repercussions we may face given this new situation. We were four years behind schedule.

Blast and Tesh looked at the money while Leane turned to me, her face with disdain. "Use your ingenuity instead of plundering."

"All right, we may not have done so great, but I am not sure we are entirely responsible for global warming, either. I think we have other concerns at the moment."

Leane grunted. "Who are you kidding? How many scientific opinions do you need before you listen? You and I will talk about this issue later. I'll show you the responsibility you hold in that regard. Think about the number of species you have already destroyed in the space of fifty years or the ones that will be extinct in the next seventy-five years because of your crude human narcissistic activities and the pursuit of money. And for what?" She dropped the bill to the ground and turned away, disgusted.

I remained quiet and could not debate her on that score. Leane was right. As humans before them, we were incredibly ignorant caretakers showing no responsibility.

We had a hand in destroying the environment. Our consummation patterns around the globe had left a substantial ecological footprint taxing our natural resources to the planet's breaking point. Some even said that if American consumption represented a global average, it would take four planets to sustain Earth's entire population. We needed a climate revolution to deal with saving the planet. Despite many countries' efforts to produce renewable resources, reduce carbon dioxide emission from fossil fuel, and breakdown or absorb and reduce waste products, we remained far from the changes needed to slow the impending climate disaster. We were, in many ways, already too late. By 2025, the scientists said we would be way over our heads.

But we had more significant problems right about now. I had to tell them. "I would like to know everything you have implemented in your time, but I think there are more important things to discuss right now." Shifting my eyes away from Leane toward Tesh, what I saw mesmerized me. There was no other way to put it.

Blast's hand holding the money glowed with an energy field. The shimmer at the tips of his fingers concentrated on the edge of the bills. It grew and bled onto the dollars. The shimmering spread, and within the next minute, the twenty-dollar bill replicated itself into multiple copies, slowly transforming into a thick wad now in his grasp. A smile spread on his face as he murmured, answering my question,

"Oh, we don't need yours. Would you like some? In our time, we use credits."

"And how do you do all of this?"

Blast handed the bills to me. "This process is simply molecular transference."

"Simply?" I whispered, frowning. I seized the wad and flipped through the notes. They were perfect, and I couldn't tell the difference between Chase's bill and the rest of them.

"Well… That beats all the other things I've seen so far," I said, shaking my head. The awesomeness of his power held much danger if abused. It could topple economic systems. "Don't let them know you can do that… Ever. They'll put you in jail and throw away the key," I added, with a grim look on my face.

"They would have to catch me," Blast said.

We all looked at each other, and our smiles dropped. The silence that followed between us lasted longer than I felt comfortable with, so I added, "I am worried about you guys. It is so…" I didn't even have a word for it."

"You're worried about us?" said Blast, surprised.

I shrugged. "You should be too. Guys… Oh, shit. It is difficult to say." It may be unexpected for me to admit this to the guy I didn't trust, but I was suddenly terribly concerned about their well-being. "Yes. What I have experienced with you threatens everything we know. It challenges what we can do at this time. You must realize this. If anyone finds out your capabilities, they won't care about the tablet; only what you all can do, and you'll be lab rats. You are wise to keep your skills quiet, yet it might help if I know more. How can I help and protect you otherwise? But all of this is not even the tip of the iceberg."

Tesh moved toward me, sensing my unrest. "What is it?"

I shook my head... "Oh... Shit, I'm just going to come out and say it. It is not 2018. We are in 2022. Your plan to remain nonexistent in our timeline may very well be completely torpedoed now. The damn Sphere kept us locked in for four years."

Tesh's face registered shock. "What?"

I repeated, this time more forcefully, "It's the year 2022. We are May 15th, 2022."

"NetWash... This latest news beats it all. We remained in this Darnet Sphere for four years. HellNet, I hate this place," Blast exclaimed, furious.

"Oh... No, whispered Leane. Our friends..."

I ran my hand in my hair, distraught. "Your friends, my parents, the Center... It's all fucked up. How is it even possible?"

Tesh took a deep breath. "The Sphere is more like a time suspension, different but like cryo. We knew things might not work out our ways, Chase. We will figure this out. Still, we are here now, Blast. There is no point in deliberating what we cannot change. We need to know everything we can as quickly as possible, Blast. And Leane, now we have to move immediately. Chase, how did you find out?"

I grunted. "My phone and my laptop. Also, this place... I thought something was wrong when we entered. It is way dirtier than how my friend keeps it."

Tesh nodded. "You need to deal with your family, but we also need you to reach out to the Center."

"I know... But how the hell do I explain my absence?"

Tesh looked at me. "You need to think of something...."

"I have to go and limit the damage," I muttered, wondering how I was going to manage that.

"Easier said than done. I think we may be too late for that," said Blast.

"No, freaking kidding," I yelled. "Can you maybe come up with a solution instead of stating the obvious?"

Blast shrugged, turning to Tesh. "It's not my job. It's hers." Then, looking at me, he continued, "Wait up a moment." His hand landed on my arm, holding to the fold of my shirt. A glow at the tips of his fingers appeared immediately, and a shirt, pants, and vest appeared, duplicated into a second set. Satisfied, he muttered, "That should do it for me," and he dropped the clothes in my arms. "Leave them in the cabin."

"Smartass... I'm not your butler, and you forgot the boots," I muttered.

Without so much as a hint of hesitation, he grabbed the pair of boots on the ground. "No, I didn't."

Picking up the boots, he dropped them into my arms with a satisfied grin. "Here, since we're in a hurry. Don't get anything for me."

"This works so long as we don't wear these when we are together," I clipped. "I don't care to be your twin."

"You should be so lucky," Blast said. In the next second, my teammate changed the color of his new attire to black.

"This lacks imagination...." I muttered, moving quickly outside his reach.

As if on cue, the sound of a helicopter stopped our conversation. It flew to the east of the town, moving low over the treetops toward the mountain's side. It was another Halo.

Blast's face lit up, his topaz eyes shimmering brilliantly. "You don't need me here anymore," Blast said, following it with assessing eyes. He smiled, a dangerous expression on his face. His light blond hair, which sometimes almost appeared white, moved when he cocked his head, looking at Leane. "You'll join me?" He added, oozing confidence.

Leane stepped forward, gently resting her hand on his chest. "Are you going to do something insanely stupid?"

His smile widened. "Absolutely."

Tesh smiled. "About time..." she clipped, and knowing he needed this action, she added, "Make sure you're crazy successful at it then."

Blast winked at that before turning away from us and using the small wooden door to the forest path.

I followed Blast in haste with Tesh and Leane, in tow and watched him disappear in the underbrush, moving fast on the forest floor. He shot away from us with such speed that his departure resembled the path made by a fallen star traveling across the night sky. As he sprinted between the trees, he left behind the slightest trace of green - a blur that lasted the split of a second before it vanished in the air.

I turned toward the girls. "Well, I'll be damned... The Jackass is not even using his boots."

Leane chuckled, "Yeap. I'll be joining him if you don't need me here?"

Tesh grinned, "Go."

"You sure?" Leane said, looking between Tesh and me.

"Yes, Chase, and I can finish here. I'll come up as soon as Chase leaves for the East coast."

Leane nodded, a reserved expression on her face. "I'm sorry about your family. It's not right. Any of this. We will see you soon."

"You be careful up there," I nodded with a crooked smile. It was hard not to like Leane.

She turned around and followed the path Blast took moments ago, leaving this time a faint bluish trace under the forest canopy.

Witnessing another one of their powers confirmed how much I didn't know or how limited we were in comparison. Their presence here was such a fantastic discovery. I realized how lucky I was to be in their company.

Yet, the danger was ever-present. It was everywhere.

23
INTRIGUE
Logan

Sommerville Mansion, MA - 2018

The uneasy feeling settles in my gut as I enter the bathroom. I wonder if it is my imagination or is something going on with the Center? DAINN Annals - Summer 2022.

The bathroom was enormous. It was a room one would expect in a mansion. The countertop, walnut framed mirror, fluffy towels, a wicker laundry basket, and a small love seat on one side adorned the place.

I closed the door behind me and took off my jacket. Then I washed my face and dropped the towel in the basket after drying my hands.

Another hour to wait before I met Jonathan, and I desperately needed to get a grip. But the information I gathered from the files had made me uneasy. It would seem logical that the confidential nature of the project required a thorough evaluation of the personnel. And maybe I was overreacting. Perhaps it was the way of things when one got a job in research these days, especially when it was so secret that no one knew about it. I supposed these guys needed to understand their employees. Admittedly, this was all there was to the whole thing.

Patience was not my strong suit, and tea would have to do to keep me busy until my meeting. Resigned, I walked out of the bathroom and heard voices. Usually, I would have proceeded ahead, but the urgent tone of the conversation stopped me. From across the hall, two distinct voices stood out.

"Hell… You have to do better than that, Sinclair. The lab results are obvious. We possess something of consequence."

I recognized Jonathan's voice, eager to hear more about the conversation; I stayed put.

"We need to remain under the radar… Spallberg. The implications otherwise would be immense. We've taken all precautions. Our team has created social profiles and activities for everyone. No one will be missed."

"Good. But we need to make allowances," said Jonathan. "The town is small. We can limit access to it."

"Spallberg… It's going to take time. If one scientist gets recognized as it is now, we can't afford the others to be. Any amount of publicity would be too much. Too many questions bring awareness we do not want."

"I know, but… Our personnel need the ability…."

"Not after what happened. We had to develop a brand new profile and disseminate fake activities all over the internet. We can't afford to have a duplication of this."

"Most of the scientists have settled into their labs. They are eager to work and impatient to meet their team. So, I don't see this as a problem in the immediate future, added Jonathan, thoughtful. But many of our graduates are young. They are not used to confinement."

"No one is… But these graduates have everything they need within the Center."

"Still, we need them motivated."

"Their salary should do that. Nature is abundant around there. This research gives them something they will find nowhere else, a ticket to tomorrow. They can build their reputation on this project."

"Let's hope it works out that way…" whispered Jonathan. "I think we must revisit this issue soon, Sinclair."

"I think you have chosen the right candidates for this operation," said Sinclair.

"So, now, the hard part begins, murmured Jonathan.

"Have you heard from Chase?"

"No, nothing. Chase was quite upset the last time I saw him. I expected Chase to arrive tonight, but I have heard nothing."

"Keep me informed on that. We will keep the charade going for as long as we need it. Misinformation is the game that keeps us under the radar. I know Chase had reservations. He will have to come around."

"I'm not sure he will. But I've already expressed my thoughts on that," said Jonathan, frustrated.

"We will keep the illusion going, even from Chase."

"Once again, it's a mistake," said Jonathan.

"We can't let the world know. We can't risk a leak, Spallberg, and that's final."

"A little trust would go a long way."

"This issue is closed. When do you want the plane ready?"

"Tomorrow. Make it nine."

I heard their footsteps walking away and pondered on the conversation going back to the library. What were they talking about behind the scene? What misinformation? It was intriguing. I had no idea, and this worried me.

Spallberg did not agree with everything they were doing. That much was obvious.

Jonathan had told me they founded the Center to pave the way for a better tomorrow. The discussion had corroborated that point, but left me with many questions.

Once again, I entered the library and sat on the sofa, puzzled about what I could ask Jonathan to understand their conversation.

This Sinclair guy appeared to have some pull. I wondered what his connection was to the operation? Scientific research comprised at least eight thousand different areas with various degrees of importance. Jonathan had selected some of the brightest minds to influence our future. I could ask about the other fields besides mine.

Experienced scientists would lead the project. We would support them. They were already at the Center waiting for us. Many came from all over. Indeed, the team was world class, and while I didn't know all of them, those I knew about were impressive.

In my conversation with Jonathan, he narrowed down several areas of study. The Department Heads covered Geosciences with Rich Sand; Clinical Medicine with Philip Sognier; Biological Sciences with Lauren O'Brian; Chemistry and Materials Science with Mark Burke; Physics, Astronomy, and Astrophysics with Andre Lacroix; Mathematics, Computer Science and Engineering with Roger Mendelson; Economics, Psychology and other Social Sciences with Ursula Scheller. Apart from this information, I possessed no further details.

What could have caused the distribution of misinformation about one scientist? So, they recognized him... Considering they wanted the facility to remain off the grid, it could make sense that they distributed false data to lead people away from the location. Still, I wasn't sure what to make of this.

Although I was on board the moment, Jonathan expressed that they would have unlimited means to conduct my research, the files, and this tidbit gave me pause. I grimaced.

Instead of a sense of excitement at meeting the brilliant brains of the next generation that would carry on the work we did inside the facility, I felt hesitation. The research would influence our very future, and our group, the graduates from universities around the world were to meet here tomorrow. And here I was, waiting in this house for Jonathan, with anxiety. It sucked big time.

I poured myself some tea, wanting something a hell of a lot stronger.

Jonathan needed our team of graduate students to think outside the box. It was how he explained our importance in the selection process of the Center. Providing older scientists with new viewpoints became our mandate. While brilliants, they were set in their ways. Conceiving new paradigms and challenging concepts remained our purpose. Our mentors could soon find themselves in the path of our progress. This job was possibly the best opportunity I expected to get, but instead of enjoying all its perks, I was thinking of all the things they were hiding.

The door opened, and Jonathan Spallberg walked in with a smile on his face. "Logan, I see they already took care of you. How was the trip?"

I got up and shook his extended hand. "Fast."

He chuckled at that. "You brought your bike?"

"Always."

I sat back down and said, "Talking about that… It's coming with me, you know. My bike, I mean."

Jonathan raised an eyebrow and sat down. "I'm not sure you'll get a lot of use where we're going."

"Oh, don't worry about that. I'll find a way to use it."

"Hum… It may not be easy." But Jonathan thought better of that and shrugged, "I suppose we can make adjustments…."

With a tight grin, I said, "You're the man in charge of this operation; I'm counting on it, Jonathan."

"Yeah, well, there is a lot to it, but we're not here to discuss this now, are we…"

"No. You wanted to see me."

Jonathan hesitated a moment, but then he said, "You know how important this is."

"From the look of it… it's much more than a job. It's almost a life commitment," I said, a bit sarcastically.

"Yeah, well, it is for some of us. You're quite right, Logan. How did it go with your family?"

I grimaced. It has not been easy for my family. My parents counted on me to join the business since I was young. But, I finally convinced them that I needed to do this. "We came to an understanding."

Jonathan nodded and said, "Great. I wanted to meet you in person. We didn't get to discuss everything during our conference call. You were supposed to work directly with Lacroix, but he is involved with something else inside the labs. I need your eyes for the excavation site."

Surprised, I said, "Excavation?"

"Yeah... I'll need you to jump right in when we get to the Center."

"I see. Okay, but... Tell me about the excavation?"

"Huh... you will learn all about it when we get there. We need you to identify something in the caves."

"The caves?" I schooled my face to look blank. "How accessible is that?"

"We are working to secure the area. It should be ready when you get there."

"I see." This information, combined with what I overheard moments ago, rendered me cautious. "What am I looking at?"

Jonathan continued as if I had said nothing, not that I just said much. "I gathered that you enjoy a bit of a challenge?"

"What type of challenge are we talking about?"

"The usual when people excavate a site, I suppose. I haven't seen the area myself yet. But I plan on joining."

"You do?"

"Of course... I just saw pictures of the site, but you will find it quite exciting."

"You have pictures?" I said, suddenly more interested in hearing this. Can I see them?"

"These are confidential data, but we are not yet prepared to share it. I can't have it spread among the other scientists. Not until we know for sure what we have found. So, I will give you access as soon as we reach the facility. Once there, you will work away from the labs. There is some climbing involved, and it's not efficient to go back and forth."

"How isolated are we talking about?"

"You will work with the excavation team in another part of the structure. Don't worry; we are just talking until we crack the object."

I observed Jonathan as I inquired, "So, there is an object?"

He looked pretty thrilled when I said that. "Oh, there is...."

"And the others do not know?" I said, curious.

The faces of the other graduates floated in front of my eyes. Among them were all the recruits, Chase Davenport, Axel Summers, Gen Aubrey, Anders Quinn, Zoey Silas, Ronan Phelps, Brielle Brown, Liam Donovan, and Veronica Smooth. These were all people I would meet and fly to the facility with, and for now, they would remain at arms' length.

Gen Aubrey's face stuck with me because I had met her earlier. She was the girl in the car I almost collided with on my way here. So, she was part of this entire expedition, too. It was good to know that I would soon meet a familiar face.

Now I understood why Jonathan wanted to see me alone.

I nodded while wondering what this recent development meant for me. "Why am I given this assignment?"

"I believe you will find this fits your field. It is a critical assignment. But we have a protocol in place, and not everyone will be privy to the same information."

"Why not tell the team? Jonathan, keeping things from the other members of the project, seemed obsessive. The other graduates were my age. We would bring energy into the midst. Keeping information from them didn't sit well with me. I insisted again. "I thought we were all working toward the same goal?"

Jonathan watched my face for a moment in silence. "This is important to the success of the project. I need you to be discreet."

I paused. Jonathan had made up his mind. Did I have a choice? No. But I was curious enough to go along with it for now. "Fine."

"Good. I can tell you this much…" Jonathan's face reflected his excitement now as he continued, "We have found an alloy unlike anything we have ever seen, and we need you to tell us its composition."

"Where did you find it?"

"When we get there, my friend… When you get there."

"Is this part of components from Earth?

"This is what I want you to tell me."

A part of me was still skeptical. "Where else could it come from, Jonathan?" Then I thought again as I watched his face. "Oh… You think it's from space?"

"In due time, my boy. But now you understand why this is top secret."

24
CLASH
Blast

Facility Perimeter - 2022

The recon served its purpose. We know what we are up against around the perimeter, but now we understand the activity's extent. Inside of the facility is another matter, though. But we still had time to break in tonight. Blast Vlog - DAINN Annals — Summer 2022.

I ducked behind the shrubs, and within seconds, made the foliage grow around me, forming a great natural barrier to curious eyes. My palms glowed with a greenish hue, allowing the energy transfer, and the plant responded to the wave emanating from the tips of my fingers. It now formed natural protection extending outward by several feet in each direction.

Through the NetComm, Leane said, "I'm on my way."

"NetRoger that," I murmured. Conscious that we still had people working the perimeter, I whispered, "There's still a lot of activity. I'm hiding behind a cluster of bushes."

The energy from my hand holding the branch continued to expand the hedged field, now harboring enough room for all of us. In seconds, it became denser with thick fresh leaves, the branches passing over my head.

The guards' voices resonated in the forest's silence, not far away from my position. Their trajectory as they walked brought them closer to my location.

I heard their approach and grimaced. Leane might come upon them if they didn't move on. I quickly typed a warning on my NetComm.

Their physical inferiority played tricks on my ego compared to our extended abilities. I had no doubts about that fact, and Chase was probably responsible for making me feel this way. HellNet, the guy drove me nuts.

The capabilities of ordinary human beings, who until now were at the top of the food chain, paled compared to us. I was sure Chase was more a hindrance than a help. Shaking my head, I couldn't even presume to understand him. But I also knew how I would react in his place. I morosely contemplated what would happen in a conflict scenario between his people and us. It wouldn't be pretty. HellNet, I liked the power, but I wasn't one to enjoy inflicting harm on others, although I did what I had to do for my people. But these Nonets would undoubtedly suffer if we turned to be dominant and in search of power. Thankfully for them, it wasn't our purpose.

I glanced beyond the cover of the leaves. The guards approached my position, moving with noise in the underbrush.

I hoped Leane was not coming up too soon because there was every chance she would stumble on the security team if they didn't move away from the area.

I glanced toward the lower slope, looking for Leane and suddenly saw her running full steam in my direction. I quickly typed, "Stop. The guards are at ten."

Getting out from the open ground took her a split second. But by the time she ducked under the thick foliage, her shimmer still swirled between the trees. She was not stealthy.

Voices echoed behind me. "Hey, did you see that? You... Saw it, right? Over there, between the trees?" Steps stumped the terrain behind us.

"Yeah... Like a shadow that disappeared...."

"No, it was more like a light that lifted off...."

Leane rose her EmVat and made a face on my visor. Her words formed "NetShit."

"Shoot..."

"Where?" the first guard said, looking all around.

"I'm reporting it..." the second guard announced.

With its cloaking device, the EV now kept her from being seen. She positioned herself behind a tree, watching the guards.

The guards stood around, looking as if they had seen or heard ghosts—one of them, not taking any chances, reached for its comm device. "We have...."

I couldn't let that happen. I got out of the hideaway cloaked and moved in the blink of an eye. My body, capable of lethal force, appeared behind them. My mixed martial arts and combat style were my own, and I was good at it. I barely touched the ground as I positioned myself over the shoulder of the first man. Whatever I did was amplified by air fighting, hovering behind both guards now. I knocked the one reaching for his communication device with a swift move of my right hand, striking a blow against the guy's neck. I inflicted blows that would not cause permanent damage.

The guard fell to the ground at my feet, unconscious.

The other guard turned at the noise, "What the hell...."

He instantly joined his partner.

Leane chuckled and began her walk toward me.

"Darnet... It is too much fun," I whispered as I watched Leane's approach.

Leane bent over to check on the unconscious guys. Her face guilty, she said, "They'll wake up in a few hours with a major hangover."

"Huh... Huh... And I will be in trouble with Tesh."

"Yes, but it was my fault. I had too much fun running," Leane continued sternly.

Then, she turned toward me with a smile, "You haven't lost your touch with this maneuver."

"How can I? I perfected it," I boasted with a proud smirk.

Leane glanced in my direction. "I know your reputation for your forceful maneuver with the flip of your hand. I also know that you can gracefully inflict an instant knockout on the biggest assailant. You can paralyze a much bigger guy than this one with just two moves," she finished, proud of me.

"Yeah, but I am scared of our fearful leader. What does it say about me?" I said with a grim face. I then glanced at Leane, remaining still beside me. Her expression revealed nothing.

"It was my mistake. I'll let Tesh know," Leane said, appearing calm while getting on the NetComm. "Tesh, we need you for a wipe."

Tesh's face appeared on both of our visors. "What happened?" she said, in control.

"Two guards," whispered Leane. "They saw my trail."

Tesh nodded, showing no reaction. "I'll be up in a moment." It was as if she experienced a stakeout in a different time zone a million times before, but we knew better. We understood how much she hated what she would have to do.

In our way, we looked formidable and fearless. Our capabilities served us differently as events unfolded.

I shook my head, looking up the hill. "So, they have been at this for four years. I'm not sure what triggered this much security up there, but it must be a major find. The bulk of the teams arrived already and reinforced the entire area. And they're intense."

I lifted both guards and carried them down the hill, away from the fence.

Leane kept watching the grounds behind me. "Maybe they are preparing for the new arrivals?"

"I need to get inside," I concluded.

Leane watched the security feed on her visor. "The biometric system is pretty advanced even if we can breach it, but the scan would probably pick you up and set the alarm. Let's find a different way in."

"There are ground motion sensors that will trigger an alarm. I don't know where they are yet. The gate system engages visual iris patterns, touch, and voice recognition. A bit of an overkill... If you get my meaning," I said. "You touch it or come near it, and it will activate, and if you're not in the system, everything goes crazy."

"Maybe we can give the patrols something to go crazy over...." Leane said with a thoughtful expression. "This way, we can get closer?"

"We always have our suits," I said.

Leane smiled in my direction. "I need to stay close to the mountain for a scan. It'll make it easier."

My eyes went to her face. I hated these and the effect they had on her. They kind of shook me up. Part of it was my aversion to close quarters, but a correct assessment had to do with Leane herself. A scan contained risks none of us could estimate.

Hesitantly, I nodded. "All right, but while we wait, there is something I want to do." My EmVat disappeared.

The night had settled around us, wrapping us in darkness. We were out of the way of the patrols. So, I pulled Leane against me. "Drop your suit," I whispered.

Leane's face registered surprise. "We already have a mess on our hands." she whispered, but she dropped her suit in the same breath.

My hands lifted to encase her face, and I tugged her a step closer. Her body set against mine felt right. Looking into Leane's eyes, I said, "HellNet, we slept in cryo for too long. We stayed inside the Sphere for four years. Darnet, I won't wait anymore. We are on our own here. We don't have to give an account to anyone. I want this...."

Leane's eyes never left mine until I stopped talking, and her gaze dropped to my lips. It was enough of a signal for me to move. I closed the gap between us and kissed her.

Her head tilted as my lips touched hers. Her mouth opened under my own. Carnal need rose in me, and I knew this was right between us. I wanted more, but this had to be enough for now. It was the first step toward something more.

With a ragged breath, I slowly released her.

25
SURVEILLANCE
Tesh

Off-Grid Facility, CA - 2022

There is no alternative. The time lost in the Sphere plays against them. Tesh and her Conclave must infiltrate the Center to get their people out and make a play for the Sphere itself. And they must locate Streak. Tesh Vlog - DAINN Annals — Summer 2022.

After Blast and Leane departed to survey the activities on the mountain, I reviewed the surveillance feed Blast had placed around the perimeter of the cabin and positioned one of the last Custodians near the back gate. It was part of our defense system around the property, since these grounds were now our new location.

The evening air, balmy, smelled of a sweet scent of pine. The forest sounds reached us at night, forming a cocoon of noise I had never heard before. My senses, heightened by the novel experience, registered everything, classifying each one for recognition and reconciliation into our database.

The silence, a welcomed relief since we exited the Chamber, allowed me to process everything that had happened since we awoke.

When I finished calibrating the sensitivity field, I inquired, "What are you going to do?"

Chase stood by my side, indecisive. "I'm not sure. If I go to my parents, I will have to deal with my family. They think I'm dead." He shrugged and continued, "Who knows when I will be back? I suppose I can call them, but it's lame. Jonathan must be here. I must assume he stayed on schedule, which means who knows what. If I am here, I might do some good, discover what they have and slow them down."

Mage got up from the porch and joined us in the backyard.

"Mage wants out," Tesh said. "Let him."

"Okay." Mage ran to the back gate. "Go, boy," I said. He quickly entered the edge of the forest. "You're not worried he could get lost?"

"No. Mage will be fine. You will need to take sides at some point, Chase. I am sorry about your family. I am... For everything they went through since you disappeared. But we need you here, at the Center."

"What are you saying? There is a line I won't cross, Tesh."

Chase turned away, frustrated. He disappeared inside the cabin to reappear with two beers in his hands. He handed me one. "Here, try this. It's beer. You drink it."

"I know what beer is, Chase," grabbing the can. The beer was refreshing and tasted smooth on my tongue.

"You have it in your time. Good to know we haven't destroyed everything worthwhile." He said as he sat in one of the wooden chairs behind me.

"Yes, although it comes in different packaging."

"Look, Tesh; this situation can quickly become untenable if you expect me to spy for you. As of now, I have been out of the loop for four years. I'm not sure what you expect for me to do."

"The Earth got nearly destroyed... Our future was nothing like what you grew up and lived through, certainly nothing like this, Chase. You can't begin to comprehend the ravages we witnessed in our lifetime. Every day was a fight for survival. When DAINN came along, things got better. But the generations that came after you never got it easy. You did a Darnet job at disseminating enough garbage on this planet that, in the future, it no longer is the home you know."

"Will you show me?"

How could I show the destruction we faced on our planet by 2098? In truth, I didn't know how to explain its scope. "It's a lot to take in."

"Come on, Tesh. I can take it. Besides, it may help to know what is truly at stake."

Tesh hesitated for a moment. "Fine, but don't say I didn't warn you... Come here. It may be better to sit down for this journey," and her voice resonated with irony.

I joined her near the two wooden chairs on the veranda overlooking the backyard. With a swap of her hand, she moved one chair in front of the other and sat down.

Eager for the experience, I dropped in the other and waited.

"You will feel the same thing we did on the mountain, only this time I will do the sharing, like when I showed you the various images of my childhood. Just relax and stay open to me."

Chase nodded, his face getting whiter when he suddenly became anxious at the idea of experiencing another reading. I registered his hesitation and said, "I won't be reading you this time, just sharing. Close your eyes and relax."

The plunge into Chase's mind did not take long, as I had already learned his pathways. But the sharing with him, filled with intensity, took me by surprise.

The experience left me shaken, living once again our planet's losses. It hurt to contemplate our destruction, especially now that we saw how beautiful our Earth had been, even if I witnessed it daily in our future. How does one prepare for such a loss? How does one accept the destruction? It was an impossibility not to feel sick about what we had done. With my stomach reacting and nausea filling my throat, I slowly withdrew from Chase's mind.

When I finished, Chase got up abruptly, obviously shaken.

The silence between us continued, longer than I expected, and then he whispered, "Maybe some other time you can explain how… Right now, I just need to process all of it."

I remained where I was as he walked away from me and finally said, "Chase, the fact is, you own us. All of you do. So, if I'm insensitive to your family dilemma now, well, you'll have to excuse me. But you can't go back, Chase. Not now."

Chase nodded and began making a list on a small notebook. "I'll leave this on the kitchen counter. These are items that might be helpful to have on hand."

Although we only used it on occasions, our replicator hidden inside one casing could provide almost everything. Most of the time, we took advantage of Blast's gifts. "Chase?"

He looked at me, deep in thoughts. "There are a few things I should explain before I go…."

"You can't go see your family, Chase."

I wondered if it was wise to let Chase even go to town. His usefulness served us better within the walls of the Center. At least for now… It would give us someone to call upon if the need arose.

Chase nodded, "I'm not going anywhere… The priorities have changed. But I need some time to call my parents." He looked thoughtful and sad as he sipped from the can, looking at his cell phone."

I took the device in my hand and looked at it. "We're not going anywhere besides the facility." It was an antiquated model of communication that appeared rather rudimental. "I can always contact you without it."

"You know how I enjoy that…."

I smiled at him. "All you need is to focus on me when you want to talk."

He shook his head. "How far is your range, anyway?"

I frowned, wondering if I had a range. "I never had to ask myself."

The disbelief on his face spoke volumes. To change the subject, I asked, "Where are your parents?"

"Boston, Massachusetts. Well, we shall test it soon."

I teased him. "Protective already?" *Darnet.* I suddenly hoped I had remained quiet, feeling a blush rising on my face under his insistent eyes. So, I looked away. HellNet, it was a dumb thing to say right now.

Chase smiled back. It was an uneasy smile, but one nonetheless. "I have a stake in the outcome, and you reminded me of a debt." He shrugged as he half-joked.

"I'll leave you to it," and dropped the cell phone back in his hand. With that said, I stepped into the yard and went looking for

Mage. The call Chase was about to make was not straightforward. So, the least I could do was give him privacy.

The last rays of sunlight were now gone. The evening descended over the canopy of leaves. Muffled noises of life and the soft tussle of branches in the breeze whispered through the woods. Mage ran back towards me, his behavior satisfied from exploring the nearby grounds. He carefully dropped a small cat at my feet. The kitten shook his head and waddled on his little legs.

I looked at Mage and smiled. "You found a friend?" I said, picking up the stray and stroking the little kitten. "Is it ok if he keeps it?'

Mage barked.

Chase looked away from his phone, relief on his face. He struggled to reconcile everything and attempted to develop a likely story for his parents. But now, he glanced between my dog and the cat, "Huh... Does Mage picks up stray often?"

"He is a protector. It is in its DNA. The kitten was likely lost."

I realized Chase needed time to make his call as he got up and moved inside the cabin. "Sure... I'll get some tuna."

I tasted the outside with every breath, with each beat of my heart, but remained on the porch. The dark of the night surrounding the cabin suited us. It was an excellent spot to hide.

While Chase set up things for the kitten, he talked about the infrastructure of his time through the open doorway. And as he explained things, a picture of his world formed in my mind. It correlated to what I had grasped from the MindLandscape, giving me a deeper understanding of this world.

This environment was ours now as we inhabited these parts. I learned more about people and how things worked by listening to Chase.

Chase was thorough. He talked for the better part of the hour and then headed into the backyard, his phone in hand.

Once alone in the cabin, I monitored the progress of Blast and Leane for a little while. Then, I dove into finding out more about this time to facilitate dealing with our mission. In all of it, I was giving Chase his moment with his family.

While I perused the television programs that provided insights, giving me access to some cultures and values. I absorbed everything I could in the next hour. Most of it appeared, at first, superficial with self-absorbed tendencies spread across social media platforms. Nonsensical trivial things seemed to hold the attention of most networks until the news began. Traditional media focused on a crisis, dealing with issues relevant to a current pandemic the world faced. The struggle appeared to start in 2019 while we were in the Sphere. It resembled one of the many challenges we met in the future, notably the pandemic of 2040. At the moment, all networks got lost in the data as the death mounted around the globe. It appeared in a cursory fashion that nothing else competed for attention.

Going back through our history, I understood that these new global health issues pushed the development of our Nanotechnology and implants. Undoubtedly, faced with this type of global impact, our world scientists began to consider other advantageous solutions to a worldwide health crisis.

The survival challenges we contended with during our time did not take center stage here. Climate change, if mentioned, did not yet matter much, at least not the way we dealt with it in our time, as the long-term importance to the health of our planet remained our daily focus. This indifference to the state of Earth triggered the path for the worst. I knew this from our history.

The SRC Conclave would influence this in a big way. Some geopolitical issues found their way into the news cycle but only warranted a few hours of exploration and discussions. The news focused instead on business interests and updates due to the pandemic and its impact on the economy, including the activities of particular leaders. The Company Conclave would enjoy running circles around some of these guys. I learned much in these instants. Yet, the key events that would soon topple our world remained obscure. The Institute Conclave will identify the issues directly influencing the outcomes we faced in 2098. The insight I gained in the quiet of the cabin was valuable.

A plan formed in my head; I knew what to do once we retrieved all our members. Once the other Conclaves joined this timeline, we would affect the flow of information. It is where we would begin.

But there were many other causes, like the drive for higher economic returns, the chase for power, and greed. Even in the future, it remained the root of our problem. The state of our world in our time was a clear example that we had learned nothing.

I noted the companies' names and CEOs; we would soon need to impact these. Their organizations' activities would serve as a strong starting point now compiled in our database. Wherever they affected change for the worst, we would intervene. We would seek to trigger events that would do the opposite. Achieving positive results would require our entire team—all five Conclaves, working together to shift the emphasis and the tide of a future otherwise without hope.

I smiled. Benevolence influenced public opinion. These steps appeared to be the best way to derive outcomes without using the bulk of my powers.

The Company Conclave would also enjoy this. Because from what I could surmise, so long as the enterprises and their CEOs held the reins of power, satisfaction would remain guaranteed. Determining agendas and providing a little competition in the right direction couldn't hurt. I knew who was precisely suited to do just that within our Conclaves.

My visor opened on Leane. Her face appeared strained, but she was straightforward as she said, "Tesh, we need you for a wipe."

I schooled my face. "What happened?" I said, in control.

"Two guards," whispered Leane. "They saw my trail."

I nodded, showing no reaction. "I'll be up in a moment." Once the NetComm was off, I got up to get my gear. It was time for me to join the others.

The door opened, and Mage grunted from his spot near the kitten who had wrapped itself near his head.

Chase appeared in the living room doorway, his face set in a stern look. "All done here," he said.

"Leane called in. I have to go."

"Want some coffee before we hit the road?" Not waiting for an answer, he walked into the kitchen. "Did you eat anything?"

"No. I learned instead."

"Oh?"

"Yeah, I watched the news and went through your internet."

"Not all of it, I hope?"

"Enough… There is a global pandemic. Many of your people have died."

"Really? How bad is it?"

"Bad… It is not as bad as what we saw in 2040, but it seems to spread easily. No wonder we adopted Nanos as quickly as we did."

"Really? How does it work?"

I walked over to the door. "I am going to meet the others."

Chase poured his coffee and served me one. "I need fuel. I'll show up at the gate and ask to see Jonathan."

I took the cup and looked at the dark liquid. "I'm not sure… We don't drink it like this."

The black liquid didn't look too appealing, but smelled good. I took a sip and grimaced. "Nope." It was way too bitter for my taste.

"What do you put with it?"

"All kinds of things."

"With milk then?" Chase took the cup back and poured the milk into it. "Try this." He handed me a cup.

I did. It was slightly better, but still lacked something.

Chase saw that in my face and retrieved the cup from my hand. "Sweet it is…." He poured a spoon full of sugar and added it to the mix. "I think this should do the trick."

I tasted the coffee again, and this time found it more to my liking. "We add a few things to coffee."

"What else do you use?"

"You know, huh, this and that?"

Should I tell him that our additions to the coffee concoction gave us optimum performance based on our metabolism and were the norm in my time? Probably not, and so I remained silent. Instead, jokingly, I said, "At this rate, if we are to show you all the things we can do, you may be ancient before you get to see them all."

Chase grimaced at the thought.

I immediately regretted my joke because I could see Chase's neurons turning. Now embedded inside Chase's mind, a notion existed and flashed an alarm bell. "You get old, now, don't you?"

"Well… We age… But we don't change," I whispered, now ill at ease with the subject.

"What? You mean to tell me I'll look like your father twenty years from now, and you won't change at all?" Chase looked at me to gain confirmation.

I heard the disbelief in his voice and cringed.

The disappointment pummeled him. "How is that even possible?"

"Nanobots, genetic engineering, and implants," I answered matter-of-factly. "It also keeps us healthy. We no longer suffer the effects of a worldwide pandemic. We just don't get sick anymore."

His reaction to the news left him completely silent.

I could see that he was affected, although he tried to hide it. But knowing this reality about us was better for him. Chase had a crush on me because of the link. But there couldn't be a future for us. Chase would grow old while I remained the way I appeared today. I sighed.

Melancholy settled on Chase, his hope and desire dashed. His daydreaming about me became a stupid fantasy in a flash, an instant that ultimately killed the dream. It was better that way. Eradicating any ideas, he may have in his head was indeed a good thing. Since Chase had met me, he had held some hope; I could feel it growing between us. I intended to destroy it now before it went any further. "I won't change. It is also why we were discouraged from entertaining any relationships with Nonets. It can't work. Besides, our people paired us."

Chase's face fell. "Nonets?"

I shrugged. "People from your time. People without Imps. People not connected to the System."

In one statement, I disintegrated any hope in his mind. The disappointment trickled down from his eyes to his mouth, which tightened when he clenched his jaw. His hope vanished like grains of sands carried away by a wave on a day at the beach.

I held my stare steadfast in the moment. *It is better that way.*

Chase walked to the door and turned on his way out, looking like he may say something more. After a beat, he then whispered, "I assume you are going up ahead?"

"Yes. My team needs me, but I can give you a lift?"

"No. I need to deal with my family and time to think about the walk-up. I will contact you when I can."

"Okay…"

Chase nodded, his eyes focused on mine. "Be careful."

I smiled. "We always are."

Satisfied with that, Chase headed toward the forest, dialing his phone.

I watched Chase leave with Mage at my side and then said, "Okay, boy, you stay here and keep watch." I left a small window open for my dog to access the backyard if he needed it. Then, with Mage inside, I locked the door behind me and ventured back into the forest, cutting away from where Chase moved ahead as he talked to his family.

It is better… Better… Why do I feel like NetShit?

In the dense part of the forest, the ground soft under my feet called for stillness. I stopped my advance. The deeper I went, the stronger the pull. So, I stood surrounded by thick tree trunks, some of them by their looks, at least three hundred years old. The branches, encouraged by the soft breeze, bristled their song. The hum of the leaves lightly shifting created a melody that filled my heart, soaring inside my genes, allowing me to recharge. No wonder Leane was so in awe of the place. If I could feel this way, she must get this tenfold.

I closed my eyes and focused on listening. The surrounding nature soothed my body into calmness. In the stillness of my surroundings, I reached a perfect clarity of thoughts. I pushed away all emotions and became present, aware, and knowing.

While connected to the forest grounds, I saw our path. My eyes settled on the sky above when I emerged from my meditation. For the space of an instant, I watched the dance made by the leaves under the breeze. I breathed the fresh air. I admired the few stars devoid of the angry cloud patterns we found in our time. The experience freed me. It was like escaping our training in Ang. It reminded me of flying over the buildings to reach the high canopy of the dome. Only here, I didn't need our EmVats to achieve the same satisfaction.

Refreshed and reborn, I followed the promise of an answer to our dilemma, for the shape of my thoughts led me to our next move. Determined, I now ran up the forest grounds to get back with my team, leaving a streak of gold behind me.

Each step confirmed how much this environment differed from the life we had left behind. The Earth under my feet remained the same. It was still my planet, and yet it showed itself to be so different, composed of many nutrients nonexistent in our time.

Suddenly, I heard the surf. The ocean was near, and I could listen to it. It was the ocean we explored with Leane when she scanned the cave. I wanted to see it from the cliffs above, so I followed my instinct as it cried out at me. I reached the ridge and looked down. The water crashed into the sand below, but it looked beautiful even in the dim light. In no way did it resemble anything like our ocean. It was not tumultuous and dreary. It was not angry and ugly. It was instead a mighty ocean, serene, pristine, and blue.

I dropped, lured by something on the cliffs, leading to the stretch of sand below. My feet hit the sandy beach in no time. I loved its feel under my boots and its gentle golden hue. The light color mixed with small pebbles and slightly more massive boulders spread among seaweed in places, and the smell of salt overwhelmed my nostrils. The remote expanse of the beach followed a near-perfect croissant as it hugged the rock formation of the cliffs. Dark shadows appeared against the ridge, forming gaping holes in the backdrop of the mountain.

Drawn to them, I walked to find an entry to the caves. I resisted going in because Leane and Blast waited for me, and I had already meandered too much. Still, this was a place to explore next.

I darted fast up the cliff and through the forest. My freedom of movement enhanced my speed. Exhilaration filled me. A surge of adrenalin coursed through my entire body, and I laughed. My voice echoed in the trees as I progressed fast on the grounds.

This place didn't belong to us, but it did, part of an inheritance based on our ancestors going back centuries.

I increased my speed and ran faster, leaving a golden trail behind me.

As always, we turned this into a game. Our way of coping. The impossible situation that brought us all here for what may be forever gave us new freedom. In this quest... Nothing seemed out of reach because of our powers. We could do almost anything except reveal what set us apart and disclose who we were.

The playground stretched ahead.

I glided up the slope. The landscape released the pressure of the last few hours. It will keep our sanity in the days ahead, allowing us to maintain a semblance of normality, and helping us reconnect with ourselves again. For a moment, I forgot the bounds that anchored us here. Our people, our family, and the tasks that our mandate dictated we perform.

I knew this was what had happened to Leane. She forgot because, for one split second, she was carefree. I would not begrudge her that. I slowed and turned on my EmVat, disappearing under the trees.

Identifying the events that would destroy everything would not be easy, but I had to believe that we could do it. We would succeed because there was no other choice. I couldn't imagine the destruction of this place in the years ahead. I wouldn't let it happen. I couldn't.

I looked around, trying to spot Leane and Blast. My eyes searched between the trees.

I ran up the slope to higher grounds in stealth mode until the forest changed, leading to rocky paths and boulders. Further away from civilization, it felt as if this side of the mountain belonged to us.

And then, I saw them as I came upon them against a tree. "Hum…"

Leane's hand flew to her mouth. Her cheeks flamed under my gaze when she saw me standing there. The blood rose to her face again, transforming it into a blush that couldn't go unnoticed.

I said, "Well, I hope this is not what triggered why you need my help."

Leane's eyes rolled up, "No… Never."

"Hum… Okay, then." Having witnessed their exchange, I paused, waiting for an explanation.

They parted, avoiding looking at me.

When neither of them gave me an answer, I added, "I know you enjoyed this obviously, but I'm sure you didn't get into a fight deliberately, so... Where are the men you knocked out?"

Blast shrugged, feeling guilty. I could see that in his face. But he was not upset about kissing Leane. He disliked having me clean up a mess they caused by inadvertence. "They can't remember us, Tesh."

"I was careless, running," said Leane.

"I need you to heed me, Blast. Unless this is indispensable, we cannot engage," I insisted, "I won't go poking in people's brains every time you exercise your fighting skills."

"I avoided a bigger problem. The guards could have reported Leane's trail and created more questions in these parts."

I nodded, "I know, and that is the only reason I'm not cross with you about that. But I am crossed about you not telling me about you two." And I smiled. "It's about time if you want to know what I think."

Leane and Blast both reacted with surprise and guilt. They were still processing their moment.

I had pushed Chase away. Streak and I may never be together. But at least someone in our team would be happy, and they both deserved it.

I had just given them a nudge and my approval.

They were now smiling as they looked into each other's eyes.

Within seconds, I forgot they were even there and focused on both men on the ground, hidden by shrubbery.

I was a Shaper. I penetrated minds and removed their memories. If I wasn't willing to do this for our mission, the implications were significant for all of us. It would make things so much more difficult. But for the first time since we landed here, I understood that while it should remain my decision and not what the Institute expected me to do, my role was crucial. I understood I would have to make more sacrifices for my team and this world's well-being. I was all right with that, and maybe that is why the leaders chose me.

When I finished, some time had passed. I hugged Leane and Blast and moved up the slope without a word.

Forest Grounds, CA - 2022

The images replay in my mind. There is no way to comprehend how badly we mismanaged Earth until one faces the extent of the devastation. Our planet dies slowly, taking with it millions of species. It is humankind's accomplishment, our ultimate legacy, and slow extinction, unless.... ChaseVlog - DAINN Annals – Summer 2022.

The sharing did not hurt physically, that is. But they did not prepare me for the immense chock of watching a devastated Earth in the years ahead. I could not have imagined the horrid impact we had on our environment. The emotional ramifications hit me hard, yet the evidence of our actions lay plain in front of my eyes and could not be denied.

The experience, far from the reading, progressed smoothly. It was like watching a film on the walls of my mind, except for the emotions that surged through me as the images flashed by in my thoughts, providing much more than what I was eager to see. I cringed inwardly as the mosaic of moments sped forward, more painful than I could have imagined. It left me shaken to no end.

Tesh brought me into the world of Ang, at first. Under the domes, each with their specialized utility serving the community, things appeared organized and beautiful. "We have come far to protect what we hold dear, but it is not enough," she said in a disturbingly low voice.

It became quickly apparent that everything had a purpose within Ang. Our technical advancement spoke of extraordinary achievements made by necessity. The domes, clear under a turbulent sky that kept changing colors under heavy winds and severe thunder, brought me awe. "It is truly amazing," I whispered.

"It is necessary," she replied. Until this moment, I did not know how much.

Indeed, the domes were transparent, but their force field held strong. Inside, the day appeared clear, almost sunny apart from the changing hue that played havoc over our heads as the clouds drifted fast across the expanse of the domes. Within the city, the ravages of climate change seemed at first inconsequential. But we did not stay inside the domes.

Once outside, my eyes adjusted to the difference in light. The pastel tones shifted to dark hues. Black charcoal swirled with deeper blues.

The never-ending winds assaulted us, tumultuous and unruly swelling around us like demons. The arrowing gale never lit up, casting small ground fragments, sand, pebbles, and shards everywhere.

Tesh anchored herself to the ground with her adjustable boots to withstand their force, fighting to move forward. I saw her shifting on her feet as a large piece flew in her direction, extending a shield to block it. The rounded field spread wide, protecting her. The projectile bounced around, lighting the net, and moved on with the gust, carried to another destination. There was no ending to the turmoil. But it was not the most drastic of site.

Tesh's eyes shifted, and her head moved to the right. Barely discerning shapes ahead, I focused on what she wanted me to see.

Beyond the whirlwind, the deserted landscape with specters of what used to be trees stood like phantoms of a time past, their trunks twisted by the elements. It was a foreboding sight, to be sure, but not yet the worst of what would occur on this journey to our future.

A blanket of night surrounded the city, with hundreds of thousands of golden lights shimmering within the central dome protecting the Golden Ghetto and Water's Edge. It was a beautiful view with the other domes extending past it, bringing different colors peaking within; the green of Emerald Field, the slight blues of CliffsTop, and the subtle orange and purple of ArchWay Pass. Ang stood like a jewel in an isolated island of peace. Our people appeared safe, but it was not to be for the tranquil vision changed abruptly.

I saw Tesh run from her bed to the balcony of her room as an alarm resonated within the city walls. At first, I did not notice the change. But the dome field, weakened by the pelting rain and rising seas levels, flickered in the distance. It suddenly crashed by the shoreline. Simultaneously, above the GG, the tenuous threads of the canopy faltered, assaulted by the still pounding rain. In the next moments, I witnessed droves of shuttles taking flight from the Presidential tower in the direction of Water's Edge.

Within minutes, a flood from the ocean rushed toward the Plaza, tumbling over the streets, washing away everything in its wake. It toppled structures, crashing over doors and windows, invading buildings, swirling around corridors and spaces, changing order into chaos. Its water mounted swiftly, toppling trees on its way and penetrating further into the city. The roar of the water became quickly overwhelming.

Tesh moved quickly, getting her gear on in seconds and making her way to a small platform where an Airbike waited. She jumped on it and took flight toward the buildings pounded by the ocean. "What are you doing?" I murmured, but she never answered.

I could not tell what Tesh planned. But as the dome dropped its protective envelope on the city, I understood that she played a vital role in the unfolding scene. There was little room to control the rising panic between the winds and the untamed sea as the screams rose in the night. While the high winds picked up, Tesh maneuvered her AirBike over the tumult erupting below. In that next instant, I came to understand her function. Her face held a resolute concentration as her eyes moved over the ruins. One hand on her bike, the other stretched ahead of her as if to encompass the entire scene; she whispered, *Hold on, we are coming. Calm yourselves, go up into the buildings. The EHAF is sending relief.*

In her social role as a Shaper of Thoughts and a Phenom to boot, she communicated with the people of Ang city. She brought reassurance and order in a chaotic moment, issuing information, chasing fear and loneliness, giving direction to save those now stranded in the debris and the floundering structures. Turning suddenly in a different direction, she narrowed her focus on a separate area near the river banks. *Streak, people are cut off near the Water's Edge Park. They need extraction.* The echo of streak's voice responded quickly, *NetRoger that.*

Tesh's Airbike wobbled in the high winds and lost its altitude. She quickly pushed the engine to rectify her position, but it did not work. The small vehicle swayed some more, and she lost control, tumbling toward the rushing water below.

A sturdy frigate flying nearby swiveled on its axis and opened a rear cargo door. As Tesh's body tumbled, she let go of her Airbike and pushed the NetJet of her boots to stabilize her fall. In the screaming wings, she oriented herself toward the door. Test twisted her body and launched her head down into the cargo hold in a magnificent display of control and purpose.

The shuttles fought the winds and the pelting rain, evacuating civilians and rounding up the broken bodies. Soon, I witnessed a number of them toppling in stiff gusts and crashing to the ground with horror. Some even impaled themselves on buildings losing control as they attempted a landing to board evacuees. The entire city landscape had turned into a complete war zone.

They were soon replaced in the sky by robust cruisers and battle frigates, more prominent in their sizes and less maneuverable among the skyscrapers. Flying over areas near the shoreline revealed more broken structures and flooded streets, bodies floating among the debris and beating the jetty. But it was not all…

Tesh took me to another place where the panorama diverged entirely from what I knew. The snow of icecap regions was no more. The artic white immensity of land we were used to was no longer there, replaced by vast water areas. The ocean was all that remained, much higher in this unwanted future. It covered the old habitats of over two hundred species no longer alive.

I witnessed images of multiple cruisers and carriers. They dropped over small remnants of receding land, rescuing with ZNets herds of Porcupine Caribou and reindeer, penguins, white polar bears, arctic wolves, foxes, weasels and hares, brown and collared lemmings, ptarmigans, gyrfalcons, and snowy owls. Later, I saw some of these species inside an artificial habitat under out-of-the-way domes within Ang city. But the number of these various animals did not represent half of what these were once. Perhaps they had not adapted to their new location. Maybe the food was simply lacking, or something else I did not want to ask happened.

As we moved south, forests decimated by fires spread for many kilometers or miles. While some remained in places extending over the land, they looked anything but healthy. *We are fighting an infestation that destroyed over two billion hectares. We have lost over fifty percent of the thirty-one percent that covered our planet. We are slowly losing that battle despite our efforts.*

A kaleidoscope of shores came up next, now invaded by higher seas around the globe. We had lost entire coastal cities, and what remained were now skeletal structures abandoned long ago. These included the vestige of some of our most significant metropolises. *We have lost many cities, like Miami, New York, Tokyo, Shanghai, Kolkata, Dhaka, Osaka, Mumbai, Guangzhou, and Shenzen. Many others have been drastically affected, like Norfolk and Hampton, Virginia, Ocean City Maryland, Galveston, Texas, Redwood City, San Mateo, and Alameda, California, Cambridge, Massachusetts, Pompano Beach, Hollywood, Fort Lauderdale, Davie, Hialeah, and Plantation, Florida, Mount Pleasant, Hilton Head Island, and Charleston, South Carolina, as well as Honolulu, Hawai.* Instead of hearing a maybe in all of this, I saw the results first-hand, and it brought a new perspective of what awaits us.

But the journey was still not over for we made another stop this time within Ang city again, and I got a different appreciation of what Tesh's people were doing and what Ang truly represented.

We approached a series of domes interlaced closely together. As we entered the first one, a group of four people walked carefully beside a short platform. They slowly maneuvered toward a stretch of sand near a water area. It looked like a small pond, but it behaved like a sea as the water softly pounded its shores. I stopped to look further. The stretcher or metallic gurney was lowered to the ground, and the people moved back. After a few minutes, the small form moved its head, and I recognized a small seal. The little creature looked around, slithered off the metallic platform to the sand, and purposely made its way to the water.

Tesh smiled as she watched its progress. *They rescued it about four weeks ago. We did not think it would make it, but Leane was called, and she brought it back to life. A team at the SRC dedicates a lot of time to do this. They venture out regularly to rescue the animals that remain once DAINN identifies a location.*

Tesh brought me next to a giant aquarium filled with seawater under another dome. It looked serene and not so artificial. Indeed, amidst coral reefs, all kinds of sea life thrived there. Fish of all sizes swam in pristine blue water. I watched dolphins, orcas, sharks, and many others unknown to me. *We maintain this as a preservation park for the species that can no longer survive in the current acidity of the oceans, but we cannot do more. We do not have the resources.*

Farther ahead, we left the water park and moved to a giant aviary, where all kinds of species of birds made a cacophony of sounds. The noise was deafening, but somehow, after the eternal winds outside, it became a reprieve stemming from life, and I welcomed it. *We are rounding more species daily, but there are so many we have lost. The SRC dedicates a lot to these programs despite our dwindling reserves.*

Tesh turned toward a giant wall blocking the view to another area. As we approached, we walked up a sizeable mounting pathway, reaching the top of the structure. When we arrived at the top, I could see a vast plain with all kinds of vegetation and within meandering streams, and calm lakes. I observed many animals of various sizes, including elephants moving slowly on the ground, giraffes reaching high among branches, panthers, lions, zebras, and so much more. We remained there a long time in the serenity of this moment as life spread at our feet. *This preserve is not by any means enough land, and we are expanding as we can with our resources, but it is a balancing act. Many of our scientists within the SRC work here. It was one of my favorite programs growing up.*

A long sigh escaped Tesh's lips before she turned away saying no more. *I can share many other things, but we do not have all day.*

The images faded from my mind, and I faced a wall of darkness before I understood that the show had ended. When Tesh left my mind, it took me a moment to come back to reality, although I opened my eyes abruptly and got up, impatient to get away from the visions. My heartbeat thundered in my chest, and my voice was raw with sadness when I whispered. "Maybe some other time you can explain how. Right now, I just need to process all of it."

When I returned to the present, unsure how long the visions lasted, I did not have a voice to impart the realization that hit me. The conclusion was simple in its scarcity of explanation: our beautiful world as we knew it was gone. Ang city served as a refuge for those who remained. Part of me wondered how many other cities still stood just like this one?

Dominique Luchart

27 ASSETS
Logan

Sommerville Mansion, MA - 2018

We are in the room to meet and celebrate. But somehow, it doesn't feel like a party. The research holds murky challenges and hidden dangers for many of us. I can feel that. DAINN Annals, Summer 2022.

"A toast every one… To the Center. We will pave the way to a better tomorrow," said Jonathan as he entered the room, a glass of champagne in his hand.

I heard that, and my mind raced. We knew so little about the research or the terms of the program. It left me with a bunch of questions. How far were these people willing to go for the sake of the research?

Scientific discoveries continued to expand in many areas. While I recognized some fields Jonathan selected to focus on, they did not appear the most beneficial to our society, but what did I know? Yet, based on the emphasis the Center gave them, they would be dramatically influential in our future.

Today, instead of getting answers, I only had more questions. The puzzle pieces formed a tapestry I still couldn't quite make out, and here we were, leaving in a few hours.

The room filled with recent graduates, and those who arrived here were from all over, excited by the opportunity offered to them. I observed a lot of pretty geeked faces as they entered and moved toward the center of the vast area.

Gen looked around, searching for someone, eyes drifting over the crowd.

I lifted my eyebrows and glanced at her with a question.

She shrugged, with a smile, as she bantered with Zoe Silas, a slip of a girl who did not fit among us. Her arts and humanities background made me wonder what Jonathan had in mind when he included her among our team. Moments ago, she had stood alienated until Gen brought her into our group after none of the other scientists deemed her worthy of their attention. Left on the sidelines, she remained alone and would probably still be there if it had not been for Gen. Our brilliant non-conformist made a B-Line for her and dragged her into our midst.

I smiled at the memory. Gen was one of the most exciting additions, a brilliant self-deprecating woman. I dare say there was something between us as we looked at each other.

I didn't have the heart to turn m back on a pretty lady in distress and promptly obliged. Since she had joined us, Zoe's face had opened up, and after two glasses of champagne, the girl seemed to relax. It suited me just fine.

Zoe was now frowning as she attempted to figure out a problem. "Jonathan told me that the department heads were already at the facility, except for our group. But I do not know what he expects from me."

"Yes, most have already begun their work, but I'm sure Jonathan has something in mind. He may want you to be the historian among us," said Gen, smiling reassuringly.

"Well, that maybe, but it's not like he had to go as far as he did to find someone like me. I mean, Oxford is not next door, right?"

I laughed. "I wouldn't worry about that. Jonathan wants an international team. It gives the project credibility."

The others watched our group with disdain as if including Zoe in our circle influenced their opinion and somehow made us less worthy. Although she was from Oxford, and that was something. Sometimes, I forgot how arrogant and "click-ish" scientists were, especially young ones. But, as always, there were some exceptions.

Besides us, Axel Summers was a pleasant guy that fit right in. He was soft-spoken and an ace in aeronautics and astronomic engineering from MIT. I had more in common with him than any of the others. The conversation turned on what we expected at the Center, and I got silent. Who knew?

Our talk got interrupted by one late arrival among the group. Veronica Smooth just appeared at the entrance of the room. She stood there, waiting for an audience, and got quite a response.

The team of scientists quieted down after appraising her. Their gazes told quite a story. Some opened their mouths and remained awe-struck for the better part of a minute before conversations resumed.

I chuckled at their reaction and hid my smile by taking a sip of my drink. Not fast enough, though.

Veronica caught me laughing and raised her chin. While she didn't make a move, her eyes stopped on me after a glance at the crowd.

Comfortable in her lovely skin, she now moved with no hurry toward us, a smile planted on her beautiful face.

Like the others, I watched her slide across the floor. Sure of herself, she knew the unmistakable impact she had on many of us. Veronica would give any woman an inferiority complex and knew it. So, intelligent and gorgeous to boot did not somehow qualify as sufficient attributes when it came down to her.

My glance slipped to Gen and Zoe. These two felt it, and I could see them fold on themselves by her very approach. Competition among women was deadly in most cases. Damn… None of us needed this.

Veronica stopped by our group and pushed her way in, settling across from me. "Hello."

Her voice, exquisitely modulated, sent butterflies to my stomach as she joined our group and introduced herself. And all the while, her gaze never shifted from mine.

Axel standing beside me, murmured, "You hit the jackpot… Or so she wants you to think."

I jabbed him in the ribs. "Who says I want this?" I muttered behind my glass.

Axel laughed and said, "Make them believe it…" looking toward Gen and Zoe.

Oh, brother… The girls were now looking at me as if I had let them down. Figure that one out…

"Will you be a gentleman and get me a drink?" said Veronica as she cut through the others and landed her hand on my arm, ignoring everyone else.

Caught in her snare for at least a moment, I could have said no, but then, I would have genuinely been a pig, and I couldn't do that to any woman. It was not my style, not that Veronica was my style. She was too obvious, too confident, too much of a predator for my taste—a player's player. The girls would not know that.

Resigned, for now, I accepted the idea that I would have to make that clear to them later while the male contingent looked at me with daggers in their eyes. As if I cared… "Why don't you come with me?"

Axel snickered behind us, and I turned toward him. "Don't fear. You'll get your turn."

With Veronica at my side, I made my way toward the bar. "What would you like?"

"Champagne."

"Of course…" Stupid question, undoubtedly.

I ordered the glass and looked around while listening to Veronica talking about her trip. "I thought I would never make it on time."

Already, I could see a path toward my freedom.

A large guy, whose name I didn't remember, but belonging to the Bio-X project, watched us with interest. His look of envy gave me an idea. Veronica mesmerized him, so I signaled him to join us.

He didn't hesitate and cut across the crowd without looking back.

"Hah, here you are, old chap…." I said. Have you met Veronica?"

His eyes roamed her frame with the look of a predator. "My pleasure… I'm Ronan."

These two would get on famously. Relieved, I extricated myself from Veronica and Ronan as he introduced his list of achievements and headed toward the exit.

"Where are you?"

Cutting her off, I said, "There's something I have to do, Veronica... Excuse me."

I walked away from them and stopped near our group to find that Anders Quinn had joined Axel in our group. Axel turned to me and said, "Meet Anders Quinn; he has a degree in Applied Physics and Mechanics from ETH, Zurich in Switzerland."

I smiled at Anders. "Nice to meet you. How is it going?"

"Me, pretty good. I'm not sure about one of our colleagues until about recently, thanks to you," said Anders.

"Oh, how is that?"

He laughed. "You lured away Ronan Phelps, who was a jerk with Brielle Brown Henot. She was just about to send him packing."

Our group looked around and saw Ronan close to Veronica. "Oh, yeah... I met him, and he appeared to be a bit of a hound," I murmured.

"Oh, he is a total prick," said a female voice as she entered our circle.

"Meet Brielle; she has an Economics, Architecture & Science of the City degree with Finance, EPFL, from Yale University, said Anders.

"If it had not been for Anders, I think he would boast a broken nose," Brielle added, without a hint of hesitation.

"Well, at least he is on the other side of the room," said Gen, with a genuine smile.

Brielle laughed at that and said, "Let's hope he stays there. I think he found his kind of company."

She was beautiful, with a mane of long blonde hair framing a face with high cheekbones and blue eyes. She waved at a tall guy talking to Jonathan, who had just entered the room, followed by an older gentleman. Behind him came Steven and another guy.

I grabbed the first drink shooting by me from one of the serving trays. The catering guy went on to the next group. Without hesitation, I took a sip. Then I grimaced because it was not a Scotch. "What in the hell was that?"

"I don't know, but you looked like you could use one," said Anders.

Gen turned toward him and smiled, then inquired at me. "What happened to you? Did Veronica lock you in a closet?" Her voice was teasing, and relief showed on her face. Maybe she was happy to have me back in our group.

I said, "Right," and offered a crooked smile in her direction. "I escaped."

"Good to know," she replied with another smile.

The crowd quieted down as Jonathan and his team finally walked to the front. There was no doubt we were about to learn more about this well-guarded project.

Jonathan smiled and waved at all of us. "Welcome. I trust you have met each other by now, and I hope you've enjoyed the food and the drinks. There is still plenty to go around, so don't stop on my account. But I wanted to take this opportunity to tell you how thrilled I am that you are all here. Tonight, we officially begin our journey on this grand adventure. As we embark on this path of shaping a better future for humanity, I have a late introduction to make, as he joined our group just a couple of days ago. Please welcome among us Dr. Jon Belsor Jorgensen," who just arrived from Oslo. You all know how important our research is and how much we count on every one of you to take us toward new frontiers. Well, Dr. Jorgensen, here will lead the charge."

The older scientists beamed at us, ecstatic, as Jonathan continued. "He will head our new department, which we just enhanced with new funding. His research will focus on space and propulsion for interstellar travel. But I do not wish to dull this party with a long speech, so I encourage you to talk and enjoy the festivities before we board the plane. We will leave in about two hours, and Steven beside me will give you the details on the way out."

"What?" exclaimed Gen, looking around the room, hoping to clarify what she had heard.

"Whoah?" Brielle said, outspoken.

"They want to engage in space travel research?" Axel muttered with a questioning look. "I knew space became the trend with the shuttles and space stations, but our technology is far from being ready for deep space travel."

"Yeah… It seems far away," I whispered.

"Maybe not with what they found," I murmured.

"Do you even know what they found?" Axel inquired.

"Hum… I do, at least some of it, but I cannot discuss it now. Regardless, it was enough to mount an expedition, so obviously, they think it is," I said.

Anders was fixated on me now. I looked toward Gen, morosely standing to the side, observing us both, a frown on her pretty face.

"You don't say?" Axel's curiosity ignited. "So, it's the real thing? Not of this world?" His excitement overcame his doubts.

"It appears so," I said morosely.

Gen nudged me. "What did they find?"

"I can't talk about it," I added, watching Jonathan.

"Come on. Why don't you explain?" Gen said. "I will tell you something you don't know if you open up."

"Really? Why would you tell me?" I said, smiling at Gen.

The girl's eyebrows furrowed together, and her mouth tensed. "We need to stick together."

It surprised me, but I had a feeling that Gen was full of surprises. "So, you have questions too?"

With a serious look, she said, "Plenty."

I nodded. "Me too. Who were you looking for earlier?"

"A friend. He should be here, and he is not. It worries me," Gen said, still searching the room. "He watched my back."

"I see. You think it still needs watching?"

Gen's eyes met mine. "In this crowd? Absolutely."

I nodded. "Well, since Chase is not here, how about I watched yours?" Then, as an afterthought, I asked, "Would his name be Chase, by chance?"

"Yes. You know Chase?" Gen's face lit up. Perhaps a little too much for my taste.

"No, but I heard Jonathan say earlier that he had not heard from Chase today, so he may not make it."

She appeared to think about it for a few minutes. "Okay. You watch mine, and I'll do the same. I know a few things that could be of interest, including the fact that some of the scientists working at the Center have disappeared from their previous labs," Gen whispered in my ear.

Another piece of information appeared to fit right into the conversation I overheard. Uneasy, I murmured, "Now is not the time. Maybe I can give you a bigger picture later. But not now," I said.

The murmurs of the surrounding voices increased as everyone questioned what they heard only moments ago. The only person who did not react as I expected was standing across from me. Gen remained steady, assessing what she had just learned.

I frowned, wondering what else she knew.

28
DOMINANCE
Blast

The Gate Promontory, CA - 2022

None of this feels right. Why are we just now waking up? The Sphere has an agenda. What is it? What has happened? DAINN Annals – Summer 2022.

The guards were still unconscious when Tesh implanted recent memories into their minds as they slept. It was a simple procedure. By the time they woke up, they would be confused and not remember what they saw. The process took her a few minutes, and during that time, Leane and I monitored what was taking place at the facility.

As soon as Tesh finished, I turned to her. "I want to reach the Center and position our tech to get inside."

"Okay, lead the way," Tesh said.

I ran up the pass, but I went around it instead of going by the forest trek, keeping to the mountain. This way, we would approach the gate from above.

Knowing that my green shimmer would lead the way for the girls as they followed me, I sprinted ahead. The blur appeared and disappeared behind the rocks on a path much less traveled by the security team. A strike of moss with deeper shades joined by shimmering sunlight stayed visible only a brief instant before it disappeared in the air. But I knew my team would see it.

Joltingly beautiful, the feeling of freedom in this place could get into one's head. I glanced behind me and saw Tesh and Leane follow my path.

Tesh's mark dissipated differently from mine as she moved around the boulders on the narrow pass. It floated near the rocks' base, creating a golden flash of light, rapid and robust. Leane's was a straight blue pattern, narrow and focused, that quickly burst forth like a laser before it vanished.

We reached the narrow pass and landed on the mountain's upper part, above the gate. It overlooked the fenced area. A series of steep rocks paved the way down to the gate, and we now stood feet above it, facing the heliport.

I slowed down and approached the edge, lying on the ground to observe the area. "The guards have been at it all night. The activity intensified in the last hour as they brought more workforce and security forces," I whispered. "You'll be able to review all this from our feed," as I signaled her to drop on a small rock formation.

Tesh crouched beside me. She witnessed patrols surveying the grounds around a yet unmarked perimeter to the East. The watch expanded outward, way past the landmarks shown to us by the Custodians earlier. "This is a wider perimeter... isn't it?" Tesh whispered at my side.

"Yes, and it looks like it's not over."

The rigor of the operation surprised me.

"Something triggered these measures," Tesh murmured, now flat on the rock at my side.

"Nothing that we can determine on the surface. That's why Leane wants to run a scan inside the facility."

"Leane, where do you want to do this?" Tesh asked as Leane looked around the grounds in her EmVat with the invisibility shield up.

"I think right here…" she said as she got to her knees, her hand extended over one of the solid rocks situated right above the gate.

Tesh watched Leane and said, "We need to get eyes in there… But nothing deep. Just get the lay of the facility."

"It appears to be state-of-the-art for this time. I'll find out about the operating mechanism at the gate and follow the corridors. It's bound to get me into the labs and see what they are working on," murmured Leane, mentally preparing for her scan.

Beside us, Leane focused on the gate, and we could feel her mind slip away from us. Intent on exploring the infrastructure under our very feet, she held on to the rocky surface and released her hold on the moment, leaving her body. In an instant, she stopped being Leane, as we knew her.

This time, Tesh did not tie herself to Leane, as she would typically do on a more in-depth scan. Leane only needed to penetrate the underground corridors and the installation without losing herself.

"Maybe we should put our EmVats on," Tesh suggested. In the next moment, she disappeared from the landscape.

I complied while muttering at Tesh's side, "We landed here hoping to escape scrutiny and instead found prying eyes. How is that for planning?"

"I suspect we are here because we need to be, Blast. For now, it's just a feeling, but I think it will transform into certainty," Tesh murmured. "The weaving of this web holds no coincidences."

"Interesting saying," I said.

"My dad used to say that when we found no answers to our questions other than disjointed facts that appeared unrelated. In his viewpoint and experience, it precisely was why we needed to pay attention," Tesh said.

"So why has the Sphere released us after four years?" I inquired.

Tesh chuckled. "Has it been four years for us? It certainly doesn't feel like it. I thought it was just a few days."

Blast shook his head. "Are you saying what I think you are saying?"

"Huh, Huh… I've been wondering the same thing, but I think it has to do with this below," murmured Tesh. "I believe we will have our answers soon."

"You're talking about time dilation, aren't you?" inquired Blast.

"Yes. I think the Sphere can slow time in its vicinity. I believe that only a few days have passed for us, but I cannot be sure. If I am right four years have passed for the planet. The question is, why?"

"Do you have a theory?"

"Not yet."

We observed the main grounds of the facility, watching over the clearing and the gate. A flurry of movements started near the fence. "We need to go down," Blast whispered. "Here they are," I said. "Look at these crates."

"They chose the location well," Tesh whispered. "And have a lot of equipment," she said with a thoughtful expression on her face.

"And they are taking it down through this... Look at the system."

"It's a bunker gate," Tesh murmured, "Like in the history books."

The covert nature of their operation suggested that people in town did not know their presence on the mountain. Yet, the workforce at the gate conveyed the importance of the endeavor. They remained hidden for a reason.

Our vantage point lay just above the gate, hidden behind an outcropping of rocks, but we soon found ourselves with guards coming up the path. Two of them moved up the rocks as we did a while ago. They would quickly be up behind us, and Leane remained engrossed in the scan.

Tesh edged closer to Leane to protect her if the need arose. She monitored Leane's vital signs to avoid encountering a problem. During that time, I watched the security guards.

"I'll take care of them," I murmured, standing up to position myself in front of Leane and Tesh to face the guards.

The guards were thorough. I gave them that.

While our EmVat allowed us to remain unseen, the way these two advanced on the path put them on a direct approach with us.

One guard asked his companion as they arrived on the landing where we were, "What have you seen?"

"I'm not sure. I just want to check the area out," answered the other.

The first guard, waving his firearm's nozzle from left to right and back, moved toward us.

I stepped aside.

He kept going, as if testing the terrain ahead of him.

I kept moving back, but Tesh and Leane were soon on his pathway.

HellNet. I stayed put.

He hit my EmVat. The metallic sound resonated on the small peak.

"What the hell…" exclaimed the guard.

So much for stealth… Tesh's voice echoed in my head as she grimaced beside me, her resigned comment coming my way.

I engaged, reacting quickly instead of retreating out of reach. I now held the man's neck with one hand as he unhooked his communication device and landed a quick blow to the side of his head.

He went out like a neural net deprived of nods.

His companion, looking around frantically, grabbed his comm device and spoke, "Huh… We've got…"

But I sent the second guard flying several feet away with one of my kicks. As powerful as it was quick, the action winded the guy, stopping him from alerting the others, but it was already too late.

Whether it was his call or his flight across the sparse grounds, some guards running point below us rushed in our direction.

While I anticipated the outcome in our favor, I didn't relish facing them for what followed. It would require Tesh to use her powers again. I grimaced at the idea, thinking about her reaction to what she would have to do.

I held on to my first victim, reminding me of the picture hunters took with their game. It was like those I saw during our historical research. "Yeah… I just made you mad, didn't I?" I whispered, looking at the guard's gear and then at Tesh.

She shrugged. "It cannot be helped. They suspect our presence. I think remaining stealth is going to be difficult. So, let's make the best of the opportunity."

"NetRoger that," I said with a grin. I was pleased to go into action mode.

In each category of hand-to-hand combat, I had gained the Phenom level. I followed a series of rituals to maintain a particular acuteness and a strict code of conduct and did not use a weapon most of the time.

The best solution was not to give them a hint that we even existed, and we had just failed at that. But then again, this strategy came to be when we believed we had just landed here.

While the second guard landed with a loud thud, I released the first, unconscious at his side. He dropped to the ground like a dead robot. "Let's do then," I whispered…

"HellNet, you enjoy this too much," Tesh muttered as she chuckled under her breath, contending with the possibility that our discovery up here hinged on what we still didn't know they had found down below.

It was something we all had hoped to avoid. Arriving here and dispersing in the crowd, unbeknown to all, was not meant to be, it seemed.

I understood why Tesh felt the way she did about her Shaping abilities, but it was her gift and burden. We all carried them. Although mine may be better than most, after all, I was a Molder of Things; but even with that gift, I still had to fight and protect others.

Tesh had a different kind of legacy. She could influence crowds to do her bidding even if it wasn't by choice that she did it. The Institute had nurtured that gift for their purpose, and they had done this to all of us. Their action taken for the good of our entire society built the next generation of leaders. We were part of all that.

"What do you want to do, Tesh?" I asked, looking at the three guards halfway up the slope. "I should have extended the Custodians perimeter."

Tesh shrugged at the thought. "It's my responsibility as much as yours. Engage." She bent down to the guard, unconscious on the ground, and focused on the moment his gun hit my EmVat, removing the experience from his memory. She would do the same for the other guards.

Tesh would only touch the memory she must remove to keep us safe. For as long as I had known her, she resisted her gift for fear of hurting others.

Tesh said, to my surprise. "We are going down there as soon as Leane finishes her scan. I want to know what all this is hiding."

Our training required that body and mind work together, using our enhanced capabilities and superior powers with each of our gifts. No matter what these were, they demanded advanced mental focus and a different level of consciousness. Practicing these was an art form in our world. Tesh had demonstrated these abilities early on. She was better than most at it.

We still waited for Leane to emerge from the scan. As I looked in her direction, a sheen appeared on her face, and she looked pale.

Pulling her out of her scan at this time was not a risk either Tesh or I wanted to take. Not unless we had no other choices. At the moment, we could handle whatever they threw at us.

The three guards were now upon us. I launched toward the first and sent him to the ground in one move. By the time the other two guards frantically looked around to decipher what they faced, the encounter was already over. Three moves and swings, fist, elbow, and kick. They all lay at my feet.

Tesh moved near the second guard, remaining invisible to the eye and executing the same action by reshaping his memory and inserting a fresh one to replace the old one. She then tackled the remaining three unconscious guys.

Tesh's job on the two guards' memories was a patch, a quick fix that would probably not last long. Their lack of consciousness at the moment did not allow her to do much more than that. Eventually, they would figure out that someone tempered with their memories. But by then, we will have disappeared from these parts. And since they had not seen us, we didn't care.

I shrugged, uncomfortable with our performance. In the space of the last hour, Tesh already had processed seven individuals. MindShaping them all should never have taken place, because they should have never met us.

The Custodians covering the surrounding area notified us of more ground security now on alert.

Tesh leaned over the edge and glanced at the fenced area below. "Chase is arriving," she said.

Indeed, Chase walked up to the fenced perimeter as if he was out on a stroll. But my attention got diverted to Leane.

She slowly lifted her hands from the ground and took a deep breath. "The blueprint of the facility spreads underground close to one of our Chambers," whispered Leane. "It's not good."

Looking at Leane, I reached for her. "You need to rest. What else have you found?"

"I've recorded a log of their faces," added Leane. "This way, we can keep track of the personnel on the inside."

"We'll need time to match their names. The database is basic," I said with a chuckle.

"I need to do a deeper scan," added Leane, frowning.

Tesh appeared conflicted as she stood on the ledge. "What have you seen? What could be so Darnet important that you need another scan this close to the first?"

Leane grabbed Tesh's hand. "We can breach the underground access with Blast's abilities, but what concerns me the most is that they are digging."

"Digging where?" My voice went up a notch.

"Not where… What. The Center's team is digging to get to what appears to be one of our Chambers." Leane opened her mind and shared her memory of the scan.

"So, could they possibly know?"

"I'm not sure. These guys may not understand what they have found. Regardless, we must get our people out before they breach the outer disk of the Chamber."

I crouched next to them. "We go in now."

I nodded. "We have to."

"Fine," Leane whispered, looking relieved.

"They are searching, but the excavation is really near the edge of the outer disk of our Chambers… Since the entire underground shifted, I am not sure which one it is…"

"Blast is right. You need some rest, so first we are going down there. I have questions to ask." Tesh observed the area below.

Chase waited by the fence, his arms over his head as the guard patted him down. His voice carried loudly, "I demand to see Jonathan Spallberg. Tell him it's Chase Davenport."

315

The guards surrounding the parameter appeared to be waiting for something or someone as they communicated between themselves.

"Let's wait and see what is happening," I said. "What story is Chase going to tell them?"

Tesh smiled. "Your guess is as good as mine."

Surprised, I said, "You didn't discuss it?"

"The closer to the truth, the better."

"They're going to think he is a flake," I muttered, already anticipating the reactions of the team below.

"Look, they are letting him in," Leane said.

We watched Chase move inside the perimeter of the gate. Two guards escorted him now toward the structure.

The noise of an alert broke the silence.

"The gate is opening," I said.

As Chase approached the bunker, he disappeared below the overhang.

"I hear a helicopter approaching." Tesh stated and added as an afterthought, "I miss our transports."

Leane shrugged. "I miss a lot of things. But I worry about our friends," gesturing toward the area under our vantage point.

I moved around the guards and looked in their pockets. Checking each one, I found nothing of significance in the first two guards, but the third carried a plastic key. "I lifted this from him," I said, handing the small badge to Tesh after examining the plastic badge that boasted the insignia and name of the Center. "It could come in handy."

Tesh grabbed the plastic card and looked at the logo and pass number under its transparent plastic envelope.

My eyesight, enhanced with implants, saw the details otherwise invisible to the naked eye. "It must access something, but what? I'm not sure."

Indeed, a code embedded into the surface tied to the guard's identity most likely corresponded to a security clearance.

"No personal identification? Apart from the Communication device and gun, only this pass," said Tesh.

I nodded. "You can see fingerprints. I can lift them." My ability as a Molder of things allowed me to duplicate the pass in seconds. On the one hand, he now held the Center's original I.D. card. Within a few minutes, a duplicate pass, identical to the first, manifested in the palm of my other hand.

I handed Tesh the copy, and she secured it in a compartment of her EmVat. The original made its way back in the guard's pocket.

The sound of the helicopter grew louder.

We turned to watch it land.

29
GATE
Chase

The Center, CA - 2022

The four years spent inside the Sphere overwhelm Chase Davenport. His disappearance causes significant sorrow within his family and repercussions with his work at the Center. DAINN Annals – Summer 2022.

A year ago, I held a piece of tomorrow in my hand and a promise of future discoveries. But in reality, a year turned into five years. Who could have foreseen it? Still, in my mind, it was only a year ago. I tried to reconcile with that, but my mind did what it wanted. It gave me a runaround. We had spent four years inside the Sphere. Now I was twenty-five with no memories of these last years.

When I grasped the tablet after finding it inside the cave, I didn't know it represented a future that meant our demise. The key to a destiny we did not want any part of, yet that was already ours, even if unknown.

The device, now in possession of the Center, belonged to Tesh's people. It had been in Jonathan's hands for four years. I still couldn't reconcile that I had lost four years of my life.

Did they decipher the codes? I was obsessing about that, wondering what this meant or if they had succeeded.

The device's response to my touch remained vital for me. I was determined to find out what it meant. Only now, I needed to retrieve the tablet and understand the link between me and the technology before turning it over to Tesh. However, I had no idea how I would make that happen.

I still felt the aftershock of the MindLandscape. Tesh's probing hurt.

I resisted her probe, somehow protecting my link to the tablet, and I never told Tesh the extent of my connection with it. Funny, I didn't even know how I accomplished that. My guess... The bond forged with the tablet allowed me to withhold that piece of information. My desire to figure out this tie seemed the only logical decision, and how could I do that if I couldn't interface with it?

Determined to access it, I now had to reintegrate the Center and, more importantly, talk with Jonathan. Only my explanation of what happened would be a challenge. While Tesh and I had discussed the plan, I now needed to persuade Jonathan of my whereabouts these last four years. Tesh and I agreed that Jonathan could not know the truth anyway because no one would believe it.

As I walked the forest grounds, making my way to the facility, my conversation with my family remained an emotional rollercoaster. It had been weird seeing them over WhatsApp, especially knowing that I deliberately agreed to stay here instead of going to see them. Choosing not to make the trip to visit them after a ghastly four-year absence certainly felt awkward. No doubt, my guilt in that regard plagued me. The wedge between my parents and me grew greater, and for now, there was little I could do about it.

Once I reached the fence, I would demand to see Jonathan. I hoped that my past relationship with him would become the factor that would get me back on the project. My ace in the hole was part of our plan to provide Jonathan with information to enhance the project.

This entire endeavor was Jonathan's most significant research ever. I followed his path through my father as a kid and more closely as a teenager, so I knew something about him and his accomplishments.

Our time had a different meaning for us within the Sphere than what others experienced outside. It felt like we went into the Sphere yesterday when we woke up. The time dilution became apparent only when I accessed my phone after charging it. I confirmed it once I checked my laptop to look at the date. The difference between the clock inside the Sphere and the one outside regimenting our world arose relative to the velocity between them. The lack of synchronicity could also be due to the difference between the locations' gravitational potential. The Sphere impacted the environment of the mountain. Why and how remains the factors to uncover.

Getting closer to Jonathan proved of utmost importance now. During the four years, my absence from the organization created a distance in our relationship. I needed to bridge that gap fast. It would be hard to overcome. I needed a reason to narrow the distance quickly to become an indispensable part of this team once again and access what he knew. By-passing Steven was also the plan since we never saw eye to eye.

The ground landscape changed the closer I got to the fence. Security personnel present on the grounds accounted for that.

When I arrived at the fence, I knew getting inside would be tricky. The guards surrounded me quickly as they began to pat search me down. It was an overkill, but I submitted to it, asking to see Jonathan. I insisted on seeing him. The guards were not playing around, and it took some convincing for them to call their superior. They didn't know who I was, and too much time had passed. So I waited and pondered about what I left behind four years ago.

I grimaced, wondering if Gen joined the Center despite my recommendation not to. I felt somehow responsible for her. Great. Now, I had another thing to consider. Although quite intelligent, she had been vulnerable. I feared this environment's toughness inside the research center, primarily due to Steven's team, would lead to a change in her. Still, so many things were beyond my control at this point. If she chose to join, I would see her soon, and I anticipated she would have questions. I sighed.

Gen's curious personality would require answers.

I shrugged… Tonight would be interesting for sure.

I contemplated the changes since college and the women in my life. Tesh and Gen. Gen was a beautiful girl, but I had never met someone like Tesh. HellNet… Both different… Both were interesting in their own right. Both…. Hah, terrible idea.

The whole exercise was futile. These women were both puzzles. I better keep clear of that line of thought.

I felt Tesh just as I was thinking of her. It happened in an instant, and it was just a flash. Strange this communication with her. She appeared and disappeared just as quickly. Maybe this had to do with my concentration. Perhaps I wasn't doing what I was supposed to do. A moment later, I still couldn't reconnect to her, so I waited, immobile, eyes wide open, looking ahead and seeing nothing in particular.

Nothing happened.

The facility entrance lay ahead. Once inside, everything would speed up. My explanations would be challenged and would demand proof.

The research will take a momentum of its own. The Abyss where the Sphere lived might come into play. If so, our scientists inside the Center would be called to decipher it, moving us into the next phase of the plan—the most sensitive one at that. But it would lead them away from Tesh and her people. I hoped so.

Inside the Center, I would get to the tablet, my connection to it remaining unknown to everyone. So far, I had kept this knowledge wrapped inside me protectively. The Nanos Leane injected in me on the mountain top might strengthen that link, and I was impatient to test that theory.

This device weighed heavily on my mind. With it, the unknown powers it may reveal terrified me. Were we ready for them? Would they only trigger our demise faster? Now that I knew Tesh and the circumstances of our encounter, it proved even more critical. The total experience left a burning impression on my brain. Her arrival confirmed the need for the investigation that began over a year ago. It also answered many questions. But the Sphere's role in that scenario left much to be uncovered.

Why was it here? Why did it release us? What would it do next?

Tesh and her team left their world on the brink of extinction and reached across time to find the key to saving it. So, along the way to the life we had paved, something went very wrong. In the years and

322

decades ahead, we would continue our negative impact on the planet and cause this world's destruction. And if the help I gave Tesh changed, I gave it gladly. *How could I not after what I saw?*

Here it was again. Suddenly, the sensation of forest grounds and rocks entered my mind. It stopped me in my tracks. This feeling came with Tesh's imprint because I could sense her at that moment. How did she do it?

I shook my head, wishing to understand it. I half expected her to reach out and talk to me even now. It was odd since I asked her to butt out of my head before. She hadn't tried to reach me again since I left her. I realized I missed her presence in my mind. *Oh, brother...*

Somehow, my survival in the cave landed me in the middle of this. My instincts screamed at the significance of that fact. I took deep breaths and coughed, choking as I remembered the entire chain of events. I thought about the way things had happened. In my book, destiny outlined my meeting with Tesh even if, deep down, I believed in hard science, which coincidentally denied the possibility of chance. But then I laughed. *Nope. Not a coincidence.*

Our moment at the cottage did not qualify as romantic, but damn, we had a moment, and it had been hot, and they added since I met her. These moments, well, I could not explain them. Were they even real? They felt that way. I didn't know, but I wanted to be with Tesh. I couldn't wait to see her again. I attempted to convince myself that it would be fine once we talked. She would explain these feelings. But I lied to myself. It was crazy, so I looked at the gate, wishing for it to open. Still, there was so much to consider that thinking about these moments alone with her appeared like a phantasm. It probably was. *Shit, none of it made sense.*

This abnormal relationship unfolded beyond expectations, as our link strengthened between us, and it did not bode well. I would age. Tesh would not. She was physically stronger than me, probably faster and brighter, too. I needed something of equal value to offer her. It was impossible. I shrugged, knowing full well that I would take what I could get. That did not sound too foolish to me, even if the balance in a relationship was way incredibly lopsided. Our thing was indeed exceptional. I knew she felt it also, although we avoided talking to each other about it.

Tesh's presence came to me again. This time, the sensation brought me closer to the ground as if I looked at it inches away from it. It was abrupt. Had they jumped?

I frowned.

These visions lacked clarity, fluctuating unevenly. I breathed deeply, attempting to relax. I needed to remain open to receiving and reading them correctly.

Then, I remembered... Tesh could read my mind, and if I thought of her hard enough, she could decipher that I missed her. But this also meant that she could probe further. In a defensive reflex, I shut out my thoughts.

Tesh invaded my mind again. Only this time, it was more precise.

The ground moved. My curiosity increased, but I remained still, worried that I would break the link that had opened between us a few minutes ago. *What are they doing?*

Within seconds, it stopped. I lost the connection.

My frustration increased as I attempted to recall it. A sound this time overwhelmed the silence. An alert. The gate... They were near the entrance.

I looked around, searching for them.

They were nowhere to be found, probably wearing their EVs in their invisibility mode.

The impression lasted only a few seconds and then disappeared. Frustrated, I took a deep breath. Learning how to do this was paramount. I focused. *Tesh… What's going on?*

I closed my eyes and laid my head back, trying to relax, waiting by the fence.

I attempted to recapture the feeling by concentrating on the instants where the visions occurred.

A gentle push in my head startled me. Tesh had answered. *Chase…*

Tesh…

Now, she was in my head again. *What's up?* I asked, faking a nonchalance I didn't feel.

Tesh's voice sounded strained. *We've moved up our timeline.*

My concern for her rose. *What happened?*

We're getting our people, Chase. All of them.

My face tensed. *Did you find Streak?*

Not yet, but we found a way in underneath the facility.

I frowned. *What about the Entity?*

When you get inside the Center, contact me.

It didn't sound right. The hesitation in Tesh's voice resonated, showing a hint of uncertainty. Okay. Then I realized I could feel her hesitation. I took a deep breath. *Tesh…*

Yes?

Will you go for the tablet?

It's part of the plan.

325

Her kindness contributed to my guilt. Pulling down at my collar, I shifted on my feet. *I need to tell you something.*

I don't have time right now. Later, okay?

I released my breath. *Fine. Be careful.*

The information I withheld could not help her right now. Remaining quiet about my relationship with the tablet once again made me feel that I had broken an unspoken rule between us. And yet, the timing was not right. I was better off not telling her.

We will. Just get inside. Don't forget about Mage, right? Tesh's voice trailed.

Of course. I will take care of Mage.

It's just that… Mage will be at the cabin with Cian, and I don't know when I will make it back. He seems to like you.

Who is Cian?

Oh, I forgot to tell you. Cian is my domestic bot. He will take care of the place while we are away.

A domestic bot? How advanced is his programming?

Pretty advanced. Why?

You better make sure it doesn't go into town. We're not there yet.

Yes, of course.

Something concerned her. *Tesh… Are you okay? How danger…*

She interrupted me. *I have to go.*

I will look in on Mage as soon as I can. Wanting to reassure her, I kept my thoughts and doubts.

I heard her intake of breath. *Thank you. It's just that Mage doesn't know anyone else, and he, huh, likes you. I'm counting on you,* she added with relief.

Play it cool. *Tesh… wait. I… Be safe.*

Her chuckle resonated in my head. *Always.*

In the next second, she disappeared.

The gate opened. I waited and stared at it. Would Jonathan emerge from it, or would I face Steven?

Tesh would find the cause, the key that led to the destruction of their world. I believed it. She would stop it. Their knowledge and their advances far outreached ours. The Center might help too if only we could all work together. For now, a lot of questions still plagued me regarding Jonathan. My presence at the facility would bring answers; I questioned if I would like them. Overall, I doubted my judgment regarding the Central project.

Anger at me surged. It was a welcome ally, for I had gone through various emotions since my eyes landed on Tesh. The MindLandscape, the dive from the mountain, the help extended at the cabin, and Tesh, most of all, left me unhinged. Trapped somehow. And yet, I wanted to be a part of it. *It was contradictory; I know.* Even in my state, I could see that.

I began walking back and forth, waiting for the gate to open. It took longer than I hoped for since my request to see the guy in charge. What was Jonathan doing?

Tesh's powers intimidated me. Their influence, especially Tesh's influence on me, spun a reaction as a team. I had not come to grips with it, and I grimaced. As real as it felt, my connection to her did not dictate my actions. I did that myself. I preferred to ignore it, yet could I blame them for not trusting me?

Finding their way down the labyrinths of paths in the soil, going from the darkness into the light, and emerging at a different time would probably destabilize anyone. Yet Tesh had let me go. My mind remained my own. She chose not to change my memories when she possessed the opportunity to do so.

Part of me rebelled still, and I demanded some payback in my need to re-establish some control. The realization hit me. I felt like I screwed up. *Damn…*

They possessed powers we could not deflect if they used them. It was terrifying if I thought about it long enough. A moment ago, Tesh gave me the answer I gave Leane. She just teased me. Thinking about it, I relaxed. She wouldn't do it if they were not confident in what they were doing, now would she?

I felt the cell in my pants pocket and shrugged. Tesh was right. Who needs a mobile phone when you have this ability? I laughed. How has life changed?

Beyond the gate, the field dropped, and Steven crossed its threshold.

Damn… I grimaced at the thought of facing Steven. It was no secret. We didn't like each other. He kept me at arm's length from Jonathan, purposely. I stepped toward the small fenced door with resignation and waited for the guards to give me access.

Under their eyes, I entered the gate's immediate perimeter, walking toward Steven, who waited for me, only feet away from the main entrance to the facility. "Steven," I said when I stopped in front of him.

"Chase," Steven said, observing me. "Well, it seems you have some explaining to do."

A tight smile came to my lips. "Yeah, and I'll do that with Jonathan. Where is he?"

Steven remained silent for a moment. "He is inside. You'll have to go through the gate first." He turned around and led the way back to the biometric system.

He expected me to go through security. I should have thought about that possibility and hoped the Nanos I had in me would not get picked up somehow.

Without a word, I began to follow him when I heard the noise of a helicopter overhead.

30
MINDSHAPE
Tesh

The Gate Promontory, CA - 2022

We now reside in action, a home away from home. It is where we excel, for we have trained for this. Their minds belonged to me; they were my domain for a short time. DAINN Annals – Summer 2022.

Leane and Blast took positions on the rock overlooking the entrance beside me. With our EmVats, we thoroughly blended in with the mountain, invisible to everyone around us. Our NetJet boots, ready to activate at a moment's notice, provided a tremendous evasive maneuver. But we would not use them in this particular instance.

I saw Chace waiting by the fence. He would soon be inside, and I felt confident about that. He had too much to offer the Center. I linked with him. We quickly connected but, Leane called for my attention.

I sensed Leane's need to convey the information she had garnered moments ago from her scan. I opened my mind, and we established a link.

The cave was relatively small, and the ceiling stood fifty feet high, with the rock formation on one side broken halfway up by a smooth metallic surface. Twenty men slowly dug around it to clear the object embedded inside the mountain. Recognition hit at once. This sphere protruding from the cavern's wall and carved into the rock formation was one of our missing Conclave Chambers.

I focused on the perimeter. From our vantage point, the outside compartment appeared intact. I strained to make out a symbol to identify which of our Conclave compartments it was, but nothing visible to the naked eye gave any information on its provenance. The coloring could have helped identify which Chambers lay nestled inside the Earth's crust, but the lack of light muted any markings. The designs covered by dust and pebbles rendered the hull dull, providing no insights into its origin. "I can't make out the Conclave."

"Me neither. It will take the Center some time to dig it up, even with this many men. They won't get in easily. The only way to avoid a confrontation is to go around them, and this means using your power, Tesh," Leane said.

"Or we find a different way," I murmured.

Chase moved past the fence and walked toward the gate to meet someone.

The alert from the gate broke the silence. The sound resonated in a series of brief bursts, creating a signal we had not heard before. It beeped at regular times at regular intervals before it stopped. The gears of the massive portal disengaged, grinding the teeth of an iron wheel. One after another, the latches gave way, and twelve individual pops freed the outer doors' mechanism.

Chase stopped inside the perimeter of the gate. Would he need to be screened, or would they give him access?

Chase began a conversation with an additional guard who did not look happy on the ground below.

The entrance now stood open.

Leane continued giving me information. Next came a schematic of the facility, highlighting the lower floors of the facility. The corridors held the research labs hidden behind large biometric activated doors. This glance into the place's layout, below the main open communal areas, provided the first glimpse at the location we needed to raid—this was our access to the secret research held within the Center.

Most of the crates' contents immediately transferred upon arrival on a mid-level floor locked with plastic security key cards remained inaccessible. These were like the card we lifted from the guard to secure entry into the facility.

Leane was upset. I could feel it in the fluidity of her movement. Imbued with the energy of water, she naturally moved with harmony. And it served her well. Only now, her motion beside me was abrupt as she reviewed her gear. "I hear a helicopter," she said.

I looked, and it didn't take me long to see it flying toward us.

"Notice how it makes a huge evasive move to avoid the town. These guys don't want anyone to see them," Leane added.

"We can perhaps use this to our advantage at some point," I said as I adjusted the fighting gear to my EmVat.

Our technology was an assortment of things we used in combat operations. The Znet we always carried got hooked first to my left shoulder. The NetArray grapple, several Custodians, a FreezeLaze, and some Recon Nanobots were wrapped on my back. I expected Blast would use some of his when he got near the gate. By the time we were ready, the sky had turned darker as we still watched the arrival below from the ledge.

We stood on the promontory and waited for the helicopter to land. The screen of my PVZ broadcasted its arrival based on the feed from the Custodians. Our drones surveyed the forest area, watching for any other activity on land. They monitored the areas around the town.

Blast had positioned one of the Astra Custodians, a smaller, incredibly nimble sphere with high visual acuity by the cliffs, overlooking the ocean. They captured anything that moved, alerting us way before the threat reached our vicinity.

The huge bird flew above our heads and descended by the main gate.

Leane turned to me. "Do we find Streak, then move on to the Chamber?"

"We will know more after I interrogate these guys. Regardless we remain in stealth and improvise when we have to..."

"Works for me." Blast wore a scowl that didn't bode well for whoever would get in his way. "Our friends here will provide the way."

I shared with Blast the plans of the underground facility as Leane saw them. The transfer of information occurred in seconds. "It appears they are digging here."

"Huh… Huh." Blast's lack of reaction did not surprise me. He was ready to move.

"What if we wake the EHAF?" Leane suggested.

"Getting to the pool first makes sense. We know where it is," said Blast.

"The water surrounds the chamber. The entire area is unstable. How long would you need?"

"A few hours, but I'll mold a passage and hold it while you wake them."

"Then, this is where we begin," I said.

"I expect a certain resistance without Streak." Blast creased his forehead and looked at me. "But you are at the head of the Origin Program, Tesh. They must follow you."

I shook my head, concerned that the information we received from President Langden would cause friction among the ranks with the other Conclaves. He specifically told me that I could trust the EHAF but that there was a traitor among the other Conclaves. "We go for the EHAF."

Blast shrugged. "Without Streak, the other Conclaves will still have to answer to me."

Blast looked intense. "Are you worried about the EHAF's allegiance?" His frame created an aura of power as he prepared for action, and the green hues of his aura were now brighter than I had ever seen them as he moved impatiently.

"No, I'm not worried about the EHAF," I said. The EHAF was the logical choice, and based on what Langden said in his Vlog to me, I could trust them. "NetComm noise reduction mode."

"This is what we trained for, so let's go." Thin and tall, with a brooding look I hadn't seen on his face before, he glanced at me. "Engaged," Blast said.

"NetRoger that," Leane murmured.

My visor accessed inside the helicopter, penetrating past the outer skin. The massive machine, a Mil Mi-26, landed in the middle of the clearing. Its blades slowed with a warping sound, and the engine quieted. Four men and two women descended with bags slung on their shoulders.

Our eyes took over and replaced the video stream as we watched the action directly below us.

We leaped from the edge and dropped the distance to the ground in concert. A mere fifty feet represented a child's play for us. Jumping heights or lengths was routine. Within seconds, we stood in the middle of the clearing, watching the six people approach the entrance.

The group moved away from the helicopter while the pilot remained inside. When the six of them cleared the machine, the engine purred again, and the blades engaged, warming back up with a whipping sound, creating wind in the clearing and lifting dust into the air as it prepared to take off.

The women and men systematically crouched as they stepped away from the helipad, eager to clear it. Two of them even ran toward the gate, which until now had remained closed.

The machine lifted toward the sky and flew away, its noise competing with a biometric field signal that sounded behind us. This articulated noise was part of the security protocol barring the way inside.

"This will be fun," murmured Blast, excited, on the NetComm. "Watch them… I'll inspect their security system, laughed Blast, suddenly in his element. "First, we see what they see."

"Remember, the Center has motion sensors."

When he reached the gate's perimeter, he dashed behind one guard and shadowed him.

This unfamiliar world, one in which we possessed no hand in shaping, grated on me. The lack of freedom, the calculated actions, and even the manipulations took their toll. None of this was of our making. In our life here, I already resented hiding who I was. The first of a kind.

But it represented a necessity at the moment. I existed here in this place for a day. How would I feel in one month?

My friends stood beside me, fearless, powerful in their own right, and beautiful. All of us looked captivating in the eyes of other humans. We had seen the look on Chase's face when we first met him. Meant to appeal, we carried charisma, which influenced how receptive people were to us. They programmed us that way. People would smile, eager to help us. They would behave with deference, even though we strived to act as they did, to blend in. The engineered genetics and our very own brew of DNA created an allure about us that didn't go unnoticed. Such was the make-up of a Conclave member. Even our people back in Ang felt influenced by it.

Our knowledge provided us with advances in science that transformed our people. No longer susceptible to illnesses, we lived longer and gained special skills, enjoying gifts delivered as a birthright, with unique attributes embedded into our DNA. Technology has helped make us better in every way, and these discoveries over lifetimes accounted for our progress, and ultimately, our demise.

A Shaper of thoughts carried one of the most potent gifts around. It could read other people's minds, gently entering one's brain, caring not to leave behind traces that would betray an illicit presence, or it could be a brutal experience leaving a person with an empty mind. My mandate, shaping new realities in individuals or crowds to replace old and unwanted ones, required skills and intense training. Influencing perceptions to create different outcomes demanded an expert touch few possessed. Most trod lightly on the recesses of one's neurons. Others were not always as careful. I erred on gentleness and lightness, attempting to bring to the subject something good in return for my trespass despite what they trained me to do. Shapers came with different ratings on an advanced scale as a MindScaper. Get in, reap the knowledge, and get out.

Behind us, Chase was still there, talking to a stern guy, looking ex-military. The body language didn't bode well for Chase, who appeared tense. I could feel his dislike and decided to approach them.

Leane covered the helipad. The gate's lights illuminated the darker areas of the clearing with a purple glow.

I was distracted by a buzzing sound and observed a luminous wall oozing with a purple haze. My visor immediately picked up the components. The field encompassed lasers positioned left and right of the portal, running from ground to floor. The electrical impulse emitted an inaudible hum.

Blast would enjoy deactivating it.

I paused near Chase, watching the tall guy.

Here we were, feet away from them, walking among them without guards noticing our presence. Reading their minds became easier than reading our people, for our perceptions, enhanced on many levels, provided walls these people didn't possess.

I could shape all of them to my will, but I rejected the thought as soon as it crossed my mind.

My night vision engaged as the darkness surrounding us influenced the details. I observed the guards all around. Attuned to my surroundings, I watched their movements to perceive threats. The guy standing in front of Chase with a scowl on his face would likely give us the most information. There existed subtle differences from the others, and his presence made me pause. I observed his behavior for a while longer.

Another individual drew my attention. A woman walked by me.

Based on their attitudes, these two individuals and the general authority they carried surely possessed information we could use. The way they moved gave them away. It was subtle. One was ex-military, while the other, most likely a scientist, intrigued me.

I reached out to Chase in his head. *Chase, I am at your side. Don't react. I will help with this one.*

Chase's answer came rapidly. *Are you here?*

Yes. Who is the man?

Steven is in charge of security operations. He wants me to go through security. Is there a risk that they will pick up the Nanos?

I focused on a tall and bulky man.

I will take care of him. Just wait and see.

I drifted away from my surroundings' reality, knowing that Leane watched my back and reached into the power of my mind, pushing toward Steven.

Stop... I said to all of the guards around the perimeter. Extending my reach to those who surrounded the man I wanted to read would not have been necessary if Streak was with us. But since he was not, I carried this task. It would demand more of me, but I knew I could do it.

Leane arrived at my side, raising a mist that enveloped us, ominous and dense, another barrier protecting us from discovery.

Whenever I dove into anyone's mind, my friends became my eyes to the outside world and entered a domain only known to me.

These gifts, inherent to who we grew into, belonged to each of us. We could not transfer them to anyone, and others could not access them. Each of us possessed capabilities; no one else could achieve. Streak, Blast, Leane, and the other Conclave members were the same in that respect – unique skills beyond normal humans.

All guards ceased their movements around the gate.

We stood a few feet from them, and the mist danced around us, white, thick, and wet, providing a cover on all sides.

I appraised Steven. Invading his mind, anyone's mind, was not something I enjoyed doing. It was a disruption of a person's consciousness, and under the pledge, it was against our dictate unless circumstances demanded it. And those situations were most often dictated by the Institute. But in this case and with this person, it would be no problem.

It was now the ninth time I would use my gifts since we had awakened here. While I rustled with that issue again, the need to know outweighed our Universal Pledge demands, and I made peace with it for the safeguard of this planet and us.

To this day, my abilities never failed me. My powers worked like a spiral springing at will. For most of these men, I would make them lose their sense of time. For the one standing now in front of me, I sought to find what the Center hid from us.

My mind surged forward, purposeful, as I stood in the middle of the clearing. Reaching all the guards, I interlaced my mind with them and drew a blank space, a place where time and thoughts stopped unfolding. It resembled a moment frozen in time where they remained while I questioned the man in front of me.

Tell me what you are doing here.

A scowl appeared on his face as he fought the invasion of his thoughts. The guy was ex-military, judging by his appearance and resistance. He was well-trained. Arms, wars, deaths, and bombing. Iraq, Afghanistan, and the private sector back in the United States. Images of meetings held in off-grid locations until the Center. *I didn't pick a wimp.*

His eyes blinked.

I pushed him, strengthening my hold on him.

He hesitated another second and answered, "I am in charge of the whole security operations for the Center."

What is this facility?

Another pause. Steven released the information with a strained voice. "We seek to understand what we found."

What have you found?

"A piece of technology that does not originate from us." He fought me.

I increased the pressure. *Tell me about this technology.*

"We are not sure. But we found it several years back and are still trying to breach it. Understand it. But it led to more. A broken structure. Space and corridors. Cryo Pods. Large saucer-like disks, too. We don't know what it all means yet."

It was much more than we had thought. While it partly confirmed what we knew, we never expected these men would find the Cryo Pods. Were they from our Aurora program with underground safety rooms, corridors, and tunnels? Did some part of our underground safety quarters remain? Our scientists never expected it to be so. Did they excavate to penetrate our Chambers? These were what they called the disks. *Where? Show me.*

I could feel Steven struggling against me.

He fought my intrusion. He held back, fighting my control. Did they find Aurora? Our underground city? Or was he talking about something else like the Sphere? My thoughts rushed with hope.

I plunged deeper into his mind. Lifting the veil around his thoughts, and pressed on, getting him to release his hold on what he held at bay. The sponge-like substance parted ways under my probing.

He grimaced now, but I was more in-depth this time.

I saw images of a city. *A warning of impending doom. A piece of a tablet… And part of a name. Broken stairs, corridors, rooms, and crushed pods, hundred, no, thousands of them…. And a few intact ones, still under their independent life system.* I suddenly felt cold, and I shuddered. Our people were there, struggling to survive, waiting to awake. It changed everything for us. The images played on in my mind. Damaged buildings, fallen bridges, broken rooms, a landscape unrecognizable to my eyes, ground into pieces. Complete turmoil. Were these images from the tablet after we entered Origin? Was this from Aurora? We represented a future that did not yet happen, but we left a present still unfolding. I didn't know and wasn't sure what it all meant.

I felt his fear when he said, "Something bad will befall humanity."

The wall around my thoughts dropped for a second, bleeding into this word like an echo. The whisper reached my friend.

I heard the turmoil of Leane's thoughts at my side even as she remained still, knowing that her reaction could influence or break the link.

Where are the pods now?

Steven resisted, unwilling to share this information. "In our labs. We moved them to our facility."

Where?

"A secured corridor, on level 24."

I felt his anxiety rising. His heartbeat increased. Pushing ahead anyway, for I needed to know this, I found the thread and insisted. *Where is the tablet?*

"In one lab on the lower level. A secured area, on level 24, room 206."

Show me how to get there?

Images of corridors flew to my mind, doorways, floors, and a restricted area.

Where is the exact location of the structure?

"As we expanded the facility... Deep underground." His voice sounded raw.

Show me.

I dug deeper, impatient, and realizing that I could inflict damage, I slowed down.

Open your mind. Show me what you saw.

Steven revealed the cave Leane spotted during her scan. *Did you find anything else?*

Confused, he hesitated. "No..." His bio read showed I had reached a dangerous level for his physiology, but I thought he hid something else. *Where do you keep what you found?*

The man fought me, his physiology spiking again.

I could feel the strain Steven was under as he attempted to restrain me from his memories buried.

I had seen enough. My need to know could not supersede Steven's safety. While I couldn't deviate from my mission, I also cared for this man's mind, so I lifted the knowledge needed and retrieved it. I pulled back, implanting thoughts and creating an illusion in his mind.

You will stop searching and will kill all activities relating to digging. And you will give your men some time off. Have a party. Do you understand?

"Yes."

You will let Chase walk in with you. Help him when he requests it. Work with him and obey his demands.

Slowly, I withdrew with a light touch, carefully losing pathways as I went along, tying memories together and eliminating traces of my presence. Leaving no shadows, I avoided touching other areas of Steven's intellect, and I removed myself from his mind.

I had witnessed enough for now.

My last thought to Steven echoed between us on my way out of his mind. *You will remember none of this. You do not recognize this moment and have never heard or felt anything. Remain here for now.*

I turned and approached the woman. With a deep breath, I refocused. Pushing into her mind to probe gently, going deeper into her thoughts. Unlike my slow process with Chase, I entered her mind, passing through the barrier she erected when she felt the intrusion.

She stiffened under my grasp.

Regardless of her will against me, I penetrated her memories, keeping a wall around my thoughts. This dive remained light, grasping images and perceptions.

Her experience showed me the security they underwent to get here and enter the Center. She revealed the guards she liked because they were comfortable and courteous toward the scientific team and showed me those she could not stand. She provided the areas Jonathan set up, the personnel responsibilities, and their field of expertise. Her name was Lauren O'Brian, and she was a Dr. in Biological Science. Her personal life didn't seem to mean much, as most of the images I garnered from her mind revolved around her work before the Center. Her interview, her enrollment, and her arrival.

I then focused on her knowledge regarding the Center and saw what she knew. A map of the facility appeared, showing the upper-level floors. I saw her living quarter within the Center on the lower level of the facility. She had access to a restricted area below.

Tell me what you are working on in this place?

"The reanimation chamber."

I shuddered. Our team was at risk if these people were reanimating my people with old-fashioned methods. We needed to get inside quickly.

Her role was to monitor and analyze the subjects once they arrived at the Center. She was excited about the prospect of talking to her new patients.

Where do they come from?

"We don't know. There is a part of the mountain that contains a structure. It is big. We are working on the rest of the excavation now, but we have already retrieved twelve subjects."

Are they alive?

Yes. We have the subjects confined at the moment, recuperating.

Are they conscious?

Not yet.

Where are they?

On the 24th floor, in several labs in the corridor.

She frowned, confused. *I'm not sure I should talk about this.*

A man's face appeared and vanished just as quickly.

Convinced that I couldn't get any more helpful information, I followed the labyrinth of her thoughts backward and disengaged from her mind. I implanted new ideas and quickly withdrew.

When done, I turned to my companions and murmured on the NetComm. "We have to talk."

We now had gained vital information. I turned to Chase beside me. *Chase, the tablet is on the 24th floor, room 206. They found some of our people... Twelve of them. They are in reanimation on the same floor.*

Let me know about their status once you are inside. Just follow Steven; from now on, he will help you. You do not need to screen.

Tesh... I am sorry about your people. I will do my best to keep you informed. It will be a change, Steven helping. Huh, Good. Could you do the same for Blast?

Go now...

Be careful.

I looked at the guards surrounding us and sent them a final message: *Resume.*

The movement around the perimeter began again as if it never stopped.

In front of me, Steven turned around and began walking toward the gate, followed by Chase.

"You have everything you need?" Blast said as he continued observing the gate while he commandeered the Mave to settle above the promontory.

I nodded. "Everything, no but enough. We need the EHAF."

"This is our opportunity to get in, Tesh. We should go in now."

"I know, but we cannot... Blast, we need our team first, trust me. The Center has found the pods from Aurora. We have survivors. They also found the Chambers. We can't do it all by ourselves."

Blast's face darkened. "NetRoger that."

Steven walked straight through the field, and so did Chase.

"We will get what we need from the inside," Blast said, standing by the gate as he, in one swift move, retrieved the NanoWalkers and launched them onto Steven's clothing. He repeated the process on Chase.

The NanoWalkers attached to their clothing vanished inside the threads, invisible to the naked eye.

He then prepared the NanoWalkers for the others, waiting to get in. Leane and I watched to see the new arrivals pass the field.

On the side of the door, the display activated. The field dropped, and a wave of purple haze barred entry. The biometric system engaged immediately after Steven and Chase walked through the gate. A complicated three-step process that required iris recognition, voice sampling, and palm prints began, just as Chase had mentioned to us. The field triggered as each individual from the helicopter stepped into it; a scan took their physiology reading and cleared them.

"Let's get to it… We need to find another entry point." Blast launched NanoWalkers on each individual and moved away from the gate.

We held our breath as they passed through the security field.

The wave flashed. A signal rose.

A guard yelled, "Hold it."

The other guard by the gate stopped the process, checking the first person wearing the bots.

Another guard on the inside advanced to check on the man. Physically, he patted the guy down. "I have nothing on me." The man muttered. "I don't know what's going on."

Finding nothing, the guard waved him on.

When the next man penetrated the field, the machine reacted again.

The wave flashed. A signal resonated still.

The guards went through the same routine. Finding nothing on the newcomers, he waved them on.

The system reacted erratically but could not pinpoint the Nanos.

While not as advanced as our tech, it had identified an issue. It responded to an unknown, unable to assimilate the presence of a threat.

Good to know. Muttered Bast in my head.

The guards looked toward Steven, who had watched the process, his head cocked to the side as he observed the equipment. "Call the security company. I want this checked out."

He signaled to allow the others inside with a frown on his face. He turned several times, looking around, not satisfied with this lack of findings, as the group proceeded into the long tunnel.

The gate closed on the laser field of the scanner.

We now had eyes on the inside.

31
EARTHBOUND
Leane

The Cliffs, CA - 2022

We now possess eyes inside the Center. As the NanosWalkers, also known as SpyWalkers, penetrate the areas ahead of our intrusion, I am determined to find Streak, retrieve our people, and access our different Conclave Chambers. DAINN Annals, Summer 2022.

The plan now was to get the EHAF out. First, I wanted to scan because we still had to locate an entry point under the facility and find Streak's location. I felt the pull to do this immediately as if something called me to it. After that, we will infiltrate the Center and save our people.

We sprinted down the slope toward the east side of the mountain until the forest changed, growing thicker, all the way to the cliffs.

Blast led the way while Tesh and I followed his green shimmer, as the blur appeared and disappeared between the trees like a strike of thunder, only silent. A person had to look closely to see it, for it stayed visible only for a brief instant.

My mark, a blue sheen in the landscape, swirled around the dense foliage, sometimes mixing with Tesh, as we sprinted.

Suddenly, Blast leaped, leaving the ground below, and glided from tree to tree way above us. We were in a race, showing off our abilities, stretching our capabilities far past those of the humans that surrounded us, even though we were also mere humans. Only we were enhanced, partly engineered, and gifted. We stood out because of these differences.

Our technology gave us powers beyond the norm, surpassing typical humanoid characteristics, giving us superhuman strength, speed, health, and smarts, with intellectual processing powers reaching so much further than anything one could dream of in any lifetime.

The games we played exhibited stark differences in our varying skills. Sometimes Blast won. Well, most of the time, he succeeded in his areas of strength. Sometimes, Leane or I won, but we would have to change the game's aspects. We never felt quite the same need to win. Once in a while, we would beat him because we wanted to. It could happen through sheer power, but neither Tesh's skills nor mine called for that. We possessed different purposes.

The Custodians, covering the area ahead of us notified us of more ground security where we were now heading. Without wasting a beat, we turned on our EV suits. We moved past a patrol without detection, relying on the EmVats invisibility shields.

We aimed for a forest area located lower on the mountain slope. It stood further away from the facility's landmark, hidden among the rocks. It also led closer to the ridges overlooking the ocean. But as we left behind the gate and its fenced perimeter, our surveillance continued. We received new feeds of the grounds with our Custodian drones outside every instant that passed. Inside, the NanoWalkers gave us a look at the corridors and labs, enhancing our knowledge of the facility. These new images of the Center will help plan our break-in.

My alertness increased as we approached the cliffs. I was looking for the right location for my scan. We were now approaching the zone that would most likely give me access to a potential entry point for our tunnel. It needed to be far enough from the facility but close enough to get inside the center's lower corridor.

With the EV suits, we moved differently. The experience of the EV suits did not compare to the experience of our natural bodies. But both had their measure of efficiency. Yet, at this moment, leaving behind trails of gold, blue, or green cloud, even if they quickly dispersed in the breeze, seemed too risky.

Blast ran ahead of us. He passed the hill and lunged in the air with his NetJet Boots to reach a small outcropping of rocks.

Leane and I followed him, hearing his voice over the NetComm. "This way."

I gave him a loose location of our ultimate destination in my early scan. It was an excellent position to access the mountain's belly and set up my following deeper introspection. The isolated nature of the place, with nothing but trees and the surrounding mountain, was likely our location to begin NetPulsing the tunnel.

We jumped down a few feet without breaking a sweat and landed at a small rock formation.

This mountain scape tested us with its abrupt incline. The short hike through the underbrush trained us, like in the old days. It was a fresh ground to explore in a part of the forest so dense that it guaranteed privacy. Although we still needed to account for the

Center's security team who may venture into this area. But even with this risk, it remained a nice challenge, even if we could wish it to be otherwise. Besides, we would get bored if things were different or too easy.

Taking a quick look around the ground, I said, "Follow me." I now took the lead.

Blast muttered, "This is new ground to train here. Same as if we were at home. It is not something I would ever give up, and this place is great for that."

"Yes, it is. I wouldn't give it up either," Tesh whispered, with a smile on her face.

The run did Tesh some good.

I stopped by a boulder area. "Here," I said. It was a calm place for me to immerse myself in the scan. I didn't risk a brutal pull back away from the contingent of guards patrolling the forest in this location. "This is a good place."

Tesh nodded. "Good. Let's do it."

The Center had located our Chambers underground, and excavation was currently ongoing. Earlier, I saw that the reinforced structure of the facility spread downward for miles. The large elevator platform descended with equipment requiring assembly by caseloads. Men in uniforms incessantly orchestrated the loading and unloading of crates from the helicopter. They then delivered these two levels below.

In the last few hours, the intensity of the efforts increased. The upper corridors swarmed with the latest arrival of additional excavation specialists.

"The SpyWalkers work. I knew it," murmured Blast beside me.

When our NanoBots infiltrated Steven and Chase's clothing, along with that of the other six individuals going into the Center, they fed us the facility's layout. We could now watch the ongoing activity. For the last hour, our technology replicated and split into hundreds of SpyWalkers, latching onto walls and doorways, spreading throughout the air filtration system into new areas as deep as they could go, and penetrating all levels. In doing so, they provided us not only with hundreds of eyes within but garnered information and recorded conversations dispatched to our Network through our PVZ.

"I love these little buggers," Blast continued with a satisfied smile.

Tesh grunted, looking at the streams coming on her screen. "Focus. We might learn something more."

The multiple feeds flashing across my Visor from the SpyWalkers spread inside the facility. I focused on these particular streams since DAINN usually handled the logistics, but was presently absent.

From their positions in the Center, they communicated their feed to our Visors simultaneously. The streams now covered any movement or communications, sending updates every time someone walked by a secured lab. Unfortunately, no one entered the labyrinth of corridors below level ten.

While I prepared for my scan, Tesh and Blast monitored the different vantage points.

We watched the underground tower's activities, positioned on the forest grounds, away from the security fence. We hoped the information garnered would shed some light on the nature and scope of their operations. None of the current personnel seemed authorized to venture inside the secured labs, except Lauren O'Brian. Still, she had not left her quarters since she secured the restricted area after the personnel moved equipment into a lab. As we surveyed the landscape and the feeds, our access to the Center remained limited, thus my scan.

Blast became irritable by the minute as he watched the feeds. "NetWash… Come on, get in there."

"Chase will find a way into the corridor," said Tesh. "Give him time."

"We don't have time," Blast muttered. "We need to get our people now."

Military personnel was moving heavy equipment along chambers that looked like supply rooms. Guards organized food, materials, and equipment in one part of the building. Inside a secured area, others filled the armory racks with arms varying from firearms to drones, heavy assault rifles, fully automated mounted or portable guns of all sizes, and whatever else they had lodged in there.

The SpyWalkers pierced through the boxes with infrared vision, sending us visuals. Our PVZ's allowed us to identify the boxes' contents, giving us their weaponry knowledge, they amassed inside the Center.

"You'd think they are planning for a siege," mumbled Blast after considering the equipment.

They armed this research facility to the teeth. It was either getting ready for an attack or preparing for an offensive of its own. Still, while the amount of data to cipher through increased with each passing hour, we determined it was nothing compared to the information that awaited us once we breached the security inside the labs. Without DAINN, we expected it would take some time to weed through the SciTech they worked on inside the facility. But at least for now, we better understood the stakes we faced.

These areas remained inaccessible and lay dormant behind double steel doors boasting signs with "Restricted Areas" above them.

Soon, our team will infiltrate the corridors. We will retrieve the tablet, free our people, eliminate access to our Chambers, and locate Streak, and we will prepare for any eventuality.

Our SpyWalkers and their feeds will serve the EHAF. These secured doorways leading to long hallways detained our people. For now, these rooms delivered no electronic activity. Occasionally, we saw scientists in residence move past them but never ventured inside, so we patiently waited for the next phase of our plan. Every time we saw someone go near it, our hopes increased but then got squashed.

"We can rely on our tech, but without the rest of our team waking up and filling the ranks in manufacturing, commerce, technology, industry, and government, it will be a tough road to deliver a different outcome. Each one of us was selected to work with a specific purpose. We must be there to perform for our mission if we are to succeed." Tesh murmured. "Otherwise, we are way outnumbered. Leane, how long do you need before we wake up the EHAF? I would like to do this before the night is over."

"And so, we will," Blast assured with a tight smile. Give me two hours to open the EHAF Chamber."

"I will be quick," murmured Leane.

Tesh prepared ahead to meet the goals of our mission. It was her role. I shouldn't be surprised that she already had a plan.

Based on what Chase told us, the population of the Center amounted to three hundred people. We now could witness it on our feeds. About two hundred security personnel, both men and women, were heavily armed while the scientists and technicians comprised the rest of the people.

Tesh nodded, still focused on the streams. "Good. As soon as Leane concludes her scan here, we return to the large cave."

The facility encompassed a sizeable community room. Others, located on lower levels, served as gathering places for the scientists in residence. The Center kept the security guard areas completely separated on the upper levels. This division rendered our work easier. The personnel we surveyed remained in the common areas or inside their private chambers, never venturing past the most electronically secured doorways leading to the restricted areas and labs.

"The way the Center has this configured gives us time to search the lower levels without the intervention of the guards," I whispered. "It's easier for us."

"I think the tablet is down this corridor if I can rely on Steven," Tesh said as she pointed to an area on our screen.

"Okay. The EHAF will head there first."

The scientists in their private quarters remained the assets to tap into within the Center. These individuals possessed higher security rankings, and their workstations focused on their fields of activity. It will give us insights into the Center's research. But we didn't have time to dive into a thorough analysis just yet.

One terminal in the feed gave us access to a list of the labs, each identified with an area of research: Geosciences, Clinical Medicine, Biological Sciences, Chemistry and Materials Science, Physics, Astronomy and Astrophysics, Mathematics, Computer Science and Engineering, Economics, Psychology, and other Social Sciences. Astronomy and Astrophysics, situated in one of the most remote areas within the facility, remained the hardest to access. Tesh confirmed some of this from her scan of Lauren O'Brian.

With their higher security rankings, the Department Heads were still unknown to us, but now we possessed their names. Rich Sand, Philip Sognier, Lauren O'Brian, Mark Burke, Andre Lacroix, Roger Mendelson, and Ursula Scheller ran these departments. We needed to find out more about each of them, and we needed more time.

I kneeled on the ground. Ever since I saw the forest and tasted life around these parts, I felt reluctant to venture underground again. But, knowing they were digging somewhere below, I needed to find a path to our people. The Center prepared for a takeover of our Chambers, which would take the facility into its program's next phase under Jonathan's vigil. We needed to prevent that and remove any possibility of a strike against us or our technology.

"I can go ahead of you," pointed Blast, also looking at the feeds.

"No, we go together," decided Tesh. "The last time we split didn't prove to be the right decision. Leane, are you ready?"

"Look, once we make a PulseNet a tunnel inside, we will get what we want," whispered Blast. "The key for us at the moment is to get in, locate and retrieve the tablet before we go for the other Chambers. Hopefully, the EHAF can do this while we rescue Streak."

"The images from Steven's mind showed another structure, and it would be great to locate it, Leane," Tesh said.

I nodded. "I better get going then. We need to know what is below the building," and I began my brand of magic.

My scan needed to reveal as much as possible.

The screen of my PVZ shifted.

A Custodian planted around the grounds alerted us of the approach of yet another helicopter. It flew over the forest and descended into the clearing, landing on the low grass area serving as an unidentifiable helipad. If one arrived from the air, the unsuspecting visitors had no way of recognizing it as a landing zone.

Tonight, it saw a lot of traffic. This time, the helicopter unloaded heavy equipment. A disgruntled Blast pointed toward a massive object offloaded from the helicopter. "Look, more excavation equipment as well."

I grinned confidently at Blast, "But they do not know what we can do." I turned to Tesh. "I am ready."

These preparations triggered my need for action, just like Blast. At this moment, I understood my friend's impatience.

Focused on the mountain, I now sat directly on the forest ground at the base of rocks near a tall pine tree, with Blast on one side and Tesh on the opposite. My right hand grasped the soil, and my left fingers spread to the ground. I closed my eyes, preparing to go into the matter. "Just don't let go of our link." I took a deep breath and whispered, "I've never done a scan with this big of a matter."

"Don't worry; I won't let go," murmured Tesh.

"I won't either," insisted Blast at her side, his hand on her shoulder, with worry written on his face.

Tesh held my forearm as I dived. "I will show you the path," I murmured at her side.

Fear trickled down my back, and I tried to ignore it. I thought of Blast's smile as I took a deep breath; the first one inside the mountain. It spurred my courage. I didn't like this scan; the mountain, too big to contend with, represented a challenging risk. Put merely; it could kill me.

But we needed a direct path to our Chambers to stop whatever the Center was doing in the caves immediately.

I became a tool. My scan will provide us with an exact direction for the molding of our tunnels. Walking underground without identifying the precise location of our target amounted to utter stupidity. If there was one thing we were not, it was that. With our emitters not working and our equipment not providing a way to the other Chambers, this scan became our footprint to the exact position of any structure within the mountain.

Our mission warranted a trip inside the bowels of the Earth. Yet, there was so much more than we had bargained for in taking this trip through time. For one, we never expected to be tied to this mountain for so long. We all should have exited our Chambers by now and integrated with these people.

I advanced through the mass and kept a lookout for a signal from the tablet. I moved ahead. The first layer held my curiosity. Patterns that didn't belong here guided my quest as I searched for the Chambers.

The immediate danger our people faced in their pods under the Aurora broken underground edifice made me shiver. At least, the Origin Chambers would hold. I dared not think about what would happen if the Center's personnel got a hold of our people. This scan must reveal the positions of the various formations so we can get to all of them.

My senses looked out for forms and shapes, all foreign in this dark, damp place. Inertia surrounded me. The soft sand, the dirt, the pebbles, and the rocks all infused my sense of smell, suffocating me.

My mind searched ahead, tethering on the edge of nothingness. Losing myself here was not an option.

The scents of the Earth filled my nostrils. This particular and peculiar odor invaded my cells and then faded.

I reached the second layer, deeper into the Earth. The density increased. Slowly, inhaling and exhaling became more difficult. Keeping my center became a struggle. My mind swirled, remaining unable to form fully into thoughts. They stilled in my mind's eyes for a moment. The rock formation became heavy, unbending, and tight, too tight. Moving inside it happened in slow motion. My lungs burned, manifesting themselves like molten lava. *Breath...*

Particles danced around me.

Pushing past the impenetrable wall, I received the full impact of timelessness. This place saw through millennia—countless years of the same isolation.

I advanced through the matter, feeling stifled. The rock-solid matter of the mountain kept me bound as a prisoner inside my mind. Nowhere I turned led to an open space of any kind. I braced as I pushed through the mountain, which held me in its grasp.

Stopping meant death.

The weight of the place crushed me. I fought to breathe. My limbs felt heavy as I moved ahead in the matter. I could no longer pretend it was part of me. It was foreign, and it crushed me. I kept going, pushing my muscles to their limits.

Find a cave.

The thought came and fled. *Tesh?*

I scanned the earth around me and found more rocks. Only rocks. Desperate, I closed my eyes and lost myself in the bedrock.

An echo of a voice retrieved me. "Time remembers... Especially an intention. Nothing ever gets lost."

I tensed. Where did the voice come from?

When I opened my eyes and scanned ahead, the rocks remained, nothing but stones and stones and more stones.

Somewhere in my mind, the voice continued, speaking gently, "A link was forged between us, seared in blood. You will not die here. You cannot die here, for you are our future. Keep breathing, and keep moving."

Confusion set in inside me. What was happening? Where was that voice coming from?

Who are you?

"I am of your blood. You are from mine, linked beyond time and space to the place of stillness. So, you see, you cannot die here. Push forward."

Despite the confusion, some power fused with me. And so, I did as a yearning propelled me ahead.

Good. Keep breathing.

I knew the process. The method to use was recognizable and echoed in my memory. Experience spoke. My mind calmed and settled down amidst the overwhelming sensations that still rocketed through me and would have me scream. Whole with the mountain, and yet a separate entity, my mind refocused as I conquered my fear.

Yes… Yes… Breath.

Finally, I distinguished both size and density. I perceived details at the molecular level. As my thoughts transcended the physical plane, I broke beyond the barriers and reached the scan phase, propelling me down.

The landscape of the mountain beneath became defined as my mind followed the formations, looking for unusual patterns. Solid rock surrounded me everywhere, straight ahead, above me, below me, and on all sides. Deeper and to my left, the mass of a structure appeared, corridors, rooms, shafts, levels upon levels of it. All were regular, Human made. It was the Center, more significant than I had expected.

Further into the ground, beyond the facility's outline, almost immediately underneath existed an emptiness created by rocks forming a natural cavern. There was no sign that something else remained lodged under the concrete edifice — just some void. Still, I believed something else existed, somehow pushed by knowledge beyond my own.

A disk... Broken. There it was, the promise of one Chamber. Only, it was not sitting on its normal axis. I could see rough edges. It was like a disk with a slight deformity. Its contours were uneven but recognizable. Despite the darkness, I confirmed its identity as one of our Chambers and attempted to determine its origin. It was impossible from my present vantage point. Then, I saw another disc—a second Chamber, this time intact to the far left. I continued scanning, finding the last one untouched further down amidst broken structures. Relief and excitement swirled in my chest.

I had located our three remaining Chambers. My heart pumped fast. We now could plan, knowing the path to take. We would directly mount the rescue.

Probing further, I searched for other debris, ruins that did not have a place here, yet they existed nestled amongst the rocky and immovable landscape.

I saw something move way past an artificial formation. Secluded further back, it was within a wide opening of another cave. *What is this?*

My scan turned to the right of it, stretching around the edge of the far wall. There... An unusual formation. Crevasses, deep pockets, broken rocks, jagged edges. Another structure, massive, filled my vision with bridges, hallways, and rooms. Also, I observed what looked like landing zones. Could it be part of the domain protected by the Entity? We had no way of knowing at this point.

In the dense darkness of the underground, something shifted. I perceived another slight movement. Then another.

What is that, or rather, who is that?

It looked like a humanoid form. Then, a sense of recognition surfaced: Streak. Did I really see Streak. or was it just my imagination? What is he doing here?

I wanted to speak, but I couldn't. I tried to reach Streak, but I did not have Tesh's power. I focused on Tesh, but the mountain's weight proved too much. *Tesh... I found Streak.* I called her, moving ahead, attempting to get closer to the silhouette, but I lost him.

It is Streak. I felt it deep down.

The feeling of recognition invaded me, but it was a fleeting shadow, as happiness still filled my heart. I had just found Streak.

The surprise of finding an enormous edifice spreading way below registered in my mind as an abnormality. What was it? Who put it there?

Inside this void of an empty cavern, the unknown structure competed for my attention with another disk, the last of our Chamber. Excited, I almost lost my focus. We now knew where the mountain had entombed all the Conclaves chambers.

As I prepared to withdraw and returned to the surface in my mind, something strange happened. The voice returned. Yet another mystery. From the nothingness below, someone talked to me. It rose in the mountain's darkness, compelling me and with one purpose. The sound enfolded my brain, leaving no room for evasion. It led me further down into the night, and I felt myself detached, as if my body split within me. It was a pull I could not resist, a force I could not defeat. And I watched my mirror image as a body double move away from me before it disappeared, vanishing in the bedrock.

32
MIRROR
Tesh

Forest Hills, CA - 2022

The scan lasts a while. Part of me fears for Leane. She was my friend, my family, my Conclave. However strong, stronger than she believes, she remained tied to the mountain too long. DAINN Annals, Summer 2022.

I sighed as I watched over Leane, feeling guilty about relying on my friend in that way. My unsuccessful attempts to reach Streak left us with one option - Leane's scan. Our need to find the Chambers led us to this point - Leane's scan. The recent findings from my read on Steven's mind required a further investigation, and Leane's scan provided all of that.

Thwarting the Center from its goal – getting their hands on our technology remained our mission.

Blast was on edge, worried about Leane's safety. He didn't like Leane being at risk, not in this manner, not in any way. He impatiently waited for the next phase of our endeavor. Indeed, infiltrating the

Center required his abilities. And he far preferred getting into the thick of the action.

Although I desperately wanted to find Streak, Leane and Blast were essential to our mission and me. I couldn't imagine what I would do if something happened to them. Thus, I went for the EHAF Chamber first. They were the ones trained for any confrontation.

Blast's voice reached me again. *Stick to the plan. Step one: the EHAF Chambers. The second step: extract the Conclave Chamber from the excavation site and get our people out. Then, step three: locate and get Streak while collecting the other Chambers. Step four: infiltrate the Center and retrieve the tablet. Step five: investigate the unique structures. Don't go second-guessing. I may not read your mind, but I can read your face.*

Hearing Blast laying out our plan made me smile. He knew I felt responsible for all of us.

Getting to our Chambers is a priority. Get centered, Tesh. She is counting on you, added Blast's voice in my head.

I sighed, exasperated by his prompting, although he was right in this case. So, I muttered, "I can think and be centered."

He chuckled. "That's better."

Blast will lead the way to the underwater Chamber next. NetPulsing his way under the facility until we reached the other Conclave Chamber, we saw protruding from the wall inside the small cavern. But without a map of the underground, we would waste too much time. If we couldn't locate Streak, the Chambers must be our next destination. Although getting him was essential to the entire mission, we may have to wait. I hoped that Leane would locate Streak this time around because we were not complete as a Conclave without him.

The scan appeared to go all right for now. Leane advanced through the layers, with her vitals registering as normal.

After finding out what was going on inside the Center, the circumstances justified our search scope. With the surveillance implemented with the Custodians, we accessed the patterns surrounding the outside of the facility and could execute a breach. Knowing the path to take under the mountain would cut down on time and increase our success rate.

Blast's assessment of the situation was right. We needed to act now. The Center had found not just a broken structure, but our pods and our Chambers. What was the broken edifice? Who built it in such a place? Was it part of the Entity's universe? Questions without answers plagued our quest.

Blast voice called my attention to him. *All good?*

I nodded. But with the night wrapping itself around us, Leane's continued search made me nervous. It was taking too long. The wait rendered me impatient.

My mind went back to the unknowns we faced. The instruments we retrieved from our Chamber indicated that the continents had shifted due to the cataclysm. The center of the Earth realigned itself. We didn't know how bad of a shift. The entire landscape of the Earth had moved as the tectonic plates deviated from their position in 2098. We had awoken to a new planet's configuration, so we were blind to the other Chambers' positions underground.

Our compartments had broken up. Origin's underground facility we entered back in 2098 had protected us. But, from what we observed in the cave, the infrastructure twisted under the blunt force of the Earth's movement. Corridors were shredded and ripped apart. The new position of our Chamber inside the mountain intimated as much. The discovery of the EHAF Chamber surrounded by water near our own confirmed it. We suspected the SRC, Faculty, and Company Chambers were still intact, but they were nowhere near our initial calculations. If only DAINN were available to us, it would provide the exact coordinates. The System would give the precise shift in the Earth's axis, but we were on our own to find them.

The in-depth survey of the topography of this place demanded a considerable amount of energy. So, I provided Leane with an anchor. I gave her a beacon if she got lost during her probe by tying my mind to hers.

My experience with this type of thing remained limited. Would Leane suffocate? Would she panic? I wasn't sure. I never dealt with inert objects, which made the experiment somewhat unpredictable.

It was Leane's special gift. She selected the area and determined that this location would bring us just under the facility from the Center's layout.

I lifted my eyes to our Custodians, positioned among the branches of the trees, guarding the open area above us, and my gaze stopped on Blast. His role was to maintain a lookout on the ground while shielding us from view with his EmVat invisibility shield.

Our years of practice at the Institute gave us an understanding of Encharging. Now, the energies we emitted individually were recognizable patterns. They were also comforting. They would help Leane remain grounded to us, a trace that served as a safety net and reinforced the tie we shared. This process, connecting us at a different level than my mind's power, linked our bodies to each other's chi.

In that way, Leane could track her way back to us not only with the MindLink I shared with her but with the energy pattern our bodies produced.

Our connection gave me the ability to follow her progress, and keep up with her mind so she would not feel cut off from us as she ventured into the unknown of the mountain. Otherwise, she could lose herself in the matter. My gift intervened like a thread in a labyrinth to find the way back to the surface.

The lack of signal emitters from the Chambers rendered our task to identify the Conclave structures impossible. Not until we were close and saw them, would we know which ones they were. Leane would locate their positions. She would confirm what our equipment established, the presence of human-made patterns deep inside the Earth. These surrounded the research facility. If a more significant edifice lay underneath, we needed more information. Was it another edifice tied to the Sphere? Speculation would not provide answers. This investigation might.

I glanced briefly up ahead and breathed deeply, trying to keep myself tied to the surface as Leane went deeper inside the mountain. From our position, we were out of sight with the clearing, far enough from the cameras not to pick up our movement, and undetectable under the blanket of darkness.

DarNet Blast. He got me out of my moment of contemplation. When I was unsure about things, my tendency to ruminate about everything took over.

My attention went back to Leane. Conducting a scan wasn't something difficult to accomplish. However, this entailed a significant amount of energy when the scan was a mountain. It wasn't a process easy to describe, either. Training demanded a particular affinity for everything surrounding us and a vision and perception beyond the obvious. It required an ability to perceive matter in its infinitesimal microscopic state, along with the capability of creating fusion at the source. The key amounted to not losing oneself. It was the gift of a Seer, a Seer of Life, and all that was in the universe. It was Leane's legacy, her special gift.

I followed her progress as she plunged ahead. *Remember, weight does not exist. It's only in your mind.*

Blast's worried gaze crossed mine. I smiled reassuringly. In my head, I reached out to him. *I won't let anything happen to her.*

Suddenly the mountain swallowed me. I surveyed the rocks. My hand touched the ground. The clearing disappeared around me, and I stood in the immutable strength of the hill. The soil and rocks beneath me felt rough. The dirt, leaves, grass, pebbles, and sand were inside my mind and replaced everything.

My intake of breath was abrupt. Leane pulled me inside her mind, and suddenly I saw and felt through her. Everything dimmed around me. The sounds, the wind, and the fresh air on my face remained behind me until they were no longer there.

Blast murmured, "Nothing can touch you in there, and we have you out here." His touch reassured me. He anchored us both in this place.

Suddenly, inserted into the solid rock foundation, I merged with the hill in some primal fusion. I felt old. Ancient, like when time itself began. Then the feeling disappeared altogether. We became a matter, with no figment of cells. A mountain just is part of the interconnectedness of things. It merely exists with no anchor in time as to its beginning or end. It was energy, chaotic, synchronized but only a speck in the immutable fabric of space, a simple dust particle in the universe.

These were Leane's feelings and emotions, only not quite Leane's, as I knew them. These were sensations she passed on to me as if they were my own.

I'm here. Breathe.

I recognized Tesh's voice from far away, but it was my voice perceived by Leane.

You have no density… Don't fight it.

Deeper breaths opened my lungs. No longer choking, my mind cleared. My thoughts stretched, seeing through the barrier of the mountain and into the next layer. Deeper still. The heaviness present with every step ahead surrounded me. The darkness encircled me.

You are okay; we are here. Keep breathing… Tesh's voice, my voice, reached me again. But I was Leane. It was odd. I never lost myself like that before.

Unable to respond, too ensconced in the overwhelming sensations, I was also too confused to read thoughts, mine or Leane's, at the same time.

The odd feeling persisted. I became agitated.

Leane seemed confused, almost fighting toward something.

My mind became muddled, unable to process input.

My voice resonated in my head and beside me, echoing against the wall of my brain, but no words formed. I tried to say something, but impaired by all the layers of matter around me, weighing me down, I struggled even to breathe, a persisting sensation hard to overcome.

Too much… I can't.

She had been there long enough.

Leane, come back… Come back now, I said in my head.

370

I can't come back... Not without... No. Don't pull me out...

Intense emotions flooded me. Something was wrong... I sensed fear. Leane's fear and felt compelled to pull back. A surge of adrenaline rushed through me as I reacted.

Leane moved ahead in the dark corridor she crafted inside the mountain.

I had to control this emotion.

Leane resisted, pushing ahead and away from me.

Another pull. Then a tug.

Sensing all this, I followed, holding on despite my reluctance. I would not let Leane go without me. The pressure on our mental link intensified. Leane was getting away... My breath escaped in gasps, uneven.

I felt Blast squeezing my shoulder. No, not my shoulder, Leane's.

I held on to the thread, refusing to go on. There was too much fear emanating from Leane. I firmly pulled back and found myself further away from her. "Get back." I heard my voice occupying two distinct people: Leane's body and my own.

She fought it and disintegrated from me.

The rupture happened.

Emptiness followed in my mind. I had lost her. How could this happen? Almost in a panic, I focused on my breathing. I searched for her in darkness, attempting to reach a calm I was far from feeling. I grasped around for Leane, reaching out to get a hold of her, but too late. She had disappeared entirely from me.

There was no way I could go back without her, so I stayed. Still, in the darkness of the bedrock, I went into a meditation state and waited. She knew the way she took through the mountain. She would get back down the same path, and I had to believe it.

Leane would find me.

I am unsure how long I remained that way. But suddenly, I found a trace of her, and the link strengthened, retaking hold. Now that I felt Leane's mind in my head again, my heart pounded. Relief and joy invaded my chest. *Where were you?*

I, Huh… I lost the link.

Hold on to me.

This time determined to hold on to Leane; I pulled back on the link with power, overshadowing her own will.

I recognized Leane's resistance, and I ignored it, but she finally gave in. I could feel how tired she was.… But I also felt something else in her mind, something I could not place.

The process began, against her own volition.

Regardless of Leane's desire, the physical change in the MindLink affected her biology. Because of my tugging, I triggered a retreat from this place. And Leane lost her connection to the matter. Pulled away with me, she retreated from her probe despite herself.

Slowly, I felt myself coming back from far away, and as she made the journey to the surface, so did I.

The fusion process with the mountain broke.

I suddenly felt like my old self again. I called the scan to stop. Usually, the process always occurred through physical contact. It required an electrical shock, an emotional connection pulling at the subject, or a mental prompt like I used. Indeed, any of these devices retrieved a Seer. It became standard procedure if circumstances showed the Seer had run into difficulties during a scan.

I pulled on the string slowly, evenly, resurfacing ahead of Leane, who moved back on her journey little by little. A sudden jolt was never right, and guilt hit me. I could have lost her in my determination to bring her back before instead of coaxing. We usually avoided doing that, and I was angry at myself for risking Leane that way. But aware that the link could break like it did when I tried initially, I still did it. Why? Was it my fear driving me?

Emerging first from the mountain, I whispered, "She's coming back."

Blast nodded and looked relieved that this entire experiment was about to be over. "Good," muttered Blast. "What in the hell happened? You were there too long, and both scared the HellNet out of me."

Leane slowly withdrew, following my lead.

I kept my focus on her, impatient to see her back with us, and as she peeled one layer at a time, I wondered where she had disappeared when the link dropped between us.

Leane gasped at her return among us. Her face was covered with sweat, and she leaned forward, her head almost on the ground. A few seconds passed while she took deep, uneven breaths. Abruptly, she moved away from us and threw up.

It was an unusual reaction, but I don't think she ever attempted something this grand before.

I felt her heart beating unusually fast and her mind rolling.

"Are you okay?" asked Blast.

I read her jumbled thoughts, awe, frustration, and impatience. Then disappointment... She was upset. "I'm fine." Taking a breath, she paused and added, "I found our Chambers."

I frowned. Leane did not look fine. "Why are you upset?"

She lifted her head and turned to me. "I'm okay. I need a moment."

Leane looked far from okay, her face pale and withdrawn. "I felt you were in distress. Why are you so upset?"

"I wasn't... I saw Streak." Leane said, barely emerging from her scan, "At least, I think I saw him...."

"Where is he?" Stymied, I groaned. "You saw Streak? I didn't know... I was worried about you."

She was upset. "Why did you pull so hard to get me out? Why did you ignore me?"

I misinterpreted Leane's emotional state. "Oh, gosh..." HellNet, I read distress instead of surprise and read fear when I should have concluded excitement. "Oh... No. What have I done? I'm sorry. What did you see? Was it really him?"

She still breathed hard, and her eyes focused on something far away. She still had not recovered from the experience. "Streak... is in some structure, very similar to our Chambers... But it's not our Chambers," said Leane, her voice gruff as she attempted to readjust her emotions to the surrounding reality.

"Are you sure?" inquired Blast.

"Was he okay?" My eyes teared up, and my voice sounded tense in my ears.

"Of course, I'm not. But I'm pretty sure it was Streak. He is inside a compartment located way below the Center. Not directly under, but to the right of it."

"Anything else?" insisted Blast.

"Not really. Except I think Streak was attempting to connect with me. I'm sure of that, but I lost him."

"Can you get us there?" Blast insisted, disregarding how weak she felt.

Leane closed her eyes, wiped out. She looked completely out of sorts.

"Give her a moment," I murmured.

Disappointment struck Blast's face.

Guilt ate away at my heart because I just screwed up the scan. I ignored Leane's hints out of fear. My eyes looked away from her face as I took a deep breath. I would have to forgive myself and learn a lesson in that so I would never do it again. But as my vision reached the ground while I thought about all of this, I saw something in Leane's hands that shocked me. Unable to make sense of it, I closed my eyes and reopened them. Thinking it was a mirage, I grabbed one of her hands and reached for the other.

"What is this?" I said, my voice shaking.

Blast leaned in to see what I was looking at and reached out toward her arm, "What in the HellNet?"

Leane looked up at us, her face remaining blank, without showing surprise.

For the first time, I felt her withdraw from us. Her eyes did not meet mine, nor did she look in Blast's direction.

She slowly rose and walked away from us without an answer.

Blast looked at me, one eyebrow raised. "What was that?"

I shrugged, worried.

We quickly got up and followed Leane, seeking answers to her strange behavior.

Leane's hands were tattooed with symbols we had never seen before and remained clinched as she walked away from us.

33
BLOOD
Leane

Unknown Temple, Uruk - 4000 BC

The darkness lifts under the lit fires provided by torches ensconced in the walls. The surface is smooth, unlike the walls of the caverns we walked inside the mountain. Instead, this place is beautiful, glistening under the flickering light with smoothly polished marble floors. DAINN Annals, Summer 2022.

In front of me stood the silhouette of a woman, immobile as she watched me with a smile. She wore a simple shift, wrapped on her shoulders, hanging gracefully down her body and held with a simple belt. Where was I? What was this place?

"Welcome."

Blood flew loudly in my ears. My mind attempted to understand what was happening at this moment, but confusion filled me. "Who are you? What is this place?"

"My name is Anuti. It means star in the old tongue." She looked up to the sky above, and her face brightened with happiness. Her demeanor relaxed for a brief moment, and then she glanced in my direction, waiting for something from me.

Confused, I followed her lead anyway.

The stars shimmered under the dark canopy brighter than I ever witnessed before. There was no roof above our heads to reduce their impact, no transparent dome to dim their brightness. A deep breath escaped from my lungs. I looked at the walls surrounding us from all sides, and still confused and filled with questions; my eyes returned to Anuti.

"Do not fear me. I am one of your ancestors. You are here as a rite of passage. Your blood talked today, and I am here to guide you across centuries."

"What do you mean? I do not understand."

Anuti frowned. "It is unusual. Perhaps there is an answer to that quest if you do not know. Please approach."

There was no fear in me, only questions as I moved forward and stepped onto the dais. "What is this place?"

"This is the place where it all began. The place where magic was born."

My voice trembled. "Magic?"

She smiled again, and her hand reached my face, her fingers barely touching my cheek, her fingertips warm against my skin. Concentration filled her eyes as she looked at me, with the bluest of piercing azure eyes color I had ever seen. It was as if she was passing right through me and looking beyond the ages to find the thread of my life. "You were recently unbound. Do you remember it?"

"Oh…" A sign of recognition built within me, and in that instant, I remembered my last day in Ang city, right before we departed, the day my grandmother Manaha released the power I held within me.

I search for my memories. If my magic was bound, Mahana had done it. She was the only one with the power, for I did not recall my mother capable of such feats. But perhaps Mahana had also bound my mother because our leaders hunted down those with extraordinary powers since they considered them dangerous. It must have occurred before I was born, since I never witnessed my mom do anything out of the ordinary. How could one relinquish such a gift willingly? Thinking back to what we had endured at the Institute, I recognized that this was a course filled with wisdom if one wanted to live a somewhat normal life in our society. The Institute was not kind to those whose nature had gifted them with unprecedented abilities. These were capabilities people wanted to control and curb, so the Conclave's leaders worked in darkness to dominate. It did not differ from enslavement in a society that proud itself of incredible achievements. Yet, the reality was quite different.

For a moment, the knowledge that I now possessed astounded me. What would happen if others learn of it? What would my Conclave do if they found out about my super powers? How would Tesh, Streak and Blast react? Would they trust me still? Would they attempt to subdue me? These were questions that circled my mind without answers.

If indeed, the women of my family carried our powerful bloodline, one that began centuries ago…. *AkkadEtanaEra*. I whispered the words: "AkkadEtanaEra."

Her smile grew wider, if it was even possible. "AkkadEtanaEra," she repeated after me. "I am here to welcome you, my child, and release fully the power you hold in your blood with all the hidden knowledge it possesses so that one day, you can pass it to your children. Don't use it too much. Use it wisely. Use it rightly."

"I do not understand… How is this possible?"

"Magic is powerful, Leane of the lineage of Anuti, the lineage of Aelia, the lineage of Aisling, the lineage of Alice, the lineage of Albin, the lineage of Ann, and all the others that came after the early matriarchs of our families. The blood and wisdom of the ages befall you now."

As she spoke these words, symbols floated in the air between us like golden butterflies. They increased in numbers in front of me with each name she pronounced, surrounding me with light and power. When she finished, they landed on my skin, melding within me on my forehead, my neck, my hands, and my limbs. I now felt them over my entire body, sharing space on my chest, tummy, hips, and back, all surging with power. They ignited briefly and settled on my skin in blueish hues.

"They responded eagerly to your line and power. Your elemental gifts are strong, child."

I was now covered in shimmering blue sigils, positioned all over my skin. My brows furrowed, contemplating how I could hide these from my team. They would trigger a lot of questions.

"These are the keys. Use these elemental powers with care. Rely on the wisdom of the ages. Command, and they will respond. Hold their secrets with care. They are your heritage, your lineage, your gifts."

Awe entered my heart and soul, for I felt this power subtly humming inside me now. It was beyond anything my grandmother Mahara ever shared with me growing up. And I finally understood all that she had imparted to me in the early days of my childhood. Still, I did not know all that they truly represented. I would need time for that.

I nodded to Aelia. "Thank you."

She inclined her head and said, "Farewell, Leane, AkkadEtanaEra."

"AkkadEtanaEra, Anuti."

As I speak these words, she faded away along with the temple I stood in, and I glided back inside my body and amid the bedrock of my scan.

I search for the symbol on my skin with my mind's eyes but could no longer see them as they no longer appeared on my body. Realizing that this was a boon for me, as this way I did not need to fear people knowing about my powers unless I revealed them, I sought to find in my memories the exact moment when Mahana had bound me. Somehow, it seemed important to understand what prompted her to do this so early on, without teaching me any of the things I needed to know about my powers to use them properly.

I remained in my head, unable to focus on the moment, recalling my childhood. I remembered voices raised in anger and frustration. There were cries, too.

My mother objected, but my grandmother was adamant. "You do not want them to use her. They will find out."

"Her evaluation is not for another year. She has time."

"So, she can learn about a power she can never use? Shara, it would be cruel. Let her grow up as normal as she can be."

"I hate that she will never know."

"It is better this way. They always find out, you know. Somehow, they do. The only reason I escaped their attention is that I was older when they did the assimilation."

"But it is part of our lineage, mother. How can we ignore this for her?"

"I fell into the crack. Apart from working with potions and herbs, I never practiced once we discovered what they did to those they identified with special powers. Do you want this to happen to Leane?"

Regretfully, my mother answered, "No."

And just like that, the powers within me disappeared, until now.

34
DIVE
Gen

The Flight, US - 2018

I am in the middle of a storm and feel the madness of the crowd surrounding me. We are all here, some carrying doubts, others with blind excitement. Either way, it is our own doing, and no matter the outcome, I chose this. DAINN Annals, Summer 2022.

The madness of the crowd or the popular delusion was real and not just a notion. I witnessed it a while ago, and part of me is still reeling from it. It was hard to comprehend what happened at the mansion earlier, and reconciling the events was only the beginning.

Chase never showed up, and it was on my mind. He was the only person I felt connected to, although Logan became a kind of lifeline. He was friendly, and I felt comfortable around him.

Earlier, we learned the Center included a department dedicated to researching interstellar travel. I thought I was dreaming! But the crazy part about it was that no one, within the crowd of scientists present, questioned it. Indeed, they all took it in stride. Even more so, their excitement became quickly contagious during the party. It was like a big wave of smiling faces across a living room canvas. Even Logan appeared to be thrilled at the idea.

I knew many companies endeavored to venture into that sphere to commercialize space travel. But a difference existed between us going to the moon to establish a base and taking a journey through the galaxy. The cosmos was a vast unknown. At least, it was my perception, and I stuck to it.

So, the notion of crowds' madness had a definite appeal when I considered my colleagues on the flight. Indeed, it was all I could come up with to justify the elation existing around me as we boarded the jet.

We were all mad, but I had one justifiable reason – my mother.

Just before our departure, Jonathan had introduced each one of us, specifying our degrees and field of expertise. He also set some expectations for each of our departments.

After the brief formal introductions took place and everyone connected over the buffet set for our benefit, Jonathan made another announcement that surprised us. For the next three weeks, Jonathan mentioned that we would prove our meddle based on a series of trials he would announce on the plane.

Not only did Jonathan outline a tight schedule, but he also intimated that we were to meet additional requirements. We still had no idea what these were, nor did we know what they would demand from each of us. And, as the gauntlet dropped, our competitive nature surfaced.

Tension mounted in our ranks as he went on. And from that point on, everything went sideways.

Suddenly, we were not just enjoying the party and taking part in food and drinks. We were a bunch of driven scientists eager to make our mark. Our focus changed from a friendly one to assessing each other to determine our strengths and weaknesses. We were to be judged. Joyful. If we had to use each other to help our goals, it was par for the course. None of us would be surprised by it as concurrence among us heightened. Indeed, understanding the stakes benefited every one of us. Starting a new job, one could expect as much, but Jonathan enlightened us on that fact without a doubt.

Curiosity rose in our midst. Our outburst filled with questions did not garner many answers. "I will explain the details on the plane," said Jonathan. "But, you will compete for your research budget."

This announcement was new. Among the surprise that resonated in the room, Jonathan also offered the opportunity to back down and not join the team. "You are here because you chose to be here. We are glad you joined us, but you are free to go if you doubt your ability to perform in this endeavor. Should I have Steven plan your departure?"

The tension in the room increased another notch. Then, it became clear that this room was filled with triple AAAs who very seldom lose. No one wanted out. We just wanted to know if there would be any rules, so we knew which one to break. At that moment, I felt the buzz and determination. Facing new challenges and beating the competition for the prizes, yeah, I could do that. I never worried about second place. It would never be civilized.

People surrounding me closed off, putting on their game faces. There was no longer any friendliness in the room as if we were ever friends. Under a veneer of reserve and indifference, we all waited for Jonathan to reveal the rules.

In the end, no one volunteered to leave.

When Steven announced the moment to head to the airport for our flight to the Center, everyone found themselves eager to depart.

We were all anxious to get to the plane and determine what the competition truly entailed.

The moment arrived to depart. We split into small groups into three BMW SUVs. I got inside with Logan, Zoe, and Anders. Immediately, we left for a private airport.

Our little group remained silent inside the car. Thoughtful and calming notions filled my mind fighting uneasy conclusions on the way as I sat by Logan. His proximity made me doubt myself. My determination to stay friends wavered as his arm touched mine and as his leg pressed against my thigh. Could we do it when we competed for a grant? Could we remain civil and transparent? Some of us would certainly be able to do it. Others not so much...

Logan and I glanced at each other several times on the way, and his gaze trailing to my lips left nothing to guess about his thoughts. I could feel myself blush and turned away several times, but his easy smirk betrayed him. He was testing me. I ignored him. Too many things flew in my head to contemplate getting involved with Logan. At least, the competition among us excluded Zoe, and I was suddenly glad she sat near me.

The ride went by quickly.

Shortly after arriving, we saw our bags loaded aboard the private plane. Jonathan's team handled the transfer and everything about this trip effectively. Even Logan's bike made the trip and was one of the last items to get on board.

The plane was a sleek Boing 3 jet, one of the most expensive aircraft made. A separate cabin and an area with a seating arrangement near a bar awaited us.

We took our seats, impatient to know more about the significant explanation that would provide the terms of the work for the next month. The moment Jonathan moved to the front of the plane, we knew we were about to understand the implications of this new competition.

He smiled and said, "When we reach the Center, we will assign you your quarters and work details. But as you begin, you will need to define the research you will undertake to get your grant based on your area of expertise. Giving you a budget only makes sense if it benefits the Center. We will provide two grants after selecting the projects that stand on their own merits. So, within two weeks, you will submit your plan. We will then decide which of you wins."

"But you said we would have access to a grant when we joined the Center," said Brielle. "You never suggested that we would need to compete for it."

Jonathan smiled, "You do. You just need to have the best projects to get it."

Confronted with these new terms, we remained silent. Tempted with an unlimited budget for our research was indeed an offer none of us could pass up.

Jonathan had not discussed this before, nor had he addressed the process, but it was undoubtedly the equivalent of qualifying performance tests.

"Jonathan, you never made that clear when you hired us," said Axel.

"You're playing in the big league now," continued Jonathan.

He hired us to do research and development. Yet, now, we had to prove ourselves. The Center was not clear about anything. Everything I suspected about my employment became somehow reaffirmed by this new information. I had to shove aside my doubts once again. *I am here to find my mother.*

"Great, and I thought we had just finished with tests," exclaimed Veronica.

"You're not alone in this," muttered Anders, with a laugh.

"Well, since I can't do any research, that leaves me out," murmured Zoe.

"Consider yourself lucky," said Logan beside me.

"Rather than feeling cheated, you have an incredible opportunity to impress us, so do it," added Jonathan, feeling the resistance to the news.

"You hired us to work as a team," said Liam. "Don't you think this will defeat the purpose and create unwanted conflicts?"

Instead of taking the statement at face value, Jonathan turned Liam's question against all of us. He exclaimed with a laugh, "You can't break under the influence of nerves, fear of the unknown, or competition. Do you fear being ridiculed when faced with a challenge? We hired winners. If you doubt your capabilities, you don't belong among us."

With that statement, Jonathan disarmed the whole issue. Like a master with a confident smile, he stepped into the private cabin ahead of the plane. In a matter of seconds, he had diffused further questions, leaving us with a feeling of unease. The idea that we would compete against each other for two grants made us all appear insecure, and none of us wanted that.

Logan, at my side, took it in stride. He leaned back in his seat with a big sigh and shrugged.

Our eyes crossed.

He smiled and winked at me.

I followed his lead and reclined my chair.

Ronan and Veronica walked toward us as they grabbed their drinks at the bar and promptly returned to their seats. Their voices drifted toward us as they walked away. "Well, I guess we better focus on our project. Do you have an idea of what you will submit?" said Ronan.

"Even if I did, I wouldn't tell you," laughed Veronica.

Ronan chuckled, "A guy can try."

"Great," muttered Logan as he stretched in his seat. "Now, everyone will focus on the competition instead of working together."

"You didn't think it was going to be that easy, did you?" I said, bringing with me two drinks from the bar. I handed one to Zoe and the other to Brielle. "I think you can use these."

"Thank you," said Zoe as she took it and downed it, surprising all of us.

"Whoa…" I smiled. It never dawned on me that this slip of a girl could handle her alcohol like this.

"I have three terrific friends that are more like brothers, and we've had a bit of practice," said Zoe proudly.

Logan opened one eye and said, "I don't suppose there is one for me?"

I made a face. "Hold on… Only two hands here. I'm going back to mine. Scotch…" I smiled."

Logan chuckled at that. "When you know what's good, you know."

I smiled at Logan's comment. "Oh, shut up," I said, heading back to the bar.

Brielle took her glass and thanked me, but she only took a small sip.

We laughed, already forging a stronger bond despite the upcoming competition.

I returned to my seat with two drinks and sat down. My fingers touched Logan's as I gave him his drink, and my gaze slid over him briefly.

The liquid burned my throat on the way down, and I coughed, but it settled my frayed nerves.

Zoe laughed at me. "Logan converted us. Even you drink that now."

The people on the private jet were still strangers, even Logan. While I learned to appreciate his personality and just barely began to trust him during our brief time together, it was still a recent relationship. How do I really know I can trust him?

Regardless, a part of me felt uneasy. Where was Chase? I asked Jonathan, but he told me briefly that he did not know. He had not heard from him in a couple of days. I could not stop thinking about him and wondering what had happened. Chase appeared committed to the Center. I knew how much he wanted to be part of this expedition. The reality that Chase did not answer my calls, although I left him messages, was yet another worrying factor. Still, despite my concerns and doubts, I was here, among them.

When we first boarded the plane, Axel Summers whispered, "I hate flying. I look at a plane, and it stresses me, and it doesn't even have to leave the ground for me to feel that way," joked Axel with Anders Quinn.

It was kind of ironic. Axel possessed an aeronautics and astronautics engineering degree. With a degree in Geological and Planetary Sciences plus Applied Physics and Mechanics from Caltech, Anders made for a pleasant companion for Axel on this flight. They talked about computational mathematics as they lounged in two side leather chairs, a small table between them. Axel nervously glanced from time to time outside, past the jet's fuselage, but otherwise, the conversation kept him occupied. They were an interesting pair.

I observed my peers as we flew toward our destination. Everyone sat according to their affinity with each other. Already, allegiances were forming.

Veronica sat with Ronan and Liam upfront. Engaged in a conversation, they laughed a lot. Veronica Smooth was beautiful and self-assured. No doubt she was good at what she did, for she landed here, among our group. Her degree in Biotechnology, Bioengineering, and Robotics, from EPFL- Ecole Polytechnic Fédérale de Lausanne in Switzerland, fascinated me somehow.

I didn't think she and I could ever become friends. It was just a feeling more than anything else, but I had seen girls like her before, and they turned out to be, for me, enemies. Some people... Well, they were impossible to befriend because it just didn't click. I felt she was one of them.

Liam Donovan wore a short blond beard and mustache over a face that could have appeared in a Men's Health magazine. I guess it made sense considering his degree in Life Sciences and Medicine. I had learned earlier that his studies focused on Neurobiology, Bioengineering, Computation and Neural Systems, and Molecular Biophysics at Cambridge. He was impressive, and not only in appearance.

Liam kept to himself mostly, but Veronica insisted he stay with them. I guess they had plenty to talk about in their fields of expertise. He appeared calm and non-committal about Ronan's behavior. At the moment, Liam remained engrossed in a magazine. Reading an article was an excellent way to distance himself from Ronan, who sat near Veronica.

Ronan Phelps was a bit of an enigma. I couldn't read him but didn't like what I saw. He appeared outspoken, boisterous, and opinionated, past his disheveled outer appearance, which was also significant. His bulk was above average, more suited to be on the football field than in this plane if one asked me. So far, he kept his thoughts hidden. His degree from Stanford in Biological Engineering under the Bio-X initiative had provided him with an unusual opportunity to work with some of the most brilliant people on the planet. Whereas he seemed ill-suited for it, he made a name for himself, at least as much as I could surmise.

My brief contact with him made me grateful. While he addressed me a few times, my monosyllables' answers drove him away, and he moved on. I owed that to Logan's presence around me. Logan seemed determined to keep him away from me. I could only deduce that they felt the same way I did. Logan's behavior made that abundantly clear earlier on. Regardless, there was something about him I didn't trust.

Logan must have read my thoughts, for he leaned in my direction and said, "He is the bully type."

I nodded, "There is something about him that makes me uneasy. Why would they pick him to be on this project?"

"I'm not sure. The Bio-X initiative experience says a lot about him. We'll have plenty of time to find out when we get to the Center."

I nodded again. "Why is Ronan focusing on Anders and Axel? I caught him watching them."

"Yeah. I noticed it too," said Logan. "Listen, we will be in close quarters when we get down to the Center. And I don't mean to scare you, but be careful with him, okay?"

Looking at Logan more closely, I said, smiling, "Are you getting a bit too protective?"

He shrugged, and I could tell he was about to make a joke, but he thought better of it, for he smiled at me. "Maybe a little," he said, pulling away.

"Thank you." But I needed to ask if everything was fine. Are you all right?"

Logan's hand covered mine and squeezed it before he returned to his conversation with Brielle.

Seated in the center, near the part of the fuselage that was the strongest, I glanced over toward Axel.

He was opposite me, and our eyes had met several times, but we had not yet exchanged a meaningful conversation. Still, I had to concentrate on keeping up with their ongoing chat. My curiosity and thoughts about the odd mix we formed came back to the surface. *What does their specialty have to do with time research or even Anthropology and Neuroscience?* Was Jonathan planning to build a time machine of sorts? It appeared so farfetched that I chuckled.

"What's funny?" Asked Zoe, sitting to my left. She was the odd duck among all of us. But I related to her immediately. Her degree did not fit with ours. She stood apart from the scientific minds collected in this venture. It was what had drawn me to her. I felt like I had been there before.

She was a vibrant slip of a girl with black hair and big brown eyes. She seemed kind and perhaps was a bit of a dreamer. I didn't see her role in all this, but obviously, she had one.

"Just an odd thought," I said.

"You want to share it?" asked Brielle. "We can all use a brief laugh right about now."

"Sorry, guys, it's not for public consumption," I said, smiling at her.

"What do you make of all this?" asked Zoe.

"What do you mean?"

Zoe leaned toward me and said, a little discouraged, "Looking at all of you with all these science degrees, I understand even less why I'm here."

"Didn't Jonathan tell you anything at all about your role?"

"He was very vague about it… Talking about making history," said Zoe. "What about you?"

I turned to observe her… Somehow her line of thought had met mine. "The same… I think it's what Jonathan said to all of us. Her involvement in all this was unusual, though. Maybe she was here to record the future from a historical standpoint from now on. "Maybe he wants you to record all of this for posterity. You will create the annals of the Center, Zoe. Would that not be an achievement?"

"You think he wants to entrust me with such a task?" pondered Zoe for a minute.

"Seems logical. Why not?" I asked. "What else could it be?"

Already, our little group cemented with a kind of developing closeness and camaraderie that called for loyalty. Logan and I gathered with Zoe and Brielle on long sofa seats with a table in front of us.

Brielle Brown had a Ph.D. in Production, Distribution, and Consumption of Goods and Services. She had also focused on Economics, Architecture & Science of the City, with Finance, EPFL, at Yale University. The big reason she was here directly relied on her

published paper on underground space planning. The girl had style…
She was pretty too, with blond hair and a face any woman would envy.
Even the pair of glasses she wore now stressed her beauty. Seated on
the far side, besides Zoe, her attention focused on her laptop, she
remained engrossed in it, ignoring the rest of us.

Logan carried most of the conversation with her.

"Gen, sorry for my obvious lack of manners," said Logan." I
found this underground planning subject fascinating."

"I agree, especially as this is where we are headed," I murmured.
Now that I thought about it, it was crucial. So, Brielle was not only
beautiful but intelligent. *Well, she is, Gen. So, what's up with you?*

I tried not to look at Logan after that. Instead, I drifted in and
out of the conversation they carried around me, feeling somewhat
annoyed. *What is it to you?*

My eyes met Anders, and since I didn't want to dwell on my
emotions, I observed him.

Anders looked slim, almost skinny, under elongated muscles
filled his tall frame. He had dark chocolate skin and black hair cut
short. His angular face with jade eyes looped down slightly around the
corner stood over a straight nose and beautiful lips.

He seemed nice, too. His wide grin confirmed this and was
contagious as he looked back at me. I liked him almost instantly. He
remained calm under the nosy questions Ronan had launched at him
since we boarded the plane.

I would not be this nice. Ronan's behavior appeared more than
just challenging.

Finally, tired of placating Ronan with answers, Anders said,
"Hey, man, do you mind? I want to enjoy the flight. Give me a rain
check, and catch you later." After that, he just ignored him.

There was no pretense with him. He was what he appeared to be, genuine, and the guy others could relate to because they rallied around him and grunted their enthusiastic approval.

"Fine," rebuked Ronan as he turned back toward Veronica.

The questions stopped after that.

Anders glanced in my direction and winked at me.

I got utterly comfortable with him after that.

We had come from all over, and from now on, we would be together twenty-four seven. The Center would be our new home. So it was essential for us to get along. Having troublesome people among us would only make things more difficult.

I wasn't sure how I felt about living in such close accommodations. It would be a test. I had plenty of reservations about the entire ordeal, yet my curiosity had carried me. It would be great to have friends there.

Jonathan was a convincing individual. He was a man with a vision. Yet, I knew that there was more to it than what he told us, and I couldn't pass up finding out what lay behind the doors of the Center.

At least, some of us felt that way. Yet Logan held his council. He remained reserved, and while I didn't know why, I planned on finding out. However, regardless, here we were. Our group wanted to learn more and understand the specifics of this research. Our recruitment, carried with it the utmost in planning and secrecy, contributed to entice more curiosity, not less. With a tremendous amount of anticipation, I wanted to know what we would find at the Center.

The plane jerked up, aiming for the clouds over a pocket of air. It was abrupt, and I gasped.

Then we dropped.

Until that moment, our flight had been uneventful. The voice of the pilot interrupted our conversations. It rose from the speaker, methodical and cold, "Please remain seated and attach your seat belt. We are going through some rough turbulence. Hang on; it won't be pleasant."

Anders's voice faltered. "Do you think there is something wrong with the engine?"

"We would feel it by now," said Axel.

"Maybe it has to do with something else," murmured Logan.

"Like what?" I muttered. But then, I thought better of it. "I think we will. They are probably running checks."

As if the pilot heard me, the plane climbed again.

Just before the announcement, Anders had retrieved a round of drinks for the group. Anders' chuckled, "Here we go." He reached for a beer and handed one to Axel.

Logan grabbed a small bottle of Scotch from Anders and poured himself a drink. His glance returned to my face with a puzzled look. "You want one?"

I struggled to keep calm, at a loss for words. So I nodded.

Brielle and Zoe remained seated, fighting to regain their calm, no doubt. Anders handed them some wine. But I could feel Axel's stare at the back of my neck.

"Well, that was something," said Axel, with a shudder.

"It was nothing," concurred Anders. "Just an air pocket."

"I hope we passed it," said Axel. "We lost a bit of altitude, but we are gaining it back."

The activity in the cabin resumed, and I waited.

Unable to see whether we were flying over land or sea because of the darkness outside, I presumed we were by now halfway to our destination. *No doubt, we would then pass under the radar, too.*

Suddenly, lightning burst across the sky. It shimmered around the plane like a spider web. A blinding light pierced the cabin, streaking so fast that it was gone before we could grasp its presence.

The plane jerked on its trajectory as if the surge altered its course.

I looked outside, but nothing appeared around the airplane. The darkness swallowed us.

The minutes passed, but this time the plane didn't climb. The tension in the cabin increased among us.

Another burst of light stroked the ether. The plane shuddered a few times, as if influenced by high winds. The gusts buffeted the aircraft on one side and then the other.

"What was that?"

Another disturbance shimmered across our sky.

The streaks of lights appeared once more.

The jet engines sputtered and coughed a few times and resumed.

For a second, no one moved as silence surrounded us. The voice of the pilot rose again. "Sorry, folks. Everything is now under control. You can relax and resume your activities."

Calm entered the cabin, interspersed with talk and laughter. The tension I experienced released so suddenly that I giggled. The murmurs of voices dimmed, and my focus shifted back to my glass of wine.

But, caught in the downdraft, the plane's nose dropped again. The jolt pushed us forward. My drink tipped, splashing on the carpet.

"Hell, no!"

The jet banked sideways. The tension on my seat belt cut into my breasts, increasing as I slid forward. I held on to my seat, gasping. The drinks set on the table fell to the floor. Glasses, cans, and bottles rolled on the aisle.

We dropped altitude fast.

The plane gained in velocity as it fell from the sky. Our pilot attempted to regain a semblance of control over its flight pattern. But the fuselage cried against the elements, and the metal tube trembled as he fought to stabilize the jet.

I didn't want to believe what was happening, but something was going terribly wrong. Our plane jerked and dipped.

My grip tightened on the armrest.

Fear rose in the pit of my stomach, threatening to strangle me.

Logan reached for my hand. I held on to his hand, gripping it tightly.

A howling gust outside stressed the metal around the tube as the jet careened forward.

Screams shrieked inside the jet as we continued tumbling down.

Cold tendrils of fear wrapped around me, suffocating me.

The turbulence hit us on one side. Another blast found its way to the other side, and the jet careened again. Now, the airplane, with its powerful engines, was just a tube, devoid of its alluring luxury, as everyone braced for the worst.

I froze, never letting go of Logan's hand. How long before we hit the ground? Imagining the Earth getting visibly closer with each second, I closed my eyes. I did not want to picture the crash. I did not want to contemplate my death.

Admittedly, it was about to happen any minute now. But the darkness was worse as the picture of the patch of land reaching for us like a vacuum formed in my mind's eye.

I opened my lids, avoiding it altogether. I needed to face what was coming at me.

Screams rose again all around.

Another streak of light shattered the airplane walls. This time, appearing much more prominent, it grew before it split into multiple spider veins. They spread across the cabin into smaller ones without losing their intensity, crossing the space among the seats. A ball of light unfurled and grew, splitting into smaller ones. One of them stopped before me, forming a ball of light with red and white hues. It held a steady pattern for a brief moment and dissipated inside me.

Logan, seated beside me, experienced the same phenomenon. We both looked frozen like shiny alabaster statues.

Something had just happened to me, to us.

I did not know what it was. I just saw the burst of light flashing towards me and penetrating my skin.

As I stared ahead, the light vanished inside me, and I disassociated from my body.

We descended, losing altitude at a forty-five-degree angle, but my anxiety overcame everything. Only I could no longer move.

What just happened? Did it really happen? Did I see it for real? What the hell was that?

If I was to die here, was it all worth it? The answer surged in my head. *Hell, no.*

I thought of my family. Finding my mother was the most important thing, yet here I was. My time on this plane and my search for answers were not worth my life, and it was all I could think of as the plane shot out in the sky, taking all of us for a deep nosedive.

35
VANISHING
Logan

Light Strike - 2018

The disturbance comes rapidly. Suddenly, I am disconnected from my body and lose control. The light takes over and commands my surroundings. DAINN Annals, Summer 2022.

The drinks came at the right time; however, the release we sought did not last long. Even though we all needed to unwind a little, we did not get the chance. Jonathan's announcement caught everyone off guard, but he changed the rules as the CEO of the Center. While it was part of our lives as scientists to always apply for grants and chase the cheese. In this instance, it was unexpected. We all ran for these contributions to our work as fast as we could, and the competition was the name of the game, no matter the field. Just as I looked out the window, the airplane dropped. The sudden motion and its implications grabbed us by the throat. We were all on edge after that. Unfortunately, we did not enjoy our beverages.

When the plane careened downwards after the first time we hit the air bubble, everything on the table crashed to the cabin's floor. The masks held in the ceiling fell, dangling under the turbulence as soon as the plane dipped in the sky. The air pressure changed quickly, compelling us to put them on.

I reached for mine and put it on.

The others beside me did the same thing, except for Gen, who kind of froze.

The oxygen mask in front of Gen's face kept on swinging back and forth. Engrossed in panic, she looked like a mannequin watching the mask move like a pendulum. I reached out for it and tried to hand it to her to place it on her face. She looked at me with fear in her eyes.

I nodded, looking at the small device in my hand, encouraging her to comply.

She adjusted it slowly over her face, looking so frightened that a knot lodged inside my throat. The truth... I was not doing much better, but I kept it hidden. There was nothing we could do about what was happening.

Silence now floated among us. The jet fought to straighten out against its falling weight, but it failed to succeed. The fuselage did not lift. Instead, under the wind, the screams of the metal increased inside the cabin.

No matter what, this did not feel right. We faced death at this altitude if the jet did not recover. But it was not meant to happen to us, not now. I refused to contemplate that outcome. My brain fought to find a way out of this dilemma and could not find it. We ought to celebrate, not fight for our lives. Part of me knew this was a dumb thought. Yet, I couldn't help it.

I never really thought about dying before. I bet the others did not give it much thought, either. Why should we? It was not something one does when they are in their teens, barely entering adulthood. At least, these were my comments to myself. Unless, of course, one confronted depression or peer pressure. I supposed suicide was rampant among some youths. It just was not something I had ever considered much before.

In the seconds following the drop, my erratic thoughts turned to what could await us on the other side if there was another side to life. What would it be like to die? Was there even another plane of existence? Would we pass through a gateway and reach beyond what we knew to come out elsewhere? Or was there just nothingness awaiting us? Grim. I imagined myself moving past our limitations to a different dimension, reaching beyond the barrier of physical state. Maybe another plane of existence awaited all of us. Perhaps this was a sort of trial, forcing us to leave behind our minds' confines and perceptions to enter a different realm. All right, I know this was not logical. But as my anxiety increased, logic no longer held a place in my brain. Hey, I never portrayed myself as a contemplative type, but under the circumstances in this instance, I grasped at anything to reassure myself that this was not it, not the end, not a void from which no one could recover. I guessed that this paradox I entered rather willingly kept me calm and in control, at least for now.

I looked at Axel; signs of panic engulfed him. His eyes closed over a face frozen in horror that reminded me of one of those faked plastic faces, one plastered on Halloween night. He gripped the arms of his seat so hard that his knuckles were white.

Axel reached for his mask and attempted to place it on his face, but the darn thing wouldn't comply with his clumsy fingers, and it took several attempts before he finally secured it.

My hand clasped Gen's, and our fingers interlocked over her grip on the arm of her chair.

She looked at me. Lines of tension formed around her eyes, and I winked at her, trying to reassure her. "It's going to be all right," I said, over the others crying out.

As we kept our gazes locked on each other, I thought about another frontier, which helped. While my anxiety grew as the dive continued, I held on to the feeling, that belief, that new reassuring thought that something else existed past our deaths, even though I couldn't quite believe what was unfolding.

I drew a ragged breath.

The screams in the cabin overwhelmed everything.

The plane's nose did not lift. We did not recover from the dive.

Instead, the lighting struck again, colliding against the fuselage. As tendrils formed around the streaks, spreading in the isle, we watched dumbfounded, crouching for cover in our seats to avoid the sparks of electricity filling the cabin.

Suddenly, a large sphere burst inside the cabin. It hovered in place, white filaments surrounding a red core and spreading outward. It grew, splitting into several small balls of snow-white electricity, lifting in the center aisle. Each of them hesitated a split second and advanced toward us. With speed, one of them forged its way toward me.

A beat passed as I pulled back in my seat, watching the Sphere. It stopped at eye level, gliding in front of my eyes. It approached and disappeared inside me with a swift motion, entirely absorbed by my body.

I felt the jolt, and my mind ceased to be mine. In the space of a second, I lost myself in the burst of lighting. It was not painful. Instead, it felt as if a cold seeped into every cell in my body, numbing me. A loss of feeling soon followed, and a distance from my environment occurred, although I was still in the same place within the airplane.

I remained in my seat. I could feel Gen's hand in mine, but everything around me appeared now far away.

The source of light invaded my vision and my mind. Instead of panicking, I immediately felt calmer. It wasn't as if I heard words, but there were none. It was more a sort of knowing, irreversible, tangible, and absolute.

I tried to focus on what was happening around me, but nothing else seemed as natural as the strobe of light. The plane somehow was no longer my focus. My environment appeared now immaterial.

The feeling of certainty delivered yet another message in the same intangible way. I was safe. Those around me were safe. I had no idea where the news came from or what caused it to get me. It was there and no longer there.

The overwhelming emotion was gone before I could entirely bathe in it. Yet, it was enough.

In the distance, I felt the carcass of the aircraft stabilize, and the air pockets stopped. The plane righted itself, its nose lifting abruptly in the air, no longer subject to shudders, and the shrieks of metal dissipated as quickly as they had come.

The feeling of disconnection increased. The control over my limbs continued. I still couldn't move, although I tried to shake my head to clear my thoughts. It didn't work.

As I wondered if this really happened, doubts entered my mind. It lasted only mere seconds, so I was justified to wonder about it. Did I dream about it?

No.

The answer was clear. I was sure I had not dreamt of the experience. What was it then?

Something unusual, an event unlike anything I knew, took place on the plane. Something big had happened. I recognized that. I couldn't, wouldn't doubt it.

The light increased around me, creating a white barrier, thicker, and dense in its configuration. As my eyes glanced ahead, I was no longer on the plane. Somehow, I just received confirmation that I didn't dream of the event.

The light within me grew to an overwhelming, dizzying state.

I lost Gen's hand in mine, no longer feeling anything physical.

I lost sense of time and place—a white substance surrounded my mind, resembling fuzzy filaments embedded in the light.

My ability to think was lost.

I felt suddenly weightless. It was like floating from very far away, and everything concrete around me dissolved to nothingness.

Then, just as suddenly, the walls of the airplane vanished around me.

36 RESCUE
Tesh

Underwater Cave, CA - 2022

The access to our EHAF Chamber is a relief for all of us. We are finally going to see some of our team members. DAINN Annals, 2022.

We hovered above the trees, leaving behind the cliffs, and glided toward the summit irrespective of the night surrounding us. Our EmVats' excellent night vision with the destination beacon from our PVZ guided our way in the darkness. It led us back close to the peak we had departed only hours ago.

Leane barely recovered from the scan, moved behind me sluggishly, but she refused to wait any longer. We were eager to reach the EHAF Chamber to rescue our team still in their cryo pods.

Despite my multiple promptings, Leane refused to talk with us. So, Blast and I followed, disturbed that she appeared so far away from us when we needed her.

The trip to the top of the mountain took only minutes. When we landed on one of the smaller peaks, a cave's access lay open like a black hole, ready to swallow us. It led to the main cave we escaped from a while ago. This new access cut our trip by half, and Leane's scan had revealed the alternative path.

I could not help the shiver that ran through me at the idea of once again plunging into that environment.

Blast did not feel my hesitation as he dove right in, eager to begin the necessary process to retrieve our team. Glancing behind me, I checked Leane's whereabouts before I followed him.

"I'm right behind. I'm okay. Stop worrying about me," said Leane as we stood on the edge of the abyss.

"NetRoger that, but don't mind me if I monitor you. You are exhausted, even if you pretend not to be," I muttered, worried that she may not have the strength to handle the awakening of the EHAF if anything turned badly inside our Chamber.

She read my mind. "I'll be fine. Stop worrying."

I nodded, wanting to confront her about what she avoided telling us. "What..."

But she cut me off. "Tesh, I will tell you when I'm ready. So, stop."

With a curt nod, I plunged ahead, Leane trailing me.

The descent went much faster than our ascent. It reminded me of Chase, and I shook my head, determined not to think about him.

The silence in the cave surrounded us, feeling like a box closing in on all sides. Apart from the lights from our EVs, the stillness and cold sipped into me. I watched the blackness, like an enormous hand, enfolding me into an eternity of nothingness, making me disappear from the world.

Blast's voice coming from below reached me on the NetComm, "I am approaching the entrance you forged, Tesh. I'll wait for you in the tunnel."

"NetRoger that," I said, pulling myself from the gloomy thoughts that permeated my mind. "It might be better if we talked about your plan once we get there, Blast."

"Humm... Darnet, I hate to be back here again," whispered Blast. "It's simple. I am opening the Chamber and getting our people out."

Leane chuckled. "Well, go ahead then."

Blast observed the side tunnels ahead, waiting for us. He grinned and folded his visor when I reached the bedrock hole. "We're lucky; it seems pretty quiet around here."

When Leane joined us, we moved further ahead. The last time we were in this place together was after we fought the Entity and woke up from the prison of the Sphere. Nothing was touched since we left, or so it appeared. But the real challenges lay ahead.

We needed to reach our Chamber, hidden behind the wall of rocks Leane built before she joined us, and find the fork area where the other tunnels started. We had carved three more shafts beside this one when Streak was still among us.

Blast searched for the path he NetPulsed upward toward the water chute that caved the walls of this place. It had dropped him underwater and pinned him down under one of our displaced Chambers.

Streak had found him and helped free him. Although Leane, Blast, and I extracted ourselves before the collapse, it caught Streak. While he orbed out to avoid the ceiling caving on him, he also disappeared. Since this happened, we had not seen him.

What would we find in that cave now? Was our Chamber still intact? Were our teammates, okay? There was no way to know that until we reached it.

We now faced the passage, blocked by the rubble of the war we fought against the Sphere. The rocks in our path were so high that they almost reached this shaft's ceiling. The ground bore the marks of our lasers. Everywhere we looked, the charred rocks wore the remnants of the combat with the Sphere.

I remembered how cold the air felt around me as I tried to reach my team. It was excruciating looking for Leane and Blast, trying to crawl through the debris to get to them. But the fear that they would not be alive because of the onslaught of the Sphere against them ate at me at that moment.

The lightning bolt grew from white to red, building darker and looking angrier as it broke through the Sphere's inner parameters. It escaped from its center, energy bursting through its rings, in an enormous push forward, careening toward my team's location. In seconds, it pulverized the bedrock inside the tunnel, freezing everything in its path and burying my friends under a mountain of rock. They disappeared in an instant. The fear tore at me. Unable to move through the immense rubble that remained, I crawled as far as I could and lost consciousness due to the freezing cold settling on me.

When we regained consciousness, we found ourselves inside the Sphere. Much later, with no memories of how we arrived or how long we stayed in the environment of the Entity, we awoke in the tunnel.

Blast moved ahead and began to clear a path among the rocks. I stopped him when Blast retrieved his NetPulse to fuse a passage. "Do you think we should? What if the Sphere comes back? What if the Center's security team hears us?"

Blast turned to me, "You want to take these down one at a time? It will take us forever."

"Let's use our Androids," I said. Turning to Leane, I asked, "How many are still in our Chamber?"

"We've left the larger ones, the VBS5300," Leane said. "We didn't think we could use them on the outside."

Blast nodded. "I'll get the VB's. Whether or not we can use them, I want to take the rest of our equipment out of our Chamber. I never want to come back to this place."

Leane turned toward the hidden gate of our Chamber and contemplated the massive mess in front of her. "And how do we deal with this?"

"NetPulse," said Blast. "I know what you are going to say. They may hear us, but it won't be for long... And frankly, we need to move. I don't care if the Center hears us; as for the Sphere, it gave us time, so let's use it."

"I agree. The gate won't take that long to unearth. It's a risk we have to take," I said.

Without waiting for another instant, Blast began to NetPulse. This time, he regulated his device to blow the rocks in a wide berth rather than with depth, and little by little, we saw the outline of the locking mechanism of our Chamber.

The sound resonated in the tunnel as we waited for the gate to stand free of the bedrock, and I looked around with unease.

My impatience was hard to contain. I wanted to see my other teammates as quickly as possible to move to our plan's next phase. Perhaps it was time to deconstruct the Chamber and get everything to a different location. Blast may be right in that, but it would mean one of us would need to remain behind to do it. Leane's role remained at the EHAF Chamber, helping Blast. So, it left me. "I will stay back while you two go ahead."

Within minutes, Blast revealed the door.

It responded to our command in the next instant. The mechanism parted the heavy panels, opening the entrance to us. It felt so much like 'Deja Vue' that I glanced around the darkened corridor, half expecting to see the Sphere move toward us. I shook my head and joined the others as they entered our Chamber.

Blast quickly retrieved three VB's. The modules were no larger than a cube we could hold in the palm of our hand. The devices responded immediately. They glided down to the ground, opening and growing larger with each layer unpeeled. When Blast commandeered them into the shaft, they hovered behind him. The next instant, they stood on their sturdy base, deployed enormous arms, and began moving toward the rocks in an excavating formation. The first one grabbed the closest rock and passed it to the second one, which carried it away, while the third moved to get to the next rock, repeating the motion of the second one.

We had no way to know the depth of the barrier nor how extensive the cave-in was, but the androids were fast at work. At least they operated quietly.

"I will remain here to deconstruct the compartment," I said to Leane. "I will join you as soon as it is ready."

"Maybe we should do that to the EHAF Chamber as well," she suggested.

I nodded. "Yes, just let the EHAF team know we need to evacuate the area if I have not met you by the time, they exit their pods."

The advance of the androids in the tunnel proceeded as I began the deconstruction process of our compartment.

How long would it take our Chamber to finish the process? I had never observed it before, and the deconstruction in action remained a mystery.

Once it began, the process would not stop until finished. No one could reverse it midstream. The entire phase required completion before it would reassemble. Where could we reform the Chamber? We did not know at the moment, but it did not matter. The Chamber Oblong would follow us wherever we went.

I moved to the array and entered my codes, calling for the disassembly of our safety compartment. The screen responded, engaging the sequence.

I walked outside and waited by the gate. Anything we had not taken with us would remain inside our Chamber as it folded on itself in a seamless elliptic shape. The sheets of alloy, one of the most robust materials of our time, separated, disengaging from one another. Each lifted from their locked location, slid to the next surface, and attached to others until they became ten sheets, then twenty sheets, and so on, all oblong forming blocks. Each section of our Chamber continued the process, in a finite number of steps, harmoniously gliding in a continuous process. Some pieces shaped themselves into thicker oblong forms than others, but their sizes remained constant. Once completely assembled, only two large elliptical shapes remained, floating side by side at the center of what used to be our entire Chamber.

Watching this technology in action was mesmerizing, even for me. Indeed, it was an achievement for our scientists to have structured such a habitat.

Now, the inner walls of the Chamber had disappeared, folded into the outer walls. The center of the compartment narrowed, creating yet another oblong block, retrieving all displays and screens. The central array, holding some of the DAINN functions and programs, formed another brick in this formidable structure. This time, it remained more diminutive in size than the other oblong forms and decagon in shape. All shapes connected themselves, locking together, hovering in place at the center of our now empty Chamber. Our safety Chamber's decagon shape and core program positioned itself at the top of the first oblong form, adhering to the center. Each inner octagon drawer drifted away from the remaining inner walls. They followed the same process and path to become part of the compartment. Vacant of our supplies, they joined the already assembled oblong forms and locked themselves to the decagon shapes on either side of the elliptical disk. The second oval form hovered over the decagon shape and clung to it, assembling into a new structure of about six spaces by ten spaces.

This latest device remained suspended in the air as the outer walls of our Chamber detached from the bedrock. The exterior partitions gravitated toward the oblong disks and locked themselves around them, forming one seamless oblong block. The sizeable elliptical disk glided toward me in one swift move, and the outer gate attached itself as a ring around it.

Behind me, the surrounding bedrock where our Chamber was moments ago disintegrated in place, collapsing on the now empty area. Vibrations followed as the rocks fell. The noise rose like thunder, enveloping the tunnel where we stood. Stones tumbled down, filling the space, and dust particles floated in the enclosed shaft.

In a concerted reaction with Leane and Blast, I lifted my EV and turned toward the depth of the tunnel where the androids continued their advance. They cleared a narrow opening, and we walked through.

I no longer had to remain behind with the Chamber hovering in the shaft beside me. The oblong disk floated in place on the side of the tunnel. It would stay there until we got back.

Quickly, Blast launched a small Custodian at the tunnel's entry to watch for any intruders. The androids took position ahead of us inside the shaft, moving along on either side of Blast, who led the way to the upper passageway.

A trickle of water glistened on the bedrock when we reached the opening, and below us lay the underwater Chamber.

Blast dropped glow sticks to illuminate the cavern below. The dark hole glowed a deep shade of green as the androids jumped.

Without waiting around, he joined them and descended to the cavern's floor, submerged by the pool of water.

Leane followed behind him, and I dropped after her.

Blast, impatient, pushed ahead with the propulsion of his NetJet boots, driving quickly toward the vertical disk that sliced the cavern in two

I lost him in the water ahead and pressed forward to catch up with Leane.

We rushed to reach the hidden gate of the compartment.

Blast inspected the edges, trying to identify the gate's location by the time we got there, moving around the structure slowly.

Still searching for the door, he had already covered half of the width of our disk. Blast reached the ceiling, and his voice rose on the NetComm. "It's here. We need to open a larger space to get the equipment out unless we leave everything inside the Chamber as we deconstruct the compartment."

"It's the EHAF's decision. They will know what they need after we wake them up. Let's get inside," I said over the NetComm.

The entryway lodged inside a piece of the bedrock covering the ceiling required the creation of a larger opening. While Blast worked on it, Leane and I anxiously waited for his signal.

We swam upward, the weight of our EVs slowing us down, and reached Blast as he widened the hole around the entrance. The gate was below the cavern's roof, giving us barely enough space to get in and out.

Blast built a field holding the weight of the water, molding it around the entrance, giving us access to the door mechanism. "I'll hold this."

The passage inside protected by the field allowed us to approach the mechanism.

I pushed against the mechanism, and for a moment, nothing happened. I strengthened my hold on the surface and tried again.

Leane waited at my side.

Suddenly, the powerful locking system moved. The door panels gave way, and the gate slid open.

Relief flooded me. Finally, we were making headway.

I moved ahead.

The floor of the EHAF Chamber tipped to the side did not make our approach easy as Leane followed behind me until our NetJet boots engaged with the flooring. Grabbing the displays inside our Chamber to maintain our advance at an almost entirely vertical angle, we made our way further into the compartment. We ended up hanging sideways, climbing over some of the central consoles.

The safety Chamber did not automatically respond as it should have once the door opened. My first move was to check the life support system to determine any damage that may have occurred to the safety module. Its precarious position inside the Earth may have caused irreparable harm to the cryo pods. "The pod life support work," I said with relief.

"The individual units are intact," Leane said, looking in my direction as she smiled.

I crawled ahead toward the main array. "No breach?" I asked.

"Nothing that I can see," Leane continued.

"Let me check the reanimation system," I murmured, going over a diagnostic of our local DAINN—the limited Network that came with every one of our Chambers under the Origin program.

After a complete reading of the main array, it became apparent that the EHAF Chamber sustained some damage. The primary life support System could stop working during the process. Nervously, I looked at the readings. "It could fail midstream. We need to do a manual override."

Leane came to my side. As she read the consoles, she frowned. "We still have to do it."

"I know. Can you take over if it stops?"

We knew these people. I could only hope they would be okay, but we had no way to tell until we activated the process.

"We need to wake them one at a time. But it may run out of power before we finish with the last of our teammates."

I nodded and understood the dilemma. The last of our teammates might not make it. How would I choose among the four? I did not want to. These were my people, my team. One was as crucial as another as they were part of us, separate but connected. Yet some of them would have a more significant role in this world. One that would influence the result and be more necessary to the mission to pave a new future, all of us together. "I refuse to lose any of them. How do we make that happen? What can we do?"

Leane shook her head, emotionally as conflicted as I was. "I can only help one at a time if the system fails."

"I may not have your gift, but there must be something I can do to help you?"

Leane, deep in thought, finally said, "You can rely on the PodBots, maybe. Then, you can copy a physical reanimation sequence. Let me show you."

I reached into her mind and viewed the process. It was so out of my league of gifts; I shuddered at the idea of holding the life of the EHAF team members in my hands. But if the System failed, there was no other way.

With anxiety lodged in my throat, I acknowledged I had received the information. So, I manually engaged in the reanimation process with hope in my heart. The awakening inside the cryo pods began. As for our Chamber, there were four pods, each protecting four of our members.

The program of the cryo pod established by DAINN took over. Once the EHAF team awoke, they could override the Systems to address other parts of the Chamber's functions before we could safely depart.

The System began with Nis, the head of the EHAF Conclave in the Origin program. Slowly, both Leane and I followed the sequence.

Over the NetComm, I said to Blast, who remained outside, holding the force field for our team, "We started the awakening."

"NetRoger that," Blast said.

Leane reached for the PodBot, which began to move toward the pod. She took the vial of Spozor from its mechanical arm and injected the liquid into Nis as he surfaced from the long void.

Within seconds, Nis took a deep breath and opened his eyes. His face did not register any surprise as he saw Leane over him. She pulled back to give him room. He glanced over to me and said, SoulLife Tesh, SoulLife Leane."

I let out a sigh of relief and approached them as he lifted himself from the pod, his long legs reaching the ground in a smooth move. "SoulLife, Nis," I said. It was reassuring seeing him here with us. I thought about what President Langden told me that I could count on his EHAF team no matter what especially dealing with the traitor in our midst. It would be good to confide in Nis.

"SoulLife Nis," repeated Leane, after me.

It was amazing to see him again after all this time. He appeared untouched by the frozen sleep he had just emerged from as he looked at us.

Nis was tall with all muscles in the right places, broad shoulders, a powerful chest, long muscular legs, thick arms, and a defined six-pack belonging to an endomorph body type. He wore his dark hair Mohock style, shorter on the side and longer on the top of his head. His most striking features were his eyes, an unusually deep purple. The planes of his face, slightly angular, starkly stood out.

Nis added, "It is good to see you."

"You have no idea," I said with a smile, relief flowing through me as I watched his face, already alert. He was ready for action, knowing without even asking that something had happened. Our established protocols called for us to wake each other up should the need arise, and it had. Nis knew we would not be here otherwise.

As Leane moved to another pod, Nis approached me. "Any imminent danger? What is the damage?"

"No immediate danger, but we need to hurry. You need to do overrides, but showers will have to wait. We have limited time and need to get out of here," I said. "There's a lot to tell you, but we reached the year 2018."

Nis nodded. "All right. What else do I need to know?" He dressed quickly, going for his UniWear first and his EmVat second.

"We may run out of power, so we are doubling up to wake everyone else."

He immediately jumped to the array. Quickly, he manipulated the power supply and turned offline some of the other non-essential functions.

After a second of hesitation, I gave him a very concise version of everything we had encountered since we awoke. "The Earth shifted, and we are underground, but we are not alone and face two potential enemies – one human, part of The Center, and one Entity we know nothing about and which appeared more powerful than us. The compartments broke apart. We need to find the other Chambers before the Center gets to our people. The Entity plans something soon and warns of massive destruction in the area."

Nis adjusted his EV and began loading his gear, going through the Chamber as he walked the walls. "NetRoger that. I would like more details later. How long do we have?"

"We don't know. I can tell you more the soonest we are out of here," I said, agreeing with Nis that he needed the entire picture. "Select the gear you need. We already have deconstructed our Chamber. I recommend you do the same."

I turned to the third pod and watched as the PodBot started its programming to support the procedure and walked over to the fourth pod, manually jump-starting the process.

Leane watched a woman getting out by the next pod and reached for her gear. Her name was Lana, and she was the second in command of the EHAF Conclave. Looking toward Nis, she said, "SoulLife Nis, SoulLife Tesh, and SouldLife Leane."

"SoulLife Lana," Nis said clearly. "We are at protocol level five." Nis decided not to take any chances on what we would face outside.

"SoulLife Lana," I whispered, stepping closer to the fourth pod.

Protocol five required them to act quickly and called for the immediate deconstruction of their Chamber. They would soon prepare the aspects of the EHAF Chamber for a quick departure.

After retrieving some of her gear, Lana turned to Nis and said, "Protocol level five, NetRoger that."

Nis glanced my way and nodded. "Give us nine minutes."

Lana nodded and began packing some of their gear in the same type of casings we had used for ours. Everything within the EHAF Chamber would come with us. She opened a compartment that held four City Vigils. They stepped outside their cubicle and began retrieving advanced combat equipment we had not seen before. As they assembled it, I said, "Nis, I should mention we are in an underground cavern surrounded by water with NetPulsed tunnels. Blast is holding a field around us."

Nis lifted one of his eyebrows but said nothing. He gave a silent command to the City Vigil, who then turned to retrieve more casings, folding some gear back inside. "SoulLife Blast. I will coordinate with you when the Chamber is about to fold so you can reinforce the field."

"SoulLife Nis. NetRoger that," said Blast.

"Well, sounds like it's going to be amusing," said Lana.

She was of medium size, about my height, but this is where the similarity ended. While I had long, lean muscles, hers looked robust and more defined, with long legs, well-built arms, and a body type that met an endomorph's parameters. Her shoulders were undeniably broad, her waist smaller, over a tiny chest, no doubt with no fat. Her face was pretty, with a perky nose and nice full lips, but her eyes were unnerving, with a hint of yellow in them, like those of a cat on the prowl. Short, bouncy, dark blue hair surrounded her striking facial features.

Nis stepped toward the controls of the Chamber and downloaded some information.

I noted all of this while surveying the process in the last of our pods. So far, everything seemed to remain normal.

"We are good here," said Leane. "The override you did, Nis, seemed to work to give the life support system the added energy it needed."

By then, Leane pulled away from the third pod to join me.

Jolt lifted his arm for the PodBot in his compartment, which quickly injected the Spozor. He glanced around the Chamber and jumped quietly on the soft Chamber ground. "SoulLife Conclave," Jolt said, saluting all of us. "I suppose this is the welcoming committee in our new world?"

"I'm glad I don't have to activate my new founds skills," I whispered.

Leane smiled. "Me too."

Without waiting for an answer, he reached for his clothes and his EV suit.

Nis simply nodded his confirmation. "SoulLife Jolt, protocol level five. Immediate departure."

"NetRoger that, Commander," said Jolt, loading his suit with more gear than I ever saw Blast use.

Leane focused on the last member of the EHAF team, Silia.

We had never crossed paths before.

Silia joined the team as a last-minute addition.

I couldn't help but wonder if President Zane Langden removed the prior member of the EHAF team because he suspected the other one might betray us. I wondered how Nis took it as I observed her for the first time.

Each team's balance, built on the members working together, closely relied on individual actions and reactions. Instinct was never enough. A team depended on its members, working in a perfectly calibrated way based on habits and experience. Often, it was the only way to accomplish the goals of a mission.

Silia observed us, a frown on her face. "SoulLife Conclave," she said in a clipped voice, revealing little of her thought. Quickly, she hopped over one console and began to get dressed.

"SoulLife Silia, protocol level five," responded Nis, watching her a moment too long.

The latest member of the EHAF team stood out. She wore shorter orange hair over a mutinous face, whose bravado was lodged entirely in her eyes - piercing indigo eyes. She was not built like the others, but that didn't mean anything about her capabilities. Only, I did not know her and had not established a MindLandscape for her.

Her body shape was more of an Ectomorph type. Quickly, I understood why she was among them. Her movements were swift, faster than what I had seen Streak exemplify. She must have the type of gift allowing speed. In the blink of an eye, she was ready to go, EV and gear at the ready, standing by the gate. "I'll deconstruct and follow you."

Nis nodded and turned toward Leane and me, "Blast, we're ready. Tesh, lead-out."

Our EVs went up, and we stepped outside the Chamber to meet with Blast. One after the other, we moved into the body of water and descended to the ground of the cavern. We stepped through the slush and silt of the cave floor as quickly as we could. The debris and rubble would build behind us when the Chamber collapsed on itself, no longer supporting the ceiling.

I pushed ahead with Leane toward the opening of the tunnel above.

Nis sent a brief command to two of the City Vigils. The Androids quickly lifted from the ground to position themselves by the Chamber gate, right under the roof.

Nis nodded. "They'll hold the ceiling until you clear, Silia. You know what to do."

"NetRoger that, Nis," said Silia. Silia turned and gave Nis a hand sign on the visor, then with a grin in Blast's direction, "Hope you like it fast."

Blast descended to the ground and announced with a smirk over the NetComm, "Let's get out of here."

Nis turned back to Blast, looking at the environment. "NetRoger that." The remaining two Android quickly joined Leane and me to move ahead.

Blast's head tilted toward Silia, and he said, "Can't wait to test your skills. I heard about you."

We reached the opening of the tunnel. The Android climbed first. I lifted myself, followed by Leane, with Nis trailing us. Quickly, all three of us stood in the shaft, dropping water on the ground, waiting for the others.

The passageway was now wider, cleared by our Institute androids, waiting for us by the oblong disk, near the location of what used to be our door.

Lana lifted herself next, quickly stepping ahead of Nis and me, followed by Jolt. They both took the lead, slightly on either side of us. It would be so from now on. The protective bubble of the EHAF surrounding the Institute Conclave wrapped itself around us as a safety measure. It included Blast and Streak if he were here with us now.

As if reading my mind, Nis turned toward me. "Where is Streak?"

"He is missing. We must retrieve him," I said.

Nis exclaimed, "He cannot orb?"

I shook my head. "He would be here if he could."

Nis grunted. "I must catch up with what you faced. But we will get him back."

Leane answered for both of us this time, "It may not be easy, and we need your help to get him back."

"Let's get out of here first, and then we can plan the next rescue," suggested Nis.

A huge thunderous blast resonated, and the tunnel's ground shook. Other rumbles echoed within the mountain walls before they hit the bottom of the cavern below us. A surge splashed the tunnel entrance as water drifted toward us to the surface. Amid the turbulence in the water, we suddenly saw Silia's head appear in the opening as we waited for the rest of our teammates. Her EmVat, recognizable with the EHAF emblem, rose over the edges just before Blast followed behind her, dripping. Next came the android holding the elliptical

EHAF Chamber. It was the one that held the ceiling in the water when we evacuated earlier. Each bore an identifier that appeared on our visors.

A movement of her wrist and the oblong disk of their Chamber pushed upward, breaking through the rocks saturated with water of the smaller cavity. The other casings followed with one of the City Vigils that held the ceiling.

Silia's voice cut through the noise. "We lost CV3E. He got crushed under the bedrock's weight."

No one in our group needed more details as our Visors appraised us of the outcome below.

Our group had grown—our three Androids, along with the three EHAF City Vigils, added to our numbers. And we now possessed with these two teams, two of our Chambers with the EHAF Chamber casings and equipment. I could not help to think that things were looking up for us.

But we had lost a member of our team. Although different from our own, the life of an android remained a loss. They retained a citizen's status in our world, even if they were machines. They served our society just as much as any of us. Under the DAINN System, it remained duly and publicly noted.

An extended portion of the tunnel lay ahead of us as we walked. Slowly, we moved toward the opening leading to the great cave, and I couldn't help myself but wonder what we would face. Would we have enough time to get our entire team? Would the Entity rise to meet us? Would we have to fight our way out? Once again, we had invaded its territory.

I glanced at my Origin team. We were not a complete team either yet, but soon would be with Streak rejoining our ranks and awakening the other Conclaves. I'll make sure of that.

My hope fluttered in my chest. It was only a day since we woke up from the Sphere; surely, we were still within its timeline to get out of here. But it was only after that thought came to my mind that I realized how wrong I was just now.

As we reached the opening, coming from the darkness of the great cavern, a shimmer of white lights buzzed over the abyss. They drifted in a pattern I witnessed before over the black edge of the crevasse. Streaks of lightning split ahead of us, crackling within the environment of the mountain. They lit this otherwise dark, empty place.

One does not defeat a phantom. The noncorporeal being was the one that overpowers you, defeating and, often, vanquishing its adversary as it obliterated its forces under the power of its mighty light.

Our enemy was again waiting for us. We had just come full circle as we stood in front of the millions of lights.

37
MAGIC
Leane

Large Cavern - 2022

I know what we face. I understand we cannot win and realize what I must do. Unless I use my gift to overcome what we face, we will lose again, but unleashing my magic will reveal my true nature. DAINN Annals, 2022.

As we watched the Entity grow in energy, with the light dispersing throughout the cave, Nis immediately gave orders. The City Vigils powered up to combat mode. The EHAF team members prepared to defend us, but I knew it would not work.

Tesh, Blast, and I had faced the Sphere before and got totally trounced. We could not afford more delays in rescuing the rest of our team, and finding ourselves back inside the Sphere if this was indeed what awaited us was not an option.

When Blast pushed past me to take a front-line position with Nis and the other, I knew what I must do. And I had no time to explain. What would Tesh think of me? What would they all think of me? Would they feel betrayed and not accept me for who I truly was? But if I did not act now and hesitated at all, everything might be lost to accomplish our mission. We needed to survive this and so I would give myself away. I chose to believe in Tesh. I eleceted to trust our friendship at that moment, so I reached out. *Tesh, I know how to protect us.*

Tesh turned toward me, a frown on her face. *What do you mean?*

Embarrassed, I shrugged and lifted my hands.

Tesh's eyes perused the symbols shifting under my skin and looked at my face. *I cannot explain, for there is no time, but I can clear a path for us outside of this cave.*

Tesh frowned as she considered what I said. *How?*

I shook my head. *I will explain later.*

What happened to you, Leane?

There is no time. Let me try.

Tesh pointed at the runes on my skin, *It's nothing like our technology, is it?*

No. It's different. With a sight, I added, *It's magic. But I think it will hold until we reach the surface.*

After another moment, Tesh nodded. *It was the scan, right? You have been different since you came back from it. You will need to explain what is going on.*

I nodded. *Let's get out of here first. You must understand, that I needed time to process what happened. I will tell you everything, but now there is no time,* I added, glancing toward the growing Sphere and its legion of lights that advanced toward us.

Tesh grinned, a smile coming to her lips. *Hum. Magic? Different energy, maybe. But some say that any advanced tech can be identical or equivalent to the same. Is it tantamount? Fine, show me what you can do?* She then turned to the rest of our team and called a halt. "Wait."

Nis scowled, unhappy about being called on actions that were part of his prerogative in his EHAF role. "Tesh, now is not the time to interfere."

Tesh looked at Nis and said, "We have been against the Sphere before, with everything we had and lost. I do not believe that what we throw at them now will bring a different result. We need to try something else."

Nis, frustrated, shrugged and said, "So, what do you propose?"

Tesh tilted her head in my direction, a mysterious smile lighting up her face. "Let Leane try something."

"Guys, whatever you are going to do, you need to do it now," said Lana urgently.

"You're not a fighter, Leane. What in the HellNet are you doing?" growled Blast.

"We are not attacking," said Leane, moving forward among the group and taking a position in front of us despite Blast barring her way. "Fighting them did not prove productive the last time."

"Then how do you plan on stopping this?" said Jolt, grumpily. "This is not a friendly presence."

"There is a better way. Our presence threatens the Entity. It told us to get away from here. We invaded its space again. What would you do in its place?" said Leane, hands on her hips as she faced the abyss with a scowl on her face.

"What are you planning?" Nis took a position beside me.

Leane shrugged and murmured, "Be prepared to move toward the surface as quickly as you can."

The lights grew stronger, merging and advancing toward us ahead of the larger Sphere that now faced us. The reddish glimmers intensified. Remembering what we saw when we fought it, we had little time left. I needed to act now. "Get ready," I said in a commanding voice. I rarely used it, leaving it to the others to lead, but not this time.

Lifting my hands in front of me, I began the old calling to open to my magic. "AkkadEtaraEra," I murmured. My eyes focused on the cavern's width. I moved my hands slightly ahead and pushed forward the power of hundreds of women before me, which I now could call upon and possessed. The chant remained in my head, but I knew Tesh was watching and hearing it. Self-conscious as I pulled on my gifts for the first time in front of anyone, I continued calling on my magic.

Many women of power came before me. The magic felt strong within me. A taste spread in my mouth, a sort of minty tingling, and a smell of the outdoors reached my nose like waking up on a fresh morning after rainfall with the ground warming after a cool night in the early spring. The power was pure, tied to generosity of heart, unconditional love for nature, and unadulterated by greed. I could feel all of this at the moment where it surged, a willing companion to my soul.

The power within me responded. A glistening barrier lifted between the Entity and us, shimmering in the darkness. It expanded like a veil scintillating the entire width of the cavern in a sort of bluish transparent wall of energy. I smiled, recognizing my signature in all of it as it flew ahead, barricading us from the entity. "Now!"

Our team moved and propelled upward toward the surface. In a silent command, Nis ordered the Androids to remain behind, watching our backs. The rest of us lifted toward the summit's opening in an organized unit, while they covered our retreat.

Tesh, Lana, Silia, and Jolt hovered ahead of the others, followed by all our equipment, dragging the elliptic formation hiding our Conclave chambers, and the casings.

Blast remained beside me, matching the speed of my boots, as I positioned myself at the rear of our contingent. "I'm staying with you."

I glanced in his direction briefly. "Go. I will be right behind you."

Stubbornly, he growled, "No way."

When the barrier went up, the myriad of lights flashed forward, and lasers pulsed in our direction. They hit the barricade in multiple salvos, creating an infernal display of fireworks, blemishing its surface with bursts of red that transferred to deep purple hues before they coalesced into nothingness. With each strike, the energy slightly shifted as it bounced under the assault, but the magical blockade held. My power remained strong and I felt a sense of pride.

As we lifted higher, the entity seemed to slow its advance. It became less aggressive the further we moved, and relief filled me.

I rose with Blast and my NetJet boots brought me closer to the surface.

Nis followed behind me, focused on the roadblock I had created, watching for movement from our enemy. A part of me wondered if this life form was indeed an enemy. My perception shifted at the moment, as I surveyed the City Vigils coming behind us.

When none of our actions turned into an attack on the Entity, the Sphere's aggression diminished, and by the time we reached the surface, it faded away. Was that the actions of an enemy? No. It defended itself from an incursion on its territory.

When I reached the Summit, I dropped the barrier. The others were already well past the entrance and turned quickly to the emptiness below. Our team jumped under the power of the NetJet boots toward the forest grounds and I followed them.

Tesh, holding slightly behind the others, smirked. *You have some explaining to do, Leane.*

I grimaced. *Indeed, I do.*

I did not know where to begin and how to explain what I was, nor how I came into this power that only surfaced now. It was not something our world understood; the old notions of magic eroded long ago, but in truth, magic was energy. Universal energy transferred to coalesce into a purpose, a goal as pure creation.

Still, soon, I would have to face up to their inquiries, and if my gifts contributed to our success, there was nothing wrong with that. A part of me wondered if they would agree with that conclusion. I shuddered, thinking back about why Manaha insisted on the bounding in the first place. I cringed a little thinking about that. Did I need to fear something from them?

Out Of The Abyss - 2022

We are CREA.

The abyss swarmed with us. Our energy reflecting in the darkened space by the spectrum of light, the electromagnetic radiation signature within the field perceived by the human eye, rose slowly. The visible range tethered for now to this place hovered within the confines of the cave. Space shimmered among moving tendrils of a photon of light spreading outward, creating shadows coalescing into forms. Keeping the wavelength of light within parameters inside two adjacent light cycles passing a given point per second remained adequate. The lumen streaked erratically, pulsating. According to our ubiquity, they fell in uneven patterns, shattering the cavern's stillness as the lux erupted in the emptiness.

We moved at will, here and elsewhere, throughout everything and nothing, impervious to mass or nothingness, across universes, resting for millennia and passing billions of years. We were omnipresent. We existed, staying, and departing, with no beginning and no end, for the construct remained infinite everywhere. We are untouched by time, forever.

The ones moving around the terrain in the tunnel would see it. It was enough of a reminder that the time was unfolding once again. But unlike before, they did not attack. Instead, they built a wall of energy and fled.

We do not believe in destruction. We are Crea.

NEWDAWN REBOOT

Sequel Chapter Teaser

SRC Conclave,

Annals Viewing Vlog 699,344,268 – Ang City 2098

I am DAINN. Today Concordance begins. It is a day that drives anger in the heart of my people. But after many deliberations, the leaders and I have determined that we must move ahead with the day of The Concord. DAINN Annals – Winter 2098.

Many of my people opposed Concordance. Many had fought against it. Many had lost.

The Conclaves, tasked with implementing the change among their members across the planet, operated somewhat independently under the oversight of the EHAF.

It will be the third time Concordance happened and disruption occurred on my watch. For our leaders, the continuation of our civilization far outweighs the inconvenience sustained by the lives of the many. For once, it was not a matter of dwindling resources because of our population numbers. Indeed, worldwide, these had decreased substantially over the last half-century. The issue remained strictly a matter of schedule, focused on concluding the evacuation programs' build-up before the anomaly entered our galaxy.

Yet, our population suffered much more than an inconvenience with the advent of the Concord. People were repurposed, and most times, families were broken up.

The decision was not reached easily, for the demands imposed upon each soul were not taken lightly. But after many debates among our Council members, the conclusion became official. Yet, I had a hand in it.

The System indicated that we had no choice if we were to increase our chances of survival. Time was of the essence. We examined multiple options before estimating that this course of action would serve us best. But every scenario we initiated to calculate success in maintaining the schedule concluded as much. So, here we were.

My Network, stretched to the breaking point, required more resources to maintain the outputs. Our priorities shifted in the time that remained, and although everyone provided support in all the areas necessary to achieve our goals, it was simply not enough. We needed more of everything, bodies on our assembly lines, expanded supply chain and supplies, and raw materials within our manufacturing facilities. The robots and androids alone were not sufficient. Making more robots would demand reallocating resources, affecting critical sectors to implement our programs. Origin, Alpha, Provenance, and Aurora, most crucial to our survival, must continue as planned no matter the cost. More bodies meant another Concord. This solution remained the only viable option, allowing for the success of our survival operations.

The automation of the planet took place long ago. While everything ran with computerized systems, there remained the need for the workforce to oversee some of our processes or supervise the next steps. We were not dealing with manufacturing, just a few products. We were dealing with many. We created the machines to manufacture other machines, disassembling the devices and repacking them for transport. We made equipment indispensable to settle somewhere else, devices that will enhance our chance of survival in an environment we did not know. We housed pre-fabricated housing broken into parts so they could be transferred into ships and then to the surface of another planet. We stacked weapons and supplies in containers for transport and attributed them to the various programs. We ensured critical components of our engines and replacements parts found their way into every program. While the System saw it, our people ensured every resource got to the right place along the lines. Whether it pertained to raw materials, crops, seeds, animals, food rations, stasis pods, or implants, we kept producing and transporting until the last minute. And we continued to manufacture ships, a lot of transport ships.

So, now, it was time to implement the Concord. And we waited for the day to unfold. As the Planetary A.I., I knew the costs of our actions. It lay bare on the Watch Tower screens and in the System's calculations.

2
CONCORDANCE
Tesh

Golden Ghetto, Ang City - 2098

Another Concord at the planet level is once again pending. None of us have a choice if we wish to survive within a System that is changing us to our very core. Phenom Tesh, Institute Conclave – Origin Special Elite Unit, DAINN Annals - 2098.

It was the week of Concordance. The morning started like any other. But, this was not just another day. Today began the first day of Concordance or the Concord. In all the countries of our world and fields of endeavor, our population was again called upon to make a change. An alteration occurred in our way of life from professions, and expertise to the work environment and location.

The event was happening at all levels within the infrastructure of our society. DAINN established this reorganization to meet the new demands of our world market economy. At the root of our social structure, our Planetary Network ascertained the maximum effectiveness for our people and governments. The initiative instigated by DAINN applied to our workforce and our natural resources.

"Get up, Tesh. It has begun."

DAINN's voice resonated in my head as I remained in my bed, unwilling to face this day.

I lived in Ang, now divided into various Grids, both horizontal and vertical. The vast metropolis on the coast, which remained a challenge due to climatic events, spread widely on three sides.

"You are going to be late, and your team will proceed without you," continued DAINN.

"Why do we never have a day off?" I muttered to DAINN as I got up and moved to the bathroom.

"You are training. You have another month before you graduate. You have to be ready to lead."

"It's not like the Council will surrender the reins," I added under my breath as I entered the shower cubicle.

Things differed from the history books' descriptions or our elders' stories at family gatherings. Life as we knew it was no longer like it used to be. Now our planetary government was ruled under one centralized leadership. We provided to the world markets; at least up to this point, natural resources other nations didn't have. The population was enormous still, spread over our vast continent, with a land filled with many minerals in demand worldwide.

It gave us an edge… Even if nothing was like it used to be. Indeed, nothing was the same anywhere. So much so that nothing was recognizable from the old life. We had to adjust and adjust; we did. The vastness of our land just made things easier for us. *For how long, though, I ask myself?*

The shower was short, timed to save water, a supply becoming rarer as the years passed. I exited the stall, and the warm air of the device brushed against my skin. The soothing hum of the machine relaxed my sore muscles from the exercises of the previous day. As I got dressed in my Institute Conclave uniform, I thought about what the day would mean for millions of people. *I hate this role they force on me.*

The immense resources we offered our planet influenced politics and the world economy. We were perhaps the most independent of governments because of that fact. Our voice resonated high above others within the assembly. It wasn't so with the Conclave leaders, though. True to form, the Institute was the worst among all five, controlling all aspects of its membership. As graduates of the Academy, we were their puppets until the day we could prove ourselves and take our rightful place to replace them. Only today was not that day. Today was the first day of Concordance, a week-long readjustment for everyone and everything within our infrastructure. In practical terms, what did that mean?

People will be displaced today. Individuals will be moved around to other areas of our infrastructure to serve our society better. Some will find themselves downgraded; others will move up the ranks. These changes required new implants, which demanded absorption training, recalibration, and venue replacement. And as a result, families will be split apart. The Concord caused our entire society to be uprooted in drastic ways. It was the hardest thing to accept, implement, and sustain. In all of this, my part required keeping the population calm and contained. Indeed, this was the second-worst day of my life. And for our people, it was their worst nightmare.

This morning, I didn't have the heart to chat with Cian, my domestic bot, during a quick breakfast. So, instead of going to the kitchen area, I gave Mage a quick hug and headed toward the door of my quarters. My dog followed at my heels, knowingly. Mage understood my mood. He pushed against my hand, licked my fingers, and sat with its tail wagging and waiting for a reward. His reward was me, bending down one more time and giving him another caress. I murmured, "You are such a good dog. I love you. See you tonight. Then, turning, I opened the door and said, "Bye, Cian. See you tonight." When I closed the door, both Mage and Cian watched me go. It was my new normal for the entire week.

We shaped our policies up to a point. We still had the remnants of the position we once held as the world leader. Or was it just an illusion? Nevertheless, our exports generously provided other megacities with indispensable resources, so concessions were made and given on all sides. And under DAINN's guidance, the Council dictated everything.

The Elevat came up to my floor, and I stepped inside. It was too early for most, so I was alone as it made its way to the lobby. Indeed, my PVZ indicated five-thirty in the morning… A barbaric hour for the Conclave leaders living on my floor. Within the next two hours, these heads of Conclaves would make their way to their offices to announce the changes.

The lobby was empty of people when I crossed it. But the City Vigils dedicated to our security occupied their regular post behind the large reception. They were advanced robots directly linked to the Network. Two other City Vigil guards positioned at the entrance kept a watch. All in all, between our Custodians patrolling every floor and the four City Vigils forming the bulk of our immediate security, the tower was well guarded.

DAINN's formidable apparatus to promote safeguards within our world worked with our EHAF Conclave, and our President, in charge of our Earth Homeland Alliance Forces, Zane Langden.

I reached the entrance. One City Vigil opened the door and said, "Good morning Phenom Tesh."

I nodded and passed the doorway into the Plaza. The Golden Ghetto Plaza was a large park adorned with green grass and trees. Surrounded by the silhouettes of our massive towers boasting different shapes, it spread around the government buildings. The beautiful setting greeted me just as the sun rose over the ocean.

I inhaled a deep breath. I will join the others, the Shapers, who will oversee the transitions forced upon our people within the Megapolis in a few minutes. I shook my head. I still had a few minutes of quiet to prepare.

While this walk brought me to my Conclave on most days, this morning took me away from them. The three people I spent most of my days with and constituted the bulk of my Academy training were all scheduled to be elsewhere. Indeed, each of us would perform tasks based on our area of expertise in four different places. Leane was on her way to the Faculty headquarters. Streak and Blast were both on their way to the EHAF headquarters. One will work with the Elite, while the other will join the Presidential Forces. Their skills called them to oversee two distinct fields, one tactical and the other operation.

At that very moment, our leaders prepared for yet another shift in the priorities of the planet. While this mandate unfolded in all fields, from agriculture to manufacturing, from transportation to education, from high tech to science, and from aeronautic to governmental positions, it also meant a different direction for some of us within the Conclaves.

Five Conclaves oversaw all aspects of our lives. The IC, or Institute Conclave, controlled the assessment and formation of our population. The SRC, or Science Research Center, always dedicated to research and innovation, promoted our society's advancements. The

FA, or Faculty, our medical body, saw to the health of our people and monitored all implants. The CO, or Company, manufactured all our products and handled the distribution of our resources.

All five of them competed for power. Among our Academy ranks, it was no secret. And within the upcoming recruits for leadership positions, we all fought until graduation to reach the inner circle and gain some autonomy.

I now belonged to the Institute Conclave, although I grew up in the SRC Conclave with my parents as leaders. But, like a few others, I got coerced into joining the Institute. After their death, instigated by my family's nemesis, the Rat, I lost whatever position I held as a legacy of the SRC Conclave leaders. Since then, my daily fight against the System for my life and place in our hierarchy continued.

In six months, I would graduate and gain my quasi freedom— a partial one at that, but one all the same. Until then, I served wherever they wanted me. And because my gifts as a Shaper of Thoughts allowed them total control over others, my role today was to calm our population and avoid riots in our streets. If I didn't want to be subdued by a blocking implant, there was nothing I could do but comply with their plan.

My walk across the Plaza lasted but a few minutes. The Institute Conclave spread ahead of me in all its glory. The giant golden doors symbolized might, intimidating all as they passed the threshold. Soon, the quiet of my mind would fill with the cries and protests of others.

"SoulLife Phenom Tesh. They are waiting for you in the Alcove," said DAINN.

My day had officially begun.

3
CHAOS
Leane

Faculty Building, Golden Ghetto – Spring 2098

> *Perception is a shifting thing. It mutates as one moves through life,*
> *but change is never easy. It transforms what we perceive as order into chaos.*
> *Phrenic Leane, Institute Conclave, Origin Special Elite Unit.*

After the latest Imps Installs with my assigned team, I stepped out of the operating room into pure chaos. Our robots overrun the main corridors of the Faculty Emergency Center, and more were still arriving.

The City Vigils designated as our security guards this early morning were now in attendance within the walls. Their mechanical structures stood tall among our people as they attempted to maintain a semblance of order in the incoming crowd. The EHAF armor metallic steel blue Earth Homeland Alliance Force robotic frames were noticeable. Their markings alerted anyone that these androids were officially present and working under the authority of our government.

I should be with my Conclave this morning. Instead, I was here in the Faculty, but while my heart belonged there, it was no longer my place. I was part of the Institute now and belonged with Tesh, Streak, and Blast. They were my team. Only, DAINN assigned me to the

Faculty for the entire week of Concordance. *HellNet, being reminded that I used to belong here, lodge a spike in my heart. Only, the Institute deemed me too valuable for the Faculty.*

I squared my shoulders as I thought about Tesh and how she would manage her assignment this week. She hated having to control other people's minds. Yet, she was so good at it. Neither of us had a choice.

I watched the mass of people and hesitated to move further into the fray. As much as I was motivated to reach the area reserved for the surgeons servicing the ER, to change back into my clothes, I hated making my way there by going through this tangled web of anxious and aggressive individuals. But it wasn't to be helped, not today. I took a deep breath and walked further into the passageway.

Ordinarily, the City Vigils stood throughout the corridors and entryways, ready to assist anyone, serving and cooperating with our medical personnel in emergencies. This morning their assigned roles were slightly different. They were here at designated checkpoints to monitor our staff and control the crowd in the event of a disturbance. And rightly so, for at this very moment, the mass of people surging through the corridors looked anything but peaceful.

Our automated transportation Medtubes led directly into the Faculty building. Deemed necessary to service the Med Corp, it provided greater efficiency. The Medtubes catered only to our Faculty members and were accessible by personnel demonstrating the Faculty I.D. And today, it was way overflowing with members of our Faculty Conclave.

The intersection leading to our inside tram's platform appeared way overcrowded. Witnessing an otherwise friendly population, pushing and shoving, gave me pause as this was indeed an unusual occurrence. But then again, this was my first Concord, so what did I honestly know? My musing was interrupted by our City Vigil.

"This way, Universal Planetary Holders, Citizens and Residents…" said the slightly metallic voice of one of the City Vigils."

The incoming wave of attendants kept coming. Soon they would be displaced by more of our robotic personnel. Most of the lower medical staff were already required to present themselves to the Faculty's main building. They waited anxiously at the security junction for the Vigils to clear them. Their skills were no longer enough to maintain them among the Faculty body, and now replaced by androids, they were essentially obsolete. By the end of the day, they would transition to other positions in different Conclaves within our society. It was most likely to mean a loss in status, and they resented it.

I had been there before, way back then when the Institute Conclave told me they made a bid for me. My skills were too valuable to remain within the Faculty Conclave. Therefore, the Institute transferred me to pursue a different path than my vocation, based on my Evaluation with DAINN. I was a kid back then. Today, seeing for the first time, the halls where I would have typically moved around, well, it shook me. *I don't belong here anymore. I should not be here.*

I ran through a cluster of people and maneuvered to avoid the other groups arriving late. They bumped the attending interns to make it past the guards faster. They wanted to be among the first to reach the trams that would take them to the General Assembly in the hope of gaining the advantage of arriving earlier. I barely evaded a collision with a young attendant carrying emergency supplies as he tried to navigate the crowd among the mass of people.

The Official Broadcast of the DAINN Network announcing the beginning of Concordance resonated overheads.

"Concordance is here... Universal I.D. holders, Citizens, and Residents...."

On the Faculty's floating screens, the face of DAINN, our Distributed Artificial Intelligence Neural Network, called for attention.

DAINN appeared on the displays as a hermaphrodite clone, and its voice could just as well have been male or female, as it carried throughout the corridors and walkways.

Silence settled in the hospital, and everyone, out of habit, stopped watching the screen.

Our A.I. spoke to everyone at once and reached out to all the Conclaves. Its presence registered everywhere through the various grids, alerting the entire population within our city that the Concord had indeed begun. The DAINN android, chosen to inspire confidence and strength, looked either more female or male based on its political agenda of the moment. It could be either reassuring or demanding order to our population.

DAINN continued, "All personnel not formally contacted must report to your posts without fail. Those called upon for the General Assembly prepare to transition and make the shift. Follow your schedules without deviation."

HellNet, I wish it was right for me too. Instead, I found myself assigned to the Faculty because there were not enough surgeons capable of handling the mass of Imps Installs this week.

Squaring my shoulders, I made inroads down the hallway, followed by other Faculty members – all people I didn't know.

The morning had started like any other, but this was not just another day in the massive metropolis of Ang City.

Today was the day. In all the countries of our world, our population was called once again to change their profession, expertise, and work environment in all fields of endeavor. It was happening at all levels within the infrastructure of our society.

Darnet, I wish I didn't have to participate in this, and I knew Tesh felt the same way.

It was my first Concordance as a working member of our society, and it was already unsettling enough not to be, on top of it, appointed to a different Conclave for the week.

The entirety of Ang City, divided into various Grids, both horizontal and vertical, did not escape Concordance. The huge Metropolis located on the coast always faced challenges due to climatic events, but it remained the place to live.

"Walk this way, please. The trams to the General Assembly Faculty building are at the end of the main passageway," ordered one of the Vigils monitoring a group of attendants passing through.

The City Vigil's electronic eyes scanned everyone as they went by, monitoring their features through our facial recognition software. They ran through each individual, checking against DAINN's central database. It flagged those whose names appeared in the System for any number of reasons, including the conversion. Their programming instantly identified and tallied the citizens for the upcoming selection process.

"Please, come this way," said the City Vigil.

I turned, wondering if the voice was targeting me. It was not.

The City Vigil pointed at a young man as he controlled one of the latest arriving groups.

Fear spread on the individual's face inside the minor assembly of people. He reacted, suddenly attempting to evade the checkpoint.

It unleashed the City Vigil, who now moved toward him.

The crowd in the flagged faction quickly spread apart to give way to the City Vigil. No one wanted to interact with the CVs.

In the confusion that ensued, a young attendant panicked and ran. But his split-second hesitating cost him.

When the second man bolted, a commotion followed.

Now two City Vigils stepped forward to apprehend the perpetrators. One moved on to the first perpetrator of the infraction and quickly detained him. The second launched toward the running attendant.

The latter grabbed a young woman as a shield. He identified the person through her purple garb as a Phenom, hoping to use her as a barrier against the oncoming City Vigil.

So, here she was, a Phenom of the Faculty, and entirely unprepared for a hostage situation.

My training from the Institute Conclave kicked into gear, and I found myself in the middle of the fray, not far behind the young man. Sure, I could have let the City Vigil handle it. But my training caused me to react before I thought about it. I was unwilling to risk another Faculty member's life if I could help it. The Academy trained me, especially for such situations. The Institute Conclave demanded it and prepared us for almost anything.

The man had wrapped his left arm around the young woman's neck, holding her in a tight brace. His arm squeezed the breath out of the girl, using her as a shield. But he forgot to look behind, entirely focused on the oncoming City Vigil.

I moved around two people who separated me from the action and tackled the guy. I landed a blow behind his left knee and slammed the side of his head with my left hand. My right hand grabbed his right wrist and pulled his arm back in such a way that he released the girl, howling in pain. I glanced over at the City Vigil, who kept advancing on us. I flashed my Institute Badge.

The guy collapsed to his knees.

The young woman pulled away from the altercation, looking disheveled and overwhelmed.

I handed him to the City Vigil with a nod and a firm grip while presenting myself to the City Vigil, who was already scanning my face. "I am Leane, Phrenic of the Institute Conclave, member of the Elite."

"Phrenic Leane, thank you for your assistance in this matter. I will take it from here," said the City Vigil, releasing me from my charge. "Your quick cooperation is noted and will be reported in our Vlogs."

Within minutes, she became a hostage in a game she could never win for her lack of preparedness. The Faculty did not put their members through combat. *It could have been me without the Institute Academy training.*

The City Vigil got a hold of the young man, lifting him from the ground, and slipped a set of manacles around his wrists, paralyzing him in the process.

I resumed my walk toward the surgeons' changing rooms when the young Phenom woman stepped in my way.

"Thank you, Phrenic Leane. I was unprepared, and your assistance is greatly appreciated. I am Phenom Eva Bassington, and I am head of the Emergency Unit within the hospital. I do not know how to reward you for your help. But your interference probably saved my life."

HellNet! I didn't need the attention. I just wanted to get back to my routine. But the young woman appeared so thankful that I stopped and smiled at her. "I doubt very much that you were in great danger. The CV would have handled the matter with expedience, but I am glad I could be of help."

The City Vigil's programming quickly influenced its following action. He dragged the Faculty attendant away from us with one arm and turned toward the young woman who was now facing me.

"Are you alright, Phenom Bassington?"

She nodded, "I am fine, City Vigil."

"Do you need assistance to get to your destination? I can accompany you if you wish to avoid further mishaps...."

"No... I'll be fine. What will happen to him?" She said as she pointed to the limped young man, now held by the guard.

"Unfortunately for him, he is now tagged as a reluctant, which will not help his chances in the selection process," answered the City Vigil before saluting us and moving away with his charge. Effortlessly, he lifted the young man off the ground and walked back toward the tram platform. The move took less than a few seconds as everyone parted around him.

"This is such a difficult day for everyone," murmured Eva.

We witnessed one of the other guards grabbing the other man and escorting him to the departing trams. The experience of watching our City Vigils, usually so well-mannered, as they maintained order in their intractable, unemotional ways, had been intimidating. They were part of an EHAF security force that caused fear of the System for anyone inside the city today.

"Yes, it is," I whispered. It didn't sit well with me to see the City Vigil's roles today. But I was ready to resume my progress toward the Resident's room.

Eva continued, "I know you are helping us this week. Since you know none of us, you are welcome to join us later if you would like. We all go for a drink at the Faculty bar after our shift."

"Thank you, it is very kind, but I will need to meet up with my Conclave Elite members later this evening."

"Okay. If you need anything, don't hesitate to 'NetComm' me," added Eva before walking away in the direction of the transportation area.

The hospital was still a combat zone past the checkpoint. Early this morning, the influx from the Concord reassignments arrived inside these walls jamming the workload. Thus, my presence here.

Today and the rest of the week, we will process the Imps Installs. Any other surgeries were deferred and held over, which explained my presence here. The Emergency rooms of the Faculty filled with incoming patients every hour became a manufacturing belt with all surgeons busy to capacity during the entire time. It was one of the crazy aspects of Concordance.

The Faculty – our world medical body cared for an entire planet's healthcare needs. Only, this week we all implemented Imps Installs for Concordance. Today, I would behave like any other surgeon, granted access to the hospital as if I never left. As a natural healer, I hated this.

Despite how tired I felt, I headed toward the next Op room with more operations to perform.

Glossary

Android VBS 5300 – One of the latest android models, capable of lifting extreme weight, flexible in operating multi-tasks, and geared chiefly toward special rescue operations.

Alpha - A program to launch the fleet into space, along with an entire armada to safeguard the population of Ang because of an impending extinction-level event.

Ang - Angel City is one of the largest Megapolis on Earth in 2098 and known as such for the sake of efficiency and brevity. After their initial destruction, most of our major cities, rebuilt to sustain the great floods and impending massive storms, now bore new names.

Aurora – A program that created underground safety chambers for the main population to prepare for the impending cataclysm.

Astra – A small Custodian, capable of extreme speed and offensive and defensive capabilities in the enforcement of the law or strategic military action.

BeautyForm – The latest technological advancement for the reformatting and remodeling of body parts, developed by the research and development of the Company under the initial product enhancements created by the SRC (Science Research Center).

City Vigil – Robots built to oversee the security and safety of the population with advanced protocols to replace the human police force and capable of facing many situations in the city.

Custodians – Robots implement citywide security measures and enforcement policies within government buildings. They replace today's security personnel. They look like spheres of different diameters. Based on their capabilities, Custodians carry one or multiple ZNets, which are zapping mechanisms designed to put people into a sleep state. Using nets deployed around their targets, they bring their passengers to detention centers.

Council – The Council of Nations or Great Council represents multiple countries and runs the Planet and its infrastructure under a public mandate.

Cryogenic Chamber – Located inside the Institute, with a unique team of technicians who welcome those who emerge from the Cryo modules. There are many such rooms, each containing one hundred to thousands of pods. The total number of modules is unknown. We also refer to the Cryogenic Chamber as NDCryo.

DAINN – The Distributed Artificial Intelligence Neuro Network and A.I. is a planetary mind whose tentacles reach all over the globe to monitor our entire infrastructure.

DarNet – An expression that has evolved from the word "darn" or the phrase "darn it." It became "DarNet" because of the influence of the Network over people in our future.

DarNetWash – An expression suggesting "never mind," or more used to mean "nullify" this or that.

Domestic Bot – Robot or Bot designed and located inside each population quarters, apartment, or house to serve as domestic, doing chores in society's upper echelon. The Bot is programmed for basic tasks and deals with cleaning, cooking, and running errands, but can do much more. Linked to the DAINN System and Network, they monitor all our needs.

EmVats – A defensive unit or suit linked to the DNA of a user. EmVats provide protecting ambient suits with combat readiness based on specific programming.

Encharge – An exchange of energy between conclave members to unify, recharge, and strengthen the link existing within a unit and between people.

Flycar – A motorized vehicle with lower flight capability, designated for personal use to higher level conclave members. Flycars configured on-demand can carry one or two people.

Gatherer – A Gatherer, also called a Gatherer of Space, can move through time and space based on DNA, implants, and technology.

HydroSheath – Metallic tube or cylinder containing Nanos pushed through a perfusion head.

Institute – The Institute is one of the five Conclaves and the government's arm that implements the DAINN System according to specific mandates. It keeps up with A.I. and population demands.

IOGel – A gel-like substance composed of water and nutrients. An energy drink for Conclave leaders and members.

HellNet – An expression replacing "hell."

Mave – A large Custodian, extremely powerful and deadly, carrying bombs and other offensive weapons to apprehend, detain, or kill crowds or enemies.

MindTranscript – DAINN's process to a person's mind to understand a person's emotional journey or state at a certain point in time. It monitors thought patterns in different situations to learn everything a person thinks and feels.

NetComm – The planetary telecommunication network linking everyone on the planet.

NetDumb – An expression replacing "dumb" or "dummy."

NetSwarm – Nanobots capable of carrying different payloads for particular purposes, according to their programming.

NetSpy – Nanobots infiltrating spyware used in different areas to gather information for the Network.

NetPulsing – The action of using a PulseNet to carve entries and tunnels into a rock formation. It can also be used as a defensive or offensive arm based on situations, degrees, and ranges.

NetRoger – An expression replacing "Roger that" based on the influence of the DAINN Network.

NetWash – An expression signifying "Shit" or "F… It…" Depending on the inflection of the subject.

NetZapping – Custodians' tool to maintain order over individuals or crowds. Used to ensure population safety, it can occasionally serve as an offensive or defensive arm.

Nuzar – Purple drink with energizing nutrients.

Origin – A safety chamber designed to safeguard a few of the Conclave members chosen to travel back in time to prevent the future destruction of Ang.

OxyPure – A breather or breathing mask, delivering oxygen to survive.

Phenom – A title gained by accumulating accomplishments and implants to master skills and knowledge in various disciplines. Phenom is one of the highest levels individuals attain within the DAINN System.

PodBot – Robots designed to implement and oversee the Cryo process inside the Origin chamber.

Provenance - A program designed to safeguard the population and some conclave members in space facilities surrounding the planet. Using multiple space elevators and ships, Provenance began a mass exile to deliver people from Earth on the eve of an impending extinction-level event.

Pulse Device – A sonic wave pulse displaces matter and reshapes it according to pre-programmed designs. Its power creates such energy on the subatomic level that it moves matter.

PulseNet – A sonic pulse emanating from the UniBrace device on the wrist of the perfect human.

PulseTube – The level of a Pulse Device creating tunnels into the Earth based on sonic waves.

PVZ – Personal Visor Z, linked to the ZNet or Communication Network on the planet, is a system that replaces the cell phones of today. Implanted in a human being at an early age, the PVZ serves multiple purposes, including health monitoring, location tracking, and the facilitation of communication between members of the population and the DAINN Network.

Roamers – Members of the Conclave selected to become Time Travelers as part of the Origin program.

Rovers – A particular group formed to survey the timeline under assignments from the Council of Nations, enforcing specific dictates.

Seer – A person capable of performing certain gifts ranging from past or future visions. Some can enhance life cycles or perform life-giving acts and properties to various species and heal.

Sky – Advanced military Lazer-powered weapon.

Spozor – A liquid gel with exceptional qualities and nutrients developed by the Institute.

Shaper – A person capable of reading thoughts, shaping minds, influencing perceptions, and altering decision processes.

SkyFarms – Vertical agricultural complexes spread over the city and designed to grow food.

SoulLife – A greeting form used by residents of Ang City to express mutual appreciation, and based upon an Allegiance to the Universal Pledge, recognized Life Energy as a unique source of power.

The Institute developed spozor to facilitate immediate recovery in those waking up from Cryo.

SRC (Science Research Center) – The Science Research Center is the governing arm that develops all new technology and science on behalf of the government. The SRC works under the Council and the officials dictating policy.

UniBrace – Bracelet wrapped around a wrist and used as a tool or weapon with the sound wave, burst, lasers, and explosive capabilities and drawing its energy source from the user.

UniWear – Underclothing worn beneath a uniform.

UniWrap - A bracelet that wraps itself around a user's wrist, the UniWrap carries the energy and can adapt to a user's needs. It is an advanced weapons system comprising Nanobots and used as an offensive or defensive tool in combat.

VLogs/VideoLogs – A process qualifying as a work report facilitates a person's information dump into DAINN. During a Vlog, the A.I. asks specific questions about one's work. A recording of the subject is launched during the interview. Each VLog ends up in the DAINN archive.

WatGel – Water-like gel used for baths or showers.

ZDart – Disk dissolving under the epidermis used by Custodians to subdue opponents, maintain population control and order, with other offensive capabilities, like carrying a sleeping agent.

ZNet – An apparatus incorporated into the Custodians in the form of indestructible netting. Also available for EHAF ships (Earth Homeland Alliance Force).

Note from the Author

The NEWDAWN Saga continues.

To all my readers and fans, please visit the retailer's product page and leave a review on Amazon. Reviews help me with sales, as you know, and allow me to keep creating. It also tells me what resonated with you in the story and what you enjoyed the most. As my reader and the reason I write these stories, I feel blessed to share with you what I love, and I hope; I can take you with me on the adventure you seek into our future world every time you open the NEWDAWN Saga book series!

We also have our store, which you can visit: www.newdawnshop.com, and where Tesh and her team have great merchandising for you to support the NEWDAWN Saga.

As I continue taking you on this journey, thank you for your support, and please share this book with your best friends!

The world of NEWDAWN includes many facets, so please visit our sites for more information:

www.windommedia.com
www.newdawnworld.net
www.newdawnworld.com
www.dominiqueluchart.com
www.newdawnblog.com
www.newdawnshop.com

Follow this link to see more books from Dominique Luchart.

Also, follow me on Facebook, Twitter, Instagram, and Pinterest.
Also available in the NEWDAWN Saga Series:
GEN Diary System.

NEWDAWN REBOOT

Find your way to travel to the future in 2088 and beyond.

Visit Ang City in 2098.

Be the first to receive it by sending me an email at

info@newdawnworld.com.

The next novel is

NEWDAWN REBOOT

Coming to you in 2022.

REBOOT brings you to the center of the action in 2098, where everything unfolds for Ang City, its citizens, and the Conclave leaders. The planet is in turmoil, and people face impossible odds. At the height of Concordance, where the entire population undertakes a change in the world's infrastructure, a discovery threatens Earth.

You will see Tesh and her friends in her environment, facing her challenges with the governance of the Institute. You will see DAINN and the splendor of its Network. And you will meet multiple characters belonging to the different Conclaves for the first time and watch as their agenda feeds a more massive inner conflict with the leadership. You will witness the terror when an unknown force wreaks havoc on Ang city.

REBOOT places the conflict in the future and will lead you to go back in time in the lives of the characters you like. I hope you enjoy REBOOT and keep in mind that time is not linear in the stories of NEWDAWN. So have fun and get ready to uncover a new way of life!

The NEWDAWN Saga opens our potential and helps us create a better future. Some of the notions in the story do work, but only if we set the proper structure for them in real life. Others do not because they fuel the NEWDAWN Saga. Some technical and scientific advancements are based on current research and new development. Others are a bit of fantasy. Bear with me as I weave a new world and be open to a different perspective for our future. The lives we live today can be so much better if we can shape a new future with values that are dear to us. I believe we can do better for ourselves, the generations to come, and our beautiful planet and all its species.

Sign-up and receive our latest updates:
www.windommedia.com/newdawn-readers.
Contribute by buying merchandising:
www.newdawnshop.com.

Give your support at:
www.windommedia.com/newdawn-donate.

Biography

Transmute the now and transcend tomorrow. Dominique Luchart is the forward-thinking author of the NEWDAWN Saga, a YA science-fiction, fantasy, romance adventure series about the state of our world from 2018 to 2098 and beyond. NEWDAWN ROAMERS is the first volume of the series, followed by NEWDAWN CENTRAL and NEWDAWN RISING, in a chronological timeline. But NEWDAWN REBOOT was written first, culminating with the chain of events that unleashes everything in the NEWDAWN Saga. Soon after comes NEWDAWN RETRIBUTION, while in between, the adventure continues in a suspenseful epic story spanning time and space.

Dominique Luchart, the founder of WindHorse Entertainment and Windom Media, is a multi-faceted creative. As an Author and Futurist, a Media Platform Architect, Director and Producer, and Speaker, she is a masterful innovator, changing how people interact with content. As a universal storyteller, she delivers the next generation of information and entertainment networks focused on science and technology. One of her goals is to create trailblazing experiential environments delivering enhanced user experiences in storytelling. Mixing content distribution within a social network, she is working on a platform for the world of NEWDAWN, inside which the readers of NEWDAWN and SciFi lovers can take part in the stories and contribute.

"These experiences can serve as a roadmap for the future, determining what is on the horizon for all of us in the hope of building a socially conscious world where generations can thrive." Knowing what is to come is the first step to manifesting awareness and maintaining our

choices in a world where technology will run our planet. *"Only we can decide if this is the world we want...."*

Thank you for purchasing this book!

Visit our online store at https://newdawnshop.com and get special discounts on our books and special promotions.

Subscribe if you have not already!
Get a FREE ebook when you join our mailing list
Plus, get updates, new releases, deals, gifts, and more.

SIGN UP HERE
https://windommedia.com/bestemaillist

Already a Subscriber? Provide your email again to register this ebook and put you on our VIP List. You will continue to receive exclusive offers in your inbox

Other Books By Dominique Luchart

NEWDAWN

SAGA

NOVELS ROADMAP

Saga Series

Diaries Series

2018-2021

2021-2023

ROAMERS · CENTRAL SAGA 2 · REBOOT

RISING · NEWDAWN RETRIBUTION SAGA 2 · ORIGIN SAGA 3

SYSTEM GEN DIARY 1

Newdawn System (2021 – 2022)
Gen Diary 2, 3, 4 and 5.

Newdawn Academy (2021 - 2022)
Tesh Diary 1, 2, 3, 4 and 5.

2021

Credits

ISBN Number 978-1-941954-12-6